THE PERILOUS GATE

J.J. Eliyas

THE PERILOUS GATE

DOUBLE DRAGON

A DOUBLE DRAGON PAPERBACK

© Copyright 2017
J.J. Eliyas

The right of J.J. Eliyas to be identified as author of this
work has been asserted in accordance with the
Copyright, Designs and Patents Act 1988

All Rights Reserved

ISBN 978-1-78695-494-7

Double Dragon is an imprint of
Fiction4All

This Edition Published 2020
Fiction4All
www.fiction4all.com

Prologue

Snow, caught in a prism of light, cascaded through the pass, nearly taking him with it. The two thousand foot plunge would have been very unpleasant. He clung desperately to a rock outcropping, wondering why he had undertaken this venture in the first place.

Because it is the last one, the last Gate, he told himself. He swung around, his feet finally finding some purchase, and managed to get onto a relatively level ledge. He took a deep breath and expelled a cloud into the icy air. Air so frigid in fact that much of his breath froze onto his beard, made even grayer by the ice.

I am getting too old for this. But, it is the last one. He looked up through the crevasse, the sunlight almost blinding him. Pulling the hat low over his brow, he made his way up through the pass and, within minutes, was able to see what lay beyond. He knew it would be there: The Gate. But the sight of it still gave him pause.

The arch-like structure, made of a wholly alien metal, sat on bare granite, the snow and ice preternaturally giving it a wide berth. The air within the arch shimmered like a summer afternoon, distorting the glyphs and runes that covered its surface. It was by far the largest of the gates he had seen; a caravan four wagons abreast could easily pass through.

The purpose of this Gate was unknown to him. Why the mages would place it up here, on top of a mountain, was beyond him, though one scholar had suggested the Gates were created when the world was young, and the later continental upheavals would account for this one's present positioning.

He sat on a boulder and caught his breath; the air was thin at this altitude. He flexed his shoulder and winced at the pain from the old wound. He was getting old. He smiled ironically and laid his sword across his lap. The large, well-balanced blade sat there, cold, silent.

How many years had he searched out the Gates? Fifteen? He'd lost several friends along the way. Yet, he knew they would be happy that his task was almost at an end. He took off the hat and smoothed back his hair, now almost completely gray. His face was lean and weathered, and his eyes were tired. He set the sword aside for the moment and pulled two thick packages from his pack. Each had a metal seal with a rune carved into it. Magic, no doubt.

The vista up here was quite spectacular. Beyond the Gate, the side of the mountain dropped away in a sheer granite cliff. Beyond that, more snow-covered peaks and valleys. The sun slowly began to descend in a wash of cold salmon clouds and lemon rays, illuminating the side of the mountain and making him revel in wonder. He wished he could stay, put off this last task. He wondered what his life would be like without this force driving him. Other people had their own purposes; he'd just have to find one that suited him. He would have to create a new path, he supposed.

He gathered up the sealed packages and trudged through the snow. As he neared the Gate he noticed the air warming, and he could detect the faint scent of lavender.

Lavender, now that brings back memories, he thought. There was a hint of melancholy, but it lasted only a moment. He placed a satchel at each base of the arch, being careful not to touch the metals or the runes upon it. He broke the seals on each and started to move away just as he heard the sound of steel scraping on stone.

"The last one, Lord Guardian?" came an old, familiar voice.

He spun at the sound and saw a man in furs and gilded breastplate holding the sword that he had foolishly left behind.

"The last…and the seals are broken, so there is no going back."

"No," said the interloper, not much older than him, but scarred and hardened.

"I thought you were dead."

"Thought you killed me at the Great Wall?" He shook his head and grinned. "The luck of Oran was with me there."

"How long has it been? Almost twenty years?"

"And I have finally caught up with you."

"To stop me from destroying the last Gate? You're a little late."

"To kill you actually; finally."

"You're a sad person indeed if that has been your goal for the past two decades. A waste of time." In the back of his head he realized the energy was building in the satchels he'd placed at the base of the arch. He needed to get into the pass before the Gate imploded. "If you want to kill me, can we do it somewhere else?"

7

"Here will be fine. Besides, are you so sure this is the last? It will be your final thought, that wondering. Now, are you ready to die?"

"You have my sword."

"Ah, the sword of Extenn Rhinn." He lifted the blade high above his head and with all his might brought it down onto the granite outcropping. In a shower of sparks, it sank into the stone, but not before the last third of the blade sheared off and landed at its owner's feet.

He looked at what remained of his sword and picked up the shard of the blade with a gloved hand. It was still hot, and the quicksilver that shifted the balance in the blade ran out of the hollow core. It seemed as if it bled.

"You broke the sword," he murmured as he turned the twisted steel in his hand.

"You are next." Smoothly, confidently, in the manner of one totally accustomed to the arts of war, the interloper drew his own sword and began walking toward him with the broken hilt.

The smell of lavender grew stronger. Closing his eyes, thinking of all he had been through these past twenty years. The air began to vibrate from the satchels he had placed. A high-pitched keening filled the area and he wondered if he would be able to make it to safety.

When his assailant was twelve feet away, his eyes snapped open, his arm shot out, and the shard spun forward with incredible velocity. Before the interloper could react, the tip of the blade pierced the man's throat and sunk deep, followed by a momentary pause, then he dropped where he stood; there was a look of shock on the dead man's face.

"It was a waste of time."

The vibrations grew, as did the whining noise, and his time was almost gone. Ignoring the body and the broken sword, he ran quickly toward the rock crevasse from where he had entered the plateau. He had almost reached it when he heard a crack; he would not make it.

It wasn't an explosion, but rather the lack thereof. A folding inward, sending all that stood where the Gate had been into nothingness. Just as he had leapt toward the crevasse he had felt it, felt suspended in midair and in time. Then the sensation was gone and he was drawn backward to where the Gate had been. Backward and toward the cliff in a rush of air into the huge vacuum that had been created. He had escaped the implosion but not the aftereffects.

He tumbled toward the edge of the cliff, past the smooth granite where the Gate had been. There was no purchase for his hands as he encountered the ice beyond, then the edge, and over.

His hand caught momentarily on a small indentation in the stone. His legs dangled free. His bad left shoulder and arm hung numb from the initial impact.

Face pressed against the implacably cold stone, it seemed he hung there for an eternity, before his grip began to give. He opened his eyes to look upon the setting sun, then once more to the granite rimed with frost…

He smiled as his grip gave way. Lavender, sunset, and frost…

Chapter 1

Frost crawled across the window. The campus was wrapped in a blanket of snow and ice. John sighed and his breath momentarily fogged the window, hindering his view of the commons. It was certainly no night to be out. He caught his reflection in the glass, frowned and turned back to the cluttered office.

He sat in the chair and looked over his thesis, the final proof, stuffed it into a sealed envelope and put it in the box for his advisor. One journey was at an end.

John frowned. This is one place I won't miss, he thought. He was startled from his reverie by a knock at the door.

"Can I talk to you?"

He groaned inwardly, it was Lara, one of the other graduate students in the department. Attractive, red curly hair, freckles on a slightly upturned nose, she was the epitome of classic Celtic beauty.

"You've been avoiding me," she said in a soft voice: Irish accent. He didn't know what to say, because it was true. "My thesis…"

"Was done a week ago. What? You think you can ignore me?"

"I'm sorry, I've been busy with…"

"Not too busy to sleep with me."

He put his feet down from the desk and leaned forward.

"Look," he said. "You are a nice person, I don't want to hurt you…"

"But you don't love me?"

10

"Would you stop cutting me off? I only have known you for one semester."

"Oh, I see, fuck the new girl from Dublin and then dump her."

"You know that isn't true! I'm done here. Finished. You have four years to get your PhD., what would you expect of me?" He noticed his voice was rising but didn't care at this point. "I don't know where I'm gonna be in the next week, let alone the next four years."

She slapped him hard across the face. "I expected more from you!" With that she spun and was down the hall. He stepped out after her, but then noticed the heads over the cubicles, like gophers popping out of their holes, and slammed his door shut. The glass cracked with the slam.

The shock of stepping from the warmth of the building made him feel even colder inside. It had been easy to forget how bitterly cold northwestern Ohio could get in late December. As his feet crunched through ice and snow, he began to wish he had invested in a down coat instead of the fashionable leather jacket. The walk to the recreation center across campus was a long one. It gave him plenty of time to think and plenty of time to get depressed. If his roommates hadn't been waiting for him, he would have stopped at his favorite bar.

You're a real jerk, aren't you? He shook his head and picked up the pace, taking the steps to the rec center two at a time.

He saw Tom waiting for him, sitting with his usual aplomb against the far wall. Though not physically striking, he possessed what John would call a coiled energy, like that of a taut spring. Tom Smiling Wolf was half Sioux, with the facial angularity that was typical of Native Americans, set off by light sandy hair. He was dressed in wool and cotton of a coarse weave, seemingly innocuous enough for him to melt into the woodwork. Immersed in his medical textbook, his left eye scanned the pages in front of him, his right eye didn't. It was made of glass.

His friend stood as he passed through the turnstile. Tom moved with smooth, graceful motion.

"What's up with you? You look like you swallowed something bad."

"Nothing important."

"Right." Tom looked at his friend curiously, then: "Come on, you can blow off steam better on the floor."

"I guess you're right." He ran his hand through thick dark hair and frowned. Where Tom was lean and lithe, John was tall, broad and thick, his mustache accented the tightness of his strong jaw. He stood two inches taller than Tom's six feet. When he brooded, people tended to get out of his way. He had a stare, a cold aloofness, which some people would say was arrogance; but his friends knew better, knew not to confuse introspection for elitism.

"Unless of course you want to skip class?"

"No."

They moved to the stairwell and down a flight to the locker room. Bill was there, pulling on his Speedos. John nodded to his other roommate. They made a habit of working out the same night, as it inevitably turned into a social outing for them afterwards. Bill had a swimmer's build and would often be found doing laps when he wasn't doing research for his doctorate.

John keyed his locker and yanked open the metal door. He stopped when his gaze passed over a photograph of Lara and him taped to the back. He stripped it off, crumpled it and tossed it into the trash bin.

"That bad?" asked Bill.

"That bad," he replied. He looked at the other photographs on the locker door, finally stopping on the one that made him smile.

It usually made him chuckle when he saw that one. The whole gang had all been dressed up for the annual medieval festival as the Legion of the Black Skull. Only one of their group stood less than six feet tall, and all were armed to the teeth.

Tom had dressed as an explorer, with loincloth, leather buckskins, and Bowie knife. John was dressed as a Crusader and wore a white silk under-tunic, a black surcoat with a scarlet cross, and a long sword strapped to his side. Joe, who could pass for John's brother despite the beard, wore a black and purple tunic, on the center of which was embroidered a demon's skull; hence the group's name. Bill was dressed in bright colors and wore a foppish hat. The inimitable Chill hung back from the group, looking at the camera blankly. Then there was Mike. Mike was easily the tallest in the group: six-four and two-forty, he stood in the background wearing a brown broadcloth tunic and dark breeches. He carried a mace in one hand and a brandy snifter in the other. What set him apart from the others was his Manchurian style mustache, mirrored sunglasses and, of course, the ubiquitous cigarette tilted out of the corner of his mouth.

John smiled faintly and pulled the wooden bokken from the back of the locker. He tightened the belt of his hakama and nodded to Tom. Every Monday and Wednesday John and Tom rigorously studied Aikido while Bill did laps. It was a ritual. Ritual was good. He needed the ritual right now.

Joe narrowed his eyes and considered the saber. "Austrian, nineteenth century." His partner could almost hear the Germanic accent in his voice, but it was just his imagination.

"Yeah, nice. We have to pay the rent and you buy a saber."

Bad day, Joe thought. He was thirsty. He always got thirsty when he bought something this expensive. Weird.

"Don't worry I get paid next week from the museum, for the restorations I did, and I'll sign it over to you. It'll take care of it."

"How do you do it?"

Joe laughed and set the blade back in the case. "Conservator by day, fencing school owner by night? Lessee…no social life to speak of.

"Sometimes I find my thoughts wandering to the what-ifs, and that bothers me, but when I'm charging down a piste at another guy, man am I focused. Like that last match, a simple quarte that trips up the other guy. A counter-six! And the buzzer goes off as my saber hits his vest. You know what? That's what it's all about!

"It's not just men in white suits moving up and down a corridor and hitting their metal sticks together. Not just points and electric scoring. It is a metaphor for life." He looked down at the exquisite blade. "When you're behind the mask, there is relevance to the game."

"You're getting weird."

"Am I? What's wrong with that? Look at you. You don't have a career. You've been living off of daddy's income for three years now. Where has it gotten you?"

"I–" Joe cut him off. "It's not a bad thing, Chill, just who you are."

"Right," his friend just laughed. "You really have a way with insulting people and getting away with it."

"It's a gift I have." He locked the saber in a glass cabinet and turned back to his friend. "Okay, we have eighth graders tonight. They are going to be foil fencing, so that's you. Beginning fencing."

"Eighth graders?"

Joe grinned maliciously. "Yeah, and they have never handled a foil before."

Tom and John went down a long flight of stairs, past the racquetball courts to a pair of double doors. This was the combative arts room. Inside there could be heard the grunts and shouts of people learning various martial arts skills of varying discipline. Currently there were two classes practicing. A short, chubby fellow, wearing a white gi with a black belt led one class.

The two friends set their bokkens on the floor and bowed to the mat, and then to Tony Lee, their sensei.

"I thought the other class was moved to another night, Tony?" Tom queried as he nodded to the other class on the floor.

"That's next week. I had to persuade James to give us half the floor." John knew it would take more than persuasion to make a person of James's arrogance give up something.

"Line up and pair off, gentlemen," Tony called.

"Hai!" the two replied along with the other ten in the class.

Tom and John paired off. It was their habit to try to improve each other's skills, even though it was understood that Tom was the better of the two. Aikido was a relatively soft art, consisting of locks, throws, and balance. There was a lot of harmony and circular movement involved. When the sword was introduced it often mimicked the motions of the hands and body; it formed an extension. John had studied iaijutsu and kenjutsu before, and so he was a fair hand at the sword techniques. Tom, however, had studied martial arts since an early age, and had gone to Japan to study at a Taijutsu Ryu. It put him a few rungs higher up the ladder than his friend. They were probably the best martial artists in the class save their instructor.

Tonight, however, John was letting his aggression and feelings surface; he was acting recklessly. One of the students pointed this out to Tony.

"He's in one of his moods, sensei."

Tony nodded and shook his head. It would not do any good to point this out to John, at least not until the hurricane had spent its wind. One of

John's problems was his lack of focus, but when he centered himself he was truly a force of nature on the floor.

Right now he was getting sloppy. He was going nowhere as Tom managed to keep his moves tight and focused. John growled low in throat and stepped to the side, slicing low. His temper was getting the best of him and Tom just slid by and nicked him in the shin. He spun back and brought his bokken around in what was more a swing to center field than a strike with a sword.

Suddenly there was a loud crack. The tip of his bokken had collided obtusely with Tom's and had broken off. It spun across the floor and into the midst of James' students. One young student stepped onto the piece and twisted her ankle, whining as she fell.

John stared at the broken bokken. Thirty bucks, he thought.

"Lee!" James called to the Aikido instructor. Tony looked up and almost smiled. John watched as James threw his long braid over his shoulder, picked up the wood shard, straightened his gi and moved across the floor towards them. He sneered arrogantly.

"I shouldn't have to put up with this crap, Lee. I have students to teach. All you idiots ever do is get in my way."

The blood drained from Tony's face and he looked hard at the dark skinned man. John's face turned crimson with anger and he took a step forward.

"You arrogant piece of shi-"

"John," Tom said in one of those soothing tones that really irritated him. James gazed contemptuously at John. "When you learn some real skills maybe you won't make a bad parry."

John blinked his eyes slowly as he looked at the man. John was taller and heavier, but James was no doubt faster. He took a deep breath and smiled.

"I probably do need a few more lessons. "

James' eyes widened imperceptibly. John just turned his back on the man and walked away. James stared after him a moment then went back to his own students.

After an hour and a half of throws, twists, locks and more throws, John and Tom hit the showers. Tom looked at his friend out of the corner of his eye as John scrubbed down.

"What?" John said as he washed under the St. Christopher medal that hung around his neck.

"Something else is eating you. I think I'm sorer tonight than any other time we've sparred. And the argument with James, I thought I would have had to drag you off of him."

"I should have decked him."

"Maybe, but through all that bravado he does have a lot of skill. I've seen him fight. He's good."

"Could you take him?"

"Yes."

"I can take care of myself."

"I know, but with anger you tend to be reckless."

"Yeah, well, I've a lot to be pissed off about."

Bill came traipsing in just as they were toweling off. He had a puppy-dog smile on his face as he opened his locker.

"What's got you in such a good mood?" Tom Smiling Wolf asked. He watched as Bill flipped open a little black address book to quickly write something in it.

"Oh, I just met a girl," he said, his voice swelling with song. "You're a slut."

"Huh?" Bill asked, looking from one friend to the other. He had been so preoccupied with writing her number that he had missed the derogatory comment.

"Come on, what?"

"A good swimmer, Bill, you're a good swimmer." Tom smirked and began to dress.

"Okay, what's going on?"

"Kyle's," John said, feeling the rumble in his stomach. He quickly looked in the mirror, smoothed his dark hair back and checked out his mustache. He then looked to the other two for their opinion.

"Volcano pizza?" Tom asked with a frown.

"Oh yeah, and dark beer to wash the garlic bread down."

"Sounds good," Bill echoed and soon they were pulling on their coats.

Kyle's was a small pub that sat just off campus. It was a frequent hangout for grad students and non-traditional students who didn't want to be bothered with loud music, heavy drinking and lame pick-up lines. Dark woods and good cooking gave the pub a homey atmosphere; not to mention it had an extensive import list. The

19

three roommates sat in a corner booth, listening to Creed on the box. Bill's gaze followed an attractive waitress as she took an order at another table.

"Sounds like you guys had a good workout." Bill took a sip of his black 'n' tan and realized it was almost gone.

"James is a class 'A' asshole," John remarked. Tom hushed him suddenly as the door swung open, letting in a blast of snow and, speak of the devil, James. The man walked in with one of his female students. At the table he took off his long leather coat, but he left his fingerless leather gloves on. He ignored the waitress as he spoke to the student in tones too low to hear.

John grunted and took a drink of his Amber Bock. He played with a piece of pizza crust then tossed it onto the plate. "Like I said, an asshole."

Tom smiled and looked intensely at his friend. "Okay, John. What's going on? Something else is bothering you."

John sighed heavily and fingered the pealing label of his beer. "I think it's the same question that man has been dealing with from the beginning of time, who am I, and where am I going? What happens now? Do I take that government job I was offered? Joe said he needed a partner in the fencing school, do I do that? I have my ranking in kenjutsu, so I can teach. Should I still go to Japan next month? I need to get my head screwed on straight." He laughed and flipped the steak knife.

"I think we've all asked ourselves that." It was all Bill could say.

"Yeah, but you have two years until your doctorate, then it's academia. Tom has four years of med school. Me, I have this big void."

John shook his head and finished the beer in the bottle. "I think that's where my aggression was coming from today. The last thing I needed was that bastard James getting in my face."

Just as he said that Bill choked. James had gotten up, mineral water in hand, and walked over to their booth.

"Well, if it isn't Larry, Curly and Moe," the man snidely remarked. "I couldn't help but stop by. Knowing that two well-versed students of the martial arts sitting two tables away piqued my interest. Did you learn by correspondence course?" He smiled. "Oh, and I see you take your training seriously," he gestured to the beer.

"Much more seriously than I take you," the graduate student replied. Bill pursed his lips and Tom just stared straight ahead.

"You know, John, and I do mean this, your lack of skill on the martial-arts floor is truly comical. I have never seen anyone so inept at Aikido. At least your friend here has some redeemable skills. Alas, I fear that you were born with none."

"You have the right to your opinion." John slapped some money on the table.

He then got up and looked at his friends. "Ready?"

They slid out of the booth. "It did get rather stuffy in here," Tom replied. "Oh, did it?" James followed the three out of the back door and into the snow-covered parking lot. "John," he said

21

mockingly. "Going to run away." John stopped and smiled, then shook his head and kept walking.

Joe stood in his apartment, looking at the wooden frame that held a seventeenth century Dutch oil he was cleaning for an art dealer on contract. Normally he would be expected to do this kind of work in a museum lab, but the dealer had no such luxuries and permitted him to take the piece to his own studio. He just wasn't able to get that grime off the one corner. It looked like a soot smudge but it wasn't responding like one. He dabbed at it with a Q-tip. Odd, he thought. It's layered. He looked outside and watched lazy snowflakes drift down from the dark sky, wondering if this coming weekend would be his last medieval Event. He felt like he was getting too old for the events, that they were starting to attract a different breed of geek. And forget the escapism, he had to start concentrating on the fencing school.

He put on a pair of latex gloves and opened a small jar, dabbed at the clear fluid inside, and spread it on the canvas where the mark was. Nothing. He flipped the frame around and looked at the back. He saw no evidence of a burn. There was just a small Cyrillic letter; probably some old inventory mark.

He held it up to a bare bulb. Ever so faintly he could make out more writing. "Odd," he took a quick digital photo of the corner and went to his PC. In a moment he had enhanced the writing. He then brought up the site of the museum he also worked for and logged in. Checking one of the Eastern European libraries, he tried to match the symbols on the back of the canvas to the available database. He called up the file and cross-referenced it in a language program. Estimated time: 2 hours 17 minutes.

He sat back, pulled the latex gloves off and tossed them in the can. It seemed only moments went by when he was startled awake by his PC beeping impatiently. He noticed by the clock that he had been asleep for 4 hours. It was 3:30 a.m.; he had to get up at six.

He looked at what the language generator had found. Strange.

Language: Slavic, old style, derivative…
[begin]By Oran's[proper name] fire, bound in hate and blood, I call upon thee. Open the Perilous Gate [end match]

He repeated it aloud. Suddenly the edge of the painting fluoresced and caught fire where he had applied the chemical. The letters burned, flaming the painting on his table. He acted quickly, smacking down a towel on the piece, but smoky soot, peeled paint, and burned wood were all that remained of upper corner of the seventeenth century Dutch oil painting.

He was in deep shit.

Then the smoke alarm went off.

The fat, gray-haired man finally had his tent erected within the huge auditorium. It wasn't exactly the Pennsic Wars, but the Annual Battle for the Winter Crown was an event that no Medieval Society enthusiast would miss. These were the dreamers, the misfits, the history buffs, adventurers and, most of all, those who just wanted a break from everyday society.

The shelves were finally set and the workmen left to go and ready other tents by the tilting field. He looked over the texts that he'd brought out of the crate. Most were ordinary junk; the Necronomicon, a couple of Wiccan books, Hebraic text, the Gnostic Gospels, Abram's Lore and such. One crate he had acquired at an auction in London and was said to be part of the Crowley estate. That was a joke, he thought. For the price, they were probably leftovers from a druid convention. The crate was old and musty, one book in particular he'd valued at two hundred dollars. But then there was another, just a blank Book of Shadows that he would sell for twenty. He pondered on what little knowledge people possessed of history. Few knew of the great Sumerian and Assyrian scholars who wrote (and were transcribed by the English) centuries ago: famous architects, scientists, magicians and sorcerers. The crowds that came to these events ate up that stuff. He knew that he would make a killing.

Bill laughed as he drank from a glass of red wine. John sneezed and blew his nose in a tissue, hoping he wouldn't catch a cold. He chewed a vitamin C tablet while he sipped on some vodka.

John looked around the apartment, his vision blurring from fatigue and this, his third shot of the liquor. The apartment was small and not decorated in any particular fashion. A few paintings hung on the wall. The furniture was typical, blocky and crate-like. John looked into his glass of clear liquid and the lone olive floating within and thought

24

some very melancholy thoughts. He grabbed the remote for the stereo. The CD player clicked on and soon Pink Floyd whispered from the other side of the room.

"James is a real jerk," Bill slurred.

"Watch your back, John," Tom said. "He's the kind of guy who would jump you in a dark alley."

John got up and walked to the bay window to look at his Japanese Samurai sword resting on its rack. The Sword as it had become to be known. Outside the wind whipped snow around the eaves "Yeah, but maybe by the time we get back in two weeks, he'll have forgotten the whole thing," Bill interjected. John pulled off his sweater and draped it over the chair, then hefted his broken bokken, spinning it in an intricate arc. He almost knocked over the CD stand.

"Believe it or not I'm really looking forward to the Event this weekend." Bill continued as he settled into a deep chair. John remained quiet.

"So, everybody is getting back together again; the Legion of the Black Skull returns in all of its decadent glory?" Tom asked. Kiera, his pet ferret, was now crawling up one arm and tumbling down the other. This was his second Medieval Society Event and he was looking forward to it, too.

"I called for reservations. We have one room." Bill fiddled with his guitar, tuning it. "We're lucky to get that. There are several conventions going on that weekend."

"So we're all crowded in one room?" Tom asked. "Of course."

John laughed. "Where's your sense of adventure!"

People bustled about the convention center in what seemed like organized chaos. The fat man with the manuscript booth watched as the remaining tents were finally erected and a group of jugglers practiced their agility with brightly colored balls. By Friday, everything would be in place and the participants would flood in. He turned back to his tent and lit a brass oil lamp. A vision of chiaroscuro leapt into existence: the shadows hiding the unknown, the light hinting at the hidden. Leather bound tomes, dusty with age, and brittle scrolls that could be authentic, lay about the tent on oak tables. The lamp hanging over the tables swung slightly. It was ornately fashioned in the shape of a swooping dragon; he had acquired that piece in Hong Kong.

The man opened the Book of Shadows and hesitated. It was nothing more than a blank book after all, but as he flipped through the pages, he thought he saw something. Something in black. Circular?

Getting old, Zach, he thought to himself as he flipped through once more and found nothing.

Suddenly the lamp blew out. "Damn!"

The drive to his parents' house on the lake was short, but monotonous. The farms were flat and bleak, the snow bright, but the roads were well salted and dry. John downshifted to dart past the car ahead of him, then settled back into the road ahead, his small sports car tightly hugging the curves.

His thoughts wandered as he drove. He and his friends had agreed to meet at Mike's on Friday morning for the drive to Detroit. That would give each of them a few days with their families. No such luck for him, though. His parents, in their retirement, had become snowbirds.

He took a meandering drive through the town, stopping to gaze out over the Bay and watch a coal freighter angle expertly in toward the docks. Finally, his reminiscing done, he turned and headed toward his parents' house.

For him, there was always something special about coming home. He pulled into the driveway of the small ranch style dwelling and parked the car. Figuring he'd get his bag later, he grabbed his sword and headed around to the back porch, through the immaculately kept garden. Even in the midst of winter, he could make out the familiar pattern of the shrubbery, the ornamental maple, and the accompanying stonework. He smiled faintly and unlocked the door, letting himself into the home of his youth.

The silence greeted him.

He put his Japanese sword on the kitchen island. It was long for a Katana, the blade itself must have been thirty inches in length, unblemished and with a graceful curve. The fittings, the hilt and scabbard were both in good repair. The scabbard, or saya was lacquered sharkskin, sanded and polished to a deep indigo. The guard, or tsuba, was forged and carried the design of two koi amid water lilies. The magnificent blade featured a complex forging pattern and an artistic hamon, the tempered cutting edge.

The Shinto period Jindachi was signed with two Japanese characters: Mountain Pine. On the opposite side of the tang read the cutting test: Ogawa Kuroemon tested it on two bodies, 1684, 2nd month on an auspicious day.

Stationed in Japan after the war, John's father had discovered a group of officers systematically looting shrines in and around Tokyo. He had been instrumental in stopping the criminal acts and, as a reward, one of the shrines had given him the sword as a gesture of thanks. His father had given the sword to him on his twenty-first birthday.

John's passion had always been for swords. He had managed to gather a small collection of mediocre blades, but none compared to this sword. The Japanese had raised sword-making to an art. Katana, Tachi, Wakizashi, and other blade types had evolved over the last two thousand years: forging techniques had been perfected to create a blade that was resilient, surgically sharp, and wore well over time. In Western society, Damascus steel was considered the pinnacle of blade-making.

The sword had almost become a part of him; he carried practically everywhere.

Funny how certain events elicit vivid dreams. Later that night, he dreamt of the sword. Clear dreams that transcended reality. The sword was being tested. He and a Samurai stood watching the tester, a man of lower standing, who stood with the sword poised as two convicts were lined up, blindfolded and tied against a bamboo pole. Calmly the man took a step forward, the sword flashed in a lateral cut, and easily passed through the midsections of the convicts. The Samurai nodded approvingly as other criminals cleared the bodies and the tester gave the blade to his assistant who wiped it clean, examined the edge for chips or cracks, and placed it carefully in its shirasaya, or resting scabbard. It went to the swordsmith who in turn chiseled the results on the tang. The sword was then presented to the Samurai who held it out to John.

He snapped awake, but the memory of that dream stayed with him. Unlike other dreams, often fraught with fancy and inconsistency, this one had a clarity that was surprising. He shivered, not from the cold but rather from a sense of uneasiness that would persist well into the evening.

Friday found Bill practically falling down the steps of Mike's front porch. Trying to pull on his jacket, heft his Estoc, a form of epee, and walk was evidently too much for him in the early morning hours, but he finally made it and threw his gear in the SUV. John leaned against the SUV with one bag and the Sword, as everyone called it. Chill lounged on the tailgate, staring over the rim of his glasses.

Chill was about five ten, and barrel-like. Slow and methodical in all things, he nodded to his friends as he wiped his hands on his pants.

"Ready?" he asked in a gravelly voice.

"Yep, but we're missing a few," Bill answered. Tom leaned his head out the driver's side door and in an effort to see who was there and who was not. Joe seemed to be running late and Mike was still inside his parents' house.

"Are we going to be jousting at this one?" Bill asked of John. If so there was a discrepancy in the gear they needed, especially padding.

"No, we're still disqualified from the fighting."

Chill smiled and said, "It seems when we broke with the ranks of the Midwest Kingdoms and began to fight for the Northern Kingdoms it was some sort of treaty infringement."

Bill shook his head. "The King of the Midwest was an ass. He wanted us to make a suicide run for the bridge. When we turned—"

"We surprised the hell outa them," Mike announced as he walked down the driveway. He carried a bag on his shoulder, the contents of which were questionable at best. His sandy brown hair was tousled and he wore his customary shades. The ever-present cigarette dangled from the corner of his mouth.

Mike was definitely on the fringes of the norm for most people, and even for college students, for that matter. He a was recent dropout from the physics department, having left just one step ahead of expulsion for turning his major into a tool for the pursuit of the occult. He had a fascination with the uncertainty principle, and believed that it resulted from an energy field indicating a fifth dimension; hence the existence of what the uninformed call 'magic'. The only thing was, he didn't know how it could be tapped, and the dean of the school of science didn't fancy him turning the department into an alembic. So, rather than face expulsion, he had withdrawn from the University and now managed a coffee shop downtown.

"Yeah," John remembered their mock ambush. "We turned and they thought we were retreating, so they rounded on us. Then we cut them down from behind." Chill frowned, but the throaty rumble of Joe's Mustang silenced his snide retort. Joe got out and stretched wearily. The artist appeared to be tired and in a very dark mood.

"Let's get this show on the road," called Chill.

"I can hardly wait," replied an enthusiastic John. "Shut up, John," sighed Chill.

Joe opened the curtains of their fourth-floor room and gazed at the Detroit skyline. The sun had just set and the twinkle of nightlife was radiating all around the city. He turned and looked over the room. It was cramped, with two full beds, but what would you expect. They would have to play it by ear, as they had only paid for two occupants.

Joe sat down on the divan and pulled out a yellow carbon slip from his shirt pocket, scratching at his beard as he perused it. It was dated six months ago, the last Society Event. He had placed an order with a blacksmith for a hand-and-a-half, or bastard sword. Now that he would probably lose his job with the dealer, he wondered if he could get his deposit back. Probably not, he thought. It might look nice at future fairs, a piece of contemporary folk art?

"Ah, the long anticipated bastard sword. You'll pick it up tomorrow?" John asked as he handed his friend a beer.

"Yep, I am blowing money right and left lately, but it's truly a sword worthy of a Landesknecht. I had it made to historically accurate specifications."

"He had some pretty good prices on short swords."

31

"Probably for cheap-asses like you," chided Chill. "I'm not cheap," John retorted.

"You are a mooch," began Chill.

"Yeah, John, you are known for your ability to weasel out of paying for things." Mike tipped his beer back, smiling.

"I thought I was frugal."

"Ooh, kinky," Mike quipped.

"Can it, Mike, we know your sexual habits only include stray cats and raw liver," Bill tossed back.

"We should get another Game going one of these days," Chill said, directing the statement to Mike, who was still glaring at Bill. Joe, frustrated at the direction the verbal jousting was heading slipped out onto the balcony.

"When do we have time to get together?"

"Who knows?" It was last thing John heard as he followed his friend onto the snow-covered balcony, four stories up. He shivered and wrapped his arms about himself.

"Jeez, it's freezing out here. You pick a helluva spot to collect your thoughts. What's up?"

Joe looked at him, then away, toward Windsor on the other side of the river. He sighed and tossed back his beer. "I accidentally set a twenty thousand dollar Dutch painting on fire."

"Ouch. What happened?"

"Don't know. I had a very mild thinner on the edge, I found some strange writing in Cyrillic on the back. Took a digital photo and a few minutes later, whoosh, up in flames. I don't know if the chemical in the thinner reacted to the light. I called the manufacturer and they never heard of such a thing."

"What about insurance?"

"Oh it's covered. But, it just isn't the just the money, I'll pay the gallery owner. Though my insurance will go sky high. It was a seventeenth century Dutch Master; do you know how hard it is to come by those outside a museum? I'll never get a conservatory job again. Word travels. I'm screwed."

"If it's any consolation, I know how you feel."

"Yeah. Tom said something was up with you?"

John laughed. "Yeah, ain't we a pair. You kill a Dutch Master and I have no idea what to do with my life."

"I don't know, bud. I wonder if I'll lose the school. I need the job at the Smithsonian and the gallery to help keep it and me afloat, but my offer is still out there for joining me at the school." His gaze wandered down over the street, gray eyes peering through the gloom.

"There's a difference between owning one's problems and playing victim. I can't imagine you shirking that. Go in and tell them what happened, tell them it was an accident. They can't fire you because of that can they?"

"Wanna bet? They aren't very forgiving. Maybe it's time to throw myself into the school." He shook his head. He let the silence build between them for a moment, until the chill air finally began to take its toll. Finally he sighed and turned to reenter the hotel room.

"Don't beat yourself up about this, Joe. God knows we all come to a point where we question our worth. You are more accomplished than a lot of people I've met in the past two years. Keep that in mind. There's no way you will end up on the street; you have friends and family. Go to your boss, tell the truth and screw them if they don't like it. You are one of the best restorers they have. Just keep that in mind, there are plenty of museums in foreign countries that have never heard of you." He smiled sheepishly.

Joe looked over his shoulder to his friend. "Thanks for the pep talk. What about you?"

"Well, I get to spend a month in Japan, then come back for graduation.

There isn't much work for a Sociologist with just a master's degree. I've come to the realization that if I am going to do anything meaningful with my life I better start soon."

"Careful what you wish for," Joe warned as he slipped back into the room. "You may get it."

The sharply dressed pharmaceutical rep adjusted her glasses and hefted her briefcase as the elevator stopped on her floor. She frowned with impatience. It had been a long day spent in meetings and all she wanted to do was get a bite to eat in the restaurant before she went to her room to soak in a tub of hot water. As the elevator doors slid open, she gasped at the six figures standing there. Cautiously entering, she tried not to gawk as her eyes darted from one bizarre vision to the next. Twilight Zone, she thought.

The biggest stood in the rear, in some kind of brown tunic, leather boots and cape, with a

Samurai sword of some kind. A wolfish grin lifted his Manchu-style mustache, and he adjusted his mirrored sunglasses. Was he staring at her? Two others: one in a black quilted outfit with a cape and black boots, stood holding a black-sheathed Japanese sword as he talked to another, a bearded man with a purple tunic that had a beautifully-embroidered demon skull on it. His faux ermine cloak was slung back, and he had no weapon she could see. A tall, very handsome fellow with long blonde hair was dressed in bright pastels. He spoke with a sandy haired man dressed in a hooded tunic, buckskins and loose fitting pants. He had on what looked like authentic Native American moccasins and he carried a bow over his back. She shivered in revulsion upon seeing the buffalo leather cloak.

A shorter man, with shoulder-length black hair, leaned his stocky frame against the wall and smoothed his olive-drab tunic; a broadsword hung at his side. He gestured at the blonde haired guy's intricately hilted sword and scabbard and smiled slowly. The tall one laughed.

The elevator door slid open and the businesswoman stepped into the hallway. The lift continued on its journey and she went to her room, shaking her head all the way.

Freaks, she thought.

The thought of writing a check made his teeth hurt, but as the smith set the bastard sword on the table between them, Joe just smiled in appreciation. The black metal blade was about forty-two inches long and its edge gleamed with sharpness, the carved runes gently glowing in the overhead fluorescent lights. Joe hefted it – the

35

balance was perfect and the pommel was made for either one or two hands. It seemed a pity to hide such a beautiful creation inside a scabbard, but Joe had worked long and hard to create something that would accent the smith's work. The tooled leather was studded with stones and gilt wire; a fitting home for an artist's weapon. It accented the new blade nicely. He wondered if he were meant to carry a blade more akin to this than a fencing saber. He produced his checkbook, and wrote a check for the amount remaining.

"I could sure use a beer," John stated resting his hand on the hilt of his Japanese Katana.

"Hmmm?" replied the artist. "Yeah, I'm thirsty all of a sudden.

The six members that were the 'Legion of the Black Skull' sat in one of the gaily-bannered pavilions, waiting for their serving wench to bring beer and roast pig with yams. Just outside the roped-off eating area, jugglers tossed clubs, tumblers leapt about, and strolling minstrels regaled revelers with their songs. The companions ate and watched the open field in the center of the convention hall where the melee took place. A group of men in thickly padded armor with mock weapons went after each other. The group surged and ebbed as the referees called out to those that were either dead or seriously injured. Soon the field was held by a remaining small group of brightly dressed knights with the ensign of a white cross on red field.

"Those dudes are the ones that got the prize when we had to forfeit at the last joust," Chill murmured.

"I've met them," remarked Bill. "They think they're God's gift to the Medieval Society."

"Hmmph," was all that issued from Mike. His mouth was stuffed full of meat, which was probably just as well. He had nothing good to say about their rivals, either.

"They really aren't that good," observed Smiling Wolf. He smoothed down Kiera's coat and offered her some dried fruit to nibble on. She looked at him as though he were crazy and tried to nip at his finger. He just ignored her.

They all watched as the band of winners approached the King's chair and received their trophy. Joe stood up, thoroughly disgusted and turned his back on the awarding of the trophy. He picked up his cloak, adjusted his new sword and strode off. Soon the rest were done with their meals, and John, Mike and Bill wandered off to look at the booths and tents. Set off to one side, a manuscript dealer caught Mike's eye. Seemingly isolated from the hustle and bustle of the rest of the fair, the tent exuded a tranquility he found intriguing. The three walked over, curious as to what type of manuscripts and print-work the tent might contain.

As their eyes adjusted to the dimly lit tent, Zach, the proprietor, greeted them. His hands fluttered ceaselessly about the designs on his purple robe. John stood by the door, not exactly caring for ancient grimoires and such, while Bill and Mike browsed through the materials.

Mike approached one of the tables and picked up a huge, handwritten, leather-bound book that must have been centuries old. He opened and looked at the first page; it was written in Latin. He smiled, recognizing the text. It was something for the summoning and banishing of spirits to another plane of existence. When he saw the price he set it down.

"It is too much, milord?" the man asked in Society jargon.

"Well worth the price, I'm sure, my good merchant, but two hundred dollars is beyond my purse, I am afraid," Mike replied. Bill raised his eyebrow and realized why the tent was empty.

"But is the knowledge not worth it?" came the obsequious reply

"Can one truly put a price on knowledge?" Mike queried back.

The man smiled and stepped back, allowing the students to browse. Mike's eye was caught by a flutter of light from the lamp that played over the surface of a dingy black book. He picked it up, feeling the worn leather cover, noted the ragged edges of the paper. As he flipped through it, he thought he caught something on one of the pages, but when he flipped again there was nothing. Mike replaced the book and shook his hands; it felt like they had started to fall asleep.

"You know what that is?" Zach asked. The lamps flickered as if with a sudden breeze. Mike looked up and replied uneasily.

"It's a book for the recording of spells and magical notation."

"Yes, and the dealer I bought it from said it belonged to the Crowley estate." Mike raised his eyebrows. Aleister Crowley reputedly knew a great deal regarding magic and sorcery, and was also reputed to have been a most evil man. If it truly were from the Crowley Estate it would be worth a pretty penny, even if it hadn't been written in.

"Do you have a provenance?"

"Unfortunately no, gentle lord."

"How much?"

"Milord, my prices are very reasonable, fifty dollars."

"Fifty dollars for a blank book?" John said dubiously from behind Mike. "Twenty-five," Mike countered.

"Give me leave to make a little profit, young sire. Thirty-five."

"Thirty, and that's my final offer."

"As you will, but many more such deals will beggar me." The bookseller got some brown paper from below a table and quickly wrapped the book.

Bill shook his head. "You sure know how to waste your money, Mike." From the look on John's face, he echoed Bill's amazement.

"No, if the book really was Crowley's, I made an investment. If it isn't, I can still use the pages to chronicle the Black Skull's adventures. Not a bad deal either way."

Chapter 2

Somewhere, somewhen, there was a stirring. The old man slowly climbed winding stairs to the top of an imposing tower. As he reached the pinnacle, power suffused the room, and lightning flashed, illuminating his rheumy eyes. His robe was purple and the patterns on it seemed to move and shimmer. His gnarled old hand held a book, the pages filled with intricate formulae, drawings and text in some obscure language. Carefully, he chalked a circle on the floor around him and then uttered the words. They leapt from his tongue with the ease of old habit, convoluting through space and time, reaching the aether. The book in his hand glowed. The Gate was opening.

Guyle, why do you summon me? The rasp of the words filled his mind like steel on bone. He vaguely perceived the image of a translucent, membranous wing; white viscous fluid drowning something small and pink. His mind reeled and he fought for control. He touched his signet ring to his forehead.

"The Power you promised me. A Gate was triggered. I sensed it."

He almost felt the sharp teeth revealed by the apparition's evil smile. Form bespoke I none. But power thou shalt have. In number, six – for that is harmony. Yet, to white change you must, or your design will fail. I give you this, mortal:

Six is the number,, Stronger than you know; Break six asunder Thy power will grow.

"When?"

Soon, but take care, your undoing it may be. Through Perilous Gate they come. You know the summoning, you know the Path to that Gate. Look for the White Knight in the South, and there you will find the six. You know the way.

Thunder roared in the old man's ears, leaving emptiness and the faint breath of the damned. The powerful creature was gone.

Joe packed his tunic and cloak and carefully placed the bastard sword in a leather rifle case. There, all done. Now I go home and face my boss.

John pulled on his leather jacket and hefted his katana and his duffel bag. The others were already waiting at the parking garage. John gave the room a once- over to make sure that they hadn't forgotten anything and they were on their way. "You know, Joe, I could handle a life like this. Being a Knight, and my friends by my side. I sometimes wish it were so simple."

"I know what you mean, buddy, but somehow I don't think it would be quite this pleasant," said the artist as he watched the descending lights on the elevator wall. "True, there are no worries, no real hassles, but we have to face reality. You can't live life in a fantasy world."

"Right," John replied and stepped into the lobby. After they settled the bill, they met the rest of the gang in the garage. The Trailblazer was warm as they all crammed into the vehicle. Soon they were on their way.

"Where the hell are we?" Chill asked, more than a little perturbed.

"I'm not sure. Bill wanted to take a more scenic route through the State park. According to the map we should be there by now. It's hard to tell with all the snow," Tom said wearily as he squinted through the windshield.

"It seems we've been driving for hours. You know Bill, nothing's very scenic in the dark." Joe fidgeted between John and Bill. Mike sat behind them with the luggage packed all around him.

The SUV's lights illuminated a narrow strip of road columned on both sides with dark pines and coniferous growths. Fleeting drifts of snow would snag the tires every so often and pull the truck to the embankment on the right. Chill sat in the front seat peering intently at a map.

"There's a sign, Chill. What does it say?" asked Tom as he tried to make it out with his one good eye.

Chill rolled down the window. Snow suddenly pelted the interior, nonetheless he stuck his head outside trying to get a better view and read.

"Isle Royale, one hundred twenty miles. Route...can you make it out? Where in the hell?" Chill muttered.

"Oh great, we're heading north. How that happened I'll never know," Joe was incredulous as he looked at Chill. Chill shook his head; he couldn't find the route on the map.

"Man, talk about whiteout," Bill said from the cramped seat. At least it wasn't cold in the Blazer. Kiera snuggled against his stomach.

"Whiteout, it's damn wall of snow," Tom replied as he looked for a turn- around. "I still don't know how we got headed in the wrong direction–"

He was cut short as a crack filled the air and a large tree fell onto the narrow road not twenty feet in front of them.

"Shit!" Tom yelled as the others held tight; the Blazer slid into a spin.

Somewhen, the old man stood above an altar, upon which lay a flawlessly beautiful infant, squalling piteously. The book lay open to one side. As he lit the oil lamp and waved his hand over the altar, the baby fell silent. Then his arm plummeted, knife slashed, blood flowed. It was powerful and risky sorcery, yet the benefit he expected would be worth it. The flux was spun.

The SUV fishtailed out of control and sailed over the embankment. The drop seemed to last forever. The six friends were too stunned to yell.

Chapter 3

Darkness.

A feeling of free fall infused Michael's being.

This isn't heaven, he thought to himself. He had images of countless colors. "It is the Between," came a voice.

"Where am I?" the big man asked. "Somewhere, somewhen."

"Let's be specific. What happened?"

"Your bodies are lying broken and shattered at the bottom of a ravine."

"What can I do?" he had a feeling of immense potential, power just beyond his grasp.

"A bargain then?"

Bargain? "For what, my soul?"

"Hardly anything so mundane. When I ask, you must do me a favor."

"What favor?"

"That is not for me to say."

"Whatever, but when we get out of this we must be okay." There was a sigh like the wind and Mike didn't like it at all.

His back hurt and he awoke to the groans of the others. He was slumped over in steering wheel, the safety belt mercilessly constricting his midsection. Blood fell in a steady drip from his nose and he pressed against it as an afterthought. The SUV was tilted forward at an odd angle and the front windshield was a spiderweb of cracks. Tom rubbed his neck and pushed back from the wheel. Chill was out cold and Bill was groaning. Kiera jumped frantically from seat to seat.

"Is everybody okay?" John called. He sat back and a twinge of pain made him grimace.

"What do you think, asshole," came Joe's curt reply. Then: "Oh my god." Everybody looked toward where his eyes were fixed. In the dashboard between Chill and Tom was Joe's sword. Inches to the right or left and it would have impaled someone. He quickly pulled it from the shattered plastic and metal as static electricity arced over the tip. How on earth had it come from its scabbard.

"My guitar is dead," came Bill's tenor and John looked over to see him hold up a twisted mass of strings and wood.

"Glad that's the only thing," replied John.

"I guess we made it through with nothing more than bruises," Tom said as

Chill's eyes flicked over the sharp bastard sword and Joe, who was inspecting it. "Right," said Joe, who looked at the ruined dash.

Chill and Tom banged their doors open and stepped onto some water-slick rocks. Somehow it seemed a lot warmer than they remembered. They looked up the embankment, the top of which was hidden in mist. They heard the lapping of waves behind them; they must have crashed just short of a small lake.

"Where's all the snow?" Chill echoed as he looked about. The mist obscured everything beyond twenty feet.

"Michigan has weird weather," Joe responded as he crawled out the door. "Well, instead of just sitting here, I suggest we head up the hill and flag down a car. I'd say by the light that we must have been down here for some time." John looked at the sky, which was turning deep cobalt.

"That's brilliant John, who would have thought you could figure all that out on your own," Chill grumbled as he began to scramble up the steep grade. He reached the summit first and the sight that greeted him was slightly disturbing.

"Hey, guys," he said and turned to look at them make their way up. "Where's the road?"

"What do you mean 'where's the road?'" Joe began, but stopped dead when he reached the top.

They all gathered near Chill and looked around incredulously. They stood on an outcropping of grass and rock, and before them rose an immense forest. Ancient trees rose heavenward. Their gaze traveled to the right and left, but the forest followed the cliff they stood upon. When they turned they almost fell from shock.

They hadn't crashed at the foot of a small lake; the rocky shore of an ocean stretched as far as they could see.

"Jesus, this ain't Michigan," muttered Bill.

"If it is, they certainly know how to keep a secret," remarked John whirling about as he heard the distant cry of some animal. Shakily, he turned and looked back down the ravine. The SUV rested on rocks not five feet from the calm surf. In the distance, they could see the fading red glow of the sunset. As the sky grew darker and a leaden mist began to roll up the coast, their predicament began to sink in: there was no road, no icy winter, nothing of what should be there.

"I've got a bad feeling about this," Chill whined under his breath. "Where on earth are we?" Bill asked of nobody in particular.

"Oh shit!" Mike muttered and sat down heavily on the grass; he stared about blankly.

"What!?" everyone asked in unison. "Oh boy, you guys don't remember?"

"What!?" yelled Joe.

"After we crashed I blacked out. I heard a voice; I thought I was just dreaming. The voice said that our lives would be saved for a favor that would be exacted in the future. I thought that anything would be better than death.

"Anything?" Joe yelled.

Mike sat, frowning. He crossed his legs and rested his chin on a fist. "Let me think."

"Great, we'll be here all night," muttered John. "You're nuts or in shock," Chill stated flatly.

"CIA spies would be more believable," Joe retorted.

"Look," Mike started. "It all figures. I think that instead of dying in the crash, we've been transported to some alternate reality."

"You are nuts! Am I supposed to believe we are in some parallel universe?" Joe was incredulous.

"I think I'm gonna be sick," Chill whined and sat down.

"Wherever we are I'm sure we're going to find out," Tom insisted almost too casually. Kiera sat atop his shoulder, a monarch surveying her subjects.

"What should we do?" Bill asked as he looked around at his friends.

"I suggest we get our things from the truck and make camp until daybreak," said Tom thoughtfully.

"Yes," Mike concurred. "We should set up camp and rest for a while." Mike just sat there nodding his head and mumbling.

"Chill and I will get some firewood," Bill cut in, and the two immediately headed for the edge of the forest.

"Be careful," John called after them.

"Don't worry," Joe said, after the two were out of range. "They'll be scared of their own shadows."

"Well, if this is the afterlife, it's a science-fiction writer's dream come true," John said as he watched the flames dance back and forth over the heavy branches in the fire. He leaned against his duffel bag, cleaning the enameled scabbard of his katana. It was a crisp, clear night and the surf was a calm whisper behind them. The black vault above was sprinkled with brilliant white diamonds. The sound of the forest's nocturnal animals was a melody of unfamiliar calls.

"Is this our imagination?" Mike asked in a haunted voice.

"If this is one of your fantasy worlds, Mike, then we'll probably last about five minutes," Joe scowled as he rested his chin on his knees. His gray eyes peered into the darkness beyond the firelights edge.

"Not if we're careful," it was Mike's knowing reply.

"What the hell is that supposed to mean?" Bill asked. He caught the drift in Mike's voice but wanted to confirm the implications.

"It's nice to believe we could get by without weapons, but this land may be hostile to us. It may not be as peaceful as it seems."

"You've been watching too many movies, Mike," Joe countered. "I hope you're right."

"For all we know," Chill piped in, "This place could be devoid of inhabitants."

"Or," Joe began with a devious grin, "Just beyond the forest edge may lie a huge metropolis, full of horny green aliens, ready to suck the life out of us with their seductive charms."

"This is most likely purgatory," John replied.

"That's your Catholic guilt talking." Joe smiled at the thought.

"Well, that's the last of it. The Trailblazer's officially totaled." Tom threw a bundle of gear to the ground and startled the group from their reverie. He had come so silently up the cliff that they hadn't noticed him until he was on top of them. He indicated a flashlight and batteries.

"I suggest that we conserve those, and the first aid kit." Reaching into his black coat, he pulled out his knife and began to run it over a whetstone, even though it was obviously honed to razor sharpness.

"Nervous?" John asked.

"Nope," replied the Native American. "Unfortunately we have very few supplies."

"We'll have to use your bow for hunting," Mike said. The red glow of the fire made him seem right out of Dante's Inferno.

"Hold on!" Joe shook his head. "We don't even know where we are. There could be a MacDonald's just over that rise."

"I doubt it," Mike replied as he brushed a spider from his arm.

"Speaking of food, I'm starved," Chill said as he looked around. The drool almost flew from his lips.

"Be patient," Joe tried to mollify his friend. Tom tossed him a granola bar. "Well, our key concern is protecting ourselves from wild animals," Mike intoned.

"The fire's big enough, Mike, that it should scare anything away," Tom chuckled.

"Survival isn't our key concern here, we don't know where we are or how to get back. We should stick close and find somebody, or something, with good intentions to help us," Mike droned on.

"I agree, Mike," replied John as he rolled over and quickly fell asleep.

Joe pulled his wool coat on and leaned back. Soon all the others were bedding down.

"Yes, I advise rest. Tomorrow we'll go search for things that we will need to survive. Of course the natives and animals are a concern here; whether carnivorous or-"

The group fell asleep to Mike's monologue, assured that his voice would keep anything dangerous away.

The gray of dawn crept over the six sleeping figures with a tenuous touch as the pearly sun inched over the coastline and colored the sward with hints of illumination. A tiny thread of smoke wafted from the cooling embers of their fire as the morning dew stole the last vestiges of warmth from the charred logs. The constant wash of the surf was a mellow contrast to the raucous cries of the morning birds, high in their treetop homes.

Joe rolled over and something sharp bit into his back. He groaned and reached back to remove it.

"Damn stones," he muttered groggily. Instead of the expected rock, he felt the tip of a slender metal object whose sharp edges pressed against his spine. "What the hell?"

He turned over and stared at the business end of a long black lance. A fully armored man on horseback held the other end. Joe shut his eyes tightly then opened them again. The figure was still there.

"What the–!" Joe yelled and scrambled away. He looked around and saw that ten men on horseback surrounded their camp. All bore swords and lances and had the look of hard-bitten soldiers. Joe looked at them, not believing his eyes.

"I got that distinct feeling we're in deep shit," Chill said as he surveyed the newcomers through sleep-laden eyes. The rest of the group was finally awake and they formed a tight knot around their gear, waiting for the new arrivals to speak first. "Ja al, et tu?" came the first volley. The six of them stared back, uncomprehending. "Ja al, et tu?!" this time more insistent and with a raised lance.

"We better say something," Joe muttered under his breath.

"What do you say to ten black knights: how's the weather?" John replied. "Flanum, tenobis erot ne tet," said one of the horsemen and another laughed.

One stepped from the saddle and approached the group.

"Sounds vaguely like Latin," Mike whispered.

"Well, my Latin's a little rusty, but I know it when I hear it, and that ain't it," John said.

"Sprechen sie Deutsch?" Joe asked of the men. There was no response. "Good, Joe, why don't you try Klingon next." Bill shook his head.

The horseman who had dismounted sneered as he spoke. His voice was harsh, as if used to giving commands and getting his way.

"You speak the common tongue of the traveler," he spat. There was a hint of suspicion in the way he said it, as if he knew who they really were.

"Right," Joe replied, his voice almost cracking.

"Yes, we speak that tongue, and others," Mike spoke up. John looked at him with alarm.

"But nary the tongue of the Conclaveum?" the man returned. He pulled his helmet off to reveal blunt features cut harshly by a thick beard and black eyes.

"Unfortunately...no."

"Who are you and what is your business in the Regent's lands?" The man gestured behind him and the other riders dismounted.

"We are merchants," Bill blurted out. The others turned and looked at him sharply. "We were shipwrecked on the coast and survived with nothing more than what you see here."

"Merchants," the man repeated thoughtfully and shouldered aside the students to look at their gear.

"You carry nice weapons for merchants. And yet your clothes are strange."

"We were afraid of bandits, that is why we are armed," Smiling Wolf spoke up. This did not seem to be going well, for reasons that escaped them.

"The Regent Gelion holds sway over this province," the man said. "He would not be pleased to have spies from distant lands roaming about."

"Gelion," Mike said. "Do we know a Gelion?"

"I believe we do," John replied. "Two seasons ago I think."

"Right," Joe said. "I think we know this Regent of yours."

"Oh, since you know the Regent, then you won't mind being his guest?" It was not a question. He gestured to the other rider who began to stow the group's gear.

"Uh, we really should be getting back," Bill said rather lamely. "No. I insist!" the rider said sharply and mounted his steed.

The group was prodded forward by a row of lances until they came to a game trail at the forest's edge. Tall ferns brushed at their thighs as they marched ahead of the horsemen. The light that filtered from above was a golden hue, making the forest seem calm and serene. The ground didn't hinder their walking, as the turf was soft and yielding.

"How convenient," Joe said sarcastically. "We didn't even have to look for trouble. It found us. Well, Mike, this does seem to be one of your fantasy worlds...isn't it quaint?"

"Let's see what happens," the big man replied. He seemed at a loss for words.

"So much for bluffing," John said under his breath. "We don't know any Regent!"

"Go along with it," Mike whispered back. "For now at least."

"Go along with it?" Joe asked, incredulous. "Wonderful. And when they find out we're lying, they cut our throats."

"We may be able to take them," Tom said quietly as he tucked Kiera's questioning head back into his coat.

"So where is this assault rifle you've been hiding?" Joe countered. Tom glared back and was silent.

Glancing at his watch, John saw that they had been walking for about four hours when the ground on either side of trail began to rise, exposing rich, black soil. Roots twisted and turned as if they were snakes suddenly exposed by a swath of ground being lifted away. High above, the leaves ruffled in the warm breeze. As the level of the road dropped, the earth to their right rose above their heads and formed a natural stone archway. It seemed ancient, like bare bone shorn of flesh and exposed to the elements. The stone at the top of the portal was carved in the likeness of a sunburst. Living vines curled their way around it.

"I've seen something like that before," Joe mused under his breath. "Sumerian?" The lead horseman called them to a halt and the other riders sheathed their lances and stopped.

"The trail is precarious here, merchants. Be careful. We don't want any harm to come to the friends of Regent Gelion."

The group walked through the arch and peered through and down. Before them was a lush river valley. The trail dropped steeply among moss-covered stones and knee high ferns. Around them stood a variety of oaks and maples, keeping most of the area in shade. At the center of the valley flowed a wide, slow moving river and on the river sat a low, dark keep. There was some activity about the walls.

"Cute," Joe said dryly.

"Done in early castle, I think," John replied.

It took them a good half hour to reach the level floor of the valley. They approached the keep at a casual pace, watching the walls rise before them, higher than they seemed from above the valley. Two massive wooden doors swung open on creaking hinges and the group was ushered through them.

"We're gonna die," Chill whispered.

"Yeah," Joe concurred. "This is the farm, the big one."

"Keep cool," Mike uttered nervously.

John just looked at Tom who shrugged and continued walking.

As the men-at-arms watched with a mixture of curiosity and cruel amusement, the lead rider dismounted, tethered his horse to a post in front of a low hall, and gestured for the group to precede him inside. The cool darkness made them shiver as their eyes adjusted slowly to the dim light. Gradually they began to make out the details of the hall. Heavy wooden pillars supported the dark ceiling. At the far end of the hall was flaming open hearth, and in the center of the hall was a long table, a high-backed chair at its head.

They walked toward the table as several riders placed the students' gear on it then went to stand sentinel along the walls. The lead rider went to the table and began picking through their gear.

After a few moments Bill cleared his throat. "So, where's the Regent Gelion?"

The man looked up contemptuously. "I'm the Regent, you dolt." He placed his helm on the chair.

"We're dead," Chill said.

The Regent looked at them with glimmering eyes that pierced the soul.

"I am Gelion, Regent of South, and of Narntoc, the province of the Conclaveum," he said, smiling coldly. Beneath the smile was something wary and menacing. A brutality brought on by years in this far-flung place.

His finger traced a scratch in the enamel of his armor as he assessed the fine workmanship of the blades on the table. He was an experienced warrior and he obviously knew the value of these unusual weapons. He glanced over the Event costumes as a guard dragged them out of their bags, then he casually looked at the clothes his captives wore. The blue breeches, the boots, the weird blouses and coverlets – it obviously disturbed him. In all his years in the Conclaveum he had seen nothing like what they wore. These six men seemed calm and ready to spring to action. It wasn't just posturing; they looked like they knew how to fight, although they were young. And terrible liars.

A shame, he thought, they are probably spies, or worse.

He picked up a black-handled object, the top of which was shaped like a goblet with a thin piece of crystal covering it. On the handle was a depression. He pressed it and a beam of light leapt out.

His eyes widened in surprise and he looked quickly to the group.

"What type of sorcery is this, that a lantern without heat or fire may shine?" He looked to Mike who stood at the front of the group. "Which one of you is the sorcerer who commands this tool?"

No one spoke during this moment of culture shock.

Gelion smiled and tossed the flashlight into the fire. Mike rolled his eyes and Tom made a move to the hearth, but the guard behind him held him. Okay, not yet, Tom thought.

Gelion walked to Mike and put a dagger to his throat.

"Tell me, boy, who are you and who sent you? Was it Trevor?"

"Go play with yourself," Mike replied coolly.

The Regent smiled and hit him in the side of the head with the pommel of the dagger. Mike sagged to the ground in a daze.

He motioned for a guard to watch over Mike. "For each answer that I do not like, I lop off a finger." He walked over to Joe and smiled. Joe met his gaze with contempt and tried to shake off the guard that held his arm.

Only one guard apiece, they don't think we're a threat, Joe thought.

"You look like someone of the Conclaveum, yet you dress unlike anyone I have ever seen. You dress like a popinjay." With that Gelion slit open his argyle sweater.

Joe tilted his head ever so slightly to the side. Just as he was about to reply there came two loud reports from the hearth as the flashlight batteries exploded.

As the Regent turned in shock, Joe lunged, catching the man squarely in the groin with the toe of his shoe. A look of surprise, then pain crossed the Gelion's face as he fell to the floor. Seizing their opportunity, the others leapt into action.

Chill slipped free and ran to bar the door against reinforcements. Joe snatched up Gelion's dagger, just as John leaned and flipped the guard over his shoulder like a sack, and Bill ran to help Mike. The guard standing over the inert form was just about to raise his sword when Bill caught his arm, deflecting the killing blow and slamming the guard into the table.

Tom ground his heel into the foot of the man behind him. The guard yelled in pain and stepped backward. Tom struck him with three wrecking blows to the chest, and the man fell to the floor, out cold.

Gelion had rolled into the fetal position and was whimpering like a dog. Mike was just coming around when one of the guards pulled forth his curved sword and raised it high to finish Mike off. Tom grabbed one of the downed guards' spears and let fly at the swordsman. The spear caught him in the spine and he spiraled grotesquely to the ground, dead. The sword fell with a clang to the floor.

All motion ceased, and a quiet descended on the hall.

Joe looked at Tom, not quite sure what to say as the others took in the scene. Bill felt a wave a nausea coming; he bent over and vomited.

"Tom," Bill muttered. "You killed him."

"Yeah, that's obvious."

"Now what?" Joe called.

"Whatever, we gotta get out of here," chimed Chill as he peered through the grate in the door.

Where the hell is here, and where do we go? Joe's thoughts whirled in his head.

Mike groaned and stood. He felt the tender spot behind his ear and a sneer grew on his lips.

"I'll dismember the bastard!" he swore and started for Gelion. "No time!" rejoined Bill as he held the big man.

As Joe and John gathered their confiscated gear, Tom bound the unconscious men with strips of their tunics, then went to the door that was behind the table. He looked through the grate and peered down a dimly lit corridor that led to another door. "I think we should look around before going into that courtyard and getting slaughtered," he sighed. Soon they were all making their way down the hall, at the end of which was a small room that seemed to be sleeping quarters of sorts. "No one around. Maybe they don't suspect yet," Joe said as he looked about.

"It won't last long, especially if the Regent unties himself or gets that gag off. We gotta make tracks," Chill replied. He strapped on the broadsword he had worn so casually at the Society Event. Now the blade felt heavy.

They all stood and looked at one another, trying to convince themselves that this was really happening.

"Okay, normally I'd suggest we wait until dark, but that's obviously out of the question." Mike drew his Katana and the sharp edge glinted.

"As I recall, when we came into the fort, the stables were to the right of the hall. That would be that building there." Tom pointed to a low outbuilding wedged between the hall and the stout walls of the fort.

Joe cracked the doors and looked around. It was deathly still as evening drew near.

"All's quiet," John said as he adjusted his sword. Joe looked at him for a moment then outside again. "Maybe they're at the hall," the gray-eyed artist sighed.

"Whatever, we gotta move now," came Mike's voice from behind. "I don't know," started Bill.

"We can argue later," Mike called. "Right now, out of here is the only way to survive."

"Okay, John first," Bill retorted. "Me?" John asked dubiously.

"I'll go," Tom slid beside him and out the door. He looked about. The guards on the wall had their backs to him. He quickly ducked into the shadows next to the stable and the rest of the group followed.

"What I wouldn't do for a ring of invisibility," Joe whispered. "What I wouldn't do to wake up," came Bill's reply.

They crept like thieves into the musky building; the familiar smell of horses invaded their senses. The beasts shied nervously as the six moved about, especially when Tom drew near; they could smell his ferret.

"I wish I had taken more riding lessons," Chill said with a note of exasperation.

"I'd feel better in a tank," John said as they began to mount up. Tom fitted two spare horses with most of their gear.

"That sentiment is probably shared by all of us," Bill stated. As they nudged the horses to the door, they heard the shrill ringing of a bell. The shout of men and the clamor of running told them that their escape was discovered.

"Shit!" yelled Joe as he reined his horse around. The doors of the building had burst open and the entrance was blocked by a group of men. Tom slapped the rears of the remaining steeds and they charged out of the stable, scattering the men to the side as sharp hooves hit open turf.

The guardsmen fell back and drew their swords. Mike charged his horse to the side of Joe's as the others followed him. Tom was in the rear, setting fire to the stable after having routed the remaining beasts. There were about twenty men in the courtyard opposing them, and more coming from the barracks. Several stood at the gate, barring it with a timber; soon they would have the portcullis down, cutting off any escape.

John spurred his horse forward and it reared as it came to the man at the gate; he fell to the flailing hooves. John heard a crack, and an arrow slammed into the heavy leather saddle, inches from his thigh. He looked at the top of the wall to see an archer ready another arrow, draw the string, and take aim at him...

A twang and a whoosh right behind John sent his ear ringing. The archer fell from the wall clutching an arrow in his chest.

"Thanks," John called to Tom, who rode with his bow in hand.

Tom nodded and spun the horse, covering John, who dismounted and unbarred the gate. Soon the others followed him through, leaving the Regent and his men to deal with the chaos they left behind.

They followed the river as night descended. They had no idea where they were going and the terrain was but a fleeting memory from the earlier forced march. But no thought of what lay ahead could interfere with their relief at being free again.

Chapter 4

"I can't believe this is happening," scowled Chill as he pulled off his shirt and looked back to the rest of the group. It had grown quite warm over the course of the morning.

The small party sat at the edge of a clearing, watering their horses by a stream. Behind them lay the forest, and before them they could make out the distant snowy caps of mountains. A warm breeze caught the high grasses of the rolling hills and sparse clouds raced overhead.

They were basking in the warm sun, not used to anything but snow and wind- chill factors. Joe scooped some water from the stream and splashed his face; it was cool and refreshing.

"What a great reception to the land of our dreams," he said and rubbed his sore buttocks.

"Better than being tortured," John smiled as he shoved his sweater into his pack. He breathed deeply and the air tasted sweeter with the intoxicant of freedom.

"Too bad none of that oxygen is getting to your brain," needled Chill. "Mike, could you hand me my sword?" John asked innocently.

"Sorry, I don't want to see you break it on his head." The big man adjusted his sunglasses and he heard Bill laugh, then choke, no doubt from swallowing some toothpaste.

"Besides, John, if you did something that might harm the group I would have to retaliate," Mike had that pseudo-macho tone of voice.

"That's real brave of you, Mike," Joe snarled as he tossed a twig at the big man. Then: "I swear to God. You win one fight and you think you're a demigod. I'd like to see you handle it all on your own."

"Oh, I don't know about that," started Mike, ready to launch into one of his long, drawn-out spiels.

"Oh no," John muttered, realizing how lengthy that process could be.

"You never agree, Mike. You can't admit you're wrong, face it," Joe retorted. "I can, when the proof is there," he replied.

"Proof! Who's proof? Can't you take my word for a change?"

"Watch it, Joe," said Chill. "That's two questions. He'll spend the rest of the day answering them...with other questions." He laughed and sat down in the shade, chewing on a piece of grass.

Tom, who had been rummaging through one of the saddlebags, turned abruptly and produced a thin piece of paper.

"Hey, our luck is just too good. I found a map."

"Is it Triple A?" asked Joe sarcastically.

The group gathered around Tom as he spread the parchment over a rock. Kiera jumped from shoulder to shoulder in the huddle, her frenetic actions irritating most of the group. After much pondering they discerned what must be the Regent's fort.

"This would be the river we followed," Joe pointed out.

"This writing doesn't help," Mike intoned, "But we should be about here."

"What's this?" Bill piped in as he pointed to the black square surrounded by a circle.

"Another keep, maybe a town. Looks like it's across some border," Joe looked at John. Just like the war games, he thought. "Think they're friendly?" Tom asked.

"Either that or they're worse than Gelion."

"Great."

"It doesn't look too far, maybe a day by horse," Tom stated after he assessed the scale on the map.

"Well, we should get started then," said Chill as he stared at the hard leather saddle.

"Fortune won't find us, we have to find it," Mike cheerily replied.

They moved out from under the comfortable shade of the trees and into the more humid plains. It seemed like any other summer day and they could almost succumb to the tranquility and forget the previous night, almost.

"I gotta take a dump," announced Mike.

"Well thank you for sharing that with us." Joe rolled his eyes. "Who the hell's around to care?" the big man replied.

"Watch what you wipe with," called Tom matter-of-factly.

They waited for what seemed like an endless period while Mike tried to be discreet behind a group of bushes. The horses danced impatiently, wanting to move along brisk pace. Tom noticed a dark line of clouds outlining the trees of the forest behind them.

"Looks like a storm, guys. I hope that is a town on the map." John nodded and trotted his horse up to Joe's. "Quite idyllic."

"Mike taking a shit?"

"No, the land."

"Yeah. No pollution, no crowded cities, no environmental problems. Just a bunch of bloodthirsty mercenaries trying to put you in their dungeon."

"Right." John smiled crookedly.

Mike walked from behind the bush and mounted his horse. "Everything come out all right?" John queried.

"I hope that leaf was poison ivy," snarled Joe.

As evening drew near, the air cooled rapidly, warning of the impending storm. They rode at a fast canter, alert for any type of shelter but finding none.

Ahead they saw the farmlands. Low walls surrounded each partition of land and far to the rear were farmhouses; thin wisps of smoke trailing from chimneys. To the west was a small town and, at the center of the town upon a hill, sat a castle. The keep was a sharp contrast from the last. Tall and of stone, it was a castle in the true sense, not a dark keep like the last.

They rode quickly along the dirt road that led into the town. The last remnant of the setting sun speared through the deepening clouds and through the gaps of the castle's two towering spires, casting long, diminishing shadows over the village and silhouetting the keep.

"Quite a change, eh?" Joe said wistfully.

They moved cautiously along the road as it wound through the village. Most of the buildings they passed seemed to be businesses and were closed for the night. A few shutters betrayed the glow of soft lamplight. As they neared the center of town, Tom pointed out what looked like an inn. They proceeded in that direction.

"I hope these folks are friendlier than the last," Bill said as he dismounted under the horse shelter and tethered his beast. No one was out, most likely due to the impending storm.

"Before we go in, can I make a suggestion?" John turned to his friends. They looked at him expectantly. "I think we should change into our Event costumes."

"That's one good idea you can claim," Joe replied as he pulled his outfit from the saddlebags. Soon they were all changed into their medieval garb and ready, if necessary, to descend into the depths of hell itself. Luckily it was only a tavern.

"Let's remember not to make waves," Joe reminded them as they stepped to the door. The wooden portal opened just as lightning flashed above, illuminating them all. Joe leaned to John and whispered: "Helluvan entrance, eh?"

All motion and noise within the tavern ceased, and all the patrons looked to the group that stood at the door.

"I think we're overdressed," Chill muttered, noticing the patrons of the bar. They were a swarthy lot: land laborers and shop owners, dressed in the most drab tunics and leggings one could imagine. Nothing remotely like what the group wore.

Tom and John led the way into the tavern. They made their way to the bar amid suspicious whispers and hidden glances. Bill sidled next to John at the slick- topped counter and turned his back on the bunch.

"Paranoid lot," Bill said.

"Look at the way we're dressed compared to them. I'd be paranoid too."

"Strangers," came a deep voice. The bartender stood in front of them, his massive arms resting on the bar. He had a thick beard and keen eyes that looked at them with distrust.

"We need a table for six, and a round of ale," Joe said quickly. "Do ye ave shenks?" drawled the burly man.

"Shenks?" Bill asked. "Money," John replied.

"Yes, we have those." Mike pulled out a silver coin and handed it to the man.

"Where did that come from?" Chill raised his eyebrow at the sight of the pouch.

"Off of that dead guard. He had no more use for it." Then, "It is enough I trust."

The man bit down, "Aye, 'tis more an enough, ye sit down, I'll send a girl." They seated themselves at one of the corner tables and surveyed the place.

Soon the regulars seemed to have forgotten their guests and returned to a normal level of conversation.

"Well, what do you think?" asked Bill. He nervously fingered the hilt of his

Estoc epee. Chill looked about, then slowly at each member of the group. "I don't know about you guys, but I'm scared shitless."

"Ditto," Joe smiled nervously. He looked up sharply as a serving girl approached the table with their tankards of ale. She was about their age, maybe younger. She had fair skin and shoulder length, dishwater blonde hair. She smiled nervously and set the ale on their table. Then: "Is there anything else?"

"How about some food?" Chill asked, his stomach had been rumbling a lot lately. She smiled nervously, almost tripped as she turned away and headed back the way she came.

"Bit nervous," John remarked.

"Why don't you do a study on that?" Mike said acidly. "Why don't you shut up," John snapped back.

"Okay, okay, don't squabble in front of the natives. They might not like it," Joe said it too soothingly and earned a look of contempt from the both of them. Bill tilted his tankard back and took a swig of ale. Then he spewed the contents across the table into Mike's face.

"Ugh, what is that shit?" he scowled at the bitter taste that was left in his mouth.

Joe tasted it cautiously. "It is very crude, and very weak beer."

Mike wiped his face and gave Bill an accusatory glance. Then they eased back as the girl returned with a plate of bread, cheese, and a smoked sausage.

"What's the charge?" Mike asked, feeling free with his pilfered money.

"Oh, milord, there is none. That silver shenk was quite enough. It is not often that we see shenks with the Conclavium's stamp." She smiled and

69

retreated once more. They listened then, as they chewed the hard bread and strong cheese, to the conversations that flowed in the room.

"Aye they be from the Conclaveum. Did ya see their shenk, silver it was. We dinna need their kind. Trouble follows im."

"Aye, Konner. They slowly wirk their way soud, and takin more of the land wit them. Did ya see how the fair Trianna warmed up to im. Soon they be takin our women folk too."

"She could use a good man."

"Aye," he laughed lowly. "But she probably sluts aroun wit Duran in gud Lord Trevor's keep. If 'e adn't av saved Trevor from the Deep, thin I doubt they woulda stood im ere long."

"Duran's a foul viper I giv ye that. E probably as Gabrielle in his arms ere night too. Im and his Conclaveum folk."

"This is some good stuff we're getting," John said to Joe, who just smiled as he struggled with a piece of sausage.

"...ever since Trianna went ti wirk fur Gabrielle, she as had high airs about er."

"Aye, Konner, she could be taught a lesson or two." The man cracked a gap-toothed grin and rubbed his unshaven face with a dirty mitt. His friend, Konner, winked and quaffed his ale; wiping the froth from his chin with the back of his arm. The tunic he wore was covered with filth more from the gutter than the farm.

The two turned their conversation to more mundane things, like the weather and tariffs. The six friends listened to some of the other tables.

70

"...business is bad. Trade wit the nord has gone sour. Gelion's behind that I'll wager, you don't see im comin from Ord or Tarn Hold much. That Gelion, he never got along with Trevor. No doubt Duran is his lap dog."

"Ye cannot git much worse an that."

"Aye," said a third. "An now it looks like more of their ilk have found der way to Galfeon Yor," he said it with contempt, not even trying to keep his voice down.

"Cut their throats, I say."

"Wonderful," Joe said to John as he eased back in his chair. He nervously fingered the hand-and-a-half pommel of his new bastard sword. He was itching to try it on any smart-ass that got in his way.

"Christ, they think that we're somebody else," Chill remarked as he nursed his ale.

"This Conclaveum, it must be some type of ruling class or something. Taking the land slowly?"

"Colonizing like an empire," Mike cut John off. "Let them think what they will of us, it will gives them a mystery to worry about."

"Well, these Conclaveum guys aren't well liked, Mike," John replied. "So–"

"So," Bill took up. "This Conclaveum is represented by our buddy, Gelion. Remember, he's the one who wanted your balls for Christmas tree ornaments. If you haven't been listening, Gelion dislikes this Trevor which, in my book makes Trevor a good guy."

"Right," Tom interjected. "If we could get help from Trevor, then we have a place to start in getting home. We have to be careful though. We can't risk letting them know who we really are.

"We don't need their help," Mike said, shaking his head. "We don't?" John asked.

"No we can handle things for ourselves, we'll figure out a way-" John leaned forward impatiently and cut him off.

"Figure what out, Mike? We already know that we're here because someone, or something caused us to be here. We already know that we need help because we made a very powerful man very angry. We already know we want to find a way home, and the only way we're gonna do that is to get some help from powerful, but friendly people."

"I don't think that's necessary," Mike extolled. "I think I can figure it out on my own."

"We need a base of operations," Tom rejoined. "Yeah, with decent food," Chill commented.

"We can handle things on our own," Mike insisted.

"Yeah, right, we'll set something up, Mike. Get a keep on our own, and get servants and stuff," Joe said facetiously.

"I think we can do it, but it requires teamwork," Mike persisted. "Then we can gather the information we need to figure things out. We all have the ability to function properly in this world. I think we have the ingenuity to get-"

"Ourselves killed," John shot at him.

"Be real, Mike," Joe sat there and shook his head. "We have to start somewhere, and it isn't at the top. As in our world, you have to work to get what you want and I have a feeling that it isn't

72

gonna be any easier in this world. Now, I think we should seek help at this keep, first thing in the morning."

"I agree," John said. And as Chill and Tom agreed, Mike only shook his head. "What about you, Bill?" Mike asked of the former graduate student. "Where do you stand?"

"I have to go along with Joe, it is the only reasonable solution."

"Fine," said Mike. He had that look of betrayal on his face. "Of course, you guys are right. I'm wrong."

John rolled his eyes and Tom shook his head. Bill just got a little agitated. "Don't pull that guilt trip shit on us, Mike, we've known you too long. You know the facts outweigh any personal opinions in this matter. We won't live long enough to get out of here if we don't get the help we so desperately need," Bill said. Mike looked resigned to an uncertain fate.

"So, what do we do?" John asked. "Do we just walk up to the castle, knock on the door and ask them if they can beam us home?"

"It would be a start," Bill replied.

Mike grunted and sipped at his ale with distaste. He then sighed and leaned forward, resting on his arms.

"Well," he said. "We could say that we are from another country across the sea, that we were lost in a storm and shipwrecked. We can say that Gelion accosted us in his woods and that we would like refuge.

"I think that it's important to keep up the facade that we created."

"Sounds good," Joe replied as a devious grin spread across his face. "We should assume other identities than John the grad-student or Bill the rock star."

"Why don't we stick to the personas we had in the Society, they're pretty good. You know – The Legion of the Black Skull," Chill said as he picked his teeth. "Yeah," Mike continued, "and we give ourselves titles, that way people won't treat us like commoners."

"Right–"

"Look at that," John cut off Chill as a man entered the Inn. They all turned to see who had entered.

He was of medium height, somewhat good-looking, and wore his hair in a ponytail high on the back of his head and walked to the bar, casually surveying the taproom. His tunic covered chain mail, and he carried a sword at his side. He walked to the counter and spoke to the proprietor for a moment, looked curiously at the group (who all looked quickly into their respective tankards), then looked at Trianna. She smiled as he greeted her. He spoke to her clearly and without any slang that the others in the tavern used.

"Milady wishes your company tonight," the man said. She smiled at hearing that.

"Aye, we close soon Mrick. I will be up there in due time."

"Do you wish me to wait?" he asked.

"No, I'll be fine. You go ahead."

The man turned, looked once more at the group, a curious glint in his eyes, then was gone.

Trianna went over to the bar and started clearing the tankards and trays.

"I didn't realize it was that late," Joe replied. He had noticed that many of the patrons were getting up to leave.

"This is a great opportunity," Mike interjected.

"What?" John asked of the big man.

"She works in the keep, remember. We approach her on her way there and get her to introduce us."

"Tonight?" Bill asked. "I say we get rooms for the night and head up there tomorrow."

"Let's see if they have any," Joe said and got up. He approached the bartender. Mike held him back.

"Don't you want to check the castle out?"

"It's kinda late for a house call, Mike."

"No it's not."

"You gotta, remember," Chill remarked. "Mike is nocturnal."

The bartender looked wary as they approached. He put his hands on the bar and raised an eyebrow. Joe asked him if there were any available rooms.

"No." He said it flatly and turned away from them.

"How can we persuade you?" Mike asked, hinting at more silver.

"Yi cannot, your silver is good nough fir food, naught more. We don't care for Conclaveum ilk here."

"Listen," Mike began dangerously, but John cut him off.

"No, Mike, don't make a scene. We'll spend the night with our horses." They walked out of the tavern, followed by the glances of the tavern-keeper and the few remaining patrons. Outside, the rain had stopped and the air was fresh and sharp. John would rather spend the night out here than in a smoke-filled tavern anyway. He stepped off the walkway and onto the street, ankle deep in a puddle of water. He looked down, lifting his leg and shaking it.

"Your idea," Joe said as he sauntered by. He deftly overstepped the water hazard.

They soon were sitting in the comfort of the open-front stable on a bed of dried hay, concealed from view by the deep shadows of the structure as they watched the last of the patrons leave. There was a momentary flicker near the doors of the stable as Mike lit a cigarette.

"I thought we got away from that smoke when we left the tavern," Joe said out of darkness.

"This is the only luxury I have now and I'm not giving it up."

Tom put a sleeping Kiera into a large pouch in his saddlebag, making sure she was safe, and then joined the rest of the group. Soon the last three patrons staggered from the inn. It was the three that had been so vehement about the group being from the Conclaveum. They walked across the street and huddled in the shadows, then looked expectantly at the entrance of the tavern.

"I don't like the looks of this," John said slowly. "What?" Chill was almost asleep.

"Yeah," said Mike, "What do you suppose they're up to?"

76

"Those are the ones that insulted that Gabrielle chick." Chill squinted before he realized that his glasses were off. He quickly put them on.

"The same ones that said those things about the waitress?" Bill queried.

"I don't think we should interfere," Mike began. "Whatever happens is none of our business."

"Right, the Prime Directive." Sarcasm laced Joe's voice.

"Well," Chill pointed out, "we better make up our minds, cause here she comes."

The waitress walked from the tavern and crossed the street, not paying attention too much of anything. As she proceeded down the road, the three specters followed her. Six dark shadows followed closely behind.

Joe and John crept through the darkness, being very careful not to make any noise. The moon was a wan glow behind the cloud cover and afforded no light, which was to their benefit. The rest of the group followed only paces behind.

The girl was making her way up the road to the keep, but the road veered into a dark alley. The three thugs followed her.

"She should know better," John whispered. "You would think," Joe replied.

On each side of them rose the brick and walls of buildings, eaves sometimes obscuring the sky above. The alleyway was cobble, and a gutter ran right down the center. Heaps of trash lay against the walls, and the skitter of rodents could be heard as they made their way through the darkness. It was if they had stepped into medieval London.

John stopped abruptly and cocked his head to the side, listening.

He heard a scuffle and a muffled yell. He slowly drew his knife and Joe nodded for him to go first. John smiled crookedly in assent.

They crept forward; the group was spread fifteen feet apart. John came upon a turn and peered around the corner, Joe pressing at his back. Across from them, in plain sight, were the three thugs and the girl. Two of the men held the girl's arms against the wooden wall of an outbuilding. The third faced her.

"Bit hi an mighty fir yir own good, are yi?" they heard the man drawl. The other two grinned and nodded their heads expectantly. The girl strained and tried to twist away, but to no avail.

"Konner," she spat, as if the name were foul. "You will regret accosting me."

"Not if yir tongue is out, I wilna. Wot will er ladyship do wit out yi?" He laughed and ripped her blouse, exposing her breasts. Then, as she tried in vain to get away, he sidled up in close to her. Slowly he pulled her skirt up with his other hand.

John judged the distance and the balance of his knife. Tom, no doubt, could do better, but there wasn't time. He stepped forward, holding the blade of the knife. He swung his arm, leaning into it. Joe watched as the knife thudded next to the man's fingers and deep into the wood. He was stunned at first.

"Good shot, John!"

John glanced momentarily at his companion. "I was aiming for his back." The two stepped out into the open as the three thugs turned to meet them.

The girl slid away down the alley, trying to pull her blouse about her. "Wot ave we ere, Konner?"

"Tis the scum from the Conclaveum, come to rescue fair maid," said the other.

"Aye," said Konner, "Tis them. Now we ave some guttin to do." He pulled a long skinning knife from his belt and moved forward casually, as if the two were no challenge. Then three others of the group stepped from the shadows.

Konner stopped and looked at the group before him. John and Joe stepped forward as the others crossed their arms.

"Well, gentlemen, we seem to have interrupted something."

They made a motion as if to move down the open end of the alley but Tom stepped out of the shadows, between them and the girl. Bill raised his eyebrow; he had thought Tom was bringing up the rear.

"Now, now, gentlemen, we can be reasonable," John said as he stepped between them and retrieved his knife from the wall. "Where we come from, we don't kill people like you."

The three men looked relieved, but Joe continued for John. "That's right. We geld them."

Their eyes went wide and Konner uttered a curse. One of the men rushed Tom. Tom ducked low as the man swung wide. The Sioux caught the man at the wrist and twisted it sharply. The man screamed in agony but was silenced as Tom struck the base of his neck, putting him out.

Konner swung his knife haphazardly at John. John moved with the flow of the knife, shadowing the motion. He caught Konner in a wristlock and forced the knife into the wall. Then he ducked under Konner's arm, slid in behind him, and grabbed him by the hair. John's combat knife came up and around, poised at the man's carotid artery.

"John!" Bill shouted from behind, but John just smiled. "I will grant you one wish, Konner."

"Spare me, milord," the man grunted. "Damn."

John pushed the man's head forward, into the wall. Then he drew him back and kicked him soundly between the legs. Konner fell to his knees, moaning loudly and clutching at his groin.

John turned and saw Joe whack the third man on the back of the head with the flat of his sword. It sent him to dreamland.

"Asshole ran right past me," he said, shaking his head. They all turned and looked at the girl.

Chapter 5

"I am the Lady Gabrielle's maidservant and I fear that has caused resentment in some people. They think that I have privileges which they do not." She held Joe's cloak tightly about her shoulders as they walked to the keep. The night air was still and the moon wound its way through the thinning clouds with an ethereal glow. The troupe walked up a slight grade, the sides of the street guarded by low walls that in turn protected orchards. The group clung tightly about the girl, listening to her speak.

"What is your name?" Bill asked as he trudged behind her.

"Trianna," she said, looking over her shoulder. "I am just a commoner, not worthy of notice. I am in your debt."

At the word debt, Chill perked up. Dollar signs seemed to dance before his eyes but, before he could speak, Joe interjected.

"We are but travelers from a distant land."

"Then you are not from the Conclaveum? I had thought that since you carried Conclave shenks-"

"No," Mike cut in. "We were shipwrecked upon your southern shore and very rudely accosted by a Regent named Gelion."

She drew in her breath sharply and looked at him. "And you still live? Why did he let you go?"

"He didn't," Tom replied. "Yeah," Joe commented.

"We escaped," John said as they crossed the bridge that ran over the moat which surrounded the

81

keep. John looked over the side and had to fight off the vertigo. He expected to see water maybe fifteen feet below; instead he stared into blackness. In the chasm he could see nothing. He looked pale as he moved to the center of the bridge. She noticed his distress.

"Tis the Deep, milord, the castle was built on this site because of the protection. You see, the provinces here have trouble with those governed by Gelion, though of late not nearly as much. There is still trouble now and then."

"The best offense..." Mike muttered.

They had reached the opposite side of the bridge and before them were two heavy oaken doors bound in brass. She rapped the knocker and it echoed distantly.

"Eric usually tends the door. He is quite old."

John turned, catching the look of apprehension on the faces of his comrades. He shrugged at the thought of their uncertain fate. Finally, there came the sound of metal grating on metal and the door cracked open a few inches. A wizened head, backlit by oil lamps, peeked out, trying to penetrate the gloom.

"Yea, wot do yi want?" said a voice, old and somewhat crotchety. "It is I, Eric, Trianna. I have come at the bidding of milady."

"Aye, but who are those blackguards wit yi?"

"Travelers. They saved my life, Eric. Now, get milady." He frowned at her urgent tone, but opened the doors and let them into the courtyard. The doors were surprisingly thick, and Eric struggled to close them. He ushered them across the worn flagstones to the door opposite, and soon they stood in a foyer lit by several well-placed sconces. Benches sat along the wall and the whole scene reminded Joe of an early Rembrandt.

Trianna stood, nervously waiting as most of the group sat down on the benches and leaned against the cool stone. John threw his cloak back and adjusted his sword. The Lady Gabrielle was probably an old biddy that would need to be impressed by bright young gentlemen of the court. It would probably be a long night as they tried to explain the situation to her.

The sound of footsteps preceded Eric and they all stood in anticipation. Joe turned and saw Eric, and next to him a cloaked woman. He could not make out what she looked like in the dimness, but she surveyed them with interest. She stepped forward into the lamplight. John's eyes lit up; she was stunning.

The light of the lamps struck her in the most flattering way. Her hair was deep black, yet highlighted in auburn so that the sconces caught the line of her curls and brought out the color. Her tresses fell to her shoulders in a wavy mass, held from her brow by a pearl comb.

It was her eyes though, that held John captive for the longest time. They were luminescent forest green and they danced in the faint light. Her face seemed carved from the finest artist's chisel; cheekbones high and a softly rounded chin. He could tell by the way the robe fell that she was lithe and lean.

She looked at Trianna, barely noticing the others. "What has happened?" Her voice was an even alto, full of concern.

"My Lady," Trianna nodded her head. "Konner, and two of his friends...they...they-" finally, like floodgates opening, she burst into tears and crushed herself to Gabrielle's shoulder.

"They tried to rape her," John said from the back of the chamber. "Luckily we intervened and escorted her here."

She looked past the group at John, searching his face. Then she turned to Eric and gestured to the group. "Take Trianna to her quarters. I will speak with her shortly, then give these men a reward of your discretion," she said it quickly and then turned to leave.

"We don't want a reward," Joe snapped. Mike and Chill cringed. She turned and looked over her shoulder.

"It is strange that men of the Conclaveum should not want a reward." John shook his head. Here we go again.

"Pardon me, milady," Joe spoke with a twist to his mouth that said he was patronizing her. "We are not of the Conclaveum. We were shipwrecked upon your southern shore and rudely apprehended by the Regent Gelion. Through no small effort we find ourselves here, in your fine keep. Now, since we've gotten to your little village, we've been treated rather rudely.

"We are not of the Conclaveum, milady, we have never heard of the Conclaveum. We would like to speak to the Lord of this castle." She paused, looked to Trianna, frowned.

"We cannot treat the saviors of this girl rudely now, can we?" came another, deeper voice. John looked down the hall to see a man approach. He

84

was about John's height and build, yet more muscular. As he came into the light, they could see he was a handsome man, square-jawed and dark-haired. His mustache and beard were trimmed close, to accent his jaw line. He wore a deep red tunic and boots, but was unarmed save for a stiletto. He crossed his arms and stood next Gabrielle.

"This is the Lord Duran, of Qwen. He is a guest here," she said coolly. "Come, come, Gabrielle, I am also your suitor. Or have you forgotten?"

She ignored his last remark and spoke once again. "You may stay the night and the Lord will see you in the morning. Do you have horses?"

"Yes," Tom said. "They are back at the Inn where Trianna works."

"Worked," Gabrielle contradicted. "She will stay here from now on. Eric, send two of the lads to fetch the horses. Then see to it that there are fresh bath water and linens in the guest chambers." Eric nodded and shuffled off.

"And be quick about it," Duran interjected. Eric looked at him sidelong and went off to fetch the stable boys.

"I will see you gentlemen in the morning," Gabrielle said and walked briskly down the hall. Duran glanced at them for a moment and then, smiling thinly at the group, turned and also left.

"How quaint," Joe said.

"I don't trust that fellow," Tom commented, remembering what the townspeople had said.

"He doesn't seem that bad," Mike berated as he lit another cigarette. "Yeah," Chill agreed. "Don't be so paranoid."

"I'm not," Tom replied.

John awoke with a start, trying to orient himself. He saw Joe lying on the bed next to him and groaned. He remembered now: they had decided to pair up for safety, and he'd ended up sharing bunks with the gray-eyed artist. Joe snored.

John looked about with sleep-laden eyes. The instant he had hit the bed he fell into a deep, dreamless sleep. Now, the early morning light was streaming through the balcony opposite the bed and motes of dust danced in the golden rays that arrowed to the slate floor. To his right were the door and a small bench with a pitcher and bowl. On the opposite wall was a fireplace.

John sat up and stretched. The artist rolled over grumpily, but John stood and walked to look out over the balcony past the courtyard wall.

A cool morning breeze brushed past his face as he inspected the small village at the base of the castle. Most of the buildings lay in the deep shadows of the early hour. Beyond the village were open green fields and, far away on the horizon, he could make out foothills and forest. The sky was a cloudless crystal blue.

He turned at the sound of Joe groaning to consciousness. Through half- closed eyes, Joe watched as John opened his bag, pulling out toothpaste, shampoo, and soap. As John washed and dressed, Joe grunted and went back to sleep, waiting for his friend to finish.

Joe pulled on his shirt, wondering what their hosts would think of their attire. He belted on his sword and went into the hall where the rest of the group was waiting. Mike looked as though a cat had dragged him in, but then again he always looked like that before noon.

"I see we're all armed," Mike said as he polished his mirrored sunglasses on the bottom of his sweatshirt.

"What I wouldn't do for a hot cup of coffee," John muttered.

"Well, we'll make do," Mike inquired. "It's your show," Mike casually remarked as he slouched against the wall, smoking his last cigarette.

"I think our best bet would be to go down the stairs and talk to our new friends, Trevor and Gabrielle," Bill said, not caring for Mike's surly attitude this early in the morning.

"Righto," Chill replied, and then motioned for Bill to lead the way. Bill shrugged and walked down the hall the same way they had come the night before. They came to a stairwell that overlooked an open foyer. At this hour, a rainbow of light danced through a stained glass window near the ceiling. The group sauntered down the stairs. The sound of pots and pans clanging drifted up from below. Chill perked up at the thought of food.

"I sense it, guys, there's a meal somewhere ahead," he bounded down the last few steps and onto the hard slate floor.

"Get hold of him before he hurts someone," Joe said with a rueful grin. He watched as Chill surveyed the anteroom with confusion in his eyes. Corridors lead off in four separate directions, and it was impossible to tell from which direction the kitchen sounds came.

"You know," began Bill as he looked at the medieval architecture. "This is so unreal. We're accepting this like it was an everyday occurrence yet, according to our beliefs and the norms of our society, this shouldn't be happening. Where the hell are we and why?"

"We're here, now," Tom replied as if that were the whole answer.

Mike sighed in exasperation and interjected, "There is the possibility that all those fantasy and science fiction writers, and a few scientists, were correct in their assumption that there's more to reality than we readily perceive.

"It is possible that we do not live in a universe, but a multiverse. That is, different planes, or dimensions of reality coexist side by side; like the pages of a book. The thin fabric of space and time may only separate these realms. As we learn to perceive our 'reality' as a child, we learn to discriminate our reality from so- called fantasy. So, these other realms exist beyond our knowledge because they exist in the abstract, not the concrete."

The rest of the group paused and regarded Mike thoughtfully. They'd heard variations of his theories on reality before, but now it took on a whole new meaning. It began to form a foundation from which they could try to comprehend the insanity of their situation.

"Why isn't it possible?" Mike continued. "Or rather, why should it be impossible? Why limit us to one reality? I think that notion is very egocentric. I think we have here a concrete example that other realms do exist. As Einstein said: 'If it can be imagined, it most likely is.'"

Joe leaned against the balustrade and slowly shook his head, still thinking that this could all be a dream and he might wake up with a nasty hangover and the remnants of a Dutch oil painting on his desk.

"It stands to reason," Tom said, looking around. "I know I am here. I know my friends are here. There is much, too much, that's real about this. I know it isn't a dream. And, this multiverse theory does have some historical founding. Look at Native American tradition. We believe in the spirit realm. Also look at primitive cultures around the world, steeped in superstition about the nether world."

"Yeah, but from an anthropological point of view those are just methods of coping with inexplicable events and the permanence of death," John said as he sat on the cold stone stair.

"Right," Smiling Wolf replied. "Yet, it has to have some basis. Why not this? You cannot deny the reality of the here and the now."

"Oh, I could, but I won't."

"I know this is real," Chill said, as he looked about. "Partly because I'm as hungry as all get out."

"Wonderful, Chill, you've just confirmed all our theories," Joe just shook his head.

"Well, how do we approach this thing?" Bill asked. He was just as confused as when the conversation began.

"We approach it as we would anything," Mike stated. "And how is that, Mike?" came Joe's curt reply.

"I would hope with an open mind," John interjected. He was somewhat hungry and impatient himself.

"Just remember that what we did in the Medieval Society was distilled romanticism. It didn't have any of the harshness of feudal or pre-industrial life. It was an illusion. If this is real, I fear it will be a bit of a slap in the face," replied Joe.

"Well, we could look at it like we were in another culture, a foreign country if you will. The Society is all blown out of proportion. We're incognito, so we play our part," Tom said. "And I hope we can get back to where we belong."

"I got a feeling that it's gonna be a lot harder than you make it sound," the artist said as he smoothed his hair back. He sighed.

"Such pessimism, Joe. I'm surprised," John laughed nervously.

"I think we've proved that we can handle ourselves," Mike rejoined.

"Mike," Joe began, and his tone was edged with acid. "Proved what? We barely got out of the last mess. Traipsing about with a foil or a wooden bokken is a lot different from swinging a five-pound blade and wearing eighty pounds of armor. I don't think we're in that kind of shape."

"We'll adjust," Mike replied, offhandedly. "We will find a way back."

"We were brought here by magic, Mike. Are you hiding some dark secret from us? Do you know sorcery?"

"If I'm guessing right, it won't be easy, but we probably have to find the person who brought us here and have him send us back. I plan on studying the 'magic' of this realm, and maybe I can learn how to take us back. But, right now we should settle in for a long stay."

"Wonderful," Joe said sardonically. "I have an idea. I'll just wake up and this will all go away."

They all looked at him as if he were a biology experiment. He sighed and shrugged. He knew that they wished the same, but doubted it would happen. This was all too real.

"If we play our cards right, we may not run into too much trouble. We just have to steer clear of the bad guys." John leaned his chin on fist.

"Yeah, and we've done such a good job of it so far, haven't we. A mad Regent, three rapists and what's next? Darth Vader?" Joe fingered the hilt of his bastard sword, wondering if its forging was as good as the smith promised. He hoped that he wouldn't have to test it.

"You know," he continued. "It's like we're a magnet that attracts trouble. We've been here three days and we've almost gotten killed twice. And I do have a feeling that if we face death we aren't gonna end up in another realm again. I think that next time it will be permanent."

"Nice thought for the day, Joe," returned Bill. He was about to say more when

91

Trianna appeared from one of the corridors. She greeted them with a smile. "I did not know that you had awakened."

"It's hard to sleep when you're not in your own bed," John replied as he looked at the others. They nodded.

"Well, you must be hungry," she noticed the looks on their faces and grinned. "I'll take you to the kitchen and you can get something there."

She spun on her heel and proceeded back the way she had come. The others quickly followed her, anticipating a hot meal.

"Not exactly what I'm used to," Joe said as he finished the cold gruel that sat before him. They had all gotten some dark bread, cheese and an oatmeal type cereal.

"What I wouldn't do for a glass of milk and a plate of cookies," Chill whined as he sat back. He almost gagged on the gruel; it was so sticky.

"Oh, it isn't that bad," Tom said as he bit into an apple-like fruit. It was tangy and fresh. "This is probably one of the healthier breakfasts you've had."

Chill looked at him as though he were nuts. Then gazed about the kitchen. It was a large room and they sat at a table at one end of it. There was a large hearth with many pans and grills hanging from hooks. At a preparation table, three robust women chatted merrily as they cut up vegetables. Trianna was off doing errands for the Lady Gabrielle and the castle seemed very quiet.

Next to their table was a long bay window that looked out over a garden covering a large court near the rear of the castle. The golden light of the morning danced into the kitchen through crystal panes, and the faint scent of flowers drew Joe to the sill. His eyes followed the vines as they crawled up the wall about thirty feet away, obscuring most of the stone. Roses flowered about the fountain at the center. Two buttresses enfolded the kitchen area, blocking the views immediately to the right and left. Joe sighed and watched a bee settle on a pink rose. He waited for King Arthur to come walking through the garden; instead he got Duran stomping through the kitchen.

The man scowled as he walked past the cooks; he looked as if it were distasteful to be in this portion of the castle, with the help. When his eyes settled on the troupe they widened at the strange dress and accoutrements of the strangers, but he covered his surprise with a mask of affability. Mike stood up and stretched. He towered over Duran and easily outweighed him, but Duran had a presence nobody could deny.

"Tell me, Lord Duran, when may we meet the Lord of this Keep, Trevor?" Joe asked as he turned from the window.

"I was just coming to tell you that myself. I would think that this evening at dinner would be the most appropriate time."

"I take it there's not much happening otherwise?" Tom asked.

"This is a quiet place and you may have run of it. Just be careful." He quickly exited before anyone could ask more of him.

"So we 'ave run of the place, eh mate?" John said in his best cockney. His eyes followed the dark man long after the door had closed.

93

Joe grunted and opened the door that led into the garden. A cool breeze issued in and the sounds of birds could be heard as they darted about the battlements. "Well, since we can go anywhere, I suggest we get acquainted with this oversized condo."

"Oh joy," remarked Chill as he stood and brushed crumbs from his sweatshirt. "A tour."

"Think of it this way, Chill," said Tom. "If they have anything here that might give us a clue to get us home, then, the sooner we find it, the better."

"And at least this way we know if they have any skeletons in their closet," Mike grunted. He fumbled through his pockets then frowned when he realized that all his cigarettes were gone.

Bill snorted and followed the rest of the group into the garden. They followed the path that wound its way through the shrubbery. Hyacinth and orchid bloomed amid the ivy, and there were several small fruit trees and well-pruned bushes.

They shortly came to the wall opposite the kitchen. Amid the vine-covered granite was a stout oaken door; an iron bolt held it fast.

"Do you know what this reminds me of?" Joe asked of the others as he leaned forward to examine the portal. "Remember when we played the game, that time our party of adventurers, and it was our first adventure, was put in a veteran scenario? Remember when we opened the door and found ourselves in hell, staring at a legion of demons?"

"Why, isn't that a nice thought," Bill remarked, about to throw the bolt.

"Come on, guys, this isn't the game. You don't really expect stuff like that to happen, do you?" They all looked at Tom as if he were a babbling idiot. Considering the past three days, anything was likely to happen. Even so, Tom smirked at the others and threw the bolt before they could stop him. The door swung wide to reveal a dank stairwell that led down into darkness. They all looked at each other.

"Your move, Tom," John said, reveling in the moment of adventure. Tom looked at Mike and Bill. They said nothing and Chill and Joe seemed to be inspecting the bright petals of some flower. "Great," replied the Sioux and started down the steps.

They found themselves in what must have been a gardener's storage room. A small, twelve by twelve chamber with hoes and shovels, peat stacked against one wall, and a few crates. Bags of seed and bushels of bulbs were piled against another wall. A lone lamp sat, unlit, on the bench, and the light coming from the top of the stairwell cast everything in a deep shadow.

Mike lit the lamp with his Bic and the room seemed to expand in the new light. John saw insects scurry for the darkness and immediately a shiver ran down his spine. Chill just grunted and leaned against one of the dank walls.

"What's this?" Mike asked of no one in particular and pulled tarp off of a dirty chest.

"Treasure no doubt, Mike," mocked Joe. He was anxious to get back out into the morning sun. Mike might like dank holes in the ground, but he certainly didn't. There was a loud grating noise as

Mike pulled the lid back and a foul odor drifted through the room.

"Haha, Mike, you found their manure," Bill choked as the others covered their noses. Joe's knew it was time to leave.

"Come on, guys, let's blow this place."

He turned to leave and noticed something wasn't quite right. "Hey, where's Chill? Did he leave without us?"

"No, he's right–" Tom stopped and back to where Chill should have been standing. He was gone.

"I'll bet he just took off; he was probably driven out by the smell," John began towards the stairs. He stopped as he heard a faint, muffled yell.

The others quickly went to the wall that Chill had been leaning against. They could faintly hear Chill calling out for help. Tom scanned for a lever or a trip, but found none. Then, as Mike leaned heavily on the wall, a portion of it gave way. Chill quickly retreated from the rotating wall, a look of relief written all over his face. He adjusted his glasses as Bill shoved the lamp into the secret corridor.

"Sir Chill, I presume," said the musician. The stout man only glared at him and pushed his way out of the dark passage.

"Boy, am I glad you guys got through. It's blacker than a nun's habit in there." The others peered in. The passage seemed to travel beneath the garden, roots and vines broke their way into the ceiling. The path was strung with cobwebs and the air was stale to breathe.

"Shall we?" Tom gestured inside.

"I don't know, guys," Chill said, remembering how dark it had been. "Right, maybe we should mind our own business," Joe said.

"Come on. How are we gonna find out what's going on if we don't explore. What else are we gonna do?" Bill took a step into the passage.

"We could ask somebody." John's words were weak.

"I doubt if they would know," Mike replied. "We would be best to try our luck down here. We may get some idea as to what kind of place this is."

"We're going to find answers in the basement of a castle?" Joe arched his eyebrow, and followed the rest of the group into the passage. The stone swiveled shut behind them and he shook his head despairingly.

The passage extended for about seventy feet before it came to an abrupt halt at another stone wall. Great, Joe thought, trapped forever beneath a garden. Buried alive.

"Well, that's it," John said nervously. "The end of the line."

"Shudup, John," Chill said from behind. Joe just wondered at the phrasing John had used.

"Well, if this is any type of castle at all, it should have a secret door here." Mike watched as Tom slid his hand along the surface. Nothing happened.

"We tried, at least. I guess we can't go on." Bill turned and Chill sighed in relief. He pressed up against the wall to let the tall musician get by. There was a grating noise and the wall slid aside. They all looked at Chill.

"So, I have a knack for secret doors. Sue me."

Joe shook his head and Bill peered into the blackness beyond. It was a stairwell that wound upward into inky blackness. Tom just turned, a grin of triumph on his face.

"You're first," was all Bill could say as he handed the lamp to the Native American. Tom took it from him and bounded enthusiastically up the stairs. The others followed as fast as they could.

Tom didn't fear danger. All his senses were peaked by the excitement, a benefit of his extensive martial arts training. Though the steps were steep and the way cramped, his footing was sure. He must have led the group a good four stories before he once more came to a blank wall. The group stopped behind him.

"What now?" Bill queried as he looked over Mike's shoulder past Tom. The wall before them was smooth and without any notable features. Tom ran his hand along the surface, looking for a seam.

"Get Chill up here," called the Sioux. "He seems to know how to find hidden doors."

Chill grunted as he pushed his way through the narrow passage. Joe taunted as the stout man passed. "Yeah," the artist whispered, "He got his experience from going through the back doors of sorority houses."

After a few moments of struggling and prodding on the stone surface, Chill finally shook his head and turned. The others looked expectantly at him. "What?" he said guiltily.

"Looks like his luck ran out," Mike stated flatly.

"Damn," Joe muttered and slammed his fist into the wall. There was a low rumbling and the facade began to move.

"Showoff," John said as the light from the other side pierced the gloom. The wall slid to the side and revealed a hallway. Across from them were an open door and a chamber. Inside, they could just make out the form of a man sitting at a desk reading a text. Tom saw something moving on the desk and quickly pushed his way through to the room.

"Kiera!" he berated his ferret and she quickly leapt to his arm. The man who sat there looked up sharply, then after a pause closed the text and took a pair of battered spectacles from his eyes. He pushed the chair back and stood up.

Tom estimated the man to be in his late fifties. He still had a powerful build and he really didn't show signs of age except around the eyes. He rounded the desk in two strides and beckoned the group into the study.

"Par-al to, Jal et, onia-kal tek?" he asked. After seeing the confused looks on their faces, he spoke once more. "Forgive me, I had forgotten that passage was there. I salute your ingenuity."

"Thanks," Bill replied, rather lamely, Joe cleared his throat. Tom looked at the man with distrust, his ferret chirping loudly.

"Oh, fear not for the animal, young man. I would not hurt the companion of one of my guests." He turned to the rest of the group. "I am Lord Trevor, and I welcome you to Galfeon Yor."

Chapter 6

"We come from a land quite far from here," Joe said and smiled. Boy, wasn't that the truth. John gazed out the arrow slit of the tower. The room overlooked the garden, the town and the fields. It was a spectacular view of unspoiled country.

"We were shipwrecked upon your Southern shore, at the edge of a very large forest. We made camp for one night and awoke in the morning, having been found by the Regent Gelion." Joe finished with an angry glare at the memory of the encounter.

"The man is certainly ruthless," Trevor replied. He sat back in his tall wooden chair, stroking his beard. The natural light piercing the arrow slit lighted the room, as did a small oil lamp set upon a shelf. The lamp illuminated hardwood shelves holding reams of scrolls and tomes. Some of the books were also spread haphazardly about Trevor's desk.

"Ruthless is an understatement," John replied as he turned from the view and looked at his companions. He studied the man for a moment, and went to look at the contents of the shelves. He looked back over his shoulder, at Tom who was fondly petting Kiera.

"So, how was it you escaped from Gelion? He is not one to let loose spies...or worse."

"We dealt with the situation in the manner we knew best–" Mike started. "Diplomacy," Joe finished.

"We persuaded Gelion that it was in his best interest to let us go," Tom said. Trevor smiled. "You fought your way out. How resourceful."

"Basically," John began. "When it came right down to it, it was either that or die."

"We are new to your land, Lord Trevor. We ask for sanctuary. We need a safe place from Gelion, a place where we can plan our return home." John looked at the man, then to the shadow of a cloud that was wending its way across the field. "You ask for much." Trevor sighed and placed his heavily veined hands on the desk. He pushed back from the table and walked over to place a book back upon the shelf. "Gelion and I are not on the best of terms. I would not even call it an uneasy truce.

"The lands to the west of here are a combination of baronies and citadels. Galfeon Yor is the eastern-most of the freeholds. The Conclaveum's representative in the south is Gelion. We of the free-states are in a precarious position. Do we join the Conclave, and lose our right to rule ourselves? I say not. Gelion is a harsh and brutal Regent, and would suck the life-blood from the people. First Qwen, then Paravel and now I hear that Clef is succumbing.

"If I allow you, who have damaged the pride of Gelion, to reside here, then I invite trouble. Yet, Gabrielle has informed me of what you gentlemen have done for Trianna. That cannot go without reward. I must think this over and by the evening meal I will give you my answer." He turned and opened the door that led into the hall.

"These steps are not as dusty as the ones that brought you here." He smiled and the group left the tower room quietly

"So, now what?" Chill asked as he leaned on the stone banister of the balcony that was adjacent to Joe's room. They looked out over a stone courtyard that held a well in the middle. Two boys were brushing a tall roan and chattering excitedly. On the balcony the group spoke in more subdued tones.

"We wait, what else," Joe bit. He scowled, as was usual of late, and flicked the leaf of a vine that crawled over the rail. "Until we get his approval. What else can we do?"

"What if we can't stay?" Bill asked. It was a question they hoped they would not have to answer.

"Then I guess that we move on, further west," Tom replied, Kiera cradled in his arms. The excitement was making her tired. "We all know what direction is more hostile."

"Trevor has what I need," Mike said as he came from inside the chamber. He crossed his arms and looked at Tom intensely. "That library upstairs has enough information to get us out of here. Beyond that, I'm sure this castle has other libraries. From this base of operations, we can make new contacts, magical and otherwise."

"Oh brother," Joe rubbed the bridge of his nose. "Mike, this is all academic.

First, you're going to have to learn the language; I doubt if it's written in the King's English. Second, this rests upon the good graces of Lord Trevor.

"I think the only way we're going to get out of this situation is to find the one who caused it. It isn't like we've sold our souls, maybe we can strike a bargain with whoever who brought us here."

"It isn't exactly like we can go to the local police station and fill out a missing person's report for a sorcerer who has a penchant from pulling six guys from their world and thrusting them into an actual version of the Society." John laughed without humor. "No, finding whoever is responsible will require a little more than pulling his picture from a book, or putting an ad in the paper. Mike is right, we need a point to start from."

"We'll find out tonight, won't we?" Tom placed Kiera into the muffler on his sweatshirt.

"Then let's not disappoint our hosts," Joe began. "Let's show them what they're passing up if they don't let us stay."

"The finest of the 'Legion of the Black Skull' I presume?" John inquired. "Aye, and black is in vogue this season."

John slid the curved Japanese sword into the saya. Then he looked at Joe, Tom, Mike, Bill and Chill.

They were all dressed in their finest. John in his black quilted outfit; Joe in his blacks and purples; Mike in his browns; Tom in his leathers; Bill in his minstrel's motley and Chill in his earthy greens. They were all armed to the teeth. Tom slid his knife from its sheath and examined the edge. Definitely sharp, he thought. A smith in Colorado had made it to Tom's specifications.

Joe adjusted his bastard sword and Mike his Gunto, the Japanese sword was a katana, though modern: a wartime blade that had been mass-produced in the early 1940's.

They were ready for dinner. Chill was hoping for steak.

"This way, milords," Eric drawled and led them down a birch-paneled hall. They came to two large, brass bound doors. Eric grunted as he pushed them open.

Before them sparkled the array of a well-set dining hall. The room was flanked by stone pillars and in the center was a long dining table. Above them was a chandelier holding thin tapers. Firelight reflected off stained glass windows set high, near the vaulted ceiling that during the day would spill sunlight through in a rainbow of colors. Flanking the wall were banners with various designs.

As they strode into the dining hall, John noticed Trevor, Gabrielle and Duran waiting at the far end. Gabrielle stood at Trevor's right. She was the picture of beauty; straight backed and proud. She was dressed in a low cut, ankle length gown of deep lavender. Trevor smiled cordially and sat at the head of the table, his daughter to his right.

"Ye boys kin sit down now," whispered Eric.

Joe nodded and rounded the table. As he approached the end closest to Trevor he un-slung his sword and hung it over the back of his chair. He then took a seat and the others followed suit.

Joe sat next to Gabrielle with John on the other side. Duran sat opposite Trevor. Mike sat across from her and sat next to Bill. Tom and Chill sat at the center of the table, across one another.

Trevor cleared his throat and rang the silver bell at his sleeve. The tone was clear and piercing. The group looked to their host.

"Once again I welcome you gentlemen. You have met my daughter Gabrielle, and Duran, our guest. We, though, are at somewhat of a loss. I am afraid we have not been formally introduced."

Chill shook his head, feeling like he was at a business meeting. He looked longingly at a bottle of wine that sat not three feet from him. He looked to Mike and the big man spoke first, as usual.

"You flatter, milord; but your actions belie them. I am disturbed at the evidence of mistrust." Mike leaned his heavy frame back in the chair and it creaked. His katana slipped to his side.

Tom looked. "Mike, I don't think those guards in the alcoves are just for us." At this Duran smiled; it was evidently a regular occurrence for him, Tom had informed the group as they entered the hall.

"One must be cautious," Gabrielle said in a somewhat subdued tone.

"Yet, we come seeking a safe haven," Bill replied, cocking his head to one side. He smoothed back a shock of his curly hair and frowned slightly.

"You have come armed. That may have been your mistake," she countered. "My it's cold in here," Joe muttered under his breath.

"Well, I'm sure that those few guards wouldn't amount to much of a fight—" Mike started but was cut off by John.

"These are our hosts, Mike." He turned his attention to Trevor.

105

"Milord, it is just that we are in unfamiliar lands and, considering the treatment we received from Gelion, I think that a little wariness is necessary."

"Well put, young man. The guards are merely a precaution on our part. Now that we are all full of caution, let us get on with knowing to whom this wariness pertains." Trevor gestured to the group.

"Sir Chill," replied the stout football player. He adjusted his glasses and looked to Tom.

"Uh...Tom Smiling Wolf. I'm a tracker and guide." Kiera chirped and Tom looked at his shoulder. "And Kiera, my companion."

"Bard William D'Asturien, a minstrel," Bill said, thinking he couldn't say 'Bill the Bard'. He gulped his wine swiftly; it would take a good belt to believe that this charade would work.

"Lord Michael, alchemist and swordsman."

They looked to John, expecting some trite title and name...that's almost what they got. "And I am Sir John, Lord Knight of Erie." He raised his goblet to his lips. The wine was full-bodied and slightly dry.

Joe looked momentarily at the setting before him and the reflection of his face in the polished metal plate; slightly changed by the experiences over these past few days. He looked at his goblet, took the bottle and poured the red wine into it. He handed the bottle to his compatriot, and lifted the cup to his lips.

"I am Surik Shadowlord, Master of Shades and Rider of the Black Dragon." He grinned wolfishly and drank. His friends stared at him a moment. His Society persona had come to the fore apparently.

Duran chuckled and quaffed his wine, then reached across the table and grabbed the decanter, pouring himself another. "Such noble titles for such young men. I wonder gentlemen, how did you earn them?"

"The usual way," Mike replied. A servant placed a small game hen on his plate. He looked at the bird in disappointment; it would hardly fill him. "We either inherited them, or were honored because of our deeds."

"Mmmm..." Duran smiled and slouched to the side of the chair. His glass was empty and he poured himself another; he seemed to be drinking his dinner tonight. Then he toyed with the food on his plate. "It seems that men such as you would be fairly good at arms. I wonder if we might practice in the courtyard some morning, eh?"

"Duran, is that all you think of?" Gabrielle asked, slightly upset at the turn in the conversation. Now all their plates were filled and Chill began to dig in. Joe tasted the fowl; it was excellent.

"My dear, dear Gabrielle. They are obviously men at arms, they probably know of little else."

"On the contrary, Duran," Tom offered. "Where we come from, it is best to be diversified due to the fact that combat is so infrequent. Our philosophy of the warrior is to be complete in one's mind, body and soul. This can be achieved through learning.

"I, for instance, am also interested in the healing arts and medicine; Surik, in addition to overseeing a salle d'armes, is an accomplished artist; Michael a scholar;

Chill, apprenticed to a Lord Trader; Bard William, a musician; and Sir John is also a scholar. So, the combative arts are just a facet of the whole.

"You see," Tom continued. "Through diversity, we become a more complete person. We mingle the mundane with the martial."

"How nice," Gabrielle remarked. She picked at her food and John noticed that she seemed distant now from the conversation.

"How very nice," Duran interjected. "If you'll forgive me, milord, but how is it that you have time for all this—" He waved his hand in the air as if it were some ephemeral thing.

"Obviously, we make time," Bill spoke, sensing that there was tension in Duran's probing. The man wanted an argument. "Where we come from, education is as important, if not more so, than combat."

"And where is it you come from?" Gabrielle asked. She sipped at the wine. "We come from a Republic; that's a group of states where the people rule by electing officials. We are from a province called Erie. It is on a great lake, its namesake." Mike said it all with some gravity. His plate was clean, as was Chill's and they were both still hungry.

"I have not heard of it," Trevor said.

Joe smiled, feeling the warmth of the wine flow throughout his body. "It is from across the sea. We were on an escort ship traveling to a chain of islands. There was a storm and we were separated during the night. With our navigator lost,

108

and our ship breaking up, we found it prudent to abandon ship in a dinghy.

"Next thing we know, we're sitting in Gelion's keep."

Tom smiled at the skill of Joe's story. "Our land is lost to us for the time being, but Michael is going to try to find us a way home."

"You came across the Sundering Sea? Pray, tell us how that might be, and how might you return, no ship has crossed it and none dare," Duran said with a sneer. He was on his second bottle of wine, Tom noticed.

"Mike is familiar with certain arts," Bill said. He produced a coin from behind

Chill's ear

"Parlor tricks," Trevor dismissed Bill's illusion.

"No milord, I am adept in the Grey Arts," answered Mike. "I am also familiar with the Black, but those I try to avoid. You see, sorcery is not a mere illusion, but is the tapping of universal energies. Those energies are essential to the fabric of the multiverse and, if they can be transformed and manipulated into something tangible, then they can be used; if one is strong enough."

Duran shook his head and stood. His chair slid back noisily and one of the guards to the rear of the room took a more alert stance. Duran leaned heavily upon the table then straightened. He laughed, "Oh, milords there is indeed magic, and sorcery, but I don't understand this grey and black. I don't understand much of what you said.

109

"Why is it you speak the common tongue and not the other tongues of the land or the Conclaveum...Or do you?"

"Languages that we do speak are not of this land. It surprised us that we spoke your common tongue," John replied.

"Well, that is truly a pity. Truly strangers in this land, then," he stepped around the chair, almost tripping and stood behind Gabrielle. She sat stock-still.

"I am very sorry, but I must retire. It has been a long day. Good night gentlemen, it was a very nice story you told us."

"It was no—" Bill began, but Tom hushed him with a look.

"So, I will retire," Duran looked down at Gabrielle, a glimmer lit his eye. "Would you join me for a stroll, milady?"

Trevor looked at Duran sharply and the guard in the rear alcove took a step forward. Even in his intoxication, Duran relaxed into state of readiness, hearing the guard. As the tension increased, Tom loosened his knife in its scabbard. John slid back in his seat, and Chill was ready to slide under the table.

"Duran, I think I will stay with our guests a while longer," she said, and it was in the perfect tone of voice to arrest any behavior that might provoke a fight. Duran smiled and began his walk to the doors; he walked slowly, carefully, as people often do when trying to feign sobriety.

"Maybe tomorrow, maybe next week, milady." He laughed and slammed through the door. The group followed him with their eyes.

Bill stared at his plate as the silence in the dining hall became oppressive. Then the guard who had stepped forward cleared his throat and walked to Trevor's side.

"Lord Trevor, that man is intolerable." He shook his head, his voice tight. "Quiet, Baxel, he did save my life."

"But, milord, he abuses the honor of your house. He spoils for a fight. He and his ilk are all the same, no doubt he is Conc–"

"Enough, Baxel; that will be enough. We will not disparage him." He waved his hand and suddenly he seemed a bit older. Baxel returned to his post.

"If I may ask," Chill queried. "Tell us more about the Conclaveum and Gelion." Trevor smiled, somewhat bitterly and Gabrielle spoke up. "You know its representative in the South, Gelion. He governs the lands east of here to Paravel.

He is a brutal man."

"His goal," Trevor followed up, "is to bring all of the south under the dominion of the Conclaveum. In the north, most of the city-states that exist do so under the rule of the Conclave, and I dare say that may be to their benefit, here Gelion's ministrations are be harsh and would cause the free-states and holds to wither under a heavy taxation.

"Gelion is far from a diplomat. In the past, when his overtures were met with resistance, he thought force of arms would sway us. Yet, the free-states rallied, fought a border war, and here we stand, an uneasy truce against our mutual enemy.

111

That truce is the only thing holding us from tearing at each other's throats like wild wolves.

"There is a patrol that runs the border, and is made up of men from the Western cities and holds. Galfeon Yor is no more than a small village on the borderlands. The more powerful Barons of the West think that Gelion is but an upstart, and nothing to be burdened with as they sell their wares to their neighbors. Would that were the truth, but alas, Gelion is more trouble than one would suspect. "He falls under the sway of Myella, who among other things is the daughter of the Conclavator Ironeas, himself. She is also High Priestess of Oran, and Surrogate of the South. Her reign begins at Helm and extends southward.

"She answers only to Ironeas, her father. His family has ruled the Conclave for generations." Trevor's eyes held a far-away look as he spoke. "The Conclave is the ruling body of the Conclaveum. It is made up of delegates from various provinces and cities. Each holds power in his region, as each has the force of the city guard or Provincial army to back him up. Ironeas has the largest force, his family being from the oldest and largest, Teshwa Province."

"They are decadent and evil," Gabrielle stated, matter-of-factly. "In their corruption they wish to spread their foul vices to our free-holds."

"How long has this Conclaveum been around?" Mike asked.

"Ages, far longer than any of the free holds. Its might stretched south, covering all the land. Then, with time, its power waned. Now it stretches north and east, not so much in the south, where its grasp is tenuous at best.

"There were once mighty sorcerers that ruled these lands – you can often see remnants of their presence. The Great Wall is the last wholly remaining vestige of them; for in their dominance was conflict. In the plains to the northeast was a great battle. Where once was verdant and lush land is now a warped and barren waste. And in Narntoc, to the east, all is dead in that city.

"But, I ramble gentlemen. What was before the Conclave of today is no more. When the last of the magicians' might fell behind the Great Wall, they shut themselves off from the outside and from sanity. Though their knowledge was vast, they grew complacent and sodden. Evil grew, and hate, and the Conclave that is today rules by iron will over the lands it holds. News from the north is sparse down here, and most we do get comes to us through Paravel, a city the Conclaveum is currently in the process of trying to annex.

"Since we lie south of the Doran Range, and below the Desert waste, we are thought of as naught more than nuisance. That is as it should be if we are to remain outside the influence of the Conclaveum.

"Unfortunately, of late there has been more traffic. Soldiers dare not openly cross the border bearing the standard of Gelion. But, there are others. Ord openly welcomes all emissaries and traders of the east and north. I fear that our guard lessens with each passing day.

"But, enough of an old man's prattling, gentlemen. I have some matters to attend to before

I retire. I will give you sanctuary from Gelion, for all the good it will do. It will only aggravate him the more, I fear. But, so be it. Sometimes we must stir the pot or it may boil over." He stood and looked about the hall, and to his daughter. She stood and took his arm.

"Milords," she said and nodded her head. As the two of them left the hall, the group sat there looking in slight bewilderment to one another. Joe smiled and Chill openly laughed at the absurdity of the whole situation. Bill shook his head and poured himself another glass of wine.

"I guess that means we have a place to stay," John said. He frowned and watched as the servants cleared the table.

"Yeah, and now Mike can get to work," Tom said as he carefully lifted a sleeping Kiera to his shoulder.

"Right. Trevor was very helpful. Evil or not, the Conclaveum sounds like the place to be."

"What do you mean?" Bill asked.

"I mean, that out in the boonies here, the sorcerers are few and far between. Trevor's recounting of history was probably far from complete, but he did mention that sorcerers once ruled in the Conclave and their influence is still evident in some parts of the south.

"If there are any that remain, then one of them may know why we are here." He sat back, satisfied with his deduction as Baxel walked out of the shadows to the table. Tom shot a glance of one of the other guards who was heading toward to door, the one with the long braid who had come to the

114

Inn for Trianna. The guard frowned as he looked at the group and left the hall.

Baxel cast a weary eye. John cleared his throat.

"Sir Baxel, may I ask why you have such an intense dislike for Duran?"

He looked at the group, sizing them up, and scowled. "Duran is not one of the men that I would count as trustworthy. For what you all did for Trianna, I will give you at least that much warning. Though, it seems that whenever one is saved, trouble follows.

"What do you mean?" Tom urged.

Baxel leaned on the table; he felt at ease in the company of this group. Knowing that they had bested Gelion only reinforced his liking for these young men. "One day Trevor was inspecting some work on the east wall of the Keep, the one closest to the Deep. Well, it was late and the light dim, and a rain had begun to fall. Duran had been passing through the town, and had been at the castle to pay his respects to Gabrielle, at least that was what he said.

"Well, Lord Trevor was in bad sorts. A piling that was supposed to be stout had failed and some rubble knocked him off the path and to a narrow ledge. His shoulder had been dislocated. As the rain got worse, the shoring on the battlement began to come down. Duran was crossing the drawbridge and saw Trevor. Somehow he managed to bring him up. He even reseated the injured shoulder.

"His timing could not have been better," Baxel said disdainfully. "If you asked me, Duran cursed the whole damn keep that night. And cursed us with his presence. That was five months ago, and since then he's been in and out of the Galfeon Yor like he governs the place. Nobody likes, or trusts him."

"Is he of the Conclaveum?" Tom asked.

"That or worse, your guess, perchance, is better than mine. I am nothing more than Lord Trevor's arm. Good night, milords."

"Nice," Bill echoed after Baxel had left. "Haven't we just stumbled on a nice little soap opera?"

"Duran is trouble," Tom spoke, not to anyone in particular.

"I can't tell," Joe retorted. He grabbed the decanter from the table. "I suggest a celebration of our new home." He said it somewhat sarcastically; as though it was the last thing he really wanted to do. He took a long swig from the decanter on the way.

They all filed out, leaving Tom and John alone in the large dining hall. "Well, I don't trust Duran," Tom emphasized. John pulled his katana off the chair.

"Tomorrow I think we start taking things a little more seriously," John hefted the blade.

"Just don't be too serious," Tom smiled as he replied, and they too exited the hall. "It will get you killed."

The oaken doors to the hall slammed shut behind them as the servants cleared the rest of the table.

Only Duran's plate lay untouched.

Chapter 7

"You can't blame them," Tom said as he looked over the balcony. John kindled a fire in the hearth and looked at his friend. The others were in the adjoining room, drinking heavily.

"It could be dangerous to get that out of control. I want all my wits about me." John sat heavily on the bed.

"They're just trying to numb the disorientation. As long as you and I remain clear-headed, I'm not worrying." Tom laid Kiera at the foot of the bed and quickly stripped down to his briefs. He began to stretch and commence his breathing exercises. John walked over to the balcony, a well of worry and pain cutting into his gut. He thought of his family and friends left behind. He realized that even if he weren't dead in their world they still might not get back to it. It was too real. To him it was like they had stepped right out of reality and into a fairy tale. Or worse.

Slowly he became aware of his surroundings: the balcony, the wall, and the ivy. He heard the splashing of water from the fountain in the courtyard below. He looked up to see a moon alien to him, tinted blue and with a faint white ring about it. Ice crystals, he thought, I guess physics doesn't change, or does it?

He drank in the cool breeze and noticed how the light of the moon caught on the flagstones, illuminating them and deepening the shadows. Off the courtyard he could see the yellow torchlight as it pierced through the stable windows. It was hard to discern at this angle, but it looked like someone was moving about the horses.

On impulse he turned back into the room and grabbed his tunic. Tom looked at him inquiringly. "Going for a walk."

"Be careful," replied the Native American. "Always."

"Right," said Tom as he followed him out with his good eye.

John fastened his tunic at the shoulder and trotted down the stairs. He soon came to the doors that led out to the courtyard. This foreign land, this reality, it was so unlike anything he had ever known. He walked across the flagstones hearing the water as it babbled in the font. It was a nagging feeling of having been there before, but that was impossible, of course. He stopped for a moment and took in these unfamiliar surroundings. He looked up into the sky and saw the stars with crystal clarity, no haze of city lights.

He began to walk to the stable.

A chill. A shiver ran down his back and he felt a pressure, heaviness on his chest where the St. Christopher medal sat. He turned, thinking that Tom might be watching him from the balcony. He wasn't. There was the scrabble of pebbles and he looked to the battlement.

Nothing.

It was gone then, that feeling of being watched. He looked around and the night seemed just a little more normal. It unnerved him.

He went to the stable and looked in. Nothing. He went to open the stable door and it was pushed toward him, causing him to stumble back.

Gabrielle looked at him with lucid green eyes. A quizzical expression crossed her face.

"I am sorry, milady, but you startled me." He backed into the courtyard, letting the light of the moon touch her face. She was breathtaking in the soft glow.

"That is what happens when you stalk about," she replied. She closed and barred the stable door behind her, and then she walked past him and to the fountain.

"I could not sleep. I saw the light on in the stable so I thought I'd come down." He watched her lithe form move gracefully to the fountain. Then she sat. He slowly walked over to her.

"May I?" he asked and gestured next to her. She nodded her assent.

"I thought I would run into Duran," an awkward silence followed and he saw her frown.

"Duran is not the nicest person to be around," she said, with unusual candor for a lady raised in the decorum of the court. She paused, and looked at him directly. "You and your friends are strange, Sir John."

"Thanks for the compliment," he replied. A wry twist lit upon his lips.

"It was not meant as a compliment, Sir John." The look on her face was sincere. He chuckled and she frowned.

"You can drop the 'Sir', just call me John." He looked around. The air was calm and comfortable.

"'John', it is a strange name." He noticed that her voice had strength and confidence. She seemed not at all afraid to speak her mind. "We usually see mercenaries, merchants, or brigands come through

119

here, like the ones that attacked Trianna. Or a few of the Conclaveum may pass through, and they are very arrogant. It is refreshing to have you prove that honor still exists."

"I gather that Duran is not very honorable?" She gave him a sharp look.

"His smooth manner is a facade, no doubt. There are those that have tried to court me before. I like him the least.

"His origins are doubtful. He says that he hails from Qwen, a free state. Well, he assuredly has made a home in Galfeon Yor." She shook her head and sighed, then looked at John with those penetrating eyes.

"What is your homeland like, Sir John?"

"Flat," he referred to northern Ohio. "Lots of farms. I come from a small port city. The place is different, the people are the same, I guess.

"Tell me, Gabrielle, though your father says that Gelion and the west are in an uneasy truce, why haven't your father and the other landowners of the west banded together in an attempt to drive him north?"

"Apathy. My father has told me that, when I was a little child, they made such a move. But, they were held off. It was around the time my mother died, some illness struck her."

He sensed her distance and tried to bring her back.

"I hope that we have not put you and your people in a difficult position. It seems we are lost and don't really know our way home. It's nice to know that we are welcome somewhere." He smiled and looked at her, she smiled back.

"The Regent Gelion will not like it, but I sense you are not afraid of him. Do your beliefs gird you against the fear?"

"Oh, there is fear. But it's all in the way you direct it. Positive or negative, you gotta choose. I choose the positive. It has been said that I'm overly optimistic.

"So, tell me, what do you do around here, in your spare time?"

"I have very little time to spare. I work with many of the farmers and merchants, coordinating the tithe, crops, and stores so that when the winter comes there will be enough for the village and any travelers that may pass through. Father is the diplomat, not I.

"Trianna keeps me company as there are not many of noble birth within our small province, but that doesn't bother me. Trianna is genuine, often that is not the case with noble born.

"We are currently preparing for the Spring Festival at Tonlin's hold in Ord, about two days ride from here. It celebrates the rebirth of nature. It is nothing more than an excuse for men to get drunk and women to gossip. Many of the townspeople venture there. It offers the opportunity to trade wares and information, and make bargains."

"It sounds quite ideal."

"Quite boring, you mean?" She said it and laughed.

"What of you, Sir Knight? When you are not protecting the honor of young maidens, what do you do?"

"I was a student. I enjoy sailing. In my spare time I slay a dragon or two."

"What is a dragon?" she looked at him, puzzled at the unfamiliar term.

"A mythical animal of our land, it has big wings and flies through the air and breathes fire…sometimes." Great, he thought, if they have no dragons, Joe will be really disappointed.

"It sounds like a Courier Beast, though they are somewhat dumb, and do not breathe fire." Then, as if reading John's mind she asked: "Surik, he is mysterious. Why do you call him Shadowlord?"

Good question. He hesitated. "In Erie, our 'Province', there are a group of warriors who use sorcery in combat. They conjure the shades of those they have slain in combat to confuse and thwart their enemies. Surik is the Lord over those warriors."

"You expect me to believe in magic?"

"No, but I have never seen him fail in combat."

"And you," she said, and there was that piercing look in her eyes: "Have you lost in combat?"

"Yes, but never in mortal combat, or I wouldn't be here."

"Duran says he has never lost."

"He's never fought me."

She sighed, "All men are alike."

"Yes, and no. You see, we work as a team. Separately we are all good at what we do. But together we are better. The whole is greater than the sum of its parts. We are bound by something greater than friendship."

She looked away. John couldn't begin to know what was going on in her mind. He looked at her profile, her fine jaw line, and her hair as it fell past the shoulder. Then, he looked away, knowing that he could develop feelings for this woman but not wanting to. He was not willing to trust this land or himself.

"I must go," she said, and before John could respond, she was walking toward the keep and had gone through the door. He stared after her a moment, shaking his head slightly, then he too got up and went to his room.

The shadowy figure that had been watching from the parapet stepped into the moonlight. He stroked his beard, gazing from the stable to the fountain, and then to John's balcony. He smiled as a plan began to form. Then he caught sight of a figure on the balcony, staring straight at him with arms folded. The one called Smiling Wolf, Duran knew. So be it, he thought. It is but a trifle.

A soft hand caressed John's shoulder and he sighed. Her face was inches from his and she smiled radiantly. She leaned forward and, like a feather, her lips touched his. He pulled her closer and...

Tom.

"Time to get up, Johnny boy." John cracked his eyes and saw the sun creeping along his sheets, inching its way toward him. He groaned at the thought of not finishing his dream.

123

"I don't wanna go to school!" John growled. His voice was gravelly and it tasted like something had crawled in his throat to die.

"Wake up! I think we should go into town today." Tom was already dressed in loose pants and tunic. He smiled and fastened his knife to its shoulder strap and slung it. His longbow sat in the corner, where it had been the night before. Kiera crawled over Smiling Wolf's shoulder and then into the hood of his tunic.

John slowly got out of bed.

"Are the others up?" He walked to the bowl near the door and splashed his face.

"Are you kidding? They were drinking into the wee hours. I do suppose we could rouse them though." A malicious grin split his lips. He watched as John finished dressing in jeans and a sweatshirt. He strapped on his sword and was ready.

They walked into the empty hallway to the room next to their own. Tom rapped on the hard oak, there was no reply.

"Sound asleep?" Tom knocked harder and John just looked sidelong at him. "How can you be so cheerful?" the dark eyed student asked. Then the door swung open to reveal a sad sight.

Chill belched and turned, almost falling over Mike who was sprawled on the floor. He scratched his stomach and fell face down on the bed next to Bill. It was a sad sight indeed.

"Hey guys–" John started.

"Shudup, asshole," Chill pleaded. John smiled as he realized that he held an enormous amount of power at that moment.

124

"It's morning guys, time to explore our new home," Tom said it with such enthusiasm that John doubted any of the guys could resist, but Mike just stared from the corner through his sunglasses, avoiding the light at all costs.

"You're telling us," he started, "that in a world with no flushing toilets, no toilet paper, and no aspirin, you want us to get up with the break of dawn and go looking about? You are definitely insane."

"I see you guys had fun last night," John chided. He deliberately dragged his foot over Mike's chest. The big man stirred like a bear, then rolled over, grumbling.

"Go away," Chill called. But he also was beginning to rouse himself.

"It's like bringing the dead back to life, Tom. Use the right incantation and it will work." John knelt by Bill and whispered into his ear. "Girls, and lots of them."

Bill's eyes snapped open and he growled. It was almost intimidating.

"Tom," whispered Joe as he peered at John. "Kill him."

Mike and Chill decided to stay in their chambers and sleep. Bill and Joe joined the early risers and made their second foray into the village of Galfeon Yor. It had seemed much larger at night; however, during the day they noticed that the bulk of the buildings congregated around three main thoroughfares that wound their way to and around Trevor's keep. As they walked down the road bordered by the orchard, a warm breeze blew up from the village, bringing scents of smoke and food and the murmur of people working. The village had been awake for some time and news of Trevor's guests must have spread quickly; most of the townspeople shied away, or made warding gestures with their hands. It was as if they had the plague. "Feel slightly out of place?" Joe asked. He stared back at the people and they quickly looked away.

"I don't know, Surik Shadowlord, should we?" John replied. Then he went on to inform him of his conversation with Gabrielle and how he's told her the Shadowlord controlled the shades of those he had slain in combat.

"Great, John, now I'm a Necromancer." Joe shook his head and moved under the shade of an awning. They stood in the village market. People milled about looking at fruits and vegetables, and the smiths and merchants had their wares displayed under small tents. The shops off the street were small and clean, and held everything from a stained-glass maker to a potter.

"Do you guys have any of that money Mike pilfered?" Joe asked. Bill smiled and tossed him the pouch of coins. "There's a little outdoor café over there."

They followed his gaze to a small establishment that had a few benches and tables. John would hardly consider it a café. "You guys go ahead. I think Tom and I'll go check out Omar the Knife Maker." He referred to a small stand where a man with a huge mustache picked his teeth.

"Righto," Joe said as he and Bill headed for the café. They sat down and a portly woman with a tray came to their bench.

"Wot will ye ave," she asked in what Joe decided was the uneducated slur of the townspeople.

"What do you have to drink?" Bill asked, hoping it wasn't remotely alcoholic. "Ale, mead, Adleberry wine, and goats' milk, its fresh; and hot Karo bean." The two looked at each other.

"And to eat?"

She cocked her head to the side and her apple like cheeks swelled with a gap-toothed smile. "Sweet nut bread and honey, I jus pulled it out o the oven me self."

"The milk or the—"

"Karo, lads...trust me," she smiled and smoothed back her graying hair, then after Joe nodded she went into the café to fetch their order.

"Karo?" Bill made a funny face, hoping it wasn't like the ale they had had two nights ago. As they waited for their order, they watched John and Tom at the booth across the square. The shops and street were surprisingly crowded for a town this size, but perhaps it was the warm spring day. Children splashed about in the fountain as mothers picked over the better vegetables. Soon the woman was back with the Karo and nut bread. She cleared her throat as they reached for the meal. "Oh," Bill said and held out his palm to Joe. Joe frowned and pulled out several coins. Before he could hand them to her she grabbed several and was gone. "I take it she took her tip?" Joe lifted the mug of hot brown liquid and smelled.

It reminded him of vanilla with a hint of rose and cinnamon. He tasted it without hesitation and smiled. It was less bitter than coffee would be, and

127

the flavor was just as mellow as its smell. He was pleasantly surprised, as was Bill when he bit into the warm bread. It was delicious.

"This reminds me of Germany." Joe sighed as he looked at the people, heard the sounds, and enjoyed their meal. He remembered the time he went to Bavaria to visit his aunt and spent a weekend skiing in the Alps.

"Except we can't hop on Lufthansa and fly home."

Tom looked down the length of the blade, flipping it neatly from hand to hand. It was a finely crafted knife, more for throwing than anything. The man behind the booth watched and continued picking his teeth. What remained of a blood sausage sat on a plate at his elbow.

"Ye know yer blades, do ye?" the man asked. Tom looked up and nodded. Then the Sioux pitched the knife into a wooden beam a few feet away. He frowned. "Not as well balanced as I thought," he remarked to John. The man just handed him another and gestured to the beam. Tom threw the other and was satisfied as it thunked into a knot several inches to the right of the other knife. "Better?"

"Much, I–" he was cut short as a woman screamed and they both turned and looked to the center of the square. There, a heavy-set lady was pulling a child from the fountain as the other children scrambled at her feet. Tom and John ran over and were met by Bill and Joe, who had also heard the commotion.

They watched as the woman wrung her hands over the body of the small girl lying pale and still at her feet. Someone muttered that it would take hours to get the healer. It was quite obvious that the little girl could not wait that long.

"Out of the way," Tom said as he shoved a man aside and knelt over the girl. Smiling Wolf checked for a pulse then quickly pulled her up from the ankles to let the water drain from her lungs. John cleared her mouth while Tom held her aloft.

"Demon! Get thee away from er!" the woman shouted. One of the men in the crowd made a move to stop him but Joe's sword made an ugly dance inches from his eyes.

The girl shuddered and water poured from her mouth, but still she did not breathe. Tom gently placed her on her back and lifted her head. He began to administer mouth-to-mouth resuscitation. After a few seconds, the girl began to cough, and she was soon crying out weakly for her mother. Tom gently lifted her and put her in the arms of the woman. She cried in joy as she held her baby. Tom knelt and breathed heavily, smiling as she tried to thank him. Then a whisper went through the crowd and the men surged forward and lifted Tom to their shoulders, voices swelling to a cheer. The others stood around as people clapped them on their backs. All smiled.

It was not the way John would have liked to make friends with the townspeople, but it worked.

Mike stood in Trevor's main library, paging through an old tome. Trianna had said that there were several of them about the castle, but this was the largest. Now all he had to do was learn to read the High Tongue. There were four principle languages in the Conclaveum: Common, Middle, High, and Guild. Common transcended all cultural and class barriers, though at times dialects interfered with its being understood clearly. Middle was a language often used by merchants and travelers who engaged in business transactions. Guild was a language used by any of the guilds, societies or religious organizations that existed; all of these tongues were different and secret, only known to those among that society. Trevor had explained that the High Tongue was the language reserved for mages and scholars, as well as most of the aristocracy and noble houses of the Conclaveum. Since that entity had been the dominant ruling force for the past couple of thousand years, almost all scholarly works of any value were written in that tongue. It was a strange language indeed, almost Arabic in style of writing. It was a language that consisted of forty-seven consonants and eight vowels, and something that Trevor had called Ai'jien. These Ai'jien were abstractions of thought, and it was these that gave words their power. At least that was what Trevor had said. It was very complex, with variations for gender and class standing and, like German or Chinese, some of the words could vary by pronunciation and carry a whole different meaning. As he perused the text, he shook his head. It could be worse. He grunted as he looked at the book Trevor had provided, then to the other text. He barely noticed the stout man an arm's length away.

Chill sat in a leather chair and turned his broadsword slowly. With the light that streamed through the tall crystal windows, he could note the dullness of the blade, even a few nicks. He adjusted his glasses and wiped the flat of the blade on his jeans. It was useless – he needed a whetstone.

"You gonna be here for a while?" Chill asked of the big man who had begun to pull several large books from a shelf. Mike looked up, his large arms straining under the weight of the folios.

"Yeah. I'm gonna try and learn some of the language. These books are cross- referenced in both Common and High Tongue." He went to a bench and set them down, and then he sat cross-legged on the floor and flipped one of them open. He looked back to Chill. "What about you?"

"I need something to sharpen my sword. I'll think I'll try Baxel and see where the guards take care of their stuff."

Mike nodded as Chill walked off. He looked at the words; he had seen something like it in an ancient Sumerian text. The more he looked it over and compared it with the same Common text, the more he saw a pattern emerge. This was a name and this was a vowel. It would definitely have been easier had Trevor assisted him.; however, at this point he didn't want to arouse any suspicions. He knew that their origins, if found out, would more than likely cause Trevor to distrust them all the more. So, he labored over the texts alone. It soon came to him that the one supposed to be a magical tome bore notation that was disturbingly familiar.

Quantum Physics? He wondered. Then shook his head. It couldn't be.

Chill found his way to the barracks and knocked on the open door. Baxel was sitting on his bunk talking to another guard. Baxel looked up. He was maybe in his thirties, a little taller than Chill, with a plain face and square jaw. He looked sharply at Chill and stood.

"And what may I do for you, milord?"

Chill smiled and walked up to him. He slowly drew the blade and showed it to the man.

"Call me Chill." Baxel nodded and looked at the broadsword. "It's a little dull," Chill continued. "Is there someplace around here that I can sharpen it?"

"Aye, follow me." Baxel turned and walked past the man with whom he had been talking. From the man's respectful attitude, Chill assumed that Baxel must be captain of the guard or something. Baxel led him to the rear of the chamber where a grinding wheel sat. Soon the sword was sharp and Baxel was inspecting it slowly.

"I have never seen such a blade, what is it?" He ran his finger along the sharp edge.

"It's a type of carbon steel," Chill replied and the man handed it back. "It's a special alloy, that preserves the blade. It's not magical or anything. It will just keep an edge longer and won't tarnish easily. It's not as nice a sword as John's or Joe– er, Surik's, but it will do in a pinch. May I?" he gestured to the sword strapped to Baxel's side.

The guardsman handed the long sword to Chill and he hefted it, noting that the balance was superb. In terms of quality, Baxel's blade was superior to Chill's. Chill handed Baxel's sword back.

"It's a fine blade."

"My father's." The man looked at it with pride. Chill noticed the silver filigree in the hilt and the blood-groove that dominated the center, just the right depth for balance. It was a fine blade indeed.

"Well, what have we here? Exchanging martial expertise?" Duran stood in the door with arms crossed.

"What do you want, Duran?" Baxel almost growled and Chill noticed his grip grow tight on the long sword.

"Just seeing if I could find a partner to practice a little fence and parry?" Chill then saw the elegantly hilted sword on Duran's hip. It was a narrow blade that ran from hip to ankle, long and straight, for skill more than strength.

"You won't find such here. Mrick is still hurting from the 'practice' you gave him last week."

"Come, come," Duran smiled. "It was only an accident."

"It seems," replied Baxel, with acid bathing his words, "that if you are the swordsman you claim to be, there should be no such accidents."

"Be careful, Baxel," Duran sliced back, the line at his jaw tightening. "I do not take such accusations lightly."

"Take it as you will, I have no care." He passed Duran and walked into the barracks. Duran made a move to follow then turned and looked at Chill.

"And you, Sir Chill, fence and parry?"

"I have to-"

"What?" It hinted an insinuation of his manhood, skill, and honor.

"Practice, Duran, we all need practice. If you're that desperate for a partner I'll do it, you don't have to whine." Duran's eyes narrowed and he followed Chill out of the barracks. Baxel gave Chill a warning glance as they walked by, but it was too late.

Joe looked up from the table, feeling his head swim, and he realized that later this afternoon he was going to have one hell of a headache. The townspeople had been buying the drinks and plying them for information, as well as constantly clapping them on the back for saving that little girl's life. Joe could hardly refuse their generosity and had accepted one drink after the other freely. He smiled at a plump serving wench and tipped his tankard back to taste the bitter brew. He listened as Bill recited the story of Gelion and how they had been stranded, and watched John and Tom slip from the tavern into the bright light of the afternoon.

"I'm sick of hearing that story," John remarked as he walked up the shallow grade toward the castle.

"At least we won't get it mixed up," Tom replied. "We've heard it so many times."

John smirked as he realized the scope of the story they had created for themselves. Unfortunately, if they embellished it too much with the mythos of the Legion of the Black Skull, they might end up pushing credibility to the limit.

Those thoughts were soon lost as they wound their way back to the keep. It had turned out to be a warm day; they both soaked up the sun as they crossed the Deep and entered the castle.

Chill was going to get abused and he knew it. Chill's sword technique went as far as teaching kids the basics of foil fencing. In the Society, he used a hack and slash, over-the-shield technique that was notorious in the Legions of Rome. Joe had tried to teach him a few epee techniques, generally more advanced than he taught his regular students, and for all intents and purposes they was used for competition rather that dueling or fighting, but these were almost useless with a broadsword. He wasn't even sure if he could employ a riposte or a feint.

Duran stood across from him in the open courtyard. Behind them was the fountain and before them the stables. Duran spun his blade and saluted Chill; there was an odd look on his face.

Chill frowned and saluted. It wasn't pretty.

After the first flurry, Chill realized that Duran was playing with him. His forearm was getting sore as he tried to fend off the narrow blade. Duran was obviously treating this as more than a practice match and, with each stroke of his sword, was getting closer to cutting him. Chill jumped back and grimaced in pain as Duran's blade finally nicked him. Now maybe he'll back off, Chill thought.

It couldn't have been further from the truth.

Duran lowered his blade and smiled. "Well, Sir Chill, you seem to be in need of practice."

"Yeah," Chill wheezed out, he was getting winded. "That seems to be case doesn't it?" Chill lunged at the man and almost lost his balance. Duran capitalized on this and knocked Chill's

135

sword from his hand. He poised the blade at Chill's throat and the stocky man just stared back.

Duran's eye flickered with something, but Chill couldn't decipher what. Then he lowered his blade and Chill sighed. He heard the sound of footsteps behind him. "Not nice to point, Duran," Tom said as he gestured to the blade. Duran appraised the Native American and laughed lightly. He quickly scabbarded his sword and wiped a trickle of sweat from his brow.

"It seems that your compatriot is in need of practice." He smiled and stepped to the fountain. He lowered a kerchief into the water and then touched it to his brow, feigning fatigue. Chill retrieved his sword and stood next to his friends.

"Your practice is sloppy," replied Tom. "If you were my student you would know better. Accidents shouldn't happen." He indicated Chill's shoulder and where his sweatshirt was turning crimson with blood.

"I slipped, outlander, and where I come from accidents do happen." Duran's eyes narrowed.

"Then it's obvious that you need more practice." Tom turned his back on the man and smiled at John. He was just hoping that the ass would try something. I'll make him toast, Tom thought. Duran just smiled though, and turned toward the stable.

"I think I shall go riding; anyone care to join me?"

"No thanks, one of us might accidentally fall from our mount and break a neck," John replied with a certain amount of disdain in his voice. After Duran was gone John turned to Tom who was taking a look at Chill's arm. "Smooth, Chill, real smooth."

"Boy, he sure is good."

"He's probably been using a sword since he was a little boy."

"I couldn't refuse his invitation you know? Anyway, I was playing with him." Tom smiled, "Right. I could see that." He looked at the shallow cut. "Go wash it, and pour a little honey on it to prevent an infection."

Chill slowly headed to his chambers. John crossed his arms and cocked his head to one side.

"You know," started Tom, turning back to John. "Duran reminds me of a reptile."

"Yeah, well Chill is right. Duran is very good. He was toying with Chill." John looked at the flagstones, noticed a few drops of blood. He felt, rather than heard Tom nod.

"I think that our visit to this land is going to be a bit more eventful than we hoped." Tom grinned and lifted Kiera to his shoulder.

Chapter 8

The old man laughed as he looked out through the open room of his tower. Teshwa blazed alive on this night; lightning flashed around the canopy at the summit of the Tower of Iss, the Tower of Pain. The slender pillars that supported the marble dome glimmered with each flash of light. Normally they were a deep green, laced with gold veins, but tonight there was a dark red splashed upon the smooth surface. Several bodies lay on the slate floor in their own blood.

"You are truly evil, Uncle," came a softly feminine voice. Guyle looked up, his gnarled hands clutching at the arms of the chair he privately deemed his throne. He twisted around at the sound of her voice.

"The Daemon came to me in a dream and wanted the souls of the damned. Three less whores on the streets of Teshwa." He laughed cruelly and tapped his staff. A gust of wind, gale force, swept the bodies off the railless balcony, but instead of falling, they were caught up on the currents and swept into the raging black clouds.

"Your communion with the underworld went well?"

"You should know, niece. You serve Oran." He licked his lips as she moved into the center of the chamber. Her black diaphanous gown swirled in the wind revealing her nakedness beneath. She was wholly immodest as she trailed her bare toe in the blood. He watched her. Lusted for her. He felt the stirring in his ancient loins when he saw the swell of her breasts and the curve of her hips.

"Your Daemon has spoken. Are they here?"

"Oh, yes," in a voice like sandpaper. He touched his signet ring to his forehead. To her it was a useless gesture. Communing with the likes of a Daemon was risky sorcery at best. It could take the soul of that which summoned it.

"In the South, my dear, that is where they are. Our agents have already notified us that they are making their presence felt."

"Gelion."

"Yes," he sighed. "Your father will not like the trouble we have stirred up. It is in the aether and cannot be called back."

"He is an old fool, and once the power that the Daemon promised is unleashed, he will no longer be in a position to quarrel. Then," she said as she walked to him and trailed her finger along his mottled arm. "Then a new era begins."

Chapter 9

Dark clouds dotted the brilliant hues of the sky far to the north as the sun set in a wash of red and orange. The last rays of light streaked long and low through the snow-covered peaks in the west, then slowly vanished.

Joe sighed and turned, thinking over the past six weeks. It was hard to believe that they had been here for over a month. He lounged against the parapet of the castle wall and gazed at Chill, who leaned on his elbows gazing out over the darkening plains. Whatever he thought was lost to the other.

His hair was a little longer, as was Joe's, and he supposed that now Chill's sword technique was markedly improved. Over the past month, Joe had tutored him in saber fencing techniques and John had coached him in kenjutsu. John had laughed, saying that now Chill knew more than the two of them combined. That was stretching on a few counts, Joe thought.

For the past month, Duran had left them pretty much on their own. Often, the dark man was away for several days at a time, and his presence was fleeting at best. All the better.

Joe sighed as the cobalt sky deepened to lavender and fine, brilliant jewels began to dot the heavens. A cool breeze eased the humidity but the heat of the day still seemed to radiate from the stones.

John was somewhere, probably talking to Gabrielle. She had warmed up to him somewhat. Joe couldn't understand why John wanted to risk becoming attached to anybody on this side of hell.

And they all were hoping that Mike might find something in those ancient tomes that he so readily had learned how to decipher. Yet, they were still nowhere. More and more, the only solution seemed to lie with the force that had brought them to this world, this unknown entity.

In the meantime, they had gotten to know their hosts a little better. The group had made a habit of going to town at least three times a week; otherwise boredom would kill them slowly. They had come to know the townspeople, but there were still those that distrusted them. Others, though, had become open, friendly and generous. The group had even acquired otherwise expensive items for services rendered. They had participated in first aid classes for the people, to the bitter denouncement of the local healer. Tom had shared his expertise in tanning and leatherworking. Joe had painted a bawdy mural above the tavern's bar.

Yet, Trevor had remained aloof. Oh, there were brief moments of open frankness, answering some questions and pointing out various political nuances when a courier brought the mail.

One night Trevor had left in a hurry, several of his men at arms in tow. The next morning he was back, a furrow across his brow. John had gleaned the only hint of what happened from Gabrielle.

Apparently a small party of marauders had killed the reigning Lord of Ord while on a hunt. She explained that now his son, a foolish drunk, governed the province. It did not bode well for the unity of the free-states, because all he cared for was whether the tithe would be on time and if the grapes were as good as last year's. She sarcastically noted that at least the Spring Festival would be a celebration not easily forgotten.

All this did not ease the tension that was evident among the group. John and Bill concurred that some type of release was necessary, and what better way than the Festival. Mike had grumbled some, but he was always willing to go to a party, even though it was a day's ride away. They decided to accompany Trevor and his entourage to the neighboring province, rationalizing that it would give them a broader understanding of the world in which they now lived, especially a greater understanding of some of the political underpinnings of the freeholds of the west.

At least that was their excuse; truth to tell it was also to relieve the stress that was building among them. They had all noticed it. The foremost question was if they would ever return home. Although Mike was working diligently, they were no closer now to finding the answer than they were the day they were brought to this reality.

The artist shook his head to clear it, brought out of the reverie by the tolling of a bell in the village. He smiled and patted Chill on the shoulder. The stout man looked up, surfacing from his own thoughts.

"What ya thinking of?" the self-proclaimed Shadowlord asked. "Home. And dinner. I'm starved."

Joe shook his head and the two men began their search for food.

John strolled through the musty cellar chamber. Torchlight flickered and stretched his shadow across the rock floor, making it dance like

142

a mad Russian. Occasionally, he would stop and gaze at something that would catch his fancy, and then he would move on.

He had found his way into Trevor's dungeons, if that was what you could call them, and had taken the opportunity to explore. The first time that he had found his way into the cellars, he had taken a wrong turn in one of the many halls of the castle. He had proceeded down a winding corridor, slanted at a casual grade, and had found himself facing a stout wood and iron door. It had not been locked and, upon opening it, he had stared down a dank and dark stairwell. Needless to say, he was not going to explore the depths of that cellar without a good lamp; but, he did notice that it was frequented of late, there were no cobwebs barred his path and the steps were clean of dust. The next time, he had acquired a lamp, and lit the many sconces that lined the heavy stone walls. The steps dropped into the bowels of the keep, soon leveling off and bringing him to an open area. Here, vaulted chambers lay in darkness beyond the flickering light of the lamp. Ancient blocks of granite began as narrow pillars set into the hard clay and dirt and flared to a low vaulted ceiling a bare few feet above his head.

Many of the stores of Galfeon Yor lay in these vaults: heavy casks filled with salted meats and other supplies. Enough to last a long winter...Or a siege, John thought wryly. There were a few locked chambers and, of course, Trevor's armory, through which captured his attention and drew him in.

His leather boots echoed hollowly as they tapped out an uneven rhythm. He hadn't known it was possible to get sick of seeing swords, but it soon happened. Most were not the ornate long swords that one expected, but mass-produced, plain- bladed, broad swords. He wondered why Trevor had a need for so much armor and weapons, but then this was a semi-feudal society. He hefted a crossbow; it was a heavy weapon. A two-by-four size stock with a steel bow that needed a crank to pull the string back. A small lever beneath the stock served as a trigger. He struggled with the crank, it needed oiling, but finally the bow was set and he placed a short bolt into the track. He had never seen an authentic crossbow before and he hefted it awkwardly, pointing it at the wooden door. He was about to let fly the powerful weapon when the door flew open. He jumped back in surprise and consternation, but quickly swung the armed weapon away from the new target. Duran looked up, slightly shocked at finding someone down here.

"Hello, Duran, and how are you today?" John relaxed the tension on the string and put the crossbow back on the rack. His hand lingered on the stock as he turned toward the dark man.

"Fine, Lord Knight," he replied, walking over to the outlander. "What brings you to Trevor's armory?"

"Just wandering around. And you?"

"Oh, I thought I might get a practice dagger."

John eyed the man and looked at the weapons that surrounded them. They were all dark and dusty, some even rusty from neglect. Most of the edges were dull and cobwebs spread over the crossbows and the larger ballistas from lack of use. "You have your search cut out for you." John flicked at a string that hung limp from a longbow and it shivered with dust.

"These are but the common stores, with which to arm the town militia if need be. As if they would know how to use such. The real treasures are locked up. Here, I'll show you." Duran walked to one of the locked inner doors. It was free of dust and webs and looked to have been used frequently. Duran inserted a long key and deftly opened the portal. He then produced a taper and lit the oil lamp on the inside of the chamber. Darkness fled the room and John looked over Duran's shoulder to the contents within.

The torchlight gleamed off polished blades and buffed armor. Racks of standard long swords stood against one wall and, on another, were pieces of armor. John entered behind Duran, feeling like a kid in a candy store. He smiled in appreciation for a large two-handed sword with gold cross-hilt, wondering all the while at the kind of strength necessary to wield it. His eyes wandered to where Duran stood fingering a dagger; at his feet was a small chest full of various sized stilettos and knives.

"You see, Lord Knight, Trevor keeps the very best locked tight." He flipped the dagger expertly and a shiver ran down John's spine. "These weapons haven't been used in a long time, but at least his men take care of them."

John pulled a vambrace from a rack and tested its flexibility. The vambrace was made of layered steel, like the plates of an armadillo, and reminded John of something a gladiator would wear to protect the shoulder and upper arm. The metal was polished to mirror clarity and the leather binding straps were oiled and supple. "A good swordsman wouldn't need that, Sir John," Duran said sardonically, although the muscle at the side of the man's jaw tightened as John shouldered the vambrace.

"A good swordsman knows when to exercise caution against unknowable odds," John countered. "He never assumes what his opponent is like, for if he does, he usually ends up losing. He should only make such assumptions when he knows beyond a shadow of a doubt that his opponent is weaker than himself, and even then he should still be wary." John turned and was about to leave when Duran spoke.

"Then I guess that it is a matter of philosophy. I was taught that one should use his skills, honed in practice, and forged in combat, and do anything to bring his enemy to his knees. And Lord Knight, I have done that.

"At a young age I hired out with the Jaggiers of Qwen. I sopped the blood of my first kill from my blade at the age of fourteen." He noticed the look on John's face. "You have not known battle the way I have. I am only a few years older than you, yet I have fought desert warriors in the west, and bandits near the ruins of Narn-toc.

"I killed my first Mage at twenty, and barely lived to tell of it. So, Lord Knight, while you protected the land of Erie, I fought for my life. I know of my abilities, and I am confident in the

146

inferiority of my opponent. Would you care for a bit of fence and parry?"

"Not now, Duran, I wouldn't want to take advantage of a swordsman of your caliber." John smiled and left the room. With vambrace in hand, he proceeded up the cellar stairs.

After John had gone Duran smiled. He looked down at the dagger he held in his hand and then it shot out and into the door, near where John had been standing. It shivered as it sank two inches into the hard wood.

Mike held the chain carelessly in his hand. The pure silver glimmered with a luster unknown to any other metal, even gold or platinum. He watched it swing over the bowl of dark fluid; it was a mixture of blood, urine, and milk. He watched as the chain reflected the dark red that swirled amidst the milky white, tainted with yellow. He picked up the copper and silver ornament that had been hanging on the silver chain around his neck, bought some time ago from a jeweler who specialized in pure metals and focused energy. The ornament was as long as his pinkie, a tube of copper holding a piece of unflawed quartz crystal. The tube was covered with a gold filigree and silver inlay. Stirring the contents of the bowl to mix the ingredients, he dipped the tip of the crystal in the fluid, then used it as a pen on a sheet of parchment. The runes he drew were obscure, but understandable High Tongue to him. The large man concentrated on the parchment as it dried, then took it gently in his fingers and touched a corner to the flame of the candle that lit his work. He held it for a moment to make sure it had caught, then dropped the burning paper into the bowl, watching as the ashes permeated the liquid and dissolved.

Mike sighed deeply and focused on the crystal, the chain, and the bowl. And then it happened. The liquid in the bowl began to change, to clear and harden until all that remained was a solid sphere of something akin to amber.

"Wow," Mike muttered to himself. "It worked."

A smile spread across the large man's face as he began to realize that, although in his world sorcery was almost non-existent, it could be applied in this world quite readily.

He tipped the contents of the bowl into the palm of his left hand. The surface of the transparent solid was dull, but still warm from the chemical process that had formed it. Chemical and metaphysical, Mike thought. He began to polish it with a coarse cloth. Slowly it took on a gleam and he began to make out the lines in the palm of his hand though the substance. He smiled again and wished he had a cigarette.

He noticed there was a small flaw in the orb that he had created, but it was pretty darn good for a first try; although the flaw might affect the orb's use, it would be a focus for one's attention and concentration.

The Book of Shadows he had purchased at the Event sat by his elbow on the desk, the gold-inlaid pentagram on the cover glinting softly in the candlelight. Mike opened the book and riffled through the crisp, white pages, once again struck by the almost menacing nature of their blankness.

148

He knew the link was here somewhere; he just had to find it. There was a feeling deep down in him; a feeling that his happening upon this book and their being brought to this world was more than mere coincidence. He felt that this was the path to whoever or whatever had brought them here.

Now maybe I can find you, he thought. He gently set the book down and wrapped the orb in a linen cloth, setting it aside.

Tom stood motionless in the torchlight of the courtyard. The flagstones were cool beneath his bare feet and the evening air chilled the sweat on his back. He had stripped down to a leather breechcloth for his exercise.

He had spent an hour in junan taiso, body conditioning and stretching exercises. Then onto zempokaiten, forward rolls on the hard stones, which had almost wrecked his body. Oh well, he thought.

He now stood in the ichimongi no kamae, a defensive posture for unarmed combat. He moved slowly forward, his body low and ready to strike.

The object was Fu no kata, fight like the wind. The warrior could be a buffeting attack and the opponent would never know where to strike. He moved around the courtyard, hoping John would show up so he could practice some throws. Often he had tried a new or innovative move with John, much to the other's chagrin.

After about thirty minutes of various techniques, he stopped and breathed deeply. Then he picked up the sword for which he had bartered some brain-tanned leather with the blacksmith in town.

He hefted it. It was a chokuto-style blade, which in western terms was a straight single edged sword. He favored the type in his study of martial arts, which was often shorter than typical samurai blades. John's katana was a jindachi, that is, a battle-length blade that the samurai used; it had the graceful curve the sword of the Samurai was noted for. This chokuto-style blade was about three quarters the length of the other. It had taken the smith three days to forge it to Tom's specifications and had just been finished the day before last. The edge was keen and sharp; the smith knew how to make a good blade and expressed some surprise that the outlander knew so much about what he called the Qwen style.

Tom gripped the handle just below the hand-guard and brought it up into the Daijodan no kamae, an over the head position. He swung the virgin blade down and to the left, then brought it back into Hasso no kamae, a guarded shoulder stance. It was nice to feel a decent blade. It really didn't fit with his American Indian portrayal at the Events; however, in this world it would come in handy to exercise his combat skills with the reach of this blade. Besides, he didn't have a Glock 19 to back him up; the sword would have to do.

He spun and practiced against an imaginary foe in the courtyard. Though he really had no depth of vision because he only had one eye, he had learned to compensate. His other senses made up for his lacking in that one area. His peripheral vision in his left eye was excellent and he had learned to heighten his hearing. Yet, his movements betrayed him favoring his right side,

150

and this was what he strove to correct. He did not want any opponent to learn of that flaw and take advantage of him. For that he had to learn to act as if nothing were wrong.

Unfortunately, the disadvantage was noticed. The dark figure standing near one of the shadowed entrances to the courtyard saw and noted it well. He was learning many things this day, as he had over the past month. He smoothed his beard and turned, heading towards his chambers. Tomorrow he had a two-day journey by horse and he wished to be well rested. He flipped the dagger effortlessly as he walked down the hall.

Bill lounged in the main hall of Trevor's keep. Next to him was a wide hearth and the logs within crackled as flames licked upwards toward the flue. It was nice in here, where high stained glass windows kept the sun's heat out during the day and the stones were comfortably cool. The banners that flanked the hall whispered with a draft near the ceiling, but it was not an eerie feeling, rather it was comforting, calming. He sipped at a fine wine that he had gotten from the cellar; he had asked Trianna if taking the vintage was allowed and she had smiled shyly and said yes, as long as it was shared. He'd smiled at that and had awaited her arrival anxiously. It was only late in the day that he had gotten word from Mrick that she had to accompany Gabrielle to the market. He sighed; his luck was far from changing. Companionship would have been a wonderful additive to the wine. He thought of the past and some of the girls he had known.

He strummed at the lute in his lap. Lute. He wasn't even sure if you could call it that. Mrick had called it an Ighuire. It was similar in sound to the medieval instrument, yet it had nine strings and a more resonant pitch. It wasn't quite like playing a guitar, but he had picked it up quickly enough. Mrick, the guard he had borrowed it from, had been surprised at Bill's dexterity with the instrument.

Bill hummed a tune, one he had composed for a young lady back at school. He sighed. The melody that flowed out from the Ighuire was sweet, yet melancholy. As the wine warmed his stomach, the melody warmed his heart.

Chapter 10

"I knew this was going to be a long ride," Chill grumbled and adjusted himself in the saddle. It was a cooler day than most, slightly overcast and hinting at a drizzle. The entourage had been riding for the better part of the morning but they were only a fifth of the way to Tonlin's freehold.

Tom smiled and trotted his horse up to Chill's. He leaned over and pushed

Chill forward in the saddle. A look of relief passed over the man's face.

"It's not a recliner. You'll just strain your back if you lean like that." Tom smiled and urged his horse on.

Bill and Mike rode side by side, behind the Sioux, and talked quietly. Behind them were Trevor and Gabrielle, Trianna and Eric, followed by a host of guards led by Baxel. John and Joe followed the residents of Galfeon Yor, bringing up the rear with the packhorses wedged between them and the men-at-arms. The talk among them was free and light-hearted, and every once in a while a laugh would ring out among the string of riders.

"It's good to get out," John sighed and arched his back in the saddle. Joe nodded and gazed over the open countryside. They had ridden past rolling hills and groves of tall trees. The country was rich with springs and rivers, and it had been more than once that their party had to ford a stream. As a light drizzle began to fall, Joe pulled his cloak over his shoulders and patted the hilt of his sword, as it lay strapped to his saddle pommel.

"What do you think? Did I get a good deal? Do you think it's a good blade?"

"What?" John asked as he looked at his bearded friend, slightly surprised at the turn in the conversation.

"My bastard sword. I don't know what it is, but it doesn't seem to have the weight it should. Know what I mean?" Joe smiled as he looked at John, who just raised his eyebrow.

"Look," he continued. "I know it sounds strange, but when I practice my technique it feels too light, lighter than my saber. The handling should be at least a little awkward for such a heavy blade." And it should have been. There had been several times now that he had taken up his sword just to practice, to get used to the extra weight. What he found was that it carried no more weight than his fencing saber had, at least in practice.

"What are you getting at Surik?" John grazed the hilt of his own blade with the tips of his fingers.

"I don't know, Lord Knight, you tell me. The blade seems more agile than it should. I'm hoping that I didn't get an alloy blade."

"When did you notice? I mean, has it been like that since you first got it?"

"I didn't notice it at first, but, oh hell, I don't know what I'm talking about." Joe frowned and cracked his knuckles.

"Maybe it's rusting," John smirked.

"Like your brain, shithead?" Joe barked back.

"Funny. It's probably that you're just practicing more and in doing so are getting used to the blade."

154

"You're probably right."

"Of course I am," John said and leaned over to Joe, almost whispering. "Not meaning to change the subject, but do you think she likes me?"

"Who?" Joe looked around. "Who do you think? Gabrielle."

"How the hell should I know?" Joe looked off, toward distant peaks. "Why do you want to get attached to anyone here anyway? We are trying to leave as soon as possible, why risk attachment?"

"As soon as possible, pal, what's that? A day, a week, a month, a year. You tell me, Joe. For all we know we're gonna be here the rest of our lives."

Joe glared at him and spurred his horse over a rut in the road; he bobbed in his saddle at the horse's movement. John followed somewhat more slowly.

"Listen, I know Mike is trying as hard as he can." John waved his hand in the air, dismissing that thought. "It's just that she's different from most of the women I've known."

"Of course she's different, how many Ladies of the Court do you get to meet, John?" Joe continued and looked with a piercing gaze into his friend's eyes. The former graduate student cocked his head to the side, thinking about some of the women he had known. He smiled and looked back.

"Well, she's not crazy, and she doesn't belong to a sorority."

"If you like her there must be something wrong with her." He smiled and ran his hand through his hair. "Your choice of women in the past hasn't been too prudent. Nevertheless, why take the risk?"

John grinned and shrugged.

"You just wait, Surik Shadowlord, Master of the Shades and Rider of the Black Dragon. I predict upon the Holiness of my St. Christopher medallion that you will meet..." Jokingly he pulled the medal from his tunic. He felt the sterling surface and the raised design atop it. He was about to continue...

...Darkness and then a flash. A monolithic wall appeared to rise to the heavens and, in the dim evening light, he saw leather-winged beasts flying like specks about the crest, and there was Joe, black sword awash in a purple glow with a dark-haired woman by his side. Then all was black again...

...John jerked back in his saddle and fell off his horse. The steed shied away, off the road, and Joe leapt from his mount to John's side. The fallen rider looked at looked to Joe, his head swimming.

"Jeeze, John can't even stay on his horse?" commented Mike as he pulled on the reins of his mount. He stared back down the column of riders at his comrade on the ground.

John wiped the mud off his pants and got to his feet, swearing under his breath when he saw Gabrielle and Trevor and the host of guardsman trot back. Joe steadied him as he grabbed his horse's saddle and remounted.

"Sir John, are you all right?" Trevor asked. Gabrielle looked on with concern in her eyes.

"Aye, milord, a snake caused my horse to rear and throw me." He frowned and shook his head as if to clear it. Joe looked at him suspiciously and a crease distorted Bill's forehead.

"I fear I am not quite used to this horse," he remounted and trotted the beast over to the others. Soon they had fallen into the previous riding order.

"There was no snake, John. You just fell," Joe remarked quietly. "What the hell happened, did you pass out?"

"You wouldn't believe me if I told you."

"Try me."

John smiled feebly and looked at his friend. "Well...When I touched my medal I blacked out and had a vision of a monstrous wall, dragons, you and a dark-haired woman."

"Me and dragons? You're right, I don't believe you," Joe said as he gestured to John's chest. "Touch the medal, see what happens."

With some hesitation, John touched the St. Christopher medal. He just shook his head when nothing happened. "I'm not crazy. I did see something."

"I believe you, basically because in this world I'd be the crazy one not to."

***

"Anybody who can't stay even stay on his horse in this world is doomed," Mike scowled as he looked over the countryside. He liked it when it rained; it enhanced the deep earthy greens. Their surroundings had mellowed him out a bit and, as he rode, he pondered the orb he had created. He felt he was on the path to discovering who had brought them here and the universal energies that could be tapped with ease in this realm. Creating the orb might have been a petty magic compared to

157

what type of energy it would take to create, open and maintain a gate but it was something.

Bill looked back, to make sure that John and Joe had caught up, and smiled as he turned back to Mike. "So, you created this orb through magic. What's it supposed to do anyway?"

"It's based on the crystal ball principle, as a means of seeing what normally cannot be perceived. At least I hope it functions that way. Anyway, it's more of a device that will help focus the attention and concentration of the user so that he can use the power of the mind and the aether to see what normally can't be seen.

"Of course I don't know if it will work yet. I can only hope. And as for finding the person responsible for our little adventure in this world, well, why not, anything is possible. Especially in this plane of existence."

"But, we don't seem to be doing anything really constructive. Doesn't Trevor know any magic?" Bill replied.

"Well, if he does, he isn't sharing it with us. I fear that sorcerers are pretty scarce in this part of the country, and that the Conclaveum probably has the bulk of them; probably because it's more suitable a hobby for the learned, the rich, and the elite. I am not saying that Trevor is poor, just that his hobbies tend toward the martial and not the spiritual. By the way, did you see that sword he had?"

Bill nodded his assent. Trevor's weapon was a large two-handed blade with a double hilt of gold and a bejeweled scabbard of some other rare metal. He looked at the Estoc in his own scabbard, and wondered if it, or he, could stand up to the beating Trevor could deal. Not to mention that he didn't have much experience beyond a few self-defense classes. He also wondered if he could take another's life. He doubted it; at the moment it was time to plunge the blade into the heart, he was sure he'd flinch. He sighed. It probably wasn't in his nature. Some men were made for war, and others for love. He seemed to be luckier in the latter.

"I wonder what Tonlin's freehold is like," Mike mused, bringing Bill from his reverie. "I just hope they have better beer than Galfeon Yor."

"Trianna tells me they are known for their bottled spring water," the musician said dryly.

"Great. Perrier. This gets better and better," the big man scowled and wiped rain from his brow.

"She did say they had excellent wine, and that it would be flowing freely. Apparently Tonlin's son is using his father's wake as an excuse to throw a heck of a party."

"Wonderful, we'll give you a full carafe and John a crystal goblet and you'll both be set. What I want is a good dark beer, followed by a strip steak and a baked potato."

"Tom would say that will kill you."

"Gelion almost killed me; my head still rings once in a while. No, that's just healthy eating."

"Yeah, it certainly sounds good."

"And then a smoke." At this Mike brought out a pouch and a pipe he had purchased in Galfeon Yor. After a moment he pulled at the bowl and the sweet taste of tobacco eddied over his olfactory glands.

"That'll kill you even faster."

"As I said, Gelion tried. I figure that I'm blessed. At least it isn't a carton of cigs a week."

Bill had to admit it was an improvement on Mike's diet at home. There all he would touch was a case of diet cola, a carton of cigarettes, hamburger, potatoes and beer. It didn't get better than that, Mike would say. At least in this world, the big man was eating better, healthier. Bill could tell that Mike had lost some weight, although he still maintained most of his bulk; but now it was primarily muscle, which supported his large frame.

He himself had struggled to gain weight during his tenure as a student and had succeeded in making a fairly scrawny body into a well-massed build. It had been long and difficult. He would work out five times a week, pressing weights, and he would eat sometimes four or five meals a day. He had been rewarded for his perseverance by putting on about twenty pounds of muscle. That was not to say he was overblown with it. He was well proportioned and broad shouldered; his new look had turned many an eye. He had even used it to his advantage when competing in the University triathlon and, in this world, when fighting in Gelion's keep. Back to the fighting, again, he conceded. He listened to Mike hum softly, and soon he was lost in his thoughts once more.

Bill swung the flap of the tent open, letting the morning light illuminate the interior. He stretched his taut frame and realized that last night was one of the first times he had gotten a decent sleep. Stepping outside, he felt the warmth of the sun on his bare chest. Last night weather had been rainy

160

and windy, but it had cleared rather nicely in the morning.

They had pitched camp about a league from Tonlin's hold. In the distance, he could make out vineyards and springhouses.

Their camp was set in an open field and, not far off, they could see the fluttering banner of another group of tents. As he took in the view, he realized that people around him were staring; seeming somewhat shocked at his appearance. He realized he was in nothing more than bikini briefs and quickly pulled on his jeans, all the while fighting to keep a sheepish grin from taking over his face.

Baxel smiled from where he sat at the fire, feeding the burgeoning flames. Dressed in simple tunic and riding breeches, he looked out of form; Bill had usually seen him only in armor. His sword, however, still lay within reach. As Bill approached the lanky Captain of the Guard, the man stood and handed the musician a cup of Karo. The cinnamon tantalized his senses.

"Up early, Bard," noted Baxel. "Your companions tired from the ride?"

Bill shook his head and swallowed the hot liquid. "No, they're getting up too. They're just a bit slower."

Trevor's guard smiled and picked up a piece of his armor, and began to polish it with a rough cotton cloth. As the musician sat, Tom and John left their tent and approached the fire. Tom smiled as Kiera jumped about on his shoulder and John only rubbed sleep out of his eyes.

"Good morning," Bill said in a somewhat gravelly voice. John just grunted and

Tom accepted a mug of the Karo.

"What's on the agenda?" Tom asked of Baxel.

"'Agenda'? What does–"

"Plan for the day," Tom interjected, trying hard not to confuse the captain of the guard.

"Oh...we shall arrive at the freehold this afternoon, or earlier. There we shall set up camp just outside the town. It is somewhat larger than Galfeon Yor; that is why the Festival is held there. We must honor the mourning period and remain outside the city until the black banner is lowered, that would be around sunset.

"Tomorrow night, Tonlin's son will host a grand festival at his keep. Most of the commoners will revel in the streets. The Lords and landowners of the freeholds will attend the festival at the keep. Of course, you and your companions will be invited."

"Tomorrow, wonderful," John grumbled and started to walk away. "Where are you off to?" Tom asked of his friend.

"A walk. I'll be okay." He sauntered off, adjusting his white blouse and squaring his shoulders.

"What's with him?" Bill asked of Tom.

"He's a bit moody. I don't think he slept well."

"Sometimes a man needs to be alone to clear his mind," Baxel spoke wisely and the others nodded.

John hiked through the woods near their campsite. There was a small game trail that he assumed led to the spring that Trevor had spoken of the night before. He pushed low branches aside and followed the winding path. He tentatively touched his St. Christopher medal, but it was cool and inert against his chest.

That wasn't what was fouling his mood though. It was the nightmare he'd had the night before that had disturbed him the most. He'd awakened in a cold sweat; the images still fresh in his mind. In the dream, the group had been attending a funeral; their parents and friends had also been there. He had stood to one side all dressed in black, looking into the six caskets that had been placed into freshly dug graves.

There had been mention of an auto accident in the eulogy, and the priest had turned from the graves.

John moved closer to one of the caskets and suddenly his own empty eye sockets stared up at him.

It was them in the caskets. All six of them, lying there, cold and abandoned to the earth.

Needless to say, it had affected his mood somewhat. He kept reminding himself that it was just a nightmare, but that hadn't helped much. If this world could be real, why couldn't that dream be an event that was actually happening?

God, but I don't want to be dead, even though I'm alive here, he thought. Just the idea of them not returning sent a shiver down his spine. He wasn't exactly ready to give up his normal life. Not quite ready to embark into the real world, but still wanting the known of it. Well, haven't we been given a little twist in our lives?

He tried to clear his thoughts. Finally he decided that if that was the way fate was going to treat him then he would handle it like he had just been handed a million dollars. He smiled and inhaled the fresh air, putting a more lively spring in his step. Soon he came upon the clearing and the spring. The sound of splashing water caught his ear and he approached the open glade with caution.

It could be worse, he thought as he looked at what he had stumbled on. Gabrielle was bathing in the clear water before him. Smiling rakishly, he approached the edge of the pool, sat down and leaned back.

"Good morning my lady," he said, as Gabrielle began to swim back towards his end of the spring.

She spun quickly and sunk to her neck, not wanting to expose herself. It was then she realized that the water was crystal clear and gave John a dangerous look. "Don't mind me, Lady Gabrielle," John said airily, the remaining shadows of his nightmare completely dispelled by her beauty and the humor of the situation. "You're quite stealthy, Lord Knight," Gabrielle responded. The water flashed from her dark tresses as she spun her head around. Despite her discomfort she was quite beautiful.

"Years of practice at sneaking up on people," he replied, chuckling. She smiled, and John knew that he wasn't making a complete ass of himself. She swam up to the edge of the spring where he sat, and smiled winningly. He felt his heart skip a beat. She held out her hand to him.

"Help me up," she said in a commanding tone. John grasped her hand to pull her onto the bank, but the smile on his face faded fast as she jerked on his arm and flipped him headfirst into the water. He sputtered as his head broke the surface and he tried to peer after her.

He caught a glimpse of an exquisitely formed buttock and thigh, and a very proud back as she exited the water, but she was soon out of sight in the bushes. As he pulled himself out of the water she reappeared, dressed in a light shift. It clung to her in all the right spots. John swallowed hard.

"Good move," he said as he shook the water from his arms and legs.

"I have bested the Lord Knight of Erie," she spoke and smiled. Her green eyes flashed.

"Yep, that you have."

"I will expect you to escort me to the grand festival tomorrow evening." And with that she spun and was gone.

He smiled crookedly, not quite knowing what he'd done, but knowing that he must have done it right.

"So, what do you think?" Joe asked as he nibbled at some meat on a stick. He and Chill walked through the streets of Tonlin's freehold, otherwise known as Ord to the local residents.

"I think you're probably eating lizard," Chill replied in his slow manner. A wide grin erupted on his face when the Shadowlord began to spit out the tasty morsel. Chill looked around. The cobbled streets were filled with revelers and the sounds of laughter filled the night air. Bright torches and open braziers lit the streets and light issued from every window. People dressed in colorful apparel and some in hardly any apparel at all made merry the Festival of the Spring.

"Not the food, asshole," Joe cut back as he straightened his cape and winked at a passing girl. "I mean our predicament. John seems to think that Mike will find us a way home in about three years. Right now, I don't think Mike could find his way out of a paper bag."

Chill slid to the side to avoid some running children and adjusted his glasses. "What do I think? Well, basically we're screwed. If we can get to the one that brought us here how do we know he can send us back, or will? And what were his intentions? You know this whole thing could be a setup; his intent may be malicious. We might have been better off at the bottom of that ravine.

"Or, the whole damn thing could be prearranged, even the accident. I don't know, man. I do know that if we end up crossing Gelion again we might not be as lucky as the first time. But, with what I learned from you guys lately, at least I have a better shot at besting even him."

"I think we created a monster," Joe muttered under his breath.

"What?" Chill barely noticed his companion as he looked at the tavern sign. "Nothing, how about a beer?" Joe said as he also spotted the establishment.

They began to wend their way through the crowd.

The tavern was smoky and dark, but just as loud as the streets. Joe and Chill sauntered up to the bar and ordered a tankard of ale each. It was so crowded in the tavern that there was only standing room available; it reminded them a regular college bar, almost.

Surik Shadowlord and Sir Chill leaned casually against the bar and scoped out the situation. Nobody seemed to be particularly interested in them, unlike the inhabitants of Galfeon Yor. There were so many people of different backgrounds here that even the most outlandish and conspicuous would remain unnoticed during the time of the Festival.

Chill gulped at his ale and tried not to look too bored, but the attempt failed and soon one yawn followed another. They had stood there for about an hour, drinking and watching the room fill up with smoke and even more people, when Joe opened his mouth to comment that it looked like all the women in this tavern were former Russian shot-putters. As he took a breath, it turned into a gasp as the door opened and he was completely riveted by the stunning beauty who entered.

I've got to meet that one, he thought. He left Chill in silence and made his way through the crowded bar. His friend immediately realized what was happening and ordered another ale for the duration.

The crowd seemed to part like the Red Sea. The woman stood alone, an island in an ocean of chaos. She was wearing a low cut peasant dress that clung to her full figure in such a way as to make the artist's blood surge. Her very nature exuded sexual electricity. She smiled seductively at his approach, but turned away. He shook his head and cleared his throat as he stood next to her.

"Excuse me, but don't I know you from somewhere," he cringed at the cliché but she turned back to him.

"I doubt it," she replied, her voice low and oddly beckoning. The ale must have been taking a toll because he felt lightheaded, almost giddy.

She looked at him, her eyes almost black. She was tall and deeply tanned, and her straight, dark brown hair fell almost to her hips. She arched one eyebrow in expectation of a reply from the gray-eyed man opposite her.

He took a deep breath and plunged in, "I have driven a quarrel of dragons across the Sundering Sea; stood amid demons' bones while sated on the souls of my opponents; yet such beauty as yours I remember. I do know you."

"I come from a small village in the north where such men as that are rare. And you?" she asked pouting and he almost smiled to himself.

"A small village? Surely it could not contain such beauty?" he queried. He took a deep breath, though his heart sped up. Was it the wine affecting him this way or was it her?

"It matters not, milord, I feel you have overstepped your bounds," she finished, turned away, but Joe quickly spoke.

"I currently hail from Galfeon Yor," he said, somewhat haughtily. She caught his glance over her breasts and smiled with animal intensity. She leaned back and exposed a thigh.

He caught that, too.

"I have heard of that place. What is your name?"

"Surik Shadowlord, Master of the Shades and Rider of the Black Dragon," he said it with pride, living the role.

"Surik..." she held his eyes with hers and caressed the name with a lover's tongue and he almost choked on his ale.

"Come with me," she said and grabbed him by the hand. They quickly ducked out the rear door and into an ill lit alley. To their right was the thoroughfare that many of the revelers used and to their left the alley continued on in darkness. She led him around the corner and into the shadows, yet there was enough light to allow him to see what she intended.

She began to unlace the bodice of her peasant dress. Then she pressed his hand against her chest and wrapped one of her legs around his.

Shit, he thought as she kissed him passionately about the neck and earlobe. Should I be doing this? He wondered. Then: What the hell! He responded eagerly as she rocked against him, moaning softly. He was quite aroused now and she knew it. Her eyes glinted strangely as she dug her nails into his shoulders.

He slid his hand along her thigh, beneath her dress. She panted heavily and chuckled a deep, knowing laugh. Then she reached between his legs.

And squeezed. Hard. Really hard. Too hard.

Joe doubled over in pain, suddenly feeling a wave of nausea as he fell to the dank cobblestones. He looked up through tear filled eyes, gritting his teeth against the pain.

She was gone.

Chapter 11

"All this subterfuge, I like it not."

"She wants it, the Surrogate."

"There is an easier way: two hundred men."

"Yes, and you may well have that eventually, but not now. This way it will cause unrest and chaos in the West, which will assist in putting our puppet in place. She has it well planned, you know."

"They may be young, but they're dangerous. And they can fight."

"Split them up. I know the one called Sir Chill is almost useless with a blade. Of the others, I have only seen the Wolf. I watched this tracker for some time; he is swift and careful. Of the others I know little, but I would be wary of the black blade of the one called Surik, it has an evil glare. If they can be split, then the Surrogate will then wrack them one by one."

"What does she want of them? When I reported their attack on me to the Preceptor of Helm he said that Myella took a keen interest. It was naught more than a fortnight before she and that foul courier-beast were in my stockade."

"She says they are special."

"Spies, no doubt."

"No doubt."

Duran leaned on the table and heard the echo of his words in the ill lit hall. He looked to where Gelion sat and noticed that the Regent's cast was ill, but the healer said that he should be better in a day or so. Duran could barely perceive the swath of bandages around the man's hips and loins. It must have been a horrible thing for him to come that close to surrendering his manhood: to lose one of your stones was terrible. The healer had taken care of it, with some dark spell no doubt, but by the time the mage had traveled from Paravel it was rumored that what remained to Gelion had swollen to the size of a ripe melon and he was in considerable pain. The Shadowlord had dealt him a more serious blow than even Gelion had suspected.

Now the man sat, pondering the fate of the outlanders. The yellow of the hearth gave his skin a waxy pallor, and he played nervously with the bush of beard that had grown somewhat longer in the past bed-ridden weeks.

"Ord," he echoed, in a liquor dulled voice; no doubt it was to counter the throb of pain. "The Surrogate is there?"

"Aye."

"I want the Shadowlord."

Duran chuckled. "I believe that the Surrogate has a bid on him also."

John peered through the tent flap to the cobbled wall not a stone's throw from where they were now camped. The day had not passed quickly enough for Joe, who dealt with a considerable amount of pain, but the others in the group had occupied their time with exploring the sights and sounds of the town. Now the sky, laced with thinning clouds, was now awash in deep red and orange as the sun was setting in all its iridescent beauty "Unbelievable," John sighed at the sight. He pulled on a pair of leather gauntlets and watched as Joe and Chill slowly made their way from the campfire to the tent. Joe was still limping slightly.

"That has to have hurt," Tom breathed as he watched the artist. Joe was still pale, but the night before he had been red with pain. He bore an examination by the Sioux with stoic humor and was relieved when he found out that there was no torsion, just some bruising.

Joe grunted as he ducked into the tent past John, and Chill followed. He looked about expectantly, then pulled off his cloak and laid it over the saddle stand. "How are you?" Tom inquired. Joe bit back an acid response and shrugged.

"Sore. She sure as hell got me with a vengeance." Tom nodded and Chill laughed abruptly.

"It gives new meaning to foreplay,'" Chill remarked, wiping tears from the corner of his eyes. It was probably the most emotion the man had shown since they had come to this land.

"Sorry we missed it. The most excitement we had last night was watching Tom swindle a knife thrower out of a silver piece," Mike interjected as he adjusted the hem of his tunic. Tom's mouth was the shadow of a smile.

"It isn't funny, guys." Joe's eyes flashed dangerously. "She was something. She had all the right moves."

"Yeah," Chill began, "She was his main squeeze." He laughed uproariously as Joe glared at him. The rest of the group joined in with laughter.

"You should be more careful," Mike interrupted, a quasi-serious look crossing his face.

"Anybody can lay waste to us in a moment like that. It's important to keep our guard; we do things best as a group."

"Some things you can't do as a group, Mike," Joe retorted. "Then again, you were always into that kinky stuff."

"So what if I like dead things." Mike gave them that psychotic look.

"Well, I guess I'm off then," John said as he threw his cloak over his shoulder and adjusted his katana.

"Your rocker," Chill shot back. "Funny, but at least I have a date."

"Yeah, but you won't get lucky."

"No comment." He walked briskly from the tent just as Gabrielle was exiting hers.

"Ready Milady?" he called. She smiled a reply and he casually walked to her. "Quite dashing, Sir Knight," she commented, noting the white silk shirt and

Prussian blue riding pants. His sword was strapped to his side and he had a deep blue cloak slung over one shoulder.

"And you, Milady, are quite stunning as always," he smiled rakishly as he said it. She wore a deep blue satin gown with gold trim and a single red ruby suspended on a gold torque. Her hair was pulled back in a pearl comb, but her tresses still fell across her shoulder.

John helped her onto her horse and soon they were both riding toward the gates of Ord. The rest of the group watched as they rounded the curve of the wall and soon were out of sight.

"I feel like I've lost my son," Mike moaned as he watched the two ride off.

"Oh brother," Joe said as he rolled his eyes. He would have liked to stick Mike right there, but his sword was in the tent. He had to start wearing it everywhere, especially considering the night before.

"Think he'll get–"

"No!" Joe snapped, remembering last night. "I think we are cursed and what happened to me was their sex act. We're doomed to celibacy."

"You're starting to sound like Bill." Mike smiled and lit his pipe. Red light etched out his face in the evening gloom.

"Right," quipped Bill, almost hurt by the accusation.

"What do you think? Do we go get drunk, or do we go to this party?" Mike looked at Tom and Bill, Joe and Chill.

"Both," Chill replied and they all nodded.

Joe smoothed out the demon skull on his tunic and grinned hellishly. "Then let the games begin."

"Bard William D'Asturien, at your service," Bill said as he bowed low and elegantly to the Lady that stood before him. She smiled and sipped at her wine as she looked into his blue eyes. She was quite attractive. Bill had noticed that she had been following him with her eyes all evening, and now he finally had the chance to speak with her.

"I am Drusella. I have heard of you Bard, from the Lady Gabrielle. She speaks highly of you and your companions. You come from a strange land?"

she finished with a question and looked demurely away.

The Bard nodded and began to recite, for the third time that night, about their fabricated arrival in this strange land. She listened intently and he found himself embellishing the story somewhat. She was enraptured with the tale that he wove intricately, almost like a melody. She seemed oblivious to those around her; the mingling crowd was nothing more than shadows as he told the tale.

They stood in the great hall of Tonlin's keep. The keep itself was central to the town of Ord, but far from being as grand as Trevor's. Low and heavy turrets and a dry-moat guarded ancient granite, dark with age and covered with vines. Once inside they that the outer walls protected neatly manicured lawns and small gardens tucked between the crenels. The main keep, similar in design to the low outer wall, was pierced often with balconies and high windows. Troubadours entertained the guests in the main courtyard, which was lit with lanterns of various colors. Once inside the main keep, the passage led to a main hall, and from there, passages lead off to one of the many balconies. As Bill neared the main hall, a variety of sights and sounds greeted him: sconces and torches lit the hall in gay reds and yellows, illuminating the revelers cheerily. Harsh streaks of light cut between heavy granite pillars, creating deep shadows behind them. In the near-darkness, entwined forms celebrated the festival of the Spring in timeless ritual. Music and laughter all but drowned out casual conversation.

175

Bill found himself inching closer to the young maid, emphasizing his story and the peril that they had faced. He noticed the heave of her breast and the flush of her cheeks. Dancers swirled about them with the flow of music, wine spilled from skins and bottles. A warm breeze swept in from the veranda sending the wind chimes clamoring. About them the flash of jewels, gaudy clothes, and foppish lads were lost to them both.

"And here we stand before you, paying our respects to Tonlin and celebrating the Festival of the Spring," Bill finished and looked into her eyes. She responded by stepping a little closer. He noticed the heat of her skin as he leaned close to whisper into her ear. Then the look on her face changed and she abruptly stepped back.

"My husband," she said and gestured to the man that approached. "Husband, damn," Bill muttered under his breath. He was a large older man, in his forties, and dressed like a courtier.

"Gorkas Deem," he said with a suspicious look in his eye. They exchanged amenities and, after a pregnant pause, Bill slouched back to the banquet table where Mike, Chill, and Joe sat enjoying the wine and beef.

"Second time tonight!" he growled. "My luck is taking a turn for the worse." Bill shook his head and grabbed a mug off the table. He swallowed the contents quickly, only wanting oblivion in his moment of depression.

Joe smiled as he delicately tore off a piece of duck, dipped it in a wine sauce and savored the rich flavor. My God but they're serving good food, he thought and looked at Mike who was wolfing down some beef, not even taking the time to taste.

Barbarian.

"You shouldn't try to shove yourself upon the girl," Mike responded. Being an authority on many things, he also thought he knew the finer points on the arts of love.

"I didn't force myself upon her. I was telling her about our little journey to this Godforsaken cesspool. And she was coming on pretty strong until her husband showed up."

"Not as strong as that chick with Joe last night," Chill snickered. He seemed to be getting a lot of mileage out of Joe's misfortune. Joe just gave him a dirty look because he couldn't think of a comeback quick enough.

Mike only shook his head and drank some ale; the froth lingered on his mustache. He wiped it away with the back of his hand and belched. It was loud enough to turn heads.

"Getting into the part a little too deep?" snapped Joe at the large man's outburst.

"What do you mean?" Mike replied.

"Yeah," commented Chill. "Mike is always like that." Mike just grunted and placed an overlarge piece of meat in his mouth, the juices dripping down his chin. Joe turned away in disgust.

Looking over the hall, through the smoke and the haze of the mixing revelers about the fire-pit, Joe could see even more people entering from the gardens. The conversation of his friends turned to white noise, as he was lost in his own thoughts. Then a flash of long brown hair caught his eye.

Damn! The woman who had so handily assaulted him the night before had just stepped regally into the room. She surveyed the crowd with a practiced eye, smiled to herself as if noticing something and headed toward one of the alcoves. He set down his goblet and frowned; Duran had walked in behind her.

"This isn't adding up," he muttered and moved off in her wake. Chill, Mike and

Bill just continued their talk, not noticing their companion's departure.

Tom stood casually, looking at the festive lamps that spread out over the garden. It reminded him of Mardi Gras in New Orleans more than anything else. Next to him stood Baxel, dressed in his finest; he wore a blue tunic and the gold trappings of the Captain of the Guard.

"So, what's it like living here all your life?" the Native American asked.

"I would not know, Smiling Wolf, I have only lived here nigh twelve years. I come from Albien, a port town south of here. My men and I were recruited by Trevor after most of his men were killed and routed by Gelion's raiding parties."

"I thought there was a truce?"

"There was." Baxel followed Tom's gaze over the revelers to the full moon above. The ring about the satellite was little more than a thin line. "You see the truce was only reinforced when my men, which numbered about one hundred at the time, came to Trevor's call. We held off the raiders effectively, though the toll was heavy. That succeeded in making Gelion a little more cautious."

"Has Trevor then been fighting Gelion all his life?" Tom shifted. He felt at ease with this man and it seemed he could trust him. It was good to have someone on your side in this alien world, especially one with such a wealth of experience and information.

"Not all his life," the guardsman responded, sipping from his tankard. "From what I gather, Trevor arrived in Galfeon Yor some forty years ago. His family owned much of the property there. That was when he took the Keep; it had been governed by a seneschal before that. Galfeon Yor was in disarray, what with the raids and the inability of the seneschal to maintain order. Trevor and his retainers quickly took command of the situation and brought some order, surprising most of the freeholders at that. For a time, Trevor held off the Regent with veritable ease. He had a beautiful wife, much like Gabrielle. But her health was poor and she died when milady was very young.

"You know, I think she looks with favor on your Lord Knight," he said, and Tom registered the reference to John after a moment. He gazed over his shoulder: inside, the two of them were speaking with another couple. He almost envied his friend.

"Yes, it is the first time I have seen her so readily take to a gentleman. Duran is not the most promising of suitors."

"Probably it is because John wants her as a friend before he wants to be her suitor," replied Tom.

"Hmmm...That is a thought indeed." Baxel quaffed his ale and wiped his mouth with the back of his hand. He smiled warmly. "And how do you like our freehold?"

"I prefer the wide open plains, out under the stars, or camping in the forests. I have always been more attuned to nature than civilization." He patted Kiera on his shoulder. She had been sleeping there for some time and Baxel started, for he had thought the ferret was nothing more than a part of the man's outfit.

"Your companion seems bored with the festivities."

"She's had a long day."

Tom became quiet, once again contemplating their incredible situation. He wondered what was happening in their own world and what his martial-arts teacher would have thought of this predicament. Tony had always been the first to tell him that there were far more things in heaven and earth than man was meant to know. In other words there was some weird shit going on.

Well, this is some weird shit, Tony, he thought. He looked up and Baxel was gazing into the hall.

"What do you say we bother Lady Gabrielle and Sir John?" Baxel asked with a mischievous grin. Smiling Wolf grinned back.

"Are you enjoying yourself?" Gabrielle asked, watching John loosen the collar of his tunic.

"Huh? Oh, of course, milady."

"Gabrielle, John," she said, her green eyes sparkling. She looked stunning in the flickering torchlight; she seemed right out of an Arthurian Legend. He looked into her eyes, almost spellbound and quite speechless.

"Yeah, sorry...there are a lot of nice people here."

"Don't let them fool you Lord Knight. I don't know how it is where you come from, but the nobility here can wield a smile and a sword with equal ease."

"It's the same everywhere," John replied. "Where's your father been?"

"Giving his respects to Tonlin's son. He complained of being tired and said something of leaving the festivities to the young. I fear that he is getting old."

"Trevor? No, I think he has a long life before him."

"I hope that you are right."

John paused, then: "Sure is hot in here."

Gabrielle smiled. "Would you like to step out onto the balcony?"

"That would be nice."

They made their way to a small alcove that overlooked the garden. John could make out strolling couples in the dim light of the colored lamps; the moon seemed to add just the right touch to this moment. He turned to Gabrielle. She stood close, but still seemed somewhat remote.

"Do you like me, Lord Knight?"

"Yes," he breathed, honesty gripped him. If his heart continued at this pace he would have a coronary.

"I don't believe I have ever met someone as intriguing as you, Lord Knight." She looked past him, yet at nothing, and seemed enmeshed in her own thoughts. "The feeling is mutual," he said and smiled. "My friends say that I am foolish.

181

But, I cannot know when we will return home. And, then there's you..." he trailed off. "I have had many a suitor. They have tried to beguile me with wealth and beauty. Yet, you have tried none of that."

"What you see is what you get." He took her hand and held it. She looked up at him, eyes wide, lips slightly parted.

John leaned a little closer. His lips touched hers.

"Hi, guys!" Tom called as he and Baxel rounded the corner. "We wondered where you two had snuck off to."

"I'm so glad you found us." Acid laced John's words. Baxel hid a laugh as Gabrielle raised an eyebrow.

"So, I have the Book of Shadows. That's one tool," Mike finished. He took a puff off his pipe, and Bill frowned. "I have also come across something in one of Trevor's books; something about tracing the sorcery to its roots. I haven't tried the tracing yet and I don't think that I am quite ready."

"You really think that you can trace the magic back to the one that brought us here. What if it's collective?" Bill saw that Chill held a glimmer of hope in his eyes. This world was well and good, but he preferred electricity and fast food.

"What if? Anything's possible. The power that I seem to have in this world should be able to get us back. We just have to find the bastard."

"Okay, Mike, but if you can get us back on your own, why do we want to chase down this guy.

He might be pissed." Chill raised his eyebrow at Bill's astute observation.

"Yes, but by tracking him down it might be easier. He already knows the magic. I wouldn't be re-inventing the wheel."

"And there is more," Mike continued. "I keep catching these references in the old books I've been looking at. References to gates. I'm not sure what it means, but it may be a way to travel great distances, even between worlds."

"You think we came through one of these gates," asked Bill.

"I don't know, but it's worth more scrutiny. And if indeed we can utilize these gates, it will require a bit of metaphysical power to activate them, I'm sure."

"You actually think that you have that much power?" Bill looked somewhat skeptical. He knew that Mike had good instincts and a good head on his shoulders, but magic? That was another matter entirely.

"I have yet to try anything requiring a lot of power, but I think that I can handle it. I'll just need the practice. These tired old bones aren't finished yet. I'll come up with something." He looked off, playing the martyr.

"Yeah, Mike, twenty-seven and over the hill. You better come up with something fast," Chill remarked rather facetiously.

"Hmmm..." Mike watched as John, Gabrielle, Tom and Baxel made their way toward the table. His eyes wandered freely over the young woman's figure. "I wouldn't mind getting into that skirt."

183

"It wouldn't fit," Bill snapped, upset at his friend's turn. They knew the code: no poaching. He turned to the others, "What's up?"

"Not much," replied John, a thin scowl upon his lips. Tom just smiled more widely at some hidden joke.

"Where's Joe, er...Surik?" John looked about but couldn't see him anywhere. "Off somewhere," Mike returned. "He's got a corn cob up his–"

"Something was bothering him," Bill said hurriedly, cutting off the big man before he could use one of his raunchier expletives.

"Probably that woman from last night," Chill said. He pulled his glasses off to polish them. There were some notable scratches on the lens and he wondered what he would do if he lost or broke them. He squinted across the room, not seeing clearly after about twenty feet. That would be dangerous in a world like this, especially for them. He had noticed that Trevor wore spectacles, but they appeared fragile and were probably expensive. He put the glasses back on, glad that they were not contacts. Now that would be a real pain, he thought.

"This party is getting old," Bill said, not even feeling a buzz from the wine he imbibed. He watched Tonlin's son at the head table, surrounded by advisors. No doubt, a few resented this carrying on in light of his father's death not a fortnight gone. The man bellowed for the musicians to play some rolling ballad and motioned for a boy to bring a pitcher of deep red wine.

"He's a queer one," Baxel wondered aloud. Chill gave him a look and then realized that he wasn't referring to the man's sexual preference.

"What do you mean?" Bill asked.

"His father was an excellent hunter and horseman, and to be killed by raiders, without guard? Tonlin the Second stepped right in, almost without grief. It is said that he has often pressed for his father to make overtures to Gelion, hoping that trade would ease the tension with the east. His father would hear none of it."

The man suddenly looked at them as if aware he was being talked about. He smiled when he saw Gabrielle and stood abruptly, strewing plates and cutlery in all directions, and sending the dogs at his feet scattering. John noticed that Gabrielle visibly shuddered when she realized he was heading their way.

"The man is loathsome," she said fixing a very fake smile on her countenance. They watched as the man approached, accompanied by several others. One carried a sword and sported a scar on his jaw. A bodyguard, John assumed.

Tonlin the Younger greeted them warmly and Gabrielle introduced the group. He seemed drunk, but otherwise cordial. John found him just a tad too friendly with Gabrielle.

"A drunkard," he heard the soft voice at his shoulder and turned. It was Duran. The ease with which the man sneaked upon him was uncanny. "No doubt he will soon drool upon her fine vestment." He clucked and shook his head. John noticed that the man looked fresh from riding, but also carried a bottle of wine.

185

"Ah, and the good Lord Duran." Tonlin shoved John aside and grasped the man's hands. Duran looked rather uncomfortable at the gesture, but accepted it. Then Tonlin noticed the bottle.

"Wine?"

"Er," Duran stumbled, which was unusual. "Yes, but I am sorry; it is a gift for

Trevor. I must bid my leave and wish to thank him for the hospitality of his keep."

"Nonsense Duran, wine is wine. I am sure that Trevor would not mind.

Besides, he is getting up in years to enjoy such a fine vintage." He looked approvingly at the label. Duran was very reluctant.

"Tonlin, it is a gift, respect me in–"

"Bosh! You can have the run of my cellar tomorrow, tonight we drink this!" He grabbed the bottle from Duran, who was at a loss for words, and began to uncork it.

Joe zeroed in on the dark-haired woman who had almost wrecked him the night before. She stood near one of the pillars, half hidden in darkness and looking out over the balcony. She smiled knowingly as he approached and offered her hand, but he ignored the gesture and grabbed her by the wrist, taking her to the shadows.

"What's the idea, sweetheart?" he demanded, ignoring her beauty. "Shadowlord, please," she smiled sweetly, yet tensed her muscles; Joe could tell she was no weakling.

"Please? You've got to be kidding me. I want to know why you tried to crack me last night!"

"Maybe I like pain?"

"Oh great, another deviant for John to study. Who are you, and why did you lead me on?"

"I found you attractive."

"That's the first thing I might actually believe. However–" She silenced him with her lips and he had to push her away. She began to hike her skirt up slowly, and Joe got a look at long, well-toned legs.

"I know you want me," she uttered, her voice heavy with promise. "Like I want herpes, too," he said sardonically.

She reached out with her hand and pulled him against her; she began to nibble at his neck. He had to push her away once more.

"Come, Surik Shadowlord, I know you want me. You want this." She looked down and he followed her gaze. Her skirt was hiked past creamy silk stockings and–

– slamming pain in the back of his head brought him to his knees. Flashes of light danced before his eyes and he reached out, touching the cold stone of the pillar. Blackness stole the edges of his vision. He only had a moment to hear her laugh like the sound of shattering glass, then he passed out cold.

Tom watched as Tonlin began to uncork Duran's gift. He was surprised at the man's agility considering his state of intoxication. There was a pop and Duran protested weakly.

"Where is Trevor, it is a gift you know..." He looked around as he trailed off. "He retired early," Baxel spoke. He held out his tankard and let Tonlin pour some in.

"I didn't think you would make it, Duran," John remarked as they were all poured some wine.

"I made a quick dash by horse." He followed each glass as it was filled. "Your spirits seem improved."

"Yes, I am returning to Qwen. A summons from my father." Duran frowned as

Tonlin tested the bouquet of the vintage. The man smiled in satisfaction.

"You've been holding out on me, Duran. This is a fine wine indeed. I doubt that Trevor would have appreciated it. No offense Milady Gabrielle, but I am no doubt more versed in the finer points of wine than your father."

"No doubt," she replied and rolled her eyes. John almost laughed.

"A toast!" Tonlin barked. John smiled and raised the glass to his lips. Itching.

He felt an odd pressure at his chest, then a burning where his St. Christopher medallion hung. John touched it through the fold in his tunic.

White light seared through his vision...

...The bottle opened with gloved hands. A liquid, colorless and yet all shifting colors of the rainbow at once was poured into the bottle from a glass vial. The bottle re-corked and sealed, ever so carefully. Duran and a dark-haired woman...

John dashed the glass from Bill's mouth just before it touched his lips. The wine splashed Chill, who looked at John incredulously. John dropped his glass on the flagstones and stayed Gabrielle's arm, taking the wine from her. Baxel just looked suspiciously into the un-tasted contents of his tankard.

"Poisoned!" he hissed.

Duran's face was florid with emotion as he thought quickly. Things were obviously not turning out, as they should.

"John, what the fu–" Mike began, but then he saw Duran backing up. "Curses," Duran said as he realized his plan was falling apart. Tonlin's face took on a bluish cast and he started to gag.

"Duran poisoned the wine," John said and stood at the ready as Tonlin's personal guard drew his sword. Tom slid quickly behind Duran as Tonlin fell to the floor. Gabrielle and Baxel knelt to aid him.

"That son of a bitch!" snarled Chill as he started at the dark haired man.

"It was intended for Father!" Gabrielle shouted. She stepped in the Guards way, almost knocking the sword from his grasp.

With that Duran spun, slamming his elbow into Tom's face on the blind side. Tom fell back stunned and Duran sprinted to the balcony.

"Dammit!" John shouted and drew his katana. He followed after the man; Chill and Mike in his wake. Duran stopped at the balcony rail and looked over the side; the drop, not too far, was just over one story, but people milled about below blocking his landing. He turned and drew his stiletto. John smiled and flourished his blade.

Duran grinned a death head's rictus, and flung the blade at John. John felt himself roughly shoved to the side by Tonlin's guard. The man fell to the floor with the blade sunk to the hilt in his neck.

Duran didn't wait. He leapt casually over the rail. Chill and Mike raced to the edge.

Nothing.

John peered over next to them. "Well?"

"He's gone."

"He just disappeared," Mike echoed.

"I never liked that worm," Chill muttered and turned from the rail.

Seven of Tonlin's guards stood before them, weapons drawn. The armored men did not look happy.

"Lord Tonlin is dead," one of the guardsmen said.

"Duran killed him, shit-head," Mike replied and pulled his sword from the scabbard. If they're going to get testy... he thought.

"Enough," came a very weak gasp. The guards turned to look at Tonlin's personal protector. He gasped weakly as the hilt of the stiletto moved with the pulse of his blood. The end of the blade was protruding a full two inches from the back of his neck. He lay in a pool of his own blood, and seemed paralyzed.

"Duran...poison meant for Trevor. It was Duran." He gasped loudly and his eyes rolled back.

"Duran's got some explaining to do," Chill muttered. Many of the people had gathered around now and several ladies fainted at the sight. The volume of voices had swelled to a deafening crescendo.

The guardsmen split ranks, some to Tonlin and some to the protector. "I suggest you seal the Keep," John said over the din. Then to Gabrielle: "I think you and Baxel better go check on Trevor."

Baxel nodded and grabbed Gabrielle by the arm. Soon they were gone. "This could get ugly,"

Tom whispered to John as he rubbed his cheek. "This village just lost two leaders in as many weeks."

"Right, we should go. How's your eye?"

"I'll live. The bastard really labeled me though, took me by surprise. He hit my blind side." The Native American shook his head, angry at letting the man take advantage of his weakness.

"How did you know he poisoned the wine?" Mike asked of John. He looked suspiciously at his friend. John just shook his head.

"My St. Christopher medal. Joe will tell you. That's why I fell off my horse the other day. The first time I touched it I had a vision of a massive wall. This time it was Duran poisoning the wine. And, funny, the same woman that was in the first vision was in this one also."

"What did she look like?" Chill interjected. John described her. "That sounds like the one that got Joe last night."

"Where is he anyway?" Bill asked, looking around. He expected to see the man in the thick of things with all the commotion.

"Joe? Last I saw he was over there." Mike pointed to the pillar. John saw a dark shape on the floor and frowned.

"This is some weird shit," Tom remarked. "Where did Joe get to?"

John shoved through the crowd and walked briskly to the pillar. There the group gathered around as John picked up Joe's ermine cloak.

"I don't like this one damn bit," Chill said as he looked about wildly.

"Blood." Tom knelt and traced his finger along a spattering of blood that dotted the granite floor. "A struggle? Two people, one smaller than the another carried Joe away."

"Really?" Bill asked. "You learn that at Indian tracking school?"

Tom looked at him out of the corner of his eye, "No, Boy Scouts," Tom said absently and stood.

"Okay, right, well can the tracker merit badge help tell us who?"

"Well I did get that badge with honors…an accomplice to Duran," Tom shook his head, worry edging in on him.

"That bitch! The one that blue-balled him last night!" Chill shouted, startling the others and turning some heads in the crowd that was beginning to disperse as the bodies were cleared.

"Then it's our move," Mike said as he sheathed his blade. The gray-eyed artist was gone and now they were split apart. They were vulnerable. Only luck and the unfathomable magic of John's medal had spared them from ending up like Tonlin. They had all underestimated Duran.

But why were they being singled out? Why were they such a threat? John wondered.

"The one that brought us here is behind this," Tom stated rather matter-of-factly.

"How do you know?" John asked. "I know."

"Should we wait to hear from them?"

"If we do it could be too late." John looked up, the finality in Tom's voice ringing in his ears.

"Are you sure this is the right thing?" Gabrielle asked John as he buckled his vambrace.

192

The morning calm was lost with the ruckus created by their breaking camp.

"We decided this morning with the aid of Mike's orb to go there. Chill will stay with you at Galfeon Yor, just in case Surik shows up. But all things lead to Gelion. I think he and Duran are responsible for what happened last night to Surik.

"Mike's magic is limited, but the orb did suggest that Gelion is up to something."

Gabrielle looked about her. Her hair was pulled back in a ponytail and she wore riding leathers and a short jacket. When John remembered the way she had acted last night at Tonlin's death, her courage with the guards, and her vehemence at the threat to her father's life, he realized there was much more to her than any other woman he had ever known.

"You realize that you will be outnumbered?"

"Baxel said he knows of some people here in Ord that may be able to help us. It seems that the East Quarter is a good place to meet more of the unsavory types of the West: mercenaries and the like. Tom and Mike will handle that end once they speak with your father."

"Lord Knight, I..." she trailed off. She turned from him and peered out through the tent flap at the morning light. John followed her gaze then walked over to her, he put his hand on her shoulder.

"Don't worry, we—"

"I fear that I have grown used to you in the past few months. And I do not want to lose a friend. You mean much to me and now you go off to fight incredible odds. I fear that you may not return. You do not know this land. I know you are trained, but you go against things of which you know nothing. You are up against something so much more powerful than yourselves."

John smiled and spoke, drawing her close to him. "You can count on my returning, that is my vow to you on my honor. There are other forces at play that brought us here, Gabrielle. I think that Surik's disappearance is linked to those forces, magical or otherwise."

"Be careful." She turned and hugged him tightly, burying her head in his shoulder. He held her for a long moment before he looked at her.

"Trust me." And a cocky grin twisted his lips ever so slightly.

***

"It seems that certain events are unfolding," Trevor stated as he watched his tent being stowed.

No shit, Mike thought. He rolled his eyes, but Trevor didn't notice.

Tom said, diplomatically, "It is obvious that Duran wanted to poison you with this wine and ended up betraying his hand when Tonlin took it. More than likely he wanted to cause discord among the provinces and in doing so Gelion could take advantage of it," Tom finished. Kiera sat on his shoulder as always, licking the side of his face where he had been struck. It was slightly blue but there was no swelling. "He felt us out," Mike interjected. "I think he adapted our coming to Galfeon Yor to whatever plan he had. He probably helped Gelion capture Surik.

"I think that he was using you too, Lord Trevor. Waiting and watching for the most opportune time. If it wasn't the poison, it would have been something else."

"Why did he not kill me then upon the battlements, when I almost fell into the

Deep?"

"Probably because he didn't want it to look like an accident. He wanted it to be obvious that it was an assassination, as a way of warning the other freeholders of what was to come if they didn't submit to Gelion." Tom nodded his agreement to Mike's explanation.

"And my daughter?"

"He would have killed her too, no doubt, if it suited his purposes," Baxel commented and shook his head. He would cut the man's throat if he had the chance.

"He is a foul viper. I am truly sorry that your friend has been taken. Gelion will not give him the opportunity to escape so easily this time."

Chill cleared his throat as Mike casually lit his pipe.

"That's what we wanted to talk to you about," Tom said, and Trevor turned to him with raised brow.

"Their leader is a bully," Baxel commented as he led what remained of the group through the narrow trash-ridden streets of the East Quarter. The sun was low in the horizon and light capped the top of the buildings that walled them off from the rest of the city. Beneath this tentative light, the gray stones and cobble reached cold fingers up through the soles of their boots, chilling them.

"That may work to our advantage," whispered Tom. He checked his knife and sword, then he wrapped his leather thong carefully about his wrist and hand: it would make an accessible garrote.

"If you find a weakness," replied John who walked behind the three. Mike strode next to him, a grim look on his face. Chill was bringing up the rear, cursing all the way.

"If. Mercenaries like this are not to be trusted very far, but with the time we have what can we do?" Baxel shook his head. He nodded and pointed to a tavern. Yellow light spilled from the shuttered window and they began to hear loud voices rising and falling with laughter, and shouts of anger.

Here the buildings bent into a dead end, as if this were the crux of their adventure in this strange world. Tom noticed, somewhat ironically, that retreat would be almost impossible if something went awry.

They paused for a moment outside the tavern. Suddenly the doors split open and spat forth a man, drunken and bedraggled, at their feet. The man groaned, looked up and passed out.

"Nice place, Baxel. Come here often?" John said somewhat sarcastically. "Not at all."

"I can see why."

They entered the tavern and were greeted by immediate silence, crisp as crystal. They were obviously overdressed for the party.

What light there was spilled in a yellow wash across worn brown benches. The floor was covered with the detritus of meals, drink and fights, and the sour- sweet smell of men long unbathed hung in the air. Most of the men sat hunched over their

196

tables; men more loud than others, all stilled for the moment as they stared at the newcomers. Some were caught in the act of throwing dice, others quenching their thirst. In the dim light, they all stared at the outlanders who noticed that even in the tavern the accoutrements of war were evident.

A slow murmur moved through the bar and soon things returned to normal. Baxel ushered the group off to a dark corner in an attempt to make them more inconspicuous; John doubted it had worked.

"Over there, the man with the whore," Baxel nodded to a cruel looking man who sat at a table. There was a full tankard at his elbow and woman in his lap. "Lirel is his name."

They watched somewhat fascinated as the man pulled the prostitute's blouse over and fondled a breast.

"A bit brazen," Bill noticed.

"Yes, I advise going through one of his men rather than approaching him straight away. Over there–"

Another man, with aquiline features, sat nursing ale at the end of the bar, apart from the group. He had a distant and surprisingly sober look about him. Upon this man's head was a brass helm of a different style from what they had seen thus far. Tom noticed that it covered the top of his head and was wrapped in linen, which could be brought around in a sort of veil, and a spike shot up from the center of the top. He carried a long, curved sword, similar to a scimitar.

The man himself was lean and swarthy. His beard just a week's growth, his face was weathered and lined, and there was a scar that ran across the bridge of his nose and underneath his eyes. He seemed much more formidable than Lirel, the leader, and when he noticed the group eyeing him he drained his tankard and stared at them pointedly.

"Jral-al hal. Bein et Clef, inef bar tuen?" it sounded elegant and totally incomprehensible.

Baxel turned to Tom.

"He is from Clef. He is speaking in the Middle Tongue. He wants to know what we're looking at."

Tom arched his brow and walked up to the man. "Can he speak Common?" Chill asked from the rear. "Do you speak the Common Tongue?" Baxel repeated.

The man nodded and frowned, he spoke with a thick accent. "I speak. What do you wish?"

"We are hiring."

The man smiled cynically and shook his head. "You want Lirel. He's getting whored."

The man turned and slapped two coins on the bar and stood. Raised heads and suspicious glances from the other tables met their progress through the bar. The scarred man had to duck several times to avoid knocking his helm against the low beams of the smoky room.

"This could get bloody," Mike remarked as he adjusted his belt. John just grunted and watched as the man known as Lirel looked up and belched. The whore giggled wildly and did nothing to cover herself. Mike smiled in appreciation of her well-developed assets.

"Lrl, kren jal-ahar," the scarred man said. Then: "These men wish to talk. Business."

198

"Business!" barked Lirel sharply as he stood and the prostitute fell to the floor with a thump. She sat there dumfounded and looked around. The man picked up his sword and strapped it to his side. "This is the time of the festival. Take them away, I do not wish to talk of business." He began to turn back to the girl when Tom spoke in a low voice.

"It is urgent and we do have the means to afford you." He held up a sack of gold that Trevor had loaned them.

The man quickly drew his sword and leveled it at Tom. He then brushed a hand through his greasy brown hair. As he narrowed his eyes, a cunning look came over his sallow face.

"What's to stop me from killing you and taking the gold?"

Tom smiled and turned to the side. Then the gold dropped from his hand and in a blur his blade was out and had neatly sliced the man's head off.

"That's what's gonna prevent you."

Bill stared wide-eyed as Tom held his blade out. Baxel just looked calmly around and Mike, John, and Chill could be heard swearing under their breath even though the prostitute was screaming at the top of her lungs. Tom dipped his sword to the ground, lifted and slit the sack of gold, and let spill the coins to the floor. Blood mixed with gold as it seeped across the filthy flooring.

"Anyone else?" Tom continued. There were several faces that reflected anger and the sounds of swords being drawn echoed from the dark recesses of the tavern.

John thought he could see smiles on the faces of a few. The one that had brought them to Lirel was grinning openly.

"It is not often we are hired by those willing to spill blood, or risk their own blood be spilled. Most are spineless overlords, too arrogant and weak to do their own dirty work. Unfortunately Lirel was becoming such." The man extended his sword hilt first to Tom. "I am Torec," he said, as Tom ceremoniously accepted the blade.

"I think we just hired ourselves some mercenaries," Mike sighed and watched as the rest of the patrons in the tavern extended the hilts of their blades. A few looks of anger still lingered on some faces, but most were grinning.

Chapter 12

The group awoke to another unusually crisp morning. Dew covered the ground in its ghostlike veil and an early fog was lifting to reveal the harsh yellow sun. Tom raised his face to the sky and praised the earth for letting him wake to nature's awesome beauty. He pulled his hooded sweatshirt over his hairy chest and snugged the hitches of his black BDU cargo pants; he would wear these for the ride back, his leathers desperately needed cleaning. He slung his sword over his back and affixed the knife to his belt.

"Jal et tu, an lasar ra," spoke the scarred man that had first greeted them in the tavern the night before. Tom looked up and smiled, shaking his head without comprehension. The man laughed. "Forgive me," he said with his thick accent.

"There is nothing to forgive," replied the Native American.

"I asked if we would be making an early day of it. Heading for the east?" He started to wrap linen about the brass of his helm, making a turban of sorts.

"The others are readying their horses and gear. Baxel says that if we follow a certain road it would be faster than if we went by way of Galfeon Yor."

"That would be the North Treadway." The man nodded in approval.

"Torec," Tom said the man's name, which he had learned the night before, then paused. "Torec, what do you think of our plan?"

"Well, from what you, the White Knight, and the Alchemist tell me, all things lead to Gelion's keep. He was dishonored and he perceives you as a threat. Duran probably had no intention to do you harm at first, but then you just fit into his shal- coratep, how do you say?"

"Scheme," smirked Tom as he bent down and picked up Kiera. "Yes, you were convenient to his plans for turmoil in the West."

"It seems so neat, but he left a few loose ends."

"This Shadowlord," Torec said and frowned at his pronunciation. "Does he have valuable power, wealth that they may deem important?"

"No, nothing that anybody in this land would want." Tom paused and watched the swarthy man frown in concentration.

"Torec, why is it you are so unlike most of the mercenaries?"

The man laughed and scratched at the scar on his aquiline nose. "I was not always a mercenary." A distant look shadowed his eyes. "Once, not too long ago, I was a rather wealthy merchant in Clef. Unfortunately, one day the Guard of Oran planted itself on our small island kingdom. Soon I found myself like a rat in the bilge of a felucca, smuggling myself off that island.

"I was foolish enough to speak out." He laughed somewhat cynically this time. "One night my home was broken into and my lover killed. I was blamed and my property was taken, and with it any influence I might have. I was sentenced to the block.

"Luckily, my counselor was a just man and helped me flee. He was seen and now we are both exiled from Clef. Garis was my counselor." He pointed to a fat, balding man who was rigging the saddle for his horse. "He and a few of my retainers make up about half of the mercenaries you hired. We took up with that lot without knowledge of Lirel's penchant for laziness. He would have died in his sleep had you not come along, that I can assure you."

Tom nodded understanding. He found that things were now becoming more complex than he thought they ever would in this world, this reality. It made him shiver at times to think that a place like this could exist without anyone having an inkling about these other realities. He wondered what other heavens and hells there were.

"Sonofabitch," Chill cursed as he put his gear on the horse. "How come I have to miss all the action? Why do I have to stay at Trevor's?"

"Because," John said and turned back to what he was doing. His temper was short this morning. Trevor seemed to be taking everything too calmly, Joe was only God knew where, and they were about to launch a raid on Gelion's keep. Swell, just swell, he thought.

"Because," Mike interjected, "If by some chance, however unlikely, that Gelion does not have Joe, and Joe somehow goes to Galfeon Yor, then you can greet him with open arms." Mike smiled, but his speech was humorless. His big frame lumbered over to the stout man and he placed his hands on Chill's shoulders. "And because we may not be coming back; one of us has to get through this."

"But–"

"Come on, Chill, we may get screwed. We may end up sitting on a lance, our blood and entrails spilling out onto the soil, our eyes bulging. Buzzards picking at our bones." Mike finished and grinned.

"Nice thought," remarked Bill as he passed by. "I really don't believe you, Mike. This is serious and you're getting off. Let's try a positive attitude."

"Temper, temper," Mike said as he scratched at his unshaven face. "Chill is going to keep the keep safe." He smirked and winked at John.

"Right," Chill sighed, knowing all too well that his lack of proficiency in the martial arts was the reason that he was being left behind.

"Mike, your attitude is really a pain in the ass," John bit as he pulled the saddle strap tight. "It's like the game."

John turned on Mike, his face red. "The game? You've got to be kidding me! The game was just that, a game. This is real life with real lives at stake and if you screw up you're dead. I don't know about you, pal, but I'm scared shitless. I've never had to kill anyone. I've never had a bunch of guys bent on killing me, running at me with swords and spears. This is nuts, Mike, and if you don't straighten up you're gonna find yourself on the pointed end of someone's sword."

"I'm worried about you, John. Your performance might suffer."

"Performance? This isn't a play Mike." Chill just shook his head and he and Bill went to tend their steeds.

"I worry, father," Gabrielle spoke softly as she and Trevor watched the outlanders go about getting their gear together.

"You care for him, daughter?"

"Yes. I fear he will not return. I fear that they go up against something greater than themselves."

"Aye. Twenty of our guards will go with them, led by Mrick. Then there are the thirty-eight men they have hired. They have little over sixty against Gelion's seven score. Yet, their plan is a good one: they attack at night while most sleep. I fear also, daughter, that their friend Surik may be in greater peril than they realize."

"How is that, father?"

"A feeling, daughter, nothing more."

She looked at him, her green eyes searching. She sensed that he wanted to say more...but what? Her father had been very private these past few weeks and that worried her. She was confused, and now one that she had grown to care for might be lost.

"I must bid him farewell," she said. "Yes, you must."

***

"How long has it been?" John asked as he sat down on the extended branch of a tree straddling a brook alongside the roadway.

"Six hours. The horses need a break. What's wrong?" Tom sat down next to him and watched a tadpole dart beneath the surface of the water.

"Besides my ass being as sore as hell? I don't know. Do you ever get the feeling that you're being pulled into something without knowing it?"

"Karma? Joss?" Tom asked. "It is pretty obvious have been brought here for some reason. I feel like we're way out there on Pluto."

"We're like magnets, attracting the attention of greater forces. Is there a sign on our backs saying: 'we're from out of town, kick us'?"

"I think the first mistake was saying that we were from another land across the sea, but then again, if we weren't, how would we explain ourselves? Either way we do draw a lot of attention, suspicion, and animosity." Tom said thoughtfully. "You're right. Something is influencing the course of events here. We are definitely being manipulated into stirring things up."

"I feel like I'm on the edge of a cliff, balancing. If I fall back I'm okay, if I fall forward then who knows what will happen." John leaned back against the bole of the tree and ran a hand through his dark hair. His almond colored eyes flashed. "Funny how I've always wished to be in this sort of environment. Careful what you wish for, right?"

"Yeah," the Native American sighed. "More and more I am beginning to understand how my ancestors felt and perceived their surroundings. I know how they felt when they were being driven from the places they loved. And now, I have the feeling that I'm going have to get used to the idea of fighting for my life."

"I think you already have an edge on us there," John referred to how Tom dealt with Lirel.

"Well, we have had some skirmishes. The rapists, Gelion's keep. If this is going to be a true test, I have a feeling that if we die it will be for good."

"What about our plan?"

"We hope for surprise."

"So, now we wait."

"Yep, and feed Kiera." He chuckled and stood. "She's gonna give you rabies one of these days."

"She's had her shots. Have you?" They both laughed and headed for camp.

"And I get stuck here," muttered Chill as he sat on the battlement and watched the sun set.

"Do not be too downcast," came a light voice and Chill craned his neck around. He hadn't realized that someone might be listening. He smiled and adjusted his glasses, motioning Trianna to sit down. Gabrielle's lady-in-waiting obliged.

"I'm not," Chill said after a pause. "The thing is, I know that I'm not the best swordsman around, but I think I can hold my own."

"I think that your companions know that, but they wish you to remain here as a precaution." She watched as he unfolded his thick arms and smiled.

"Yeah, I know that they're good guys. But, if they don't come back in a couple more days I may have to rescue them. It doesn't seem like two days have passed."

"It sounds like you care about them greatly."

"Surely you have friends that you are close to?" he asked, dancing around her question. She looked away and he persisted. "What about Gabrielle?"

"Yes, but in the village none of the other girls really are close. They think I am privileged. I think that the reason they left you here is obvious, they care about you."

"Helluva way to show it. I can't blame them though. I would just get in the way. It certainly isn't like foil fencing."

She turned at him, puzzled by his statement. "A sport."

There was a pregnant pause in the conversation that seemed to last forever. Chill looked out over the shadowed landscape. The sun was setting and the hills cast long, gray swaths over Galfeon Yor. In the East, stars began to punch through the blue vault of heaven. Chill's eyes followed the main road that led through the village and into the countryside. In the fading light, he could make out dim pinpoints of yellow light bobbing along the road.

"Horsemen, Trianna, I think they're back." Chill pointed to the riders.

"It cannot be. They could not have reached Gelion's hold and returned so soon."

"Maybe they found Surik and are bringing him back; maybe they didn't have to go after Gelion." The flames grew brighter as the sun set and the horsemen were only a couple of leagues off.

"I fear that these horsemen far outnumber those in your companions' party." She turned and quickly headed down the narrow stair.

Chill looked about confusedly, but then followed her down the stair. "What the hell's going on?" he called after her. The only reply was a shallow echo off the stone walls.

Mike plopped down on the ground and quickly began wolfing down the rabbit that had been cooked.

"Nothing like taking your time," Bill remarked and sat down next to him. They were in a small glade, the sun having set and twilight quickly fading. Trees bent heavy branches above them and, in the distance, the heavy trunks of the Great Forest pushed their bulk far above the canopy of the wooded fringe.

"Where are Grumpy and Doc?" Mike asked with a mouthful, sending a bit of meat flying across the space between them. He burped and smiled. Torec watched in amazement at his appetite.

"They went for a stroll." Bill picked at the rabbit, deftly stripping the meat from the bones.

"How romantic."

"Mike," Bill began, tilting his head to one side and letting his long hair fall away from his vision. "What makes the orb you have so reliable?"

"Beyond the fact that I created it? Well, according to the physical properties that I rely on for my Unified Theory as Applied to Sorcery, I feel that I have tapped into the aether, which is more readily available in this realm. When I concentrated on the orb, I had a strong sense that Gelion was involved with Duran and the poisoning."

"Couldn't that just be intuition?"

"I doubt it."

"Somehow, so do I," Bill muttered. He wiped grease from his hands and nibbled at a tuber.

"We know the place intimately," Torec interjected, referring to Gelion's keep. Garis sat down too, quite agile for being as fat in the stomach as he was. He smiled through a well-kept beard.

"We have harried the keep before," Garis said as he chewed on a morsel. "The bastards have an inclination to hang us. I really don't know what thoughts are in Gelion's head, but this would look good." He hefted a spiked mace and laughed.

"Friar Tuck, there, is my kind of fighter," said Tom as he and John approached. They sat and helped themselves to the food.

"I think we can do it," John asserted, trying to build his confidence. "Unfortunately, they have close to two-hundred men-at-arms at the keep. And we have but three score. I pray we don't end up the rabbit on their spit." Garis shook his head.

"Yes, but a castle in feudal Japan fell under the same conditions. One night a score of ninjas, assassins, infiltrated the castle and slaughtered all within. Cleanly and effectively," Tom spoke as his green eye flashed in the firelight.

"Look, here's how we'll do it," John went on to explain, before the mystified mercenaries could ask the meaning of his alien words. "We strike at night, silently. Torec, you, Bill, and Mike will come up from the river where one of the walls borders the banks. It will hide you well, and what sentries there are I'm sure you can take care of. Tom and I, plus Mrick and his men will take the gate wall." Mrick nodded from where he sat, twisting his long black hair into a war braid.

"And then?" Garis prodded.

"With any luck no alarm will sound," Tom continued for John. Several of Torec's men laughed. "We then set the barracks afire as most of the men will be sleeping. I don't think the watch will be that great a number...I hope." He smiled cynically.

"Then we hit the dungeon or whatever and get Joe...Surik." Mike looked at his empty bowl and belched.

"Looting is optional," Tom added.

"But, if the alarm is sounded, we're dead," Mike intoned and grinned. "That's a bit fatalistic, Mike," Bill remarked.

Mike just grunted and shifted, leaning his large frame against the tree. "You should read Kierkegaard's views on Existentialism."

"I'll pass."

And what's Joe doing right now? John though as he watched the fire glow an eerie red, sending sparks high into the night air. This land was truly magical. He wondered if his dream was prescient and they really were dead in their own world, or was this experience just a wink in time. He was sure that Mike would expound on it more readily; the ex-physics major could find an explanation for almost anything. John also knew that Chill was somewhat disappointed in them for leaving him at Trevor's keep, but it was necessary. He hoped that the stout man would understand their reasoning.

"We should get there late tomorrow night," he heard Torec say in the dimming light.

"And then we'll have a fine pig roast!" Garis rumbled.

John looked at Tom out of the corner of his eye. The Native American sat in the lotus position meditating. He was probably getting in the right mindset for the coming conflict. Bill had mentioned earlier that it would probably come hard to them, coming from a society that forbade such actions except in war. He himself did not know how he would react. Knowing that they weren't normal members of the herd didn't temper the anxiety that gnawed at his guts. If the gale strikes the willow it does not break, rather it bends. That was a proverb he had heard somewhere. He was just unsure if he could fight in the manner he was taught, without thought or feeling. He didn't know. Sleep eventually came, but with the hooves of nightmares edging in on his slumber.

He awoke with a start. He didn't know how long it had been, but the sound of Mike grunting and clearing his throat over and over again, to finally spit loudly roused him from a fitful sleep. He stood and stretched, breathing in the cool morning air. He watched as the dew sparkled in the morning light and wondered what could possibly go wrong on such a wonderful day.

The self-proclaimed Lord Knight pulled off his tunic and began his toilet, intentionally splashing water onto Tom and Bill; all snug in their bedrolls.

"Why are you in such a good mood?" Mike asked as he zipped his fly and scratched.

"It's a beautiful morning and–"

212

"Tonight we're probably going to die," growled Bill as he threw his covers off. "I hate pessimism," John replied.

Soon Torec and Mrick's men were saddling the horses and John sat oiling his katana. Tom sat across from him, Kiera tumbling off his shoulder. John was feeling that familiar itch at his chest and he reached inside his shirt and touched his medallion...

...black obscured his vision and was torn by white. Flames licked the sky and the ground rumbled. Screams...

"John!" Tom shouted and shook his shoulders. He looked up to see most of their party riding off.

"What?"

"Come on, we're heading out. What's wrong?"

"I had another vision, through the medal."

"And?" Tom knelt down, his interest piqued.

"I saw flame and the earth trembled. There were screams, then you brought me out of it."

"You probably saw us setting fire to Gelion's little lair." Tom stood and pulled John to his feet. "Torec, Mrick and Garis decided that our plan was worthy. If travel is good, we strike tonight." The Sioux headed to his horse and John followed, clearing his head of the vision.

He felt the medal as he mounted his horse and it was cold to the touch.

***

Baxel raced along the parapet, watching the column of riders and footmen as they advanced. He could not believe their number; easily they were

213

three hundred strong. He snapped the buckle of his chest plate just as Trevor and Chill came up from below. A bell sounded, signaling the village militia to fall back to the castle. Already the farmhouses on the fringe of Galfeon Yor were burning.

"I got a bad feeling about this," Chill breathed. He now wore some chain mail from Trevor's stores. It easily outweighed anything he had worn at a Society Event. He watched as the Lord of Galfeon Yor peered through a spyglass, trying to make out the leaders of the advancing column.

"They carry several standards," Trevor said lightly. "The Wall, Oran, and Gelion; he's getting rather brazen now that he has more swords to stand between him and danger." He looked down and watched the progress of fifty or so men as Eric let them into the keep. Scores of women and children were also falling back to the castle.

Eric, the old seneschal, staggered under the weight of plate armor. Chill, nerves on edge, did not think any of this was in the least bit funny. The men and women that he let in carried mostly pitchforks and hoes. There were a few spears and rusty swords but all were without armor.

"You don't expect to hold that column off do you?" Chill asked dubiously. They would be outnumbered if Baxel had all his men present. As it was, they were at half strength.

"We're prepared for a siege once we raise the drawbridge. I had Baxel send a rider to the freeholds to send men. And once your friends realize what has happened, they will return and fall upon them from behind. If they have any sense."

214

"Aye," Baxel called and motioned for his men to set up a heavy arbalest on the parapet. Chill shook his head and turned, not knowing quite what to say. This was certainly different from any Event. It has to be some cosmic joke, he thought. The others go off to fight the battle and the battle comes here. This really sucks!

***

The war party had left the road at sunset, proceeding into the ever-thickening forest and riding far into the evening. Once again the towering trees engulfed the riders with massive, dark pillars in a stygian vault.

"Blacker than a nun's habit, as Chill would say," John muttered. The only sound was that of the mounts tramping through the thick undergrowth.

"How can these guys tell where we're going?" Bill asked from somewhere to the rear. Mike scowled as a low branch clipped him in the head.

"I think they have some phosphorous lamp that isn't as bright as a torch. It won't give away our position." Tom squinted, but couldn't be sure. After a while, they moved into a small clearing that overlooked the valley and Gelion's keep.

Dismounting and tethering their horses, Mrick, Torec, and the four outlanders crept up top peer over the small rise.

"Can't see much," Mike complained. At first he couldn't penetrate the darkness, but then recognized the familiar low-walled structure. Finally he could make out the dim light of covered lamps that sat upon the walls and he could see shadowy figures of guards moving about.

"All is quiet," Mrick commented and slid back from the edge.

"I suggest we rest for an hour or so and then attack. By then She will be gone." Torec referred to the ringed moon that was positioned just above the tree line opposite them.

"So this is it? Jitters?" Bill said it and they could tell by the edge in his voice what he was feeling. John sat with his back against the tree and listened as they spoke in low, hushed tones. He soon drifted off to sleep.

He began to dream...

...garden enclosure of Trevor's keep. Gabrielle was there picking flowers. Chill stood behind her, but was not as they had left him. He was wearing white and there was a calm look upon his face. He seemed to be talking of home, or laughing at his own jokes, when John saw the shadows merge and creep behind the stout man. The shadows engulfed the white form, slowly staining his tunic to black and gathering him into darkness. Gabrielle was turned away, not noticing the imminent approach of the Shadows.

Why is not Joe here? John thought. Is he not Surik Shadowlord, Master of the Shades?

Soon they were upon her and she looked about in horror at the dark, faceless creatures. Her scream was silenced. John tried in vain to reach her, but the Shadows had now touched his legs, paralyzing them. The garden burst into flame and the earth trembled.

Foundations being shaken... Shaken...

John stared into Tom's face. The man had been trying to waken his friend for the past minute.

"Time to rock 'n roll, pal." He smiled coldly and began to smear some lamp black on his face. John noticed that he was dressed in his black BDU's and black sweatshirt. Kiera, as always, sat on his shoulder.

"That'll ruin your complexion," John replied, shaking the weariness from his limbs. He pushed aside the lingering unease of the nightmare and tried to concentrate on the upcoming battle. They walked to the knot of mercenaries, John carefully tightening the strap of his vambrace. Mike and Bill were already deep in conversation with Torec. John saw that Mike had his own katana out; the cold steel reflected in the dim light of the stars. His sword was gunto, a non-traditionally made oil-tempered sword brought to America by a GI. They were great cutters.

"It'll be different," he told Bill. "No bokken or mock sword. This will be different."

"You're sick, Mike," the musician replied. He was beginning to wish he had stayed behind with Chill. He hoped that he could put John's Estoc to good use.

"I won't be using that. It's dark," Tom said as one of the mercenaries brought his bow. The mercenary shrugged and pulled the string taut to let fly. An arrow struck what looked like a knot on the trunk of a tree some thirty feet away. Tom looked at the man, surprise on his face. "Well, not too dark."

Chill watched as most of the village of Galfeon Yor burned. The sounds of the villagers screaming were now carved as if by a hot knife into his brain. Red firelight reflected off the granite of the castle walls. Baxel stood in the courtyard below, giving commands to their puny force. Every now and then, they would launch a volley of ballista bolts into the air, doing little but annoying the men below. Their attackers were trying to figure a way across the Deep and, in doing so, had brought some engineers to the front to assess the situation. Chill prayed Trevor could hold them until reinforcements arrived.

"I think that we have nothing to fear as of yet," came Trevor's deep voice. Chill turned to see the man standing in a suit of scale mail with his huge sword at his side. Gabrielle stood behind him, speaking with Trianna.

"I hope, 'cause I don't want to hold all of them off by myself," the stout man replied. Strangely he noticed that Gabrielle was carrying a very long and wicked stiletto.

"I don't think it will come to that," he said and watched Baxel approach. The man looked ready for anything, but was obviously distressed by the inadequacy of the civilian force below. He had mentioned that their opponents' killing of the villagers had been uncalled for, and laying waste to the village was tactically inappropriate.

"They want something," he called to Trevor as he stopped and leaned on the parapet. "And they might get it." He handed Trevor the spyglass. "Look to the rear, those men have winches and grapnels. If the ropes are strong enough, the drawbridge won't hold."

"Yes, and they have mages too. Priests of Oran."

"I feared that." Baxel watched as the darkly armored men raised shields over their heads and the engineers and priests came forward beneath their protection. These men wore the symbol of Oran on their armor: a dagger, encircled by a ring of flame. He shook his head in disbelief when soon the grapnels strung out and defied any attempt by the defenders to cut the heavy ropes. The bridge was slowly being forced down.

"I think we're in trouble," Chill whined. Trevor swore and Gabrielle looked up, surprised.

"Gelion is a madman," Baxel commented more to himself than to anyone else. More arrows were fired, but these just ricocheted off the shields. Further back in the ranks a battering ram was being prepared.

"Sir Chill," Trevor said in a cold voice. "I cannot truly blame you or your companions. Gelion and Duran have been no doubt planning this for some time. But, I think that you and your friends have made matters worse." He turned and peered at Chill, who shrugged.

"You got me there, Trevor. What can I say, shit happens," Chill looked past him. Gelion's soldiers were now bringing up the ram; the bridge was down and now all that remained were the heavy oak doors and an iron portcullis. Down below he could hear the militia readying in the courtyard.

"Sir Chill, if things turn for the worse, I charge you to take my daughter and Trianna to the garden. Where your friends found a secret door you will find another. Eric will guide you. There is a small tunnel that goes across the Deep. I fear we will be breached."

Gabrielle looked startled. There was such a tone of finality in her father's voice. It was not like her father to give up so easily. In all his years of fighting against the border raids, she had not heard him talk so.

"Father, I cannot go. They will not get in." She clutched him by the shoulders just as there was a loud splintering noise as the iron gate was wrenched from its bolts.

"I must go!" shouted Baxel as he raced down the stair. Trevor followed a few steps and then turned back to his daughter. His hand caressed her cheek.

"You are as brave as your mother. Listen daughter, I will not lie to you, I never have. You are the most important thing in my life, not this castle or this land. Galfeon Yor is all but gone, look at the village, it is naught more than burning ruin. "Yet, you can bide your time with Sir Chill. They do not want the land. They do not care for these men and women. They seek Sir Chill and his companions. If Gelion is wise he will not kill me. If word of my death reaches the Conclaveum, he would be dead in a fortnight." He silenced her questions with a touch of a finger to her lips; he casually brushed a tear from her eye. "Not now. I will save myself, what is left of my men, but we must give you time to escape to safety. Eric will guide you, then you can rejoin Mrick."

"I cannot leave you!" she shouted and hugged him fiercely. Finally he pushed her away.

"Do as I say daughter, and remember I love you."

He motioned for Trianna and Eric to lead her away. Chill turned to Trevor. "Looks like you have your hands full. Don't worry, I'll take care of her."

"Thank you, Sir Chill."

He turned and went down the steps, following Baxel. There was shouting as black clad soldiers filled the courtyard.

As Chill and Eric escorted the ladies through the halls, he could hear the screams of the militia as they fell to more experienced blades. Then there was an outcry as Baxel and his men took up the fight.

"Come on, stop doggin' it!" he called back to Eric. They were soon across the garden and Eric was leading them into the dark chamber. It smelled of mold and mildew.

"Behind the chest," he said and motioned Chill to move it aside. He went to the wall and searched along the seam in the granite. Chill wondered how the frail old man could stand in all that plate armor, yet somehow he managed. Gabrielle seemed to be holding up okay, but Trianna had begun to sob.

"Er we go." Eric pushed a latch and the portal began to swing wide. Chill began to feel a rumbling and he knew that something was seriously wrong. The ground began to tremble from the very foundations of the castle.

"Uh, is this supposed to happen?" he called. Eric turned to him, confusion clouding his features.

"Nay, Lord. I–" he jerked suddenly and Chill couldn't understand what was wrong with him. Then a pained expression appeared on his face and a long blade shoved through the weak metal of the breastplate.

Chill jumped back as Trianna screamed and several men who had been waiting on the other side stepped into the small chamber.

"I knew something like this would happen!" He drew his sword. The men headed for the stair to the garden, but Chill backed toward the secret corridor. He pushed Gabrielle and Trianna behind him and flourished his sword. He hoped that Joe and the others would be proud of his swordplay.

He thrust the blade through a gap in one of the soldier's armor at the armpit, and the man sagged to the floor. There was another to replace him. In the close quarters and the dim light he realized that he was going to be killed if he didn't do something. He dashed out the torch and shoved the girls into the secret passage that led to the tower. He sighed as the granite closed quietly. The sound of the attackers faded.

"What now, Sir Chill?" came Gabrielle's voice.

"Good question, very good question. Unfortunately, I don't have an answer...yet." He breathed heavily and then smiled. He realized that he had handled himself quite well. Yet, he knew if the ladies could see his hand in the darkness they would realize it was shaking rather badly.

"You have a plan, don't you Sir Chill?"

"Oh right, a plan." Chill thought quickly. "Let's head to the tower."

They felt their way to the opposite end of the corridor and he hurriedly felt for the lever that led to the stairwell. That is, what stairwell remained.

About two flights up they came upon a breach, which led into the kitchen. It was dense with smoke, and flames leapt from the doorways into the keep. The raiders had set the castle afire. The timbers throughout the structure had taken quickly and were being rapidly consumed.

Several bodies littered the floor and Trianna gasped at the sight of Baxel fighting off at least six men in the garden area. Chill instinctively went to the aid of the Captain of the Guard. He ran across the burning room, Gabrielle and Trianna following, and struck heavily at the backs of the assailants, his sword flashing.

Baxel grinned as two of the men fell quickly to the stout man's newly honed skills.

"Ain't this a bitch," Chill swore as he hacked at another man. He failed to see the other soldier come up from behind. Baxel shoved himself in front of the broad axe and the blade opened his leg wide. He fell to the ground with a cry as blood pumped from the severed artery. Chill staggered as he cut at the axe-wielder, then reverted to the hack and slash in his panic. The man lunged and the blade of the long-handled weapon caught him in the side of the head.

His glasses went flying. Everything went fuzzy. Blackness.

John crept through the bush at the edge of the clearing. He, Tom, and Mrick were about fifty yards from the walls of the hold. They watched as shadows moved in front of the torches atop the watch. Mrick crawled forward on his stomach, his eyes white against the smeared black on his face.

"The signal will be the cry of the warg, Smiling Wolf. Listen carefully, it might be hard to hear at first." Tom nodded, but kept quiet. He loosened his sword in its scabbard and looked back through the bush, not really able to make out any of the twenty men that lay there. He heard John tap nervously on the hilt of his katana.

"Jitters?" he whispered. John looked at him crossly. "No, I have a hangnail. You?"

"It's foolish not to have fear, it's all in how you direct it."

John rolled his eyes in the dark and was about to make a snide reply when he heard the lonely cry of the warg in the distance. "So that's what it sounds like," he said and inched forward.

Mrick turned and waved a hand at his men. John and Tom got to their feet and, in a low crouch, sprinted the distance to the wall. They were about twenty feet apart, careful to stay in what shadow there was. John arrived at the wall first and darkness closed in about him. He watched as Tom slid into the shadows on the opposite side of the heavy wooden gate.

Tom nodded and John slid his sword from the enameled scabbard, raising it above his head. The men remaining at the edge of the forest began their charge to the keep.

Tom and John inched their way toward the portcullis that lay between them. When they stood at the large hinges, Tom stepped out in front and rapped on the wooden postern. After a pause, the door cracked open. Tom smiled and shrugged his shoulders at a leather-armored man who was more than astonished to see the nighttime intruder. The guard was about to turn and call to his companion when Tom lunged forward, grabbed the man by the hair, and shoved his knife up from beneath the jaw and into the brainpan. He dragged him outside and yanked the knife from the wound, a slow seepage of blood followed.

John peered within as the raiders crouched against the wall.

Torec looked over the bank of the river. Garis called out a wolf's howl that made Bill shiver, then they were up and running and the space between river and wall was a blur. Mike brought up the rear, his large frame lumbering. Garis signaled and the mercenaries casually tossed several grapnels over the wall. There was a clink and two of the hooks held, the third fell and was quickly discarded. Torec and Bill were the first ones to go up.

Bill went up, arm over arm, his thick muscles extending like steel bands. Soon he and the scarred one were at the top and stepping onto the narrow walkway of the waist high parapet. They waited and, after a few moments, two guards approached out of the dim light. Bored with the same routine, they were not prepared for the waiting figures. Torec's scimitar spun out of the shadows and cleaved through the man's helm and into his skull. The man dropped to his knees, his eyes glazed over as the merchant from Clef withdrew.

Bill swung the Estoc awkwardly. What was it John had said? The blade was almost too bulky to be used with any finesse? Helluva time to remember, the thoughts were fleeting as his opponentquickly brought his own blade up and the ringing sent a shiver through the outlander. Bill soon found out the guard was better at this and his sword was parried down, sinking into the wooden planking at his feet. The man grinned, but it was short-lived. Torec sent his blade through the man's back and into the heart. He fell from the wall, dead before he hit the ground.

Soon the mercenaries were all atop the wall and heading to the roofs of the barracks and stable. Mike and Garis were the last to reach the top. Mike was breathing heavily as he disentangled himself from the rope.

"Gotta stop smoking," he muttered and drew his blade. He looked to his feet, saw the death below, and was silenced.

Tom heard several dull thuds as the bodies of the guards atop the walls fell to the inner yard. He and John stepped into the gate, as the light from the torches and oil lamps sent their shadows fluttering. John began to push the heavy doors open wider and they creaked violently in protest.

Tom slid into the cover of the wall, keeping an eye on his friend. The outlander strained to push the heavy doors open and was rewarded to find it move slowly but surely.

"Hold!" came a shout. "Alarm! Alarm!"

"Shit!" John scowled and turned. Two guards were rushing headlong at him with battle-axes ready. Their well-oiled leather armor caught the yellow of the lamplight as John ducked under the two axes and behind the guards. He drew his sword from the scabbard and rammed it into the back of one of the men. The man crashed to the ground with at least one broken vertebra. The second guard spun on John but was too late to counter Tom's unexpected attack. The Native American's straight blade snaked out and bit under the man's sternum. Blood sprayed as the chudon strike eviscerated the guard. John turned as Torec's men issued into the gate. The sound of ringing steel in the courtyard had drawn their attention immediately.

Mike snapped his katana into the Hoppo-gidi, the Eight Point Cut. This succeeded in knocking four of the defenders off the narrow stair and into the courtyard. They landed entangled in one another, several crying out in pain from being impaled on their cohort's blades.

"Haha! Bastards!" he yelled and leapt into their midst. All his opponent saw was the psychotic glare in his eyes, then the flash of the blade. The cause of their demise was more the surprise at the big man's agility than the Aikido technique he used.

Bill's hair flew in all directions as he too leapt down the remaining few steps to aid the former physics student. He was stunned at his friend's ruthlessness, yet he knew they could expect no quarter from the defenders. Bill finally was beginning to get used to the unusual weight of the Estoc, and had accustomed himself to the hack and slash technique. Whenever he did let someone through, Torec or one of his men would dispatch them efficiently.

The mercenaries began to set fire to the roof of the barracks and the stable, but they left the guardhouse and great hall intact. Joe was most likely being kept in the guardhouse but, at the present moment, they were occupied with other matters as the fighting in the courtyard became more harried.

Followed by the thick white smoke that billowed from the barracks came the Gelion's guardsmen. Tom, John, Mrick and a host of their men sprinted from the gate to the inner yard and it was soon apparent that things were going badly for the men of the Conclaveum.

"Bi alal!" Torec yelled over the din of clashing blades. "They are falling back to the main hall!" Torec and Mrick's men rushed the door to the main hall, preventing the retreating guards from closing and barring it. The four outlanders closed on the heels of their allies, shoving their way through groups of fighting men.

Tom entered the hall first and spun low to avoid an axe. He stomp-kicked a man in the chest, then disemboweled him. Turning, he looked for another opponent. His clothes were thick with the blood of the slain and the wounded, but he struggled forward. He saw Mike slam his fist into another's face then cut upward from the groin. Seconds later the man lay dead on the floor. Bill looked on, rather pale, but managed to fend off another attacker. It was then that Mike spotted the Regent.

"Gelion," Mike growled, remembering the blow the man had dealt him to the side of the head. The man turned, as if he could hear Mike in the din of the closed hall, and their eyes locked. Gelion's forehead was gashed and dripped blood into his face, yet his steel eyes were cold with fury as he watched Mike approach. In slow motion, he casually killed a mercenary, and then adjusted his chain mail hauberk.

John held his breath as Mike moved toward Gelion. He edged past the fire pit, along the wall, missing most of the melee. A guardsman moved into his field of vision and he had to parry a blow over the shoulder; he sliced across the man's eyes and took him out of the fray. John saw Mike exchange pleasantries with the Regent. "Not very good, are they?" commented Tom as he hamstrung one of the last remaining guards. He frowned: something was wrong. John flicked the blood from the blade and hilt of his sword, looking up just in time to see a robed figure step out of the shadows and raise a staff.

"Navar, et'tuien!" the mage intoned. The Knight of Erie was about to make a snide retort when a bolt of energy leapt from the staff and splintered the wood flooring at his feet. He fell to the floor, sword knocked from his hands, momentarily stunned. One of Mrick's men stepped out to protect him and a bolt struck the man square in the torso. He fell to the ground, covered with third-degree burns. The sorcerer looked at John and scowled, raising his staff once more. A bolt lanced out and John felt a burning at his chest as the energy struck his St. Christopher medallion through his clothing and back lashed toward the sorcerer, shattering the wooden staff. The mage gaped at him with awe.

As John got to his feet, there was a flash of steel and the mage fell, clutching Tom's knife to his chest. John nodded in thanks to his friend and retrieved his sword.

229

There was a knot of men now near the fire pit as Gelion faced Mike. The two men were almost equal in height, yet Mike was bulkier, not as lean as the Regent. He held his katana in one hand and a sword he must have picked up in the other. The two men circled ominously. Gelion held his bastard sword in both hands, moving with uncanny agility.

"I was killing savages when you were in swaddling, boy!" he spit out the last word, showing his contempt. Mike noticed Gelion favoring his right side and saw the bandages just below the hem of his hauberk; a splotch of blood was evident on the linen wrappings. Mike ignored the man's taunting, the last thing he wanted to do was be distracted by some stupid insult and get killed.

"I may die here," The Regent of the South growled. "But by Oran I'll take the lot of you with me." He lunged and Mike slid to the side, barely parrying the great blade. Mike reversed the parry and thrust. His sword hissed a hairsbreadth past its target as Gelion drew a neat line of blood across the large man's suddenly unguarded shoulder. The katana clattered to the flagstones.

"You should take care, boy." Gelion grinned evilly, the red glow of the fire-pit turned his face into a distorted, hellish mask.

"And you!" Mike countered as he rolled, picking up his sword and wheeling low, slicing upward. Gelion tried to leap back, but without success. The sword hacked through chain mesh and bit into flesh just above the bloodied and soiled bandages that were wrapped tightly about the man's waist. The Regent clenched his teeth and staggered back, pain etching his features, but still managed to raise his sword and hack down with a mighty blow. Mike countered with a sweep of his blade, but Gelion's bastard sword carried it into the flagstones and, with a flash of sparks, Mike's blade broke off six inches from the hilt. Mike staggered, sat hard, and stared at the remnant of his only defense.

"Bad forging, that." Gelion sneered. "Unfortunate for you." He raised his sword above his head for the fatal blow.

Mike surged upward and, with all his weight, thrust the ragged shard into the Regent's groin. The man groaned, then screamed as the broken blade sheared through his already damaged organs. Mike twisted the hilt deeper and Gelion sagged to the stones, his sword clattering into the open hearth.

"Mike!" John shouted. "You did it!"

"John," replied Mike, shaking his head and breathing hard. "You have a definite grasp of the obvious."

They searched the fort and rounded the survivors into the yard. The sky had grown overcast during the fight and now the clouds let fall a steady rain. The patter and sizzle of the drops on the charred wood soon became almost white noise as the outlanders gathered in a confused knot.

"I can't find him anywhere!" Tom yelled from the guardhouse. He walked over swiftly, casting a long gaze at the prisoners huddled in the damp yard.

"Surik Shadowlord is not to be found." Garis commented. "We have searched the keep for your companion, but he is not here. The barracks were all but empty."

"We have lost five of Mrick's men and seven of our own. What is most strange is that we have slain but fifty men and wounded but twelve. What has become of the other seven score?" Torec shook his head and wiped his scimitar with the remnant of a guard's cloak. He looked weary in the dim light of the approaching dawn.

"Well it certainly was not a trap." Tom looked around, massaging his arm. Some blunt instrument had struck him during the fight.

"Do you think Surik was taken elsewhere?" John loosened his vambrace and looked around. He had a nagging doubt in his mind, but he couldn't put his finger on what was causing it.

"What would one hundred and sixty men be doing?" Mike asked, more of himself than of the others. "Duran and some bitch kidnap Joe. Duran's ally would obviously be Gelion. Yet, we weren't counted on, we just happened to get in the way..." Mike shook his head.

"Of course!" John shouted. "Duran and Gelion had something planned for Trevor before we arrived! Joe was just icing on the cake!" The companions shared a moment of stunned comprehension, and then bolted for their horses in the wood.

"A raid against Trevor," Mrick said with a note of despair.

"Galfeon Yor," Torec muttered. Soon they were all running to their steeds.

In the steel gray of an evening cloud cover, the setting sun split the horizon with a bloody smear.

The horses approached Galfeon Yor at a staggering pace, foam lathering their flanks. Even with the rain, they could make out the billowing smoke in the distance. The road that had brought the six outlanders to Galfeon Yor many months ago was much changed; it was muddy, and had deep ruts that told a tale of many carts and war machines. Torec pointed out that a force of over two hundred must have passed.

"They waited in the forest and launched their attack." Torec said it quietly, afraid of it being true.

They passed the low walls that marked the farmlands and pastures of Galfeon Yor. Here and there a body lay on the side of the road, usually a farmer or peasant who'd gotten in the way of the column of soldiers. Twisted in a rictus of pain from a sword or spear; soon after the fatal blow, the birds and other feeders of carrion had descended on the remains.

John looked away from these horrible figures of battle and spurred his horse onward. It labored beneath him, trying to keep the pace he had set. Soon they had passed through the village proper and onto the main thoroughfare that twisted its way to Trevor's castle. The buildings alongside the road were now nothing more than smoldering brick and crossbeams. Here too, death had come before the inhabitants of the businesses and homes could flee. Buildings showed signs of damage two streets deep and nothing moved save the carrion feeders and other foul things in this late hour.

Mrick choked back a sob and urged his horse into a gallop ahead of the rest of the group. Soon he and his men-at-arms had outpaced the others and rounded the road to the keep. John noticed something was wrong as he looked at the silhouette of low buildings and the castle. Then he had it. Through the haze of the smoldering fires he still should have been able to see the turrets and forward battlements of the keep, but he could not. They had been razed.

...foundations shaken.

"Hla-ilam 'eya kui tuen," Garis called to Torec as they trotted past the village square. The man nodded and removed his turbaned helm at the sight of more charred bodies. "Where are the rest of the people?" Bill suppressed a gag and brought his forearm up over his mouth to cover the mounting stench.

"This happened when we were attacking Gelion's hold." Torec twisted in his saddle. "We must be wary, they may have left some guards behind."

As they rode on, it only worsened. Near the toppled structures of the castle, stood two siege engines, smoldering in the cooling air. Rain sizzled as it struck the hot timbers and stones that were shorn away from the castle walls, right to the very foundation. Mrick sat on his steed at the drawbridge staring in disbelief; his world, or what was left of it, lay shattered before him.

John and Tom dismounted and walked through the ruined gate. Bill stooped as he crossed the bridge, fell to his knees and began to vomit violently.

"Aldi et!" Torec swore and touched his forehead with his thumb. He too had looked into the Deep.

"My God!" Mike echoed and looked. All the people of Galfeon Yor lay at the bottom of the Deep, piled upon one another.

"What beast has done this?" Torec growled.

John looked back, feeling lightheaded. "They pushed them into the Deep?"

"Aye. I cannot imagine Gelion's men alone doing this. There must have been others." Torec touched his forehead again and moved on. They stepped through the gate into the forecourt and Bill once more began to retch, but there was nothing left to come up. John turned away.

Their first sight inside the castle was a grisly one indeed. Baxel hung from a wooden rafter as if he had fallen and been caught up in some of the ropes and cables used by the besiegers. His eyes had been burnt out and he had been disemboweled. It was revealed upon closer inspection that what they thought were ropes were his entrails, blackened by dried blood. Mrick quickly went to his commander's body and, regardless of the condition, cut him down. Bill, Mike and the others moved onward into the castle, as the remaining contingent of Trevor's men stood in comfortless silence.

Nearing the center of the castle they found more bodies. Trevor's men and the militia were contorted in a dance of death with the bodies of Gelion's men and a few others in armor and dress they did not recognize. The place stank, and it was hard not to walk in some bodily fluid. They were all numb with shock, but Torec and Tom seized the lead. John was close behind, wondering if he would find Gabrielle in a similar condition. And what of Chill?

"This is some bad shit. Who are these guys?" Mike nudged a body with his boot.

"I have seen them before," Torec replied. "They are soldiers of the Temple of Oran; and some are the Black Guard from Helm."

They walked toward the kitchen and found the wall and ceiling blown out. There they found Chill.

A ring of blue fire encircled him, sending up a shimmer in the air around where he lay. Inside, he was immobilized. There were quite a few dead bodies around him and they must have overpowered him, to do what had been done. He lay on his back, a broken lance full through his chest, pinning him to the floor. His tunic was not covered with blood and there was no other wound except for a shallow gash along his forehead. He seemed to be suspended in time.

John was at his side in a moment, easily crossing the wall of blue flame. "No!" shouted Mike, but it was too late. John could not have known what he had inadvertently done. At the touch of his medal, the flame vanished and the shimmering air faded into nothingness.

Chill's chest swelled with air and a groan escaped his lips. Suddenly, blood welled up from around the shaft of the lance, and immediately his tunic was covered in red.

The rest of the company ran to him but it was too late to do anything. Chill was barely breathing; pink bubbles now frothed in the blood that was defeating John's futile attempts to stop its flow. John cradled his friend's head in his arms, smoothing back the damp hair as Tom and the others stood helplessly by. John looked pleadingly at Tom, and the Sioux just shook his head gently and turned away. Chill's face was serene, as if the last pain had long since fled his body. His eyes fluttered open.

"Oh shit, what kept you?" he whispered.

John smiled but could not speak. Then: "It's gonna be okay–"

"Shut up, John." A faint smile crossed Chill's lips, then fled. He coughed, a tearing cough, and struggled to sit up, but the lance held him in place and he sagged back. "They took them, John. I tried to protect her, but they took her and Trianna. Then they made me watch as they did that to Baxel and the villagers. But I wouldn't tell them where you had gone. I wouldn't. They think you're still in Ord. But they said they had to take Joey somewhere, I don't know where. I tried to escape, but one of the guards did this, ran me down. Duran was pissed. He killed the guy. But I knew it was too late. Some guy in a robe put the fire around me. There was no pain at all, you know. Just peace. Duran said I would make a good messenger."

"Chill, I–"

"Get that bastard...Duran."

"We will," echoed Mike.

"I guess I'll find out if home is..." he trailed off, his breath shallow, then ceasing altogether. Tom picked the man's glasses up off the floor and looked blankly at the crushed lenses. The compatriots stood silently as the clouds burst into a downpour.

Their tears echoed the rain.

Chapter 13

No more did lightning flash in Teshwa, but there was electric fury in the old man's eyes. He stared across his tower room, surrounded on three sides by the blustery evening winds of the Seat of the Conclave; before him glimmered another image: that of an ochre tent interior dominated by the powerful presence of Myella, Surrogate of the Conclavator and High Priestess of Oran. His anger mounted, his hands shaking and his voice growing metallic as the full import of her words penetrated the distance.

"Dead!?" he said, his voice winding up an octave. "How could he be dead?"

"He was mortally wounded. We could do nothing. But, I have the other."

"What happened when he died?"

"He was the weakest–"

"What do you know? I had plans even for him. Because of that idiot Duran, the power may be wasted. Must I come there myself?"

"No! I have the Shadowlord."

"Yes." He calmed somewhat at that. "Take him to your city, niece. You know how to bend him to our service. Use the Naming. As for the other, it falls to me to salvage whatever may remain. "

"Yes, Uncle."

"And what of your brother?"

"Father thinks he is coming, but I have also seen to that."

"Good. Soon no one and no thing will stand in our way."

It was a hazy, lifeless day. Not even the brief breeze blowing across the rock jetty could ease the oppressive humidity and heat. The water was gray, flat and listless, seeming as unyielding as dull iron. Here the haze obscured the definition between sky and water and made a ghost of the mainland less than half a league away. Marad, son of Ironeas and Conclavean Ambassador to the Krim, stood on the uneven tumble of rocks that were bleached white by sun and salt. The pervasive odor of rotting fish caused a slight flare of his nostril; not even a gull would brave the sweltering climate today to scavenge the carrion. He wiped sweat from his brow and looked over the sealed scroll in his hand. The wax was all but melted off and the parchment was close to cracking. He sat on the boulder and shied from the heat against his bare back. He broke the seal, his tension mounting as he recognized the familiar script of his brother.

Honored Marad,

I write this in secret. Oran's daughter is near and her conspirator nearer. I bid you hasten to our father's side; his health fails. Trouble follows upon the Helm's wind. Be wary.

Adon

Marad shook his head. His brother was not one to wax fanciful or paranoid. He tucked the scroll into the sash about his waist and smoothed back his sun- bleached hair as he rose to see the sergeant carefully picking his way across the rocks of the jetty. Time in the far North had not been generous to Kel. He was getting on in age and the sun and

239

sea had weathered him beyond his age. He had been stationed here some twenty years before, content to protect the Conclaveum from the Krim. At first, Kel laughed when Marad came to the small garrison island not two years earlier in an effort to sue for peace with the sea-raiders.

Kel firmly believed in the Dictum, which stated plainly: Sovereignty of Rule by Force. This Dictum had been established by the XXIII Conclave, over five hundred years before when the Conclaveum's long arms had reached far indeed. Marad knew that Kel was a soldier of the Conclaveum, born and bred, but he also knew that change was inevitable and that, if the raids continued, the borderlands would weaken and another crack would appear in the wall.

He looked Kel over. The man was short and lean and carried himself well. His features were aged and worn, but he was one of the best-trained warriors of the elite White Guard. Marad realized that even the White Guard was becoming an anachronism. It was one of the two remaining units guarding the borderlands of the Conclaveum. The White was the sentinel of the North and the Black was the sentinel of the South, garrisoned at the Great Wall. The Grey had been disbanded over two centuries ago, for those within no longer posed the threat that they once did to the growing and sprawling empire.

"Kel, I go south to Teshwa."

"South? But talks with the Krim are just concluded. The peace is tenuous at best and I trust them not."

"They are trustworthy enough. They are like any other people, Kel, and they are weary of the fighting. Bej-et has said so herself."

"Pshaw! A woman as emissary to the Conclaveum is an insult. That slut would seduce us and then cut our throats in the middle of the night."

"And you would do the same to her with only the smallest of excuses. She is a warrior and the one who governs the phalanx of their fleet. Remember that."

"Aye, milord. I will also remember that she and her raiders have killed more of the White Guard and ravaged wider across Tasseem than any other raider in the history of the realm."

"I will not argue with you Kel, but I trust Bej-et and our counsel enough to leave now and head to the Capital. I require you and thirty men as an escort. We should reach the Seat before the rainy season."

Kel scowled and looked off toward the mainland. It would take a month or two through the dense Northern forests of the Conclaveum, depending on the weather, which was unpredictable in the north this time of the year.

"When do we leave, Lord Marad?"

"One week Kel." Then, "Something is wrong in Teshwa. My brother has summoned me to the Seat and warns of intrigue. I like it not."

"My loyalties are unwavering, milord."

"Aye, Kel, I do." He walked past the sergeant and toward the whitewashed walls and red tile roofed garrison house. It would be hot for the next month. It would be cooler in Teshwa.

Joe's eyelids fluttered and the back of his head began to throb with exquisite pain. It was the sharp stabs in his wrists that hurt the most, though. They were bound tightly in front of him and had long since fallen numb. He grimaced and finally opened his eyes. He was on his back and looking up toward the ceiling of a tent. It was dim and warm inside and the smell of leather led his gaze to saddlebags and other leather goods on one side of the tent. He tried to sit up and failed, the motion making him realize that he had to urinate rather desperately.

He heard footsteps and quickly shut his eyes again as the tent flap was pulled open. He listened as someone approached, sighed, and then the bonds were freed at his feet. He was then pulled up and slapped hard across the face. His eyes shot open.

Duran. Flanked by two guards in black and gold uniforms with an unfamiliar symbol on the breast.

"Well, Surik Shadowlord, Master of the Shades. It seems you are in quite a predicament." Joe's gray eyes were ice, but the cold gaze only seemed to amuse his nemesis. Duran gestured, and Joe grunted as he was roughly pulled from the tent and into the daylight. Shielding his eyes with his bound hands until they adjusted to the change, he noticed the tents and the small contingent of soldiers camped. The tents were a rich royal blue, and pennants fluttered at the tip of the center poles. Further out, he could see a low range of mountains in the north, and the Great Forest against the edge of the camp. The sun was just setting, and long shadows crept over the encampment. As cooking fires flared and horses grazed, it seemed as if the normal routine had settled in, nothing out of the ordinary. If it wasn't for the pain and Duran, the setting would be rather nice.

"How long?" Joe croaked, trying to bring some moisture into his mouth.

"Six days. I do apologize for your current attire, but I fear you soiled your other clothes. My guards hated to touch the garments, but Lady Myella insisted we clean you up." He turned to one of the guards. "Balik, haq'hal etuk navar, est tuguon," Duran spoke in the same tongue that Gelion had greeted them with; it was obviously the tongue of the Conclaveum, and Joe began to see their plans unravel.

They should never have trusted Duran, and they should have suspected Gelion more. That girl must have been a ruse to take him off guard. It had certainly worked. Now one of the guards trotted off and Duran turned Joe over to the other.

"You now belong to the Surrogate of the South. She says that you and your friends are not of this world, but that you come from some fairy realm and she claims you bring powerful sorcery with you. I assume that is why Gelion is dead, but I fear that whatever power you possessed has helped neither you nor your friend."

"My friend?" Joe looked up, a dull ache of despair welling in his chest.

"Sir Chill. I fear that his fate would be much more preferable to the one that awaits you. Lady Myella can be rather ruthless." He strode off as the guard began to lead the gray-eyed man in the opposite direction.

"What about Chill?" Joe shouted, struggling in the man's grip, worry and despair gnawing at his guts. Duran just chuckled and waved, weaving his way between two tents.

"What the hell is happening?" Surik Shadowlord, Master of the Shades and

Rider of the Black Dragon shouted as he was dragged away.

Chapter 14

The wind howled through the ruins of Trevor's Keep. It was a lonely and distant sound that made John huddle more deeply into his cloak as he reflected on the events of the last two days. He sat alone amid the rubble. Their small force had set camp a stone's throw away from the once-grand castle, yet he had wandered away to sit in the ruins and think.

He cradled the St. Christopher's medal in the palm of his hand, contemplating the raised surface that depicted a man with a staff carrying the Christ child across a raging stream. St. Christopher was the patron Saint of travelers, how apropos. Now it glinted in the moonlight, almost mesmerizing him. Tell me where they are, he commanded. Nothing happened and he put it back under his shirt.

He shook his head, ruefully, and flexed his arm. It was sore and there was a ridge of blisters from the vambrace strap, just as there was a chasm in his heart from the fighting, and the death. The vambrace did not chafe half as much as the killing.

And Chill was gone. They had buried him the day before, some distance from the village on a serene hillock beneath a spreading oak. They had faced him West, toward the setting sun, and the castle. It had been just the four of them. Few words were spoken, but they each took a token from the man's belongings. A leather bracelet that Tom had fashioned for the stout man went back to its maker. Mike took the small traveler's Bible from Chill's bag, mumbling about its power as a religious tome. Bill reluctantly inherited his hunting knife. John took the broken glasses, saying it was a reminder of how vulnerable everyone was.

Now John sat and pondered. What would it be like to be dead in this world? Events were forcing him to question his own religious beliefs. They were in a world of magic and physical laws alien to their own; a world that had not heard of Christ, Buddha or Mohammed. He hoped, somewhat wistfully, that Chill had gone on to some place of comfort, but he doubted it.

In the dim light, he could make out Bill and Tom wending their way up the collapsed battlement to where he sat. Bill carried the Ighuire, Tom his ferret. John smiled wanly as they sat before him. They had lost a brother. He leaned back and gazed at the stars.

"I checked Mike's arm again," Tom spoke softly. "It's clean, but he'll have a nice scar." John nodded and looked into Kiera's eyes, she just stared back.

"We have to plan our next move," he said with a somewhat shallow voice. "Mike should be here," Bill echoed.

"Where is he?"

"He said something about trying his hand at sorcery, I think," Bill replied and struck a chord on the strange instrument. He seemed to be handling things rather well, but inwardly he must be in turmoil.

"I hope he doesn't get himself incinerated or melted or something."

"He may not fully understand the power of this land, but I think he knows enough not to cause more trouble." Tom shifted and looked over his shoulder.

"I screwed up, crossed the flames. I killed Chill." John closed his eyes and shuddered, remembering the dark power of that cold blue corona.

"No John, he was already dead. Mike said the sorcery was only a type of stasis. It could not be undone."

And what of Gabrielle? He examined his feelings for the woman. He wondered if he would ever see her again, let alone Joe. Joe had to be their biggest concern at the moment. We brought this on, we are responsible.

"We cannot blame ourselves," Tom said, almost taking the thoughts from

John's bleary head.

"Guilt is a fairly complex emotion, Tom. Responsibility for this mess is in part ours, however ninety-nine percent of it goes to the person who brought us here and Duran."

Bill grunted and began to strum his instrument. It was a sad, dirge-like melody that drifted out on dark tendrils, shunning the firelight.

"Duran had this planned before we came along, we just fit nicely into the scheme of things. I think he knows who brought us here and why."

"Maybe."

They all looked up at the sound of Mrick's approach. He stood before them his hair still in a war braid, his eyes darting from one to another. Bill looked up, but continued to play the man's Ighuire.

"What's up Mrick?" John asked, noticing the man's bloodshot eyes. Tom saw that some of the men of Trevor's guard were also approaching the fire.

"We want you to leave and take those mercenaries with you."

"What?" Bill asked, rather startled at the unexpected request. Yet, he did not miss a note and his tune pierced the gloom.

"You have brought this ruin. If we had not gone after your friend, a ruse to Gelion's hold, we would have been here. We could have helped. Almost all the townspeople are dead in that mass grave that was made of the Deep. Our life is destroyed. Now we want you to leave." His voice wavered as he tried to suppress the anger he felt. He clenched his fists. "We can only assume that Milord and Lady are dead, or worse."

"That's a pretty big assumption, Mrick. Gabrielle and Lord Trevor are probably prisoners, like Surik. I am sorry that you feel that way about us," John replied rather steadily.

"Look around, Mrick," Tom interjected. "Duran did this, not us. He had this planned long before we showed up; our arrival just gave him an excuse. And if you had been here, you and your men would just be dead with the rest."

"Damn you! Duran or not, things would be different if you had never stepped across the Deep." He shook suddenly and grabbed the musical instrument from Bill. The Bard just looked on as Mrick dashed it against the stones; it shattered and uttered a vicious noise as the strings sprung. Tom and John looked at Mrick in shock.

There was a blur as Bill shot to his feet and grabbed the man by the throat. Mrick tried to pry the hands away, but to no avail.

"Listen, you simple-minded backwater excuse for a human being," Bill growled as he clenched even harder. The man's face was turning dark and he tried vainly to tear Bill's fingers off his windpipe. "Get this straight. We saved Gabrielle and Baxel from drinking wine that had been poisoned by Duran, or don't you remember? We did not cause the destruction of Galfeon Yor. What I suggest is that you and your men look around and see what you can do about finding a clue to where Trevor and his daughter had been taken. That way we can retrieve them." He shoved the man away and the other men-at-arms looked on. Mrick sat on the ground, rubbing his neck and gulping in deep breaths of air.

"And bring them back to what?" he croaked out and looked up at the outlanders. "You can rebuild the town, but what of the people?"

John smiled cynically and stood, grabbing his sword and cloak. "Where we come from, we learn rather quickly that they, too, can be replaced." He shook his head and began to wind his way back to the camp. It was obvious to him, and he supposed Tom and Bill too, that their continued presence would only be a source of conflict.

The sooner they left, the better.

Mike crossed his legs and leaned his large frame forward over the orb. The Book of Shadows that he had obtained at the Event lay before him. It was dark and damp down here and seemed undisturbed compared to the chaotic ruin above.

The flicker of the black candles gave an eerie atmosphere to the catacombs beneath the broken keep. Outside the candle's reach, the dark was impenetrable and made the corridors that split off from Mike's chosen spot unknown in depth. The only thing that spoke of the devastation that had been wrought was a single large rent in the foundation of the keep running next to where he sat; it spilled rubble and dirt and exposed a vein of wet, red clay into the dank chamber.

Like blood, came a fleeting thought as he twisted his Manchu mustache. He rolled up his sleeves, exposing his massive forearms, and touched the orb that sat before him.

The candles flickered.

Somewhere in the distance, in some tunnel, he could hear the steady drip of water as it echoed in a deep cistern. It droned on, yet he pushed it from his consciousness, not letting the unknown put fear into his mind.

His crystal blue eyes peered out from beneath brooding brows and, as he brushed a shock of lank, sandy hair out of the way. He exposed the quartz crystal talisman that hung about his neck and it glinted oddly. Then, with a piece of chalk, he drew a circle around himself. He concentrated on the orb, focusing on the flaw at its core. The light of the flickering candles distorted it strangely, carrying him into a trance state that would facilitate the sorcery he was trying to perform. The magic would not require the utterance of words, though the High Tongue could enhance it; the formulae in this realm were simply mathematical. It all had amazing relation to his studies of Physics and Probability Theory: in sorcery there were many permutations and random variables that had to be discerned and chosen – if one looked at it another way, it was like finding the right key to place in the lock, the right chemical transmitter to go to the right neuroreceptor, etc. If the wrong variable were chosen then the wrong magic would be wrought and the outcome could be uncertain if not deadly.

The formula began to build in his mind. Three dimensional, like the ladder of a strand of DNA, it became intricate beyond reason. All his attention was focused on the construct and maintenance of the formula that would penetrate the aether and unlock power. His thoughts would become energy and form the strength he needed; it would then be a force with which to affect the fabric of reality. The three things that made up reality were not separate: Space, Time and Thought were all linked and easily accessible in this realm. It was at this moment of concentration that things became most critical and dangerous. Never before had he tried a spell, and one of this scope was extremely dangerous. The ward was essential to keep him safe. He wove the formula beyond mere intricacy and into a dimension of chaos, complex and powerful.

The candles extinguished suddenly, leaving only the darkness and the constant echo of the water dripping in the distance. Then that too stopped.

An ominous stillness settled over the stone.

He doubled his concentration on the formula, undaunted by the distraction, and the orb began to glow slightly at the center. A portion of his mind went out to the ward and found it secure. No glow there to indicate attack from powers that would thwart his efforts. So far, so good.

In the amber glow of the orb, he could clearly see the Book of Shadows. It was open now, and the pages were turning as if by an unseen hand. Something was out there, whether it was in this realm or the aether, and it was using the book to locate him. He immediately suspended his spell and closed the book forcefully; he quickly traced a Kabbalistic ward for security and protection, bridging the inner circle of his ward and the book that lay at his knee. He settled his mind and was beginning to restart his formula when he heard the scraping sound. In the dim light of the orb, he could not see beyond ten feet, but the sound grew louder.

"Well," he said to no one but himself. "Looks like I disturbed something." He waited and watched, maintaining his concentration. Moments passed, then again from the blackness came the sound of scales on stone. His spell finally finished, he sat motionless, trusting in the ward to protect him from all but the most trivial physical and mental assaults. Cold comfort though, knowing the psychological strength he would need for what was coming.

He clutched at the talisman around his neck. It was then that he saw a blank emptiness rear before him, outlined by an ephemeral blue glow. Yet, to say that he saw something would be a misnomer, to say that he perceived it would be more accurate. It was darkness deeper than the blackest tunnel and, as the form rose in the vault of the catacomb, he could make out only two bright ruby points. He heard a rustling akin to the spreading of wings and what sounded like the clack of talons on the stone. Mike shivered.

It hissed and he understood, although it was not any language meant for human ears. It was a chaotic sound that grated on his nerves: the sound of nails on a chalkboard and a knife slipping on china. It was bones being shattered and the whine of steel turbines without lubricant. It was unholy and it intruded into his thoughts, echoing vilely in his brain.

Ahhh, you have summoned me. It screamed and tears ran down Mike's cheeks as the flames of pain coursed through him.

"I have performed the summoning, yes." Mike could almost feel the hot, acidic breath as it crouched beneath the vaulted ceiling. He wondered what he had gotten himself into by reading Trevor's old tomes.

You have summoned. Yet, you are afraid. This must be important for you to risk so much.

"It is," admitted Mike uneasily.

The creature hummed in quiet triumph. Hear well, you who are less than a mouthful to me: though I can be summoned, I am not easy to command. But, perhaps for a price I might be persuaded to serve you for a little while.

"What might that be?" Mike said as he felt a tug of power at his crystal. He also noticed that the ward had begun to glow with pale phosphorescence at the edges, but it was not broken. He wondered what the creature was up to.

253

Delaying tactics to allow assault on the ward? Whatever it was, it would do him no favor, of that he was sure.

Your book, it purred. Mike looked at the Book of Shadows, instinctively knowing it was not what the Daemon referred to. Chill's Bible?

Yes! It is trivial to exchange it for what you desire.

"I would not let your touch defile it. Besides, you do not know what I want."

Power and more. Give me the book!

"I have power," Mike said dramatically and focused on the image of amber energy lancing from the orb. The creature reared back and a howl of pain echoed in Mike's mind. He glowered in satisfaction. That will teach you, asshole!

Mortal! It shouted. Disturbed by the vibrations, a scree of pebbles cascaded through the rent in the chamber wall. Lines of power between the orb and the creature arced through the air. Do not toy with me! You have disturbed me from my sleep and brought me to shape in pain. You are not of this land. You dare exert power over me? I could destroy you with a word!

"You would have to know my true Name to do that. Just food for thought, maybe I know your true Name and I know the Souldeath, that spell which would banish you to oblivion."

The creature paused, its ruby eyes narrowing, and Mike sensed it was trying to probe him. His ward wavered at the attack, fading momentarily, but then his crystal flared and the ward was reinforced. Mike smiled faintly in appreciation of his own ability; making a silent sigh of relief at the success of his bluff.

What do you wish, mortal? The thoughts were saturated with contempt and hatred.

"Who brought us here and why? Where is the one called Surik Shadowlord?"

You ask me three questions. Yet, simple answers I do not give; three questions, three answers, three answers, three riddles.

Mike hesitated. The Daemon was cunning and he had not anticipated this type of response. But, it was better than nothing and they had the time.

"Very well. Go on."

Who brought you here is he who is cast in like power, yet does not understand your realm.

His relative grand is same to brother's hand. Companions' ties, among choices, but beware if the White's Soul dies.

The Daemon paused maliciously, letting the incomprehensible words hang in the air. Then he took up again.

What is wanted is that which you possess, and what you possess is unknown.

You must create that of death.

It wields not death, but its wielder. Fire and steel bound, it is mundane Yet profound.

Once more the creature paused, giving time for Mike to memorize the verse. Then it continued again.

Surik is to be bound by will, by Name, by she who serves the dark flame. He'll be bound at the new, for the old, to serve the dark, on the Green Sea. It stopped and waited.

Great, Mike thought. We can't get much more ambiguous. He thought for a moment, but then let the light of the orb fade slightly. "You may go back to the pit that spawned you. I am finished."

Yes, you are, it hissed. Then in passing: But, beware mortal. I am not finished with you! You are now marked for all to see and know you for what you are! A searing pain flashed across Mike's forehead making him gasp.

It was gone then, leaving the air in the chamber less oppressive. Mike felt his forehead tenderly; there was a welt there the size of a half-dollar, but no blood. The candles immediately sparked to life and Mike put forth a cleansing spell that removed all traces of power from the area. He now did not have to worry about the ward. Standing, he stretched and stepped outside the chalk circle.

He did not notice the newly made blood-red runes on the topmost page of the Book of Shadows.

"Riddles?" John shook his head.

"I know, I should have anticipated that, but in the heat of the moment..." Mike sighed and threw his gear onto the packhorse. He smoothed back the bandana he wore; hiding the mark the daemon had left on his forehead. The outlanders were preparing to leave in the early morning, Torec and his men with them. The mercenaries had decided to stay in the company of the group, having acquired enough spoils from Gelion's hold to support them for a while.

"The old and the new. By the Green Sea? I wish I knew more about this land." Tom adjusted the strap on his saddle and checked the bit. Torec, who had been listening, interrupted.

"Hal, quat os Paravel," he said, and when everyone looked at him blankly he spoke in Common tongue. "The Green Sea. The Port of Paravel. It is a free city, but the Conclaveum controls a great portion of its dealings. They have a large garrison there and some say they control the governor's purse strings. This time of year, the sea plants are in full growth and the cast of the water is green."

"Paravel...and you say that the Conclaveum has a garrison there?" John questioned with a raised eyebrow.

"Yes, Lord Knight. The Lord Protector is of the Conclave, but the Governor is not. But, if one fills the Governor's coffers..." he trailed off, the allegation of corruption implicit.

"That would be our best bet then. These guys we're chasing must have struck out for Paravel after the attack on Galfeon Yor. But, why?"

"At least that would explain why we did not cross paths with them," Torec continued. "They would have taken the pass at the Tarn Range, just North of the Great Forest."

"Is there a faster way?" Tom asked.

"One other, but it is more treacherous. The Tarn route is easier, but it wends long through the foothills. If we go through the Northern Ghisik Pass, we put ourselves in the Wastes, but north of the Range. If Oran is sleeping, it would put us in Paravel nearly at the same time they would arrive, given their head start."

"Good, we'll go that way then." Tom thumped his palm into the saddle and looked to his friends; they nodded their agreement.

"Any clues as to who she who serves the dark flame is?"

"Myella," Torec sneered. "She is the Surrogate of the South, and holds

Gelion's leash. She bows to no one but Oran, a dark and evil god."

"He'll be bound by Name," Bill said. Clicking his tongue while he thought on the riddle.

"Naming magic. If you know the true name of the being, you can control it. Or kill it," Mike said matter-of-factly.

"What about the other riddles? Who brought us here?" John felt that any answer would confuse him all the more.

"Hey, let's not confuse the issue anymore that it is," Tom said, looking to

Mike. "The first riddle is ambiguous enough."

"Not really, but until we get more information about this land we can't put it together. We know that we're supposed to possess some kind of power, but what? And what is the White's Soul?" He shook his head and walked back to his tent.

"Well, that's that," John murmured, but the others caught the note of sarcasm in his voice.

"I just love being kept in the dark," Bill muttered.

"Don't we all?" Tom said, wondering if the Daemon, or whatever, could be trusted to tell the truth.

The horse stepped carefully over a twisted root and John moved fluidly with the motion, mindful of the branches that swung toward his face. His black cloak was covered with fine droplets of mist, and he could almost feel the cold clawing at his bones. The weather had taken a turn for the worse, and with the cool air came fog and rain. He could barely perceive the riders fore and aft of him and the sounds of his companions were muffled. His katana rested in the crook of his arm. Earlier, it had caught on a tree limb and he didn't want to risk losing it. His horse stumbled. They were following the trails up through the woods, into a more remote spur of the range; there was a pass there that would hopefully prove a shortcut. The deer path ran parallel to a swollen stream, its white waters rushing over dark stones and bounding down past the riders amid ferns and trees. Everything was wet and green and alive.

Except Chill.

He tightened the grip on his scabbard, and the leather gloves he wore creaked.

"Just where are we?" Bill voice echoed through the mist. He was somewhere behind John, along with Mike. Somewhere in front were Tom, Torec, and Garis.

"Near the Ghisik Pass," Garis called back, gravel in his voice. When he had said it one of the other mercenaries muttered something and was summarily hushed by another.

"Why the unease?"

"There is an old, abandoned watchtower there. We must be wary."

"Watchtower," commented Tom. "Why?"

"Years and years ago, this was a well-traveled trade route to the North. The Conclaveum built several watchtowers along the path to spy out bandits and raiders, and to garrison the White Guardsmen. Now that the North is cut off, the towers are more likely to house the raiders themselves, or worse. There is a tower in the Great Forest near Narn-toc, the dead city, and one some leagues into the Waste where a great battle took place, and the ground is scorched. Sorcery."

"Sounds lovely," John quipped, and, as the riders tightened their formation, they listened intently.

"During the Seat War, a Great Wall was erected by the most powerful mages to ward off any sorcerous or military attack. You may see a small part of it when we reach the Plains of Straw. The Great Wall is vast, and it reaches from the Doran Range all the way to Qwen. Leagues and leagues onward, a road runs atop the length, and it takes a full month on horse at a steady gait to go from end to end. No attack has ever breached it. Hundreds of years have passed since it was conjured. Those who fled from the Conclaveum now make up the cities and freeholds of the South. The Conclaveum is only a shadow of its former self and has retreated behind the Wall with its Legions. It tried to reclaim what it once governed; the Seat was in Narn-toc, but not anymore."

"Why is it called the Dead City?" Tom inquired.

"Sorcery. A great evil happened there. All the souls were lost and no one will return because the stones speak the words of the dead. It is overgrown and in ruins. "The sorcerers fled from the evil, and what was done, and went to the north and west along the coast. Little villages and towns began to pop up as the people of the middle reaches were displaced. They were protected by the Tarn Range and the boundary of the Great Forest."

"Torec, you are just a fountain of information," Mike called.

"I studied much in my youth, the benefit of being born to a wealthy family."

"You know," began John, as he pulled up the hood of his cloak to ward off the larger raindrops that had begun to fall. "I wonder if the Conclaveum is all that bad. It sounds like any large Empire, like Rome."

"The Conclaveum has been around for a long time, but I am not wholly versed in its history to the extent I would wish. All people can be good or evil, but much depends on the ruler." Torec turned his horse and forded the stream at a relatively calm point in its cascade. The path resumed on the other side. "I have never been to the interior, but I have known many of its citizens. There are those who are like you or me, and there are those who are cruel and evil, caught up in arrogance and greed.

"Evil is a very cunning thing, it is often difficult to recognize until it spits you in the eye. And then it is usually too late," Torec finished as the path widened to a haphazardly cobbled road. Middle-aged trees thrust their way up through the center of this sparsely traveled thoroughfare and the bricks were cracked and rounded with age. The riders kept the stream in sight and the forest thinned as they came upon a rocky substratum. Oaks and maples gave way to pines and firs, grasping tenuously to the meager soil, and the

261

stream became a series of rapids. The road veered away to twist through the conifers and hairpin its way up to the Ghisik Pass. Occasionally, the path would reunite with the river and they would pause to let their steeds water. The rain continued, seemingly gaining intensity as they neared the pass.

"We should be at the Pass by nightfall," Garis rumbled as he chomped on a piece of dried beef. "We should seek shelter in the watchtower."

"If it is not already inhabited," growled another mercenary, Meshek by name. He jerked his hand across his eyes as a warning. "Alqion quis tuion et ien, koris tij'el estitien."

"What?" Bill asked. He wiped away strands of rain-drenched hair.

"Folklore, Bard. Superstition," Garis replied. "There are supposed to be wraiths in the Ghisik Pass. It's named after a certain sorcerer of the Conclaveum who held the pass against a sizable force that was to supply the battling armies on the middle reaches; they ran out of food in the fight and were left to devour human flesh. It is his tower that we will spend this night in."

"Great," the Bard muttered.

The wind picked up toward nightfall and the rain increased. They had left the firs behind some time ago, and their steeds moved single file up the narrow road. On both sides, there rose the granite and basalt spine of the Tarn Range. Occasionally, a rope of mud and pebbles would slide into the path and they would sidestep their horses around it. Rivulets and miniature waterfalls fed a small stream that ran down the center of the defile and, with the increasing downpour, the cobbled road became a slippery and dangerous path. Soon the wall on their left side dropped away revealing a cataract of boulders, rapids and the remains of twisted trees, fed by a higher source in the range. The road climbed on past these rapids and soon their rumble dimmed as the party moved upward. Eventually, they came to the point in the pass where another falls cascaded straight down into a large pool. The old road passed along the face of the mountain and behind the falls. Here dead trees and rotted trunks sprung from the earth in twisted agony.

Bill noticed that they had now come to the apex of the pass. As the white water fell into an eddying pool, it spilled back the way they had come and now also flowed the way they were going by forming a new set of rapids to the North. If the weather hadn't been so foul, it would have been a sight to see, even now it was fearsome to behold.

"Here the Tarn Range shares its water with the north and south." Called Torec as they passed under the falls and to a brief respite from the storm. "The Watchtower is only a little further, and we shall follow the stream for a way more until–" His words were cut short by Meshek yelling in dismay as his horse slipped to the side on the decomposing granite. The horse scrabbled to regain its footing as Meshek instinctively reached out and grabbed the nearest thing; it happened to be Bill.

Too late. Without warning, Meshek's horse lost its footing under the falls, pulling its rider down and knocking Bill from his saddle in the process. The horse and Meshek were swept into the swirling torrent. Bill grabbed desperately for a dead limb and managed to snag it. He hung there as Meshek's horse splashed ten feet below into the water and was quickly swept away to the north with the swollen rush. He grasped at the bark but a big chunk just peeled away. He then tried to scramble up, but his feet could find no purchase on the slick rocks. With one last effort Bill pulled on the branch, but it sheared from the rock.

"Do you see him?" shouted Tom over the deluge. He slipped in the mud and was almost drawn over into the crevasse himself. Garis quickly grabbed his arm and pulled him away. The rain had obscured his limited vision; he thought he saw a dark form, but then it was gone. John shook his head and tried to edge over, but it was too risky. The waterfall was raging now and the rain was a curtain before their eyes. "Bill!" they called in unison, but to no avail. Nothing could be heard or seen through the water

"He'll be okay," Mike called and pulled the two from the edge. They went reluctantly, wondering at the musician's fate. "There was a ridge down there, if they didn't land on that, we'll just have to look downstream. There's nothing we can do out here."

"We will look for him when the storm breaks, it is too dark," Torec yelled. He turned and immediately faded into the downpour.

"They're right." Tom peered at John from about six inches away. They were soaked to the bone. "Torec went ahead to the old tower. Let's go." The two held onto each other and went along the road, leading their horses.

They almost ran into the tower wall before they could see it; looking up, they could make out its shadow, but that was about all. Bare of any exterior design, the stone was dense black. Tom and John made their way through a low portal and were greeted with a stale, dry interior. There was a spark of light and soon Garis had a small fire going as the two collapsed against the aging wall, ignoring for a moment the stream of water that cascaded over the stones from an opening somewhere above.

"Get out of those clothes," Garis warned as he stoked the fire. They soon stood naked and wrapped in blankets while their garments dried by the fire. The horses were all huddled in the back of the large chamber and they added extra warmth.

Tom sighed and set Kiera down to roam freely on the floor. John slid to his knees and absorbed the heat emanating from the blaze.

"Drink this," Torec said as he handed them a wine skin. They drank sparingly; it wasn't wine, rather it was a strong heady liquor. "Don't worry, the Bard is probably hunkered down beneath a ridge and working on a ballad."

John smiled weakly at the thought and stared into the fire. Tom looked up at the structure they sat in. In its day, it must have been impressive but now it was a hollow ruin. He looked up through rotting floorboards to the next story and beyond; nothing remained except a few nests and some rotting beams, yet it still stood more than eighty feet tall. Luckily, the roof had not been damaged or ruined otherwise they would be getting drenched. Inside, the walls were covered with moss and webs. Some of the stones were cracked, but none were in too bad shape. The Sioux looked across twenty feet to the opposite wall, noting that even in this state of disrepair it was a stout structure.

"That smells good," John whispered as he watched Garis place some dried rabbit in a stew pot. Its aroma wafted throughout the chamber alerting each man to his hunger.

"How long will this last?" Tom asked Torec, the boom of thunder was even louder and the wind howled through the top of the tower.

"I know not," the merchant replied as he pulled off his brass helm and wiped his brow with a dry cloth. He leaned back, almost exhausted by the struggle with the elements. His usually dark skin was ashen. Tom sensed something was wrong, not only with Torec, but with the weather itself.

"Torec, what is it?" the Sioux pressed.

"Never have I experienced such a deluge, never. Do you sense it?"

"Yes. The intensity." Tom almost understood the feeling. John looked at his friend trying to feel what he felt. It was vague.

"Its suddenness was astounding. One moment it is a normal downpour the next a deluge. The gods are not with us this day." Torec leaned back and watched as his men huddled close to the fire. Smoke drifted upward into the natural flue; their clothes would be dry soon.

Tom looked over to see Mike sitting cross-legged and staring right at him. This sent a chill down his spine, but then Mike gave him that silly psychotic look and turned away.

"I hope he's all right," John said in the flickering light. He laid his cloak out and curled into the fetal position.

"So do I," Tom replied. "I hope we all come out of this all right."

Chapter 15

Joe sat hunched and shackled in front of a small cooking fire. The sun had long since set and the sounds of the night played upon his ears. He looked across at his guards as they occasionally spoke in the tongue of the Conclaveum, but more often than not they just let the nocturnal sounds of the forest keep them company. Joe glanced up at the fine points of stars as the wisps of smoke from their fire mingled with others about the encampment. There was a low murmur of voices and, occasionally, a sharp command or laugh would ring out through the camp. As he looked at the men across from him, he observed their black and gold livery and the emblem of a dagger encircled by a ring of fire. He also noticed their long swords with intricate basket hilts, burnished steel flickering in the light of the flames. Tents glowed from within, hinting at a warmth that had left him some time ago.

A smaller contingent had split off from this one earlier in the day, and with them Duran. Joe felt oddly abandoned; at least Duran was a familiar enemy. Now, he had no idea who held him or why. And he was chilly. With no cloak or blanket, the air was seeping into his bones and the fire gave him no comfort. He lifted the shackles on his wrists and considered the iron links, then shrugged and drank some lukewarm Karo. He had cleared his bowl of whatever thin gruel remained, sopping it up with a hard roll, but still his stomach rumbled. At least they had let him relieve himself.

The two guards laughed suddenly and looked over to the gray-eyed artist. They were both clean-shaven and had short dark hair. Both spoke Common without accent.

"Myella will want you tonight, outlander." One spoke and the other smiled slightly. "I do not envy you."

"Why?" Joe asked, and the other looked at him with black eyes.

"You are the Shadowlord. You must know some sorcery. You would be best to use what you know to get away."

"Yes," the other replied, feeding into the sarcasm. "Or would you prefer cold steel in your heart?" They both laughed at that. Joe chuckled also, then suddenly kicked out with both feet sending the burning branches into their laps. Hot embers and coals set their tunics afire; they jumped up and away, swatting furiously at the hot ashes that burned them.

Joe was up on his feet and running.

"Alarm!" The shout brought various groups to their feet with weapons drawn and wary looks. Joe moved fast as he ran through the camp heading for the edge of the forest. Hands bound, he leapt over a cooking fire, darted between two lieutenants and butted one aside with his shoulder. Soon ten men were pursuing him between the tents. He deftly avoided the stakes and tie-downs, hearing others trip as they pursued.

The forest was ahead, a direct line, but three men with swords cut him off. He dodged to the side and around a dimly lit tent. No guards, no fire. He stopped, breathed heavily. By the sounds of it, his pursuers were going in another direction. He had to get the shackles off. He ducked into the nearest tent...

"Well, Surik Shadowlord, what do you think of my accommodations?" Myella, Surrogate of the South and High Priestess of Oran asked of the artist. Joe looked around stunned, then turned to flee but the tent flaps had disappeared. There seemed no hope for escape. He wanted to blame this mess on Mike, just for the hell of it, but knew full well that his own libido had brought him down.

"I really don't care for it." He scratched his beard and took measure of her: as gorgeous as ever. She wore a rose colored robe that had cleavage down to mid- chest. Her overtly sexual nature clung to her as tightly as the robe that strained to hold her ample breasts in check. Brushing back her long, straight brown hair, she artfully arranged herself on the divan, one leg languidly swinging over the armrest."

"Tell me about your power."

"What power?" the look on Joe's face would have been comical in another situation.

"Do not play games with me Surik."

"I don't intend to." Then he straightened rather haughtily. "You do seem to have me at a loss. What is it exactly that you want?"

"You," she stated simply. Her fingers played with the hem of her robe. "I'm flattered, but I don't have any power."

"Lies, Shadowlord, do not become you."

He was getting frustrated at this line of questioning. He looked around the tent for

270

anything that he could use as a weapon, but there was nothing. Pillows and bolsters lay on the floor in a random manner. There were also rich rugs and tapestries to ward off the cool of the night. Her divan was the only one, and what light there was came from an open iron brazier sitting next to her; the glow played on the deep burgundies and yellow ochres of the silks and linens. The rear of the tent was lost in shadow. She had obviously intended herself to be the center of his attention, he noted with amusement.

"I know that you are from another realm. I can read the aura that surrounds you and it is of a realm alien to us."

Now he was totally lost. How she knew that he came from another reality was totally beyond him. Is it that obvious? "Why did you bring me here?" he asked.

"I did not bring you here, Surik. Another had that task; but that is unimportant. What is important is that you and your friends are valuable to certain parties. You bring special qualities that we wish to harness."

"Listen," Joe began as she stood and approached him. Her hair cascaded in a wash of raw sienna and her animal beauty once again began to invade his senses. "We don't pose any threat to you, we—"

"On the contrary. Your friends have already done something that could not be easily accomplished. They have succeeded in killing the Regent Gelion and have burned his Keep to the ground. That accomplishment alone tells me there is power in you. Of course I knew something like

271

that would happen when I stole you. But I will have you and your power to use, regardless of the damage done to others."

"What if I don't want to be used?" he asked and watched as she smiled. That worried him.

"I don't expect you to do anything willingly, Surik." She gestured and his bonds fell to the floor.

"Your use of the 'Force' is commendable." He rubbed his wrists and watched her as she went to a small table and poured a glass of wine.

"What?" she was unsure of the comment.

"Never mind." He smiled thinly as she tasted the deep red vintage. She returned his smile seductively and pressed the glass into his hands.

"Drink," she commanded. He shook his head. "No thanks, I'm driving."

"Drink," she insisted coldly. He felt his hand move of its own volition. He felt it at his mouth. Then, as his body shook in trying to restrain the glass, his mouth opened and the fluid coursed down his throat. As the drink warmed him, he regained control and threw the glass across the tent. It thudded weakly on a thick pillow.

"Now, Surik Shadowlord, Master of the Shades, Rider of the Black Dragon, I bind you by Name. Baluk Nictu, et'geral ien Surik."

His vision blurred momentarily and he felt a rush. He froze, not knowing what was going on. Was he under the influence of some drug or was it magic? Probably both, he decided and watched Myella's robe drop to the floor.

"Most of the sluggishness will wear off in a few days. But, you will be totally mine. Come to me."

His consciousness fled as his body automatically obeyed her; it was the last thing he remembered.

John awoke with a start, sensing something different around him; he realized what it was. The storm had finally broken leaving a deadly silence behind. He brushed his blanket aside and sat up. Others were just waking also; Tom was rolling his bedding and tying it off.

"What's up?" John asked groggily.

"It stopped about fifteen minutes ago. I think we should go out and find Bill." He slung his knife and its sheath over his shoulder; his roll was over his back, his sword tucked into the folds. John dressed hastily and all were soon outside the abandoned tower. John shook his head in wonder. The morning sky was clear except for a few trailing clouds, and the stones of the pass were clear and free of any residual sediment.

The water level at the base of the runoff, however, had risen sharply, and where there was once a ledge was now five feet of water. It rushed in a white froth over the north edge of the natural dam. There was no trace of the Bard at all.

"I fear we have lost him," Torec remarked grimly. Garis searched the edge and found a bit of cloth, but there was no sign of Meshek or the two horses.

"Bill is a strong swimmer," Tom said as he looked down the descending path of the Ghisik Pass. The road still followed the shallow falls.

"He will have to be. There is a two hundred foot falls around the bend. Let us hope the Bard was conscious and managed to grab an outcropping or tree." Torec mounted his horse and the others followed suit. Mike, John, and Tom looked at each other and hoped, prayed, that Bill had survived the deluge.

A trail of water led from the bank of the shallows to the limp form of the Bard. Miraculously, he had dragged himself from the rapids before collapsing from exhaustion. He had nothing left but his blue jeans and Chill's old hunting knife strapped to his belt. John's estoc was somewhere at the bottom of the lake at the base of the falls.

Bill lay unconscious on the bank; his wild ride had taken him in minutes to a place his friends could never reach before mid-morning. But he was not alone.

Four figures, hidden in swaths of leather and cloth obscuring all but their eyes, crouched warily observing the fallen man. After a time, one leaned down to examine him, observing his strange breeches and boots. They rolled him over; he shuddered and, although he failed to wake, his chest rose and fell in steady rhythm. The four exchanged glances, and the one who had examined him nodded. They lifted the Bard and began careful descent to the base of the falls.

The column spread out through the plains, having left the Tarn Range behind some time ago. The Guard of Oran was making excellent speed now that the majority of soldiers had split off to the North, heading back to its garrison at the Great Wall. Now, only one hundred acted as escort to Myella on her white stallion, with Surik Shadowlord riding by her side. Every few leagues, he would lean over the side of the saddle and vomit violently, losing all he had eaten earlier that day. She smiled, almost lovingly and patted him on the back. He looked back at her, pale and drawn.

"What the hell are you doing to me?" he muttered, wiping the spittle from his mouth. He looked longingly to his sword, strapped to the pommel of her horse.

"Why, Surik, being the great Necromancer that your title implies, I would think that you would know."

He lifted his head slightly and felt a slow throbbing at the base of his skull; at least it had eased form the sheer agony that had woken him in the morning. She sighed and went on.

"The Naming is a complex spell. I used your true and full name, bound with a potion of ichor. You will be all too happy to do anything for me once you are fully bound by it; it suppresses the will and your spirit will cleave to me. I promise to reward you with infinite pleasure, but I also swear unrelenting pain if you resist. In time, you will forget your former life and come to enjoy the one I give you. At that point, I will introduce you to my Uncle."

"What?" Joe had barely followed that; his mind was clouded with pain. It seemed to race up and down his spine and reach out through his eyes.

"Mage Guyle, my Uncle. Dear Shadowlord, he is your host...he is the one that brought you here."

"Here? Where are we?"

"Hmmm." She laughed. The column moved on. It was a fortnight to Paravel.

"There's his steed!" Torec called and pointed to a shallow. He dismounted and hurried over to find the carcass of Meshek's horse still with its pack, but no rider. It floated there swirling in the eddy between two great rocks. White water rushed around the calm pool and in the distance they could hear the slow steady rumble of a longer series of rapids.

"You don't see..." John trailed off. "The Bard? No."

Tom moved himself further down the road and he too dismounted and peered closely at the ground. "Mud," he said and Mike looked at him quizzically.

"It's all over the place, Tom." The big man shifted on his horse and watched

Torec go to Tom's side.

"No, this comes from the water; it looks like someone dragged himself out. Then–"

"About four?" Tom looked at him and after a moment the merchant of Clef nodded.

"What?" John asked.

"There were maybe four people who carried him."

"Who?"

"Conclaveum, bandits, who knows. The watchtower in the wastes has a small garrison." Garis shrugged.

"Was it Bill or Meshek?" John peered hard at the spot wondering how they had gotten all that information.

"Don't know," Tom replied and mounted his steed. "We'll just have to follow the trail to find out."

The Northern side of Ghisik Pass was even more treacherous than the Southern ascent, and probably took just as long. Few trees grew on this side of the Tarn Range and the expanse that lay before them was a dusty, rolling plain. Soon they found themselves at the base of the range, riding around the eastern rim of the lake. Here there were a few trees and their leaves rustled in a moderate breeze.

John was keeping his eyes on the dirt road before him when he saw the lifeless form that lay on the banks of this small lake; it was among the rocks and reeds. He spurred his horse forward and left the others behind. Leaping from his steed he waded into the water and pulled the body to the shore. Pale and limp, he pushed the tangled mess of hair back to reveal...Meshek.

He sagged in relief and leaned back on his haunches.

"I am sorry, Torec," John said as he heard the men dismounting behind him. Torec looked at the body.

"He was a fine swordsman and a good man, Lord Knight. It was a wasteful way to die."

They realized, after they had buried the mercenary, that they had to make a decision regarding the trail of Bill. Here, at the base of the falls, Tom noted that the group that had carried Bill had split apart. Some of the tracks continued on the road running east along the Tarn Range. The others headed due north.

"Now we have a decision to make," Garis said as he leaned forward in his mount, his belly touching the saddle horn.

This is certainly no land of dreams, John thought. More like a nightmare.

Chill, then Joe was lost, now Bill, who was next?

"Listen," Tom began as he scratched Kiera's ears. "I'll take some of Torec's men. We'll follow the trail north and, with any luck, catch up with whoever has Bill. We can assume he isn't dead because they didn't take Meshek's body. You guys head east after the other two – at least that will keep you on the road to Paravel–"

"Come on, Tom!" John looked disgusted. "Separate? We're spread so thin now that it's a wonder we haven't been captured or killed. I'm not doubting your ability to track, but I think it would be better if we all went."

"And do what?" the Sioux asked quietly. "Muddle along with our heads up our ass? With just five men I can make better speed than a group of thirty. At least you, Mike, and Torec can get a start toward Paravel and find Joe, maybe."

"That's a lot of maybes," John replied, but if that was what Tom wanted to do, then who was he to argue. Tom looked around expecting more dissent, but there was none. Mike and John were at that point where the situation seemed hopeless anyway. They were grasping at straws.

Bill's first sight was that of a dark silhouette standing above him, but it soon faded and he was alone. The last thing he remembered was the wall of water that had swept him down the rapids. Then the desperate struggle for the bank, swim or drown.

He cracked his eyes open. He lay on leather and furs in some type of log dwelling. A small fire blazed in a pit at the center of the floor, warming a pot. The walls were adorned with skins and antlers, and the mantel held a collection of daggers and knives. His knife, Chill's knife, was one of them.

He didn't realize how sore he was until he tried to sit up; then every muscle protested and he sank back to the bedding. He tried to roll over and realized that his torso was wrapped in leather. Gingerly, he touched his side and winced, feeling the swelling and the pain of a broken rib. That explained why it hurt to breathe. Whoever it was who'd brought him here had done a fine job though, and he would thank him. He finally managed to get to his knees and look over the rim into the pot. Glorious food, he thought. He was ravenous. He was about to dip his finger in the pot when he heard a rustle at the door.

"I would not do that," came a husky feminine voice. It was thick with an odd accent.

"What is it," he said without turning.

"Your breeches." He looked down and realized that he was naked. He quickly pulled the furs about his waist, all the while blushing greatly. Then he turned and looked at his host.

Her flaxen hair was catching the last of the sunlight that streamed through the open door and Bill's eyes widened in surprise. She had a long thick mane swept back to one side. She was dressed rather oddly, almost mummy-like. Long strips of leather and linen wrapped her arms and

279

legs and also bound her from her hips to neck. There was a short sword strapped to her side and in her hand she held a mask and hood.

"It is not wise to travel the Ghisik Pass in such a storm, there are Kienta...wraiths."

"Yeah, well, I didn't see any of those," he replied, noticing that her clothing made her appear rather like a wraith herself. He didn't quite know what to say. She was appraising him, her eyes traveling from his chest to his arms, and from his golden hair to his feet. He returned her gaze and did the same. She would come to his chin in height and her shoulders were broad and strong. Her legs were long and well-toned and she carried herself proudly.

"Were you traveling alone?" she asked. "We were split up in the storm."

"Ah, we saw others near the lake. You are not of the Conclaveum?"

"No, we journey from the South. We were looking for the Northern route to Paravel."

"You must be careful, for the Pillagers of the North keep their Towers ever ready; their soldiers are notable." She walked past him and rifled through a chest. Then she turned and tossed him a pair of leather breeches. "Put them on."

He did what she said. She would not look away, so he turned his back to her, gasping in pain as he bent to pull them up.

"Now, I must take you before the hudef. You must give us reason not to kill you."

Tom looked at Garis and the group of mercenaries as they surmounted a small ridge and surveyed the rocky, gully filled land before them.

They had left the others some time ago, following the meager trail that the two, and now four again, had left. It was obvious that Bill's captors had only split up to confuse possible pursuers. He toyed with the idea of sending a rider back to tell John and Mike, but he didn't want to weaken what force he had. The sun had set some time ago, so they decided to set camp and have small fire. It was a waste of time to track at night; they would pick up the trail in the morning. He knew Bill well enough to hope the Bard would have a chance to leave some kind of mark or signal.

"Smiling Wolf," Garis began as he dropped from his saddle and stretched his pot-bellied frame. "It would not be wise to build a large fire. We are near the Watchtower of the Conclaveum and they have special means to detect such things."

"Where is the Watchtower, Garis?"

The fat man looked to the sky, getting his bearings from the stars. The man pointed in what would be a northwest direction. "About ten leagues in that direction." Tom looked, his impaired vision unusually clear this night. He didn't know if it was his diet or the new physical regimen, but he actually felt better and stronger.

They built a small cooking fire and shielded it. Tom chewed on what had to be a version of trail-mix while Garis spitted and roasted a rabbit. The man offered the Sioux a haunch.

"Thanks, I think," Tom said as he ate the rangy meat. Finally he rolled onto his bedding. He kept his knife extra close that night.

High atop the Watchtower, the lens of a spyglass pierced the night. It was not an ordinary glass, but one that was enhanced by magic and therefore could perceive the night as if it were day. Normally, the man peering through it would have been bored beyond belief, but this night he was not. A large contingent of troops had passed through earlier and left intriguing information of what had transpired in the south.

The guard remembered the Troop Captain. He was a tall man in black with the traditional uniform of the Black Guard of the Wall: black tunic overriding chain mail, emblazoned with the stylized Wall and Sun of the Conclave. The man had been brief and to the point, but had taken the time to water his horses and have his men refreshed. While doing so, he had told of unrest in the South, of the death of the Regent Gelion, and of the taking of Galfeon Yor. The Watch Commander had been surprised at the goings-on, and even more surprised to learn that some fools might be pursuing the column on its way to the Wall City of Helm.

So it was with anticipation that the watcher looked out through the magical spyglass atop a tower built ages ago. He looked to the west. There was nothing there except the wastes, a few herd tribes, and the mountains beyond. There were a few small villages and Tarn Hold nearer the Tarn Range, and supposedly a bandit camp not far from the Ghisik Falls. To date they had been hidden, but the bandits had successfully killed five messengers, one on a courier beast. Once they had even attempted a foray at the Tower. He smiled with a gap-tooth grin at how their score of guardsmen had frightened off a group of sixty; their mage had

282

done considerable damage with his flames. But, that had been some time ago. Now, as he sat and listened to his comrades reveling below, he turned to the south near the Ghisik Pass.

"Nothing there, ner," it was fractured Common he spoke. The best and the brightest of the Conclaveum did not serve their terms in the Watchtowers. He scratched at a cat that rubbed against his leg and peered more intently at something that caught his eye. He adjusted the glass.

"Heh, wot is this?" He watched a flicker of fire and saw a small band of men camping on the far side of a hillock, and further to the West...a village? Hidden by a grove of trees laid bare in the storm last night? Why hadn't he seen it before?

With thoughts of the Captain from the North and his tales of campaigns in Galfeon Yor, he quickly opened the hatch in the flooring, descending the ladder into a room that contained maps and arms. He then trotted down the stair and into the common room where the Commander talked with the other men.

He reported his findings of the village and the men, and the Commander made a decision.

It would not be boring much longer.

Bill stared at the group before him. All were similarly attired as the girl in whose hut he had been. They were solid men and women, yet all had that cagy look in their eyes, as if they were awaiting a fight and had to be constantly wary. Raiders? came the Bard's fleeting thought. Bandits? He looked about. Some seemed openly hostile to his presence. All told, there were about

283

eighty, including children, but there were not very many elders. Then, as the girl that had bandaged his ribs stepped aside, the crowd opened and an old woman came forth. Bill stepped back.

She stepped forward and roughly grabbed his arm, pulling him close. The grip was tight and Bill fought down a yell as pain lanced through his side. To say that she was ugly would have been an understatement. Her face was scarred and covered with intricate tattoo work. Whoever she was, her authority was obvious.

She spoke in a trilling tongue that he could not fathom. A murmur ran through the group.

Bill looked over his shoulder to the girl. She frowned, then whispered in his ear.

"Our hudef says that you are a demon and come from the Underworld. You are not of this land and will only bring death. She says that you must submit to her or die."

"Like hell I will." Bill looked at the woman and shuddered. The hudef motioned to some men who were obviously guards or warriors of some kind. They stepped forward and brandished their swords. What he wouldn't do for his estoc. Then with inspiration: "I belong to her." He gestured to the girl who looked rather surprised.

"Knowing I was not a demon, she wrapped my wounds." The crowd was evidently shocked by what he had said and a murmur ran through the group that stood in the circular yard amid the low dwellings.

"No!" the old woman grew angry and struck Bill in the side with a short stick. He cried out and crumpled to the ground in pain, clutching at his

284

ribs. The girl quickly stepped over him and stood in front of the hudef.

"Do not challenge me, Tar'elah. I will kill you!" the hudef shouted and brought forth a knife.

"You do not have to treat him so, he is injured."

"He feigns injury, he is not of this world!" with that the old woman motioned to the men and they brought Bill to his feet. He groaned loudly and his breath came in short gasps. "I shall treat him as I wish, he is bound to me!"

"No!" Tar'elah replied. "I have healed him, he is rightfully indebted to me." The hudef screamed and leapt toward the girl, her knife flashing in the moonlight. Both women twisted and danced eerily in the pale glow of the moon. Bill watched them fall and roll, too hurt to voice his objections. What's going on?

He watched as the older woman brought her blade up and was about to thrust it up into the jaw of Tar'elah who struggled to hold it off, but was wavering. Then, suddenly, the girl twisted her legs to the side and rolled on top of the other woman. She wrenched the dagger from the hudef and thrust it into her opponent's thigh. The old woman screamed, trying in vain to twist away and succeeded in tearing open the wound. Tar'elah pulled the woman to her feet and tore her cloak from her, revealing a naked and darkly tattooed body. She kicked the woman in the pelvis and was pleased to her a loud snap. The hudef collapsed with a shriek and Tar'elah deftly broke her neck.

"I will not let some mad woman challenge my authority as leader of the Bar- t'lal," she said between gasps of air. There was a murmur and one of the men stepped forward, looking at the dead woman.

"It is bad luck to kill the hudef," he remarked dispassionately. Tar'elah looked at him and shook her head.

"Lies. She was mad. Is this man not flesh? It is not a demon that we found and healed. I have tolerated her long enough. She was the one who consorted with demons." Tar'elah turned and walked to Bill. Taking him by the hand she led him to her small log dwelling amid the birch and sycamore. Passing within, he could only remember the look on the hudef's face.

"Any movement?" Garis commented as he crawled on his fat belly to where Tom lay. They had found this small gully some time ago. Amid the rocky terrain was an oasis of sorts. Here was a small village amid birch and alder, pine and fir. Strangely enough, a dead body lay in the center of the village. Tom muttered a noncommittal reply to Garis and rubbed his eyes.

"Dammit," he whispered. He couldn't understand why his vision was doing that. It wasn't hot enough to create a mirage on the dry ground below, but his vision wavered almost like a split image. Finally, it cleared and he crawled back to where their horses were hidden.

"Well, Garis, what do you think?" Kiera curled around his neck, her claws bit into skin. He'd have to trim her nails soon.

"I know nothing of the people of this area. Nor do I speak their language. However, the attire of these people reminds me of a few bandits I killed some time ago. It would be unwise to rush down there, their customs may differ from ours, but I fear we have little time. We must be cautious, yet quick. A dilemma, my friend."

"I agree, we have to do something." Tom paused, then unslung his sword and handed it to Garis. He tucked his knife under the sweatshirt and put Kiera into his saddlebag.

"I'm going to find out if Bard William is down there. You stay here and, if I need help, then you can think of something. When I am ready I will give some sort of signal and you can come down. More than likely it will just be 'Hey, Garis!'" The Sioux smiled and trotted over the rise.

***

"Another league and we should be upon them," the Commander called to his men as he rode at the front of the party. He had emptied the tower of its ranks to strike at the bandits. His personal obsession had been to rid this region of bandits; now he felt he could do it in one swift, overwhelming strike. Long had he been waiting to find their holdings and this time he would teach them a lesson by not even sparing the smallest child.

At the center of the score of horsemen rode the mage, wrapped in a purple cloak and looking bored and aloof as he prepared his mind for his sorcery. The watchman who had reported the bandits sat next to him and grinned with glee. He was not bored.

Bill rolled over on the furs that Tar'elah had prepared for him. He felt the snug and newly wound wrap that bound his ribs and wondered how long it would take for them to heal. He looked across the room to see his rescuer's sleeping form. She lay there totally naked on her furs, her hair fanned out behind her to form a sandy halo. Bill didn't know what to think at first, but he realized that raw survival had a way of banishing any concept of modesty. He looked at her exquisite form and was stirred beyond his own fears. She lay on her back, mostly in shadow, yet the play of light made him only more aware of her femininity. He sighed and sat up, trying to locate his clothes in the dim light. He casually tossed his bedding aside and yawned.

"Good morn, Bard William D'Asturien, did you sleep well?" She sat up on her furs, running her fingers through her hair.

"Yes, very well." He adjusted his leather bandages. Last night he had told her and the others his story, leaving out of course the whole "other world" aspect, but including the fall of Galfeon Yor and his separation from the group during the deluge. She had informed him, quite candidly, that this was a bandit camp and they were often responsible for the raids that took place near and about the Ghisik Pass. She seemed quite proud of it in fact. Now, she watched him for a moment and smiled.

"No, I do not have a mate," she said with a grin.

"What?" Bill stammered as she gestured and he looked down. His face quickly turned beet red

288

and he had to pull the covers over himself. "I'm so embarrassed."

"Why?" she asked sincerely. Then she nodded in understanding. "Your customs are not the same as ours, Bard. We rely less on the word and more on the sign. I am sorry I told you that I had no mate when you had no actual intent–"

"No," he added quickly. "It's not that. It's just that you are very attractive...and... well there may be intent," he finished as she crawled towards him. She reached over and adjusted his wrappings.

"Then the intent is welcome. I did not save your life for naught. But, you must still prove yourself. Tell me more of yourself, and your friends." She was near him now and he could smell the scent of her in the close quarters of her dwelling. He went over his story again, adding more detail, telling her about Duran and the Conclaveum. She listened intently and when he was finished she laid her hand gently on his shoulder.

"You have come through much. I offer the assistance of the Bar-t'lal in the effort to reunite you with your friends. But, before that, you must do something for me."

"Anything, I owe you much."

"You are a minstrel, would you sing for me?"

He smiled, wishing he had an Ighuire, but even a capella his voice soared to the sky like a dove.

Tom Smiling Wolf recognized Bill's voice as soon as he came into the stand of birch. He was singing some damn love ballad and Tom grinned as he neared the dwellings. Trust Bill to warble his way out of a life-threatening situation.

He walked to the edge of the village; the early morning sun cast long shadows through the stand of trees and flung them across the wooden dwellings. Most of the people that were out and about had turned to the dwelling from which Bill's voice issued, and to this Tom walked, being careful not to antagonize them. Bill's song finally ceased and the Sioux found himself surrounded by five men wrapped in strange leather garments. They all held their swords like they knew how to use them.

"I am Smiling Wolf," he said and held his hands up. "I am the Bard's companion and I come in friendship and peace."

"My, aren't we cautious," remarked Bill as he stepped from the dwelling wearing just jeans.

"I should have known," Tom replied when he saw the girl emerge behind him. He shook his head.

"It's not what you think, Tom. This is Tar'elah, the leader of the Bar-t'lal. She rescued me from a very mean lady. Have I got a story for you."

"I'm sure you have, but right now I–"

His speech was cut short as the dwelling near the stand of trees exploded, sending fire and timber raining to the ground. The sound of screaming filled the air as they ran for cover.

Chapter 16

Dust and flame erupted from the ground. Incendiaries? Who's got bombs in this world? Tom thought fleetingly. He grabbed Bill by the arm and they ran for cover amid the stand of trees, Tar'elah on their heels. They ducked behind and outcropping of rock just as darkly armored horsemen appeared on the ridge opposite Garis' position.

Men and women scattered from the dwellings. Tar'elah was considerably shaken by the attack and she looked about, trying to direct her people through the chaos.

"This is my fault," Bill gasped as the fire ceased and he watched a man in a purple robe stand forth.

"No, we harry them. They must have surprised our sentry. I give credit to their mage." She seemed to be regaining some of her composure.

"Okay, okay, it's okay, guys." Tom smiled crookedly. "I can honestly say that this time we have a little surprise for our friends there." Tom winked and ducked out behind Bill and the woman, heading up to the blind side of the rise and to the hillock behind. He kept low to the ground using all of his training. He avoided even what would remotely reveal him from the cover of tree and rock. He was soon behind even Garis and the five mercenaries, and he crawled upon them cautiously.

"Hi guys," he whispered as Garis made a double take to his sudden appearance.

"We thought you lost, Smiling Wolf."

"Me too. Garis, do you have my bow?" Garis motioned for one of the men to fetch it. Tom took the bow and grabbed his sword from the heavy man. He winked.

"Take care of Kiera for a moment, will you?"

"But–" Before Garis could finish Tom was gone. Soon he was behind Bill and Tar'elah, peering over their shoulders.

"What did you do to your chest, Bill?" he asked nonchalantly.

"Broke a rib," replied the Bard, wondering what the Sioux was up to. "Too bad; is it set okay?" as he pulled an arrow from the quiver.

"Yeah, fine."

"Good." He smiled then turned to Tar'elah. She looked at the newcomer, curious. "What's the situation?"

"They have my people and they know it. The mage has set a wall of flame over there and has also ringed the horsemen with a protective barrier of flame. Now he waits and toys with them. My men and women will attack eventually and die in the attempt. That will leave the children." She said it without emotion.

"Your people use bows?"

"Small ones for hunting, nothing with rage."

Bill just looked at the two as if they were insane, then his head snapped around as ten men tried to attack the horsemen; they met a wall of flame. All died screaming, their flesh turning black as they fell, twisted and burned, to the ground "Okay, when I give the signal you and your people rush the horsemen. For God's sake you outnumber them almost three to one." He turned and disappeared. Bill could hear him grunt as he began to pull himself up a lonesome oak. Then he saw the tip of Tom's stainless steel arrowhead.

Tom adjusted his position and tested the pull of the re-curved bow. He smiled appreciatively as his muscles strained to hold it taught. Then he aimed at the mage. Not now! He silently cursed as his vision blurred and wavered. He was never that good at depth, but now his vision changed...there was a strange clarity, it was like...

He paused and lowered the bow. Something about his vision. He couldn't place it. Then the thought was lost and he aimed at the mage once more. The arrow snapped from the bow as he released the string. It flew true, finding its mark in the throat of the mage. The cloaked man dropped his staff and clutched at the fletching. Then he tumbled down the rise as his magical fires were extinguished.

"Toast!" Tom shouted and dropped from the limb. Bill saw what happened and, as Tom yelled for Garis, he motioned for Tar'elah to signal her people. Those who remained attacked fiercely. The small rise was quickly overtaken; the mounted men fell back and were met by another force of the vengeful bandits from the rear. Bill watched as the leader of the Guardsmen swung his blade to the right and left, but the agile fighters easily dodged the panicky arcs. Soon he was pulled to the ground and Bill had to turn away as the short swords rose and fell more times than was necessary. At the sight of their leader falling, the remaining Tower Guard began to realize just how outnumbered they were and began to back their horses the way they had come. Most of the guard soon fell, as more of the bandits dropped out of the oaks that lined the path to retreat. Soon the fray was ended; riderless horses were corralled and the remaining Guardsmen were bound and taken to the center of the small village.

"My thanks, Smiling Wolf," Tar'elah called as she went to where they were gathered. Garis and his men looked suspiciously at the bandit, but she smiled at them too.

"What will you do with them?" Bill asked, indicating the prisoners. Tom looked from behind, rubbing the eyelid of his glass eye. His vision had returned to normal and he still couldn't figure out what happened.

"Kill them."

"What?" Bill was incredulous.

"They would do the same, or worse." She reviewed all who remained from the invading force, a total of five. Then she stopped before the gap-toothed watchman whose face was twisted in a rictus of horror. She casually took her dagger and cut his throat. She then turned and walked past Bill and Tom to where her dwelling stood.

Bill watched in shock as the man spilled his life into the dry soil. He looked at one of the other bandits, questioning.

"What did she do that for?"

"She recognized him from a previous raid. She cut his throat because he did the same thing to her mate not eight moons ago."

Bill's eyes widened as Tom nodded and walked away.

Chapter 17

Paravel was, in the greatest of terms, a cosmopolitan city. Built up through the ages from a lowly fishing village to the massive trading capital of the southeast, it made Galfeon Yor seem very provincial. The procession of the Guard of Oran passed the first defense, a wall six feet high that enclosed the tithed property of the serfs. The fields were full with crops and many peasants toiled between the rows, clearing away the choking weeds and stones. The entourage entered the city proper through the West Gate, as such processions had centuries before. The walls stood several stories tall and were angled for a formidable defense; buttresses supported massive battlements upon which the City Guard could be seen making their timely rounds. The stone itself was dark with the passage of years and the stain of blood. The people at the gate stood back as the first horses entered, the guards saluting to the leader with their pikes. From here the party entered the Port of Paravel and the riches that lay within.

Paravel was the largest city of the south since Narn-toc ceased to be. It was considered a free city and traded mainly with Clef and Qwen and smaller ports up and down the coast of the Southern Regency. Though it had a Governor and a Council, anyone who knew about the politics of Paravel knew that the Surrogate had the fat little man in her pocket; his estate was the richest in the area. The Lord Protector was also formerly of the Conclaveum and of Helm, the City of the Wall.

Now he commanded the City Guard with discipline and resolve.

Of course there were many factions within Paravel who would rather see the Governor, the Lord Protector, the Surrogate, and her Temple of Oran on the other side of the Great Wall. Yet none were willing to disparage them; many feared a dagger in the eye during their fitful and often sleepless nights.

So, like any other free city, there were merchants everywhere, but they stood respectfully to the side as the horsemen trotted their steeds to the north quarter and the Seat of the Surrogate. A drunken sot would occasionally be tossed from an inn as hollow-eyed children looked on from the gutter, playing in the offal that was thrown from the windows and into the sewers. The children turned as the procession passed and gaped at the wealth of the saddles and the horses. This section of the city was not the richest by far, and besides, these were Myella's own Guard and they were indeed a sight to behold.

Riding next to Myella, on a matching white steed, was a hollow-cheeked young man, dressed in ornate plate armor. He looked neither right nor left; a cloak slung over one shoulder and a large bastard sword at his side. A tall helm sat atop his saddle horn where his gauntleted hands held the reins.

To Joe, otherwise known as Surik Shadowlord, none of the stimulation of the city affected him. His eyes were blank as he looked ahead, barely perceiving the rider in front. On the roadside, the people glowered as the rest of the procession passed, but they did not jeer or yell obscenities. To do that was to risk the wrath of the Guard of Oran and Myella, whom even the City Guard feared. She smiled lazily, knowing her power.

"My most favorite of cities," she whispered in the High Tongue of the Conclaveum. The reason for her affection was clear: even the Council obeyed her and, at this point, she felt above the Law of the Conclaveum. Now, she had a new prize, one that in time would give her the power that would enable her and her Uncle to set in motion the series of events that would let her possess the West and more. "Surik Shadowlord," she called with a low hiss, her voice throaty. Joe turned slowly, everything that was him: a tabula rasa.

"Yes?"

"You are mine."

He looked, his hand brushing the hilt of his black bastard sword. His eyes narrowed imperceptibly.

"Of course," he replied. They rode on to the center of Paravel and to the heart of the ancient city.

"First I want to know who he is. Is he from the Interior or the West? Why has

Myella brought him here? Why should he be important? Is he important to us?

Second. I want to know why the Guard has been doubled throughout the city. This concerns me. There are several new faces on the wanted list, but the City Guard does not list their offenses. I know that this is not atypical, but it is curious.

Finally. This Surik fellow, if he proves a threat then I want three of our best to take care of him. Is that clear?"

The two men nodded and left the room. The amber-eyed man sat back and steepled his fingers, then slowly closed his eyes.

If I cannot use him, then I will kill him, thought Alaric Dirkajian, formerly of Chez, present Guildmaster Merchant of Paravel.

Marad, eldest son of the Conclavator sat alone in silence at the Inn of the Blue Heifer. He looked down at a plate that held a hard roll and chunk of cheese and sighed. Five years of field rations had changed him from a rather soft aristocrat into a lean, hard soldier. When he first came to the North, sent by his father to command the White Guard, he was impetuous and foolhardy. He'd held predisposed notions of right and wrong and had learned quickly that often the truth lay in the gray area between. He had been taught at an early age that the intrigues of the Conclave would shorten one's life considerably if one were not careful. A wrong glance at court could send your soul winging to Oran. A misinterpreted touch, a smile, a sigh, could offend a woman's honor and incite the duel. Ritual Assassination was just as much a rite of passage as it was a means of gaining a seat on the Conclave. He had managed to avoid it so far; now he must return to Teshwa, sword in hand, at the bidding of his brother Adon.

Adon was Marad's youngest sibling, but probably the wisest of them all. Determined to stay away from politics and the Conclave, he forsook the role of Counselor and dedicated his life to studies of ethics and sorcery. Though their sister looked at this with contempt and took it as a sign of weakness, their father had discreetly encouraged it, thereby fueling her anger all the more. Now, as Adon was sequestered within the Temple of Tarn and forbidden to face the members of the Conclave, or for that matter their father, he had reached out to his brother, also an acolyte of Tarn.

Marad sat in the common room of the inn now, ignoring the low murmur of his men, the watchful eyes of the regular patrons, and sat staring at his fare. He sipped the weak white wine and then casually leaned forward to look hard at Kel.

"How much longer?"

"To Ionet? I would say a good fortnight. There will be much rain in the

Northern Forests this time of year, but we can sail from there to Teshwa."

"We will have to leave the horses in Ionet and get fresh ones in Teshwa."

"Yes, milord. Begging your pardon sir, but what has your brother said that has prompted us leaving Tasseem?"

"My father is ill and I fear that the Conclave is seething with intrigue and dark plans. My brother also mentioned trouble in the city of Helm. I know naught more." Kel frowned and finished his ale, wondering if the Captain's leaving the North was a wise move. He hoped that the raider Bej-et would not take advantage of their lack of leadership and strike with her ships. Where Marad saw it as a show of trust, Kel thought it a foolish mistake. Once Tasseem fell, the Krim would have a foothold in the Conclaveum that would not be easily relinquished. Then anything could happen. Bej-et could sail down the Kipris and strike Ionet. The Conclave had already ceded the Archipelago of Bequa, from sheer lack of enthusiasm. The sergeant laughed silently to himself in wonder. Granted, the place had no economic value, but it was of strategic importance to garnering free passage among the Gangli Straights. Without Marad, or even himself, the White Guard could falter under the command of that young and brash lieutenant named Barish, another flunky sent by some Noble family within the Conclave. It was lucky that Marad had turned out the way he had, but that had been under the strict tutelage and guidance of Kel. Who was there now?

Kel looked up as Marad pulled on his soft white cloak and buckled the chinstrap on his helm. South of the Gangli Range the climate was more temperate and the weather was very tolerable under the cooling canopy of the forest; the ride North of the range had been hellish.

It was with these thoughts that Kel gathered his men about him and went to harness their steeds. They set off, Marad in the forefront of the contingent. Ionet, a jewel upon the Kipris Lake, was only a fortnight away.

***

The night air that drifted over the plain was cool and refreshing and John could only hope that Bill was alive to feel the draft as it passed on toward the wastes. Mike sighed somewhere to his right. The big man had been rather silent these past few days as he turned his thoughts inward. That wasn't what had bothered John so much; rather it was the magic that his friend was using with increasing frequency. At night Mike would pull forth the orb and gaze into it, discerning whatever lay at its depths, while absently rubbing his forehead.

John frowned. He had turned to his own medallion many times without any of the results the big man was supposedly garnering. Its properties had allowed him to save lives, but whether this was magical or divine he did not know. In turn, Mike used his amber orb to accomplish the same thing, different tool, but the same result.

They had set camp somewhere to the east of the Ghisik Pass, about a day's ride into the plains. Illuminated by the light of the ringed moon, they sat and ate.

"What do you call your moon?" Mike asked of Torec as the merchant tipped back a water skin. The man wiped his mouth and looked into the night.

"In Clef we call her, Shaj il' Cziffer. In Common it means the shield and the spear. On the eve of spring, the ring lies flat." Mike nodded and smiled, imagining the myth that such a satellite could cause in a primitive society. Back home the moon had inspired considerable mythos. Many revered and worshipped the moon; it always chased the day, never quite catching the powerful sun. It was these thoughts that led him to think of the riddles that the daemon had told him and the power that those that brought them here desired.

It wasn't much, he knew. Yet the sorcery he was coming to know was growing exponentially in his mind. It was all pattern and formula. What was really curious was that John also had some talent that had manifested itself in the man's medallion. It was as if they had each brought some piece of their reality into this world and it formed a link through the aether. He shook his head, a thought edging through his mind, elusive and fleeting. He would think on it, figuring that it would eventually come to him.

He turned to his other problem. He hadn't told John, or had the time to tell Tom, about his little project. He also decided to wait and see if it was possible before springing it on them. He knew it was a small edge, but an edge, nonetheless.

He let his fingers wander through his mustache. Life wasn't too bad. He rather enjoyed the excitement, the adventure and the lack of strict social controls. He actually didn't mind the camping, the fighting, whatever. It was definitely not the same boring routine. He slowly came back outside himself and tuned to the conversation between John and Torec.

John had stripped his sword down, and was oiling the bare blade, being careful that there was no blood under the collar or the handle. Torec watched him and leaned closer to look at the inscription on the tang.

"You sword looks like Qwen steel; what does it say?"

"It's Japanese, about two hundred and fifty years old. This side says

Mountain Pine." He turned the blade over. "This is a cutting test."

"Cutting test?"

"It is called Tameshigiri, and it is done to determine the sharpness and worthiness of a blade. There are many interesting accounts of Tameshigiri or test cutting to be found. The members of the Yamada Asaemon family were the executioners and sword testers for the Tokugawa bakufu, a government in ancient Japan. There were other schools, but theirs was best known and the others seemed to have followed similar patterns. Criminals were generally executed and then their bodies were used for testing. There were strict rules against using murderers and tattooed people, but there were exceptions. They had a system for cutting the bodies which ranked the difficulty of cut and, based on this and experience, they developed a list of swords which cut well; wazamono. The very best were Saijo Owazamono, Owazamono, Ryowazamono and wazamono in that order. I believe only twelve smiths were rated as Saijo Owazamono by the Yamada family." He showed the inscription to the mercenary.

"It says: Ogawa Kuroemon tested it on two bodies, 1684, 2nd month on an auspicious day. This sword would be Owazamono. Very sharp."

"It is an impressive blade, Sir John. You wield it well."

"Now a question for you, Torec. What is that line of lights to the northern horizon?"

"That would be the Great Wall of the Conclaveum, and atop it are the watch- fires,"

303

Torec answered as he listened to the buzz of cicadas.

"It isn't far off then?"

"On the contrary, Sir John, it is quite far, yet the wall rises as high as the cliffs of a mountain. It was built a long time since by mages and their ilk...no offense Lord Michael."

"None taken, Torec," Mike replied, suddenly interested in what the merchant turned mercenary had to say.

"I remember when I had my first voyage at trade. It was a clear blue day, unlike any I've seen since, and my father sailed our felucca from Clef and into the harbor of Paravel. Such a grand city it was that I still see the bright flags amid masts as thick as a forest.

"By and non we traded in that city, and beyond, which eventually led us to Qwen, a city-state that is comparable to Paravel. In Qwen I had my first glance at the Wall, its easternmost edge that is.

"You would understand the size of the Wall better if I told you that Qwen is on a large island and it is reached by a causeway that runs from the mainland to her western cliffs. Just to the North of the mainland plateau is the Rift; rocky, jutting formations that were left after the mages were finished raising the Wall. If you stand on the western shores of Qwen and look at the north and west, about one league, then you may see the Wall in all its glory.

"The Wall's base is cut from the earth and cliffs. A thin river runs at its base through the Rift, and into the ocean. Here the Wall rises to such a height it left me breathless. Clouds raced just a stone's throw from its highest battlement and courier beasts could be seen wheeling about the top, nothing more than specks to my eyes.

In the fall snow and frost gather at the summit, yet it is still warm at the base. Never will I forget that sight.

"If one travels many leagues west, along the Rift, he will eventually come to Helm, the Gate City of the Great Wall. This is the only breach in the Wall, which continues on to merge with the Doran Range. Here a legion of men can pass through abreast, the walls of the City rising as a mountain on either side. It is defended by the Black Guard of the South; elite troops, generations old, who guard and protect the Conclaveum from sorcerous and military attack." He traced his finger along his aquiline nose and the scar there, remembering the past. Then he smiled wanly and held out his hands.

"What more is there to say? There are many marvels in the Conclaveum. It is said that the Conclave itself is made up of a good majority of lords who spread their power throughout the north. And in Teshwa, the Conclave rules from the oldest and deepest city of the world." Torec laughed. "Alas, I prattle on and you grow tired. Sleep my friends, while I tend to my men. We will rise early on the morrow." As Torec left, John looked at Mike, who just stared back.

"I'm confused," John finally said as the big man tossed his orb up and down. "Why?"

"I thought we were the good guys and the Conclaveum had the bad guys."

"Duran and Myella are the bad guys."

"I know that, but I also thought–"

"Don't think, John, it will give you a headache. It does me." Mike sounded rather exasperated.

"I'm still confused."

"So am I."

In the shadow of a buttressing pillar the hooded figure of Alaric Dirkajian, Guildmaster Merchant of Paravel, leaned against the stone cold wall and peered into the nave before him. Myella stood before the congregation of maybe three hundred, not more because even the citizens of the Conclaveum shunned Oran. This group was mostly her Guard, designated by the dagger encircled by flame, emblazoned on their standard.

Myella, Surrogate of the South, High Priestess of Oran (Alaric had heard it was oft the wont of those within the Conclave to patronize the temples by becoming one of the clergy) stood attired in a black robe and silver circlet of the Order. The Cult of Oran had grown from a secretive religion, once banned in the far past, to an open and accepted dogma. The Temple had no altar, instead there was a low stone block with a heading sword next to it, and behind that a throne-like chair. There was also no image of the god save for a small tabernacle-like enclosure. Rarely was Guildmaster Merchant Dirkajian frightened, but the unknowns of Oran made him so; that was why he rarely came to this place, if at all.

At this moment, the congregation was in the process of filing into the temple. It was a domed monstrosity, and the vault was set with crystal panes held together by soft lead. This allowed the full light of day to illuminate the nave. Pillars flanked the walls and near the right of the nave were two large oaken doors, easily fifty spans in height. He noted that they weren't very utilitarian because they required two acolytes to open each.

Alaric was brought out of his reverie by the chiming of a bell. The crowd hushed as Myella stepped to the front of the dais and held up a hand.

"Worshippers of Oran," the High Priestess called. The crowd looked attentively on. "Today I come with you to beseech Oran to guide us. You know of the terrible death of Gelion, Regent of the South, at the hands of barbarous outlanders." Here a murmur ran through the crowd and Alaric perked up. He never really paid attention to the token ruler of the Southern Reaches before. Oh well.

"It is a special day, for with his passing we move the Regency to Paravel. We move it from the remoteness of the Great Forest and the ruined Narn-toc, to the Seat of the Surrogate. To Paravel.

"I will take the role of Regent of the South. I will dictate the will of the Conclave and the Conclavator. I will be the Judge of Keth, and the Mouth of Oran. But," she paused and looked around at expectant faces. Alaric realized the importance of this event and the ramifications it held for Paravel. "I will temper my rule with an Arch-Regent. I bring to you a new Warrior-Priest of Oran whom I shall anoint on this hallowed ground today. And, I will allow him to mete out Justice. For where I am the Judge of Keth, he shall be the Hand. People of Paravel, look on the face of Surik, Shadowlord, Arch-Regent of the South and Hand of Keth." From the shadows of the nave stepped a bearded, gray-eyed man, dressed in black plate armor and carrying a wicked looking bastard sword.

Silence reigned in that moment. Then several guards went to the rear of the nave and brought forth a man dressed in a white sleeping robe. By the gods! Alaric swore as his eyes widened at the sight of Vilidis, a very prominent merchant who owned half the wharf district. The man looked disheveled and haggard as he was dragged to the block and forced to kneel there. The guards stood as Vilidis whimpered. Alaric stepped back into the shadows.

"This man has professed sedition against the Conclaveum and has also preached separatism from the Noble families of the Conclave. Oran finds the man guilty and given to the Hand for sentence!"

She suddenly clapped her hands and pointed to the headsman's sword. It was a heavy, long blade, with a wide, flattened tip where a point should be. It had a blood-groove running down the center and a pommel that could accommodate a two-handed grip. The quillions crossed the blade at right angles. It looked very sharp. The one called Surik went to the blade and hefted it. Vilidis screamed and soiled himself.

"What is the sentence?" Myella asked.

"Death." It was a hollow echo, void of emotion or remorse, and it made Alaric shiver. Cold, emotionless, Surik placed his boot on Vilidis' back and forced his head down to the block. Vilidis cried and begged for mercy.

"The Hand has sentenced. Oran awaits." Myella looked on, dispassionate. Surik placed the blade on the merchant's neck and paused, then he drew it slowly toward him until a large bead of blood swelled and ran over the neck onto the block. Vilidis blathered and was hysterical. Surik drew the blade up and high. With both hands he brought it down.

Alaric turned away. It was a cold sound, a butcher's noise, and then the sickening gurgle of blood. Surik wiped the blade along Vilidis' white robe leaving a trail of bright red along the quivering back.

Alaric turned to the darkness and disappeared into an alcove. Before he left, he caught a glimpse of Surik; the man was staring straight through him with those empty, dead eyes. He pushed quickly into the secret passage and was enveloped in darkness.

"I want him dead," he said without pause. "I don't want to deal with him." He saw his second nod and knew that the right people would be hired.

***

"So, now the problem is to get from here to Paravel in the quickest manner possible," Tom finished explaining to Tar'elah and two other bandits. They nodded their understanding, mulling over the options.

"Easily a fortnight and a half by horse," Garis grunted as he tried to get comfortable on the packed earthen floor of Tar'elah's dwelling. This riding about was getting to him and right now he

309

yearned for nothing more than a salt bath and a down bed.

"That will have to do," Tom replied. "I suggest we head due East along the Tarn Range, following the road that Torec and John took."

"And if there are patrols we must be cautious. Myella will have reached Paravel by now and so too Torec." Garis turned to the young bandit woman. "What was the compliment of the Watchtower?"

"There will be five or six left there at the most," Tar'elah said, as she looked from Tom to Bill, who sat silent against the far wall.

"Then we must be wary," Garis commented.

"You wish to eliminate the time needed for travel so that you may rejoin your friends. This is what I suggest. You and your companions have helped us eliminate a problem that has been troubling us for some time. Now we can practice our trade at the Ghisik Pass more freely. We owe you much.

"My people have known for some time that a courier and his beast come to the Watchtower at regular times. Tomorrow night is the next run for them and, if we could be there awaiting their arrival, we could take them. We could use the beast to carry, say, the Bard and Smiling Wolf to the east. That way they may rejoin their friends quickly. Meanwhile Garis here can follow with thirty or so of my people to aid in rescuing this Surik."

Tom and Bill looked up, startled at what she had suggested. "Hold on," began the Sioux. "What led you to believe that we wanted you to help us rescue our friend?"

"Why, we can offer diversion and our swords."

"We don't want people to die, Tar'elah..." Bill trailed off. She looked at him curiously for a moment and then to Tom.

"Do you believe that you can take him easily from those of the North? Your faces will be known and likely you will be captured without aid. You have aided us, now let us aid you."

"We have thirty of Torec's men, we don't need to start a war," Bill replied, worried.

"Bard," Garis interrupted. "May I remind you of our attack on Gelion? That may have started something already, not to mention the fall of Galfeon Yor."

"But—"

"It would be much to ask you to accompany us to Paravel," Tom said, attempting to slither out of the entanglement.

"It is only right." She brushed her hair back, staring at him. "But the effort is not—"

"To assume that what we have done here will go unpunished is wrong. The Surrogate's Seat is in Paravel. Word will reach her ears and she will send a new, stronger force to the watchtower. We will send our people closer to the Ghisik falls. We hope that our aid to you will be profitable with new friends and arms."

"The Conclaveum is infinitely stronger than we are," Tom pointed out. "They are but the rock, while we are the wind." At this Bill rolled his eyes and shook his head in frustration.

311

"Now," she continued. "Do we go to the tower and wait for the courier?"

"This is getting way out of hand," Bill muttered.

"Why not," Garis replied. "I am always one for a good fight."

***

"With morning, the gates open and we have access to the city," Torec said as the mist rolled off the fields and dawn illuminated the walls of Paravel.

"I wonder how Tom and Garis are doing?" John remarked. Mike looked back from atop his steed, a grin on his face.

"I think things are going to be okay. I looked into the orb and had an overwhelming sense of calm."

"Before the storm?" John snidely retorted.

"No, I think we'll just go in there, find Joe, and sneak back out. And that will be that." Mike could be just as sarcastic.

"Well, I know it won't be that easy...You sensed calm?"

"Yeah, meaning that we are on the right path and whatever happens won't be too drastic." John looked at his companion sideways. Things had already been too drastic and it looked like it was only getting worse. He wondered what had become of Gabrielle, who'd been in his thoughts much lately. He hoped she was coping, but with Chill's death he had to steel himself for the worst. This reality seemed to flaunt death; it was indeed no fairy tale.

"We will split up," Torec continued. "We will travel in groups of two and three. Travel is high this time of year and we will not cause too much suspicion. After we are in the city proper, we will meet at the Fulchard Inn."

"Fulchard Inn, great," Mike muttered.

They split up and headed in different directions. Mike, John, and Torec continued to the western gate while the others went to the north or south posterns. "We will go to the Inn first," Torec called back. "Then I will talk to some people I know. Mayhap we can track down your companion. The Guard probably knows your faces and that may be a problem. I hope that the anonymity of the crowd will obscure us."

"If there is any trouble, we will split up and head to the Inn," Mike replied. It looked as if it would be a lousy day as low gray clouds rolled in from the north and threatened rain. John remained silent as they trotted past the fields and toward the high walls of the city. He watched as a few serfs cleared stones and weeds from between rows of corn and wheat. He would catch their eyes occasionally and they would return a look of such derision that he had to turn away.

Clearly this was not an ideal economic society, rather a harsh feudal system that pushed the profits to the top and left little for the peasants. He looked up from his saddle horn as he wrapped his cloak about his shoulders. Though the sun cast a gold sheen across them and put the Western wall out in stark relief, the impending storm clouds from the north brought cool air and darkening skies.

They came below the watchful eyes of the guards atop the battlements just as the heavy drops of rain began to fall. They passed within the gate, the walls rising on either side, and above them the portcullis hung with deadly certainty. Torec paid a tariff and they trotted their horses onto the cobbled thoroughfare. John looked back, hair on the back of his neck standing on end in that prescient awareness of being watched, but immersed in the throng he soon lost the feeling.

"They are not the brightest of creatures," Garis explained of the courier beast. "But they are fast and they obey the rider."

"What do they look like?" Tom asked, Garis only smiled. Watch, he implied. They had neatly dispatched the six guards within the tower and now waited for the arrival of the courier beast. It was now late afternoon, and Tom sat with Garis and his men in the bushes. The Native American spotted Bill's golden hair as the musician looked from the top of the tower to the ground below. Next to him stood Tar'elah, peering through the glass and looking for any sign of the beast.

"How long do you think?"

"Tar'elah said before nightfall; soon." Garis rolled to his side and adjusted his mace.

"Why did you allow them to accompany us?" Tom inquired.

"There was no arguing it. You helped them and now they wish to help you.

These bandits are stubborn people. They have lived long under the harsh hand of the

314

Conclaveum, and an opportunity like this comes only once in a short lifetime. Besides, Myella is a snake."

"What?"

"She is power hungry. She wants all the lands of the south and the west at her disposal. I do not know these bandits who help us, nor will I pretend to understand their motives, but as sure as Clef was betrayed at the hands of Myella, we must allow these people to help us."

Tom understood and how could he help but not? His ancestors were betrayed by smallpox and whiskey. His people had tried to fight back and, if they had been able to unite, then maybe the Native Americans would not have been removed to reservations and given the status of secondary citizen. For that reason alone, he respected Tar'elah and her wishes. He just hoped it wouldn't interfere with finding Joe. He looked to the top of the tower, wondering if this bandit and her people could really help them.

Bill looked back, not really seeing where Tom and the others lay hidden. "Bard," came Tar'elah's voice from behind. He turned to see her bent over the magical glass that looked to the sky.

"Yes?" he replied. Every time he saw her, his heart went aflutter. His hormones were raging.

"Why is it that you and your friends oppose our aid?"

"I guess it's because we'd rather go it alone. We don't want you and your people to get hurt. I don't want you to get hurt."

"Just being here you rally us, your aid is returned. We just happen to follow the same path for the moment."

"We feel that we are getting caught in something too big for us."

"Yes, but this way you may be assured you will get what you want."

"They are very powerful."

"Some things should be done without thought." She turned back to the glass and he frowned. Bill wondered if they would end up dead like Chill. "He comes," she hissed and Bill looked around. "Look."

He stepped to the glass and looked. He knew not what to expect and what he got was against all possibilities. "My God, it's a dragon," he breathed.

It wheeled gracefully on an updraft, spiraling toward the tower, and it was like nothing he had ever imagined. From the size of the rider upon its back, it was about thirty feet long from snout to tail. Its scales were blacker than obsidian, but as the evening light struck them they shined a deep, scintillating gold. The beast's head was long and narrow, tapering to the fanged snout. The wings spread out to catch the wind within their forty-foot span; the plating of the stomach scales undulated to the rhythm of the beating wings. The tail trailed languidly behind, but its arms and legs were pulled up to its belly with muscles taut.

Bill watched as a man wrapped in furs prodded the beast with a long shaft. The man sat in a saddle with large bags on the beast's flanks. The Bard was amazed at the skill of the rider, and the bravery.

Tar'elah called to one of her men below then waved to Garis and Tom. It would not be long before the courier landed just outside the tower.

"There it is." Garis pointed it out to Tom. The Sioux looked to see the speck glide down from above.

"We must wait for the rider to dismount, otherwise he could use the beast against us. That would not be pleasant." Tom nodded understanding and readied his bow. They watched as the beast plummeted and backwinged to alight on the ground, claws scrabbling to find a purchase, and finally coming to a halt at the tethering post near the tower. Its red tongue flicked out over the finger-sized teeth as the rider un-strapped himself from the saddle and pulled off his fur coat. Keeping the prod close, the courier tied the reins to the post. Bill and Tar'elah awaited the arrow's flight.

"Now!" Garis whispered.

Once more Tom's arrow was true as it found its mark in the man's back, just below the third rib. The man looked down, dumbfounded at the arrowhead protruding from his chest, then he fell face forward onto the soil. The beast turned one gleaming, green eye to the fallen rider and sighed. Then Tar'elah's people were out of the tower and Garis' men approached from their blind.

"Well, Bard." Tar'elah slapped the man on the back as she headed down the spiral stair. "It seems that you will be reunited with your friends soon."

"Yeah, but at what cost?" he replied. "We just managed to kill another."

317

"I do not understand you." She looked at him as she stood on the bottom step. She cocked her head to one side. "Mayhap, that is why I like you."

She passed him and headed outside and he just stared after her.

"The forces are in motion and cannot be stopped." The old man's heavily veined hand traced a pattern over his carved staff. "You have said so yourself, revenge is long in the making. Well, son of my father's whore, here begins my revenge upon you and your miserable brother for all that you have done to me."

He looked out the open facade of the room, a thin railing between him and eternity. Helm, the City of the Wall, sprawled out below him like a slumbering wolf at the feet of a giant. This room was the opulent office of the Preceptor of the City and sported quite a view of the South. As the sun set in the west, the room was illuminated with a fading red light, bringing out the deep veins in the marble flooring and the gold threads of the silken tapestry on the wall.

He turned and coldly regarded the bound man who stood near the guarded door at the rear of the chamber. His hair was illuminated by the faint glow of the sconce; the sun did not penetrate that deep into the room.

"There are many means to a man's downfall. Once the Surrogate has harnessed the power that I seek, I will use it at my discretion. Regaining what was lost will only be the first of my pleasures. The other will be to see you suffer...for a very long time." He stood and stared for a hard moment. His signet ring flashed briefly, then he simply wasn't there.

Trevor sat heavily in the nearest wooden chair and wondered if this hideous game would ever end.

The quarter holding the Seat of the Surrogate and the Temple of Oran was heavily guarded; the mounted Guards of Oran, pacing their black warhorses to and fro, patrolled the white gates separating it from the rest of the city. The City Guard often shunned the several blocks near this section, muttering of sorcery and death at the hands of those elite guardsmen, all for no apparent reason. To say the least, egress at the Portal of Osso was impossible without deep scrutiny and a very good reason. The three men who wanted to get inside the Seat had no lawful excuse, so they would have to try another, more discreet method.

Once or twice a day, the eastern postern would open and servants would cast out the garbage and detritus that the Guard and others had produced on the previous day. This done, a cart would haul it off to be disposed of in some unseen heap. It was during one of these times that the seneschal of the grounds argued vehemently with the hauler over a matter of currency and how much should exchange hands. Usually it was but a few copper shenks, but this time the hauler wanted silver. Highway robbery, insisted the seneschal, his defense of the usual cartage price causing him to miss the three shadows that slipped inside the postern and along the shrubs at the base of the wall. After a moment, the hauler gave a great show of relenting and the seneschal parted with the usual four copper shenks.

Across the yard, the three figures moved cautiously, hidden by the passage of several carriages. Soon they were inside the opulent Seat and heading for the west wing. They had it on good authority that the one known as Surik was staying there on the second floor. They paused, seeing five men with the black tunic and gold dagger symbol of the Surrogate's Guard. They smiled as these five men passed without wavering; luck was with them.

In the west wing, Joe stood at the edge of a balcony. Myella was through with him for the day and somehow he had made his way here to watch evening descend over the city. He was bathed in a neon glow as the swollen sun set behind two high spires above the Temple of Oran. A primal memory urged him, but the casting of the spell was too strong and it remained unbidden.

Faintly, he could hear the sound of street urchins playing just beyond the wall of the Seat. Laughter and the clatter of hooves on cobblestone soon faded as the sun sank below the wall and the shadows lengthened.

At the edge of the garden, darkness shifted, and three silhouettes slid free form the murk, sliding silently from pillar to pillar, then finding their way down the marbled hallway. Careful not to upset a stand or vase they all moved with grace and stealth. Their objective, the one known as Surik Shadowlord, Arch-Regent and Hand of Keth, stood in the archway of the balcony, back fully exposed, and seemingly oblivious to his surroundings.

The marble darkened as the shadows moved around the smooth wall. Flagstones issued no sound of warning; but Joe had sensed their presence. Surik Shadowlord was also Master of the Shades.

The assassins were upon him, poisoned blades drawn, when he spun. They noticed his empty stare at first, then his eyes burned into them and the bastard sword was free from its scabbard.

Consciousness flooded in; a rush of sights, sounds, sensations. Intense awareness flooded Joe's mind even as he assessed the imminent danger. Vision, hearing, feelings washed over him and he became someone, something more...

The assassins took a step back, disconcerted by the sudden change in their victim and the swiftness of the blade in motion. A usually awkward blade at best, it rippled like a thing alive, an ethereal blue glow flickering on the edge of the steel.

Joe quickly took in the unfamiliar surroundings. His last memory was that of the tent and Myella...that bitch, and then once on the road to Paravel. He must be in some castle or palace or something, and whoever these three guys were, they definitely wanted to kill him.

His sword seemed so light and stood steadfast in the way his saber had during so many competitions. Poised, balanced, and ready to thrust the fatal blow. Suddenly, they were upon him, all three of the black-clad assassins. He parried, feinted, thrust with ease. The first man screamed, or was it the blade? It surged up beneath a sternum, collapsing a lung, perforating a spleen and rending an aorta. The second man lost his head, literally. The third ran, but not before he lost two fingers.

He did not care to hear that death scream again, especially since it could only come from his throat.

Joe looked around. No noise except for the faint gurgling of blood as it fell from a headless torso and onto the flagstones. He gave no further thought to the remains of the would-be assassins at his feet. Instinctively, he knew there would be more; the important thing was to find out why.

He had to orient himself, then figure out how to rejoin the others. He smiled cynically; he would blame Mike for all this, it had to be his fault. Picking the right- hand corridor, as good a direction as any, he sheathed his bastard sword and...

...stopped. His mind clouded, leaving him only with a faint kernel of primal intent; something important that he couldn't quite remember. Slowly, his eyes empty again, he walked impassively down the hallway.

***

The great beast turned on a column of warm air; this was unlike anything Bill or Tom had ever experienced. Night coalesced into a spinning star field, bright beyond imagination. Tom laughed. Not in all his experience had he felt such a clean rush. He watched as the ground below resolved into a wide plain. Now and then, a faint yellow glow would mark a homestead and then it would be gone as the courier beast lit on an updraft and was carried aloft.

Bill clutched Tar'elah tightly with his arms, ignoring the throb in his side. The saddle strap around his waist was little comfort. She pressed back into him, occasionally turning and smiling warmly. At first, her long hair had whipped his face, but then she just handed him the prod and pulled her mane back. That was a nervous moment of trust for him and Bill relished it as Tom swore loudly, calling on his ancestors.

Time fled on the wings of the animal. Tom and Bill remembered one fleeting interval of landing and sleep, then they were up again as the beast sped on to the east. Paravel now lay in the distance, a knot of black on the shore of a tourmaline sea. It had been fast, this beast. Bill looked back at Tom, apprehension etched in his brow. Tom winked and a smile found its way to the musician's face; they both laughed in delight as the bandit guided the beast toward the city.

"What is the plan?" Bill yelled above the rushing of air. Tar'elah turned to answer as the beast dipped low.

"We will land half a day's walk from the city, we do not want to be seen on her."

Bill nodded, barely catching the words, and relayed what she said to Tom. He was hopeful that, once they got to the city, the task of finding the others would not be too great. They waited as the beast sped over the plains; the grass seemed close until a herd animal broke unto a run, thirty feet below. Then, with a clap they were sprung forward, the courier beast reared and its scalloped wings cupped gouts of air in an attempt to slow and land. They dismounted when it had settled, their muscles stiff and cramped. Tar'elah corralled the beast in a stand of trees, not far from a

323

sheepherder's farm. Bill shook his head, knowing it had to have been a dream, but Tom had a look of rapture on his face.

"This is going to be one hell of a story," Bill said as Tom adjusted his gear. Tar'elah unbound her hair and fastened her short sword to her belt. Bill smiled appreciatively, knowing that beauty could be deadly. Then, without a word, they were off, walking to the city by the sea.

Paravel.

Chapter 18

Ionet, much like Paravel, was a large city set upon the shore of a sprawling lake within the Conclaveum. It was here that Kel began to arrange for passage on the river Kipris for his men, while his Captain spoke with the local garrison commander to arrange for stabling of the mounts.

Marad stepped from the garrison house and onto the Street of the Forks, heading for the river and docks to rejoin Kel. The sun was low in the horizon and deep shadows cut their way across the narrow avenue. Most of the businesses and houses on this street were closed; it was the Holiday of Tarn (in fact, his own patron deity) and most observed it with zeal in this part of the Interior.

He adjusted his sword and cloak and wondered if he would be able to catch a bite to eat at his favorite Inn. The Inn had the sweetest sausage and cabbage north of Teshwa, and even thinking of it made a smile cross his lips and his mouth water. It was with these thoughts that he turned down the Avenue of Hig and proceeded to the river. The steady rhythm of his boots on the cobbled sidewalk was the only sound in this quarter of the city, that and the temple bells ringing in the distance to signal sunset. He passed a stand of oak and birch that was the Park of Ikn and continued on. He noticed a lone carriage and lamplighter going down the street lighting the wicks of the oil lamps. Soon a white glow guided his way.

Marad paused momentarily at a storefront and peered into the window, amazed at the cost of a crystal decanter and glasses. Then as he once more

325

strode toward the docks, he heard the footsteps behind, slightly out of sync with his own. He frowned and turned down another street as if to detour to his favorite Inn.

This street was darker and much dirtier than the last. The buildings were in a state of disrepair and the place stunk of rotting garbage. Again he heard the footsteps, this time closer. Now he smiled. From the sound it was only one, but he should expect more. He ducked into a doorway and waited.

Nothing. He must have waited a good five or ten minutes and there was no one. Maybe he was getting foolish. After all, this is the city, not Tasseem. Of course there would be people in the streets. He smiled at his own thoughts and stepped into the street.

It was only a second before a bright flash blinded him and he was struck from behind. Sorcery? He wondered if it were that or an alchemist's trick. He quickly drew his sword even as spots danced in front of his eyes. His blade was knocked from his grasp and he was jacked up against the wall. He still could not see his assailant, but it did not matter. Without his sight or his weapon, he would be dead in a second.

"Is this him?" one ruffian hissed in the Middle Tongue of the Conclaveum. "Yes," another replied. Marad felt the cold steel of a dagger pierce through his chain mail and graze along his ribs. Fortunately, it was the back of the blade, not the edge. His eyes began to clear and he saw a bearded ruffian and another, hooded man, off to the side. Marad struggled momentarily and the bearded man lost his grip on the narrow blade. It clattered to the ground.

"Blast, he's strong. Hold him still. I–" But that was all the ruffian got out as a sword passed through the side of his head and sheared off the top of his skull. He fell back with a last look of confusion on his face, as the hooded accomplice took advantage of the confusion to escape down the street. Marad looked up to see Kel wiping his blade. Marad frowned.

"You killed him sergeant. I would have liked to question him."

"Sorry, Lord Marad. The circumstances seemed to necessitate it."

"Yes. This one implied in his conversation with the other that they selected me for a purpose. It was not just robbery, I think." He stooped and picked up his sword. Then knelt and inspected the corpse. The man was middle-aged and more than likely just some petty criminal from the look of his dress and demeanor. His dagger, on the other hand, was very finely made and would have cost more than five silver shenks. He frowned and noted the maker.

"Qwen steel? House Orr." He looked to Kel, who shrugged. "Tis uncommon, but not unheard of."

"But, inconsistent with this man's accouterments."

"Aye."

Marad handed the blade to his sergeant and looked at the hole in his overtunic. He sighed; it was very noticeable.

"Have you arranged passage, Kel?"

"Aye, on the Daedalo, out of Teshwa. She's heading back with the post. We should arrive within a fortnight."

"Good. And do we have time to dine?"

"I think so milord."

"Then let us go to an Inn I know. They have the finest sweet sausage and cabbage, and a bottle of port should cool our blood after this." He gestured to the ground. Kel gave Marad a lopsided smile and they made their way to the Inn.

John sidled past a group of young men and began his walk to Paravel's bazaar. Mike walked beside him, humming quietly to himself as his fingers tapped a rhythm on the hilt of the short sword he had acquired since losing his own in the fight with Gelion. In the big man's hand was a scroll of parchment. John didn't know what was on it; whether some spell or drawing, he only knew that it had occupied Mike's attention for the past three nights at the Fulchard Inn. It was also the reason that brought them out into the public eye and the potential scrutiny of the City Guard and the Guard of Oran.

It was almost noon, and the bazaar was quite crowded. Torec had informed them that it was the height of the trading season and the streets would be swollen with many a merchant trying to barter or sell. John had never seen such an array of people in his life, not even at a Society Event. Rich and poor, peasant and beggar were all mixing with merchants and buyers. Children would dart through the crowd and then he would notice that one would divert a person while the other expertly cut his purse. He grinned, this culture was much more exciting than any he had experienced in his own world.

John and Mike strolled through the throng of people. The two would elicit an occasional glance by a guardsman or man-at-arms, appraising their weapons and gait. Mike hoped people would just assume they were nothing more than the bodyguards of some merchant, or perhaps soldiers of fortune. After all, Torec had mentioned rumors of strife in Clef (he had been very excited about this). It seemed that the Conclaveum was having a hard time holding onto what it had annexed under the auspices of the Surrogate.

Furriers, bounty hunters, slavers, sailors and dockworkers all milled about. This is great! John thought as he passed a fair maiden and her liveried attendants. He could almost forget their purpose here.

"Wanna beer?" Mike asked as they passed a tavern. What caught his eye was the burly bartender tossing a sodden drunk from the porch.

"Maybe later," John replied, dodging a little pickpocket. "What do you need a smithy for?"

"You'll know when I'm done. I also have to find an apothecary." Mike watched two prostitutes lounging in a doorway of what they took to be a brothel. He smiled as he walked past and was tempted by their cooing laughter.

"Milord," came a sweet voice and John felt a tug at his sleeve. He turned and looked at a young girl's face. She wore a light shift underneath a cloak of wool and her body strained at the tight fit. Her face was made-up with thick lip paint and rouge. "Morn special, only five copper shenks. I do

329

anything," she whispered and her tongue darted out to lick her lips.

"Uh, no thanks," he replied and took a step back.

"Hold on," Mike said and handed the parchment to John. "Where?" he asked the girl, she couldn't have been more than eighteen.

"Mike! We don't have time for this."

"I'll make time."

"Upstairs," she said and took his hand. The big man winked at John and followed her.

"Your nickel," John called after him only to hear Mike's low laughter. John sighed and leaned against the wooden slats of the building. He was tempted to take a peek at Mike's scroll, but with his luck the man had placed a ward on it and his nose would fall off. That or something worse.

Why now? He thought. You'd think he could control his libido. He frowned as he watched some very attractive dancers walk by. He looked about with feigned boredom, trying not to seem too interested in his new environment. Several merchants tried to accost him, but he waved them by, mainly because he didn't understand the language they were speaking. The minutes slowly stretched out and he began to wonder what was taking so long. His reverie was interrupted by three young men who approached him from the alley.

"Pray tell, milord, mayhap you know of a place of rest?" This was new, John thought. There were several young men dressed in tunic and hose, all of fine material. He would say they were dressed richly, with silk and lace. One even wore a hat. All of them carried what looked like epees and poniards.

"Sorry, I'm from out of town."

"We see," came the smooth voice of another. "Then possibly we can relieve you of your burdens."

John eyed the young man, trying to figure out his angle. He didn't know if they were going to try to roll him or rape him. "I doubt if you can do that," he said as he relaxed.

"No sir. You misunderstand; we insist," replied yet another.

"Listen, friend, I have no quarrel with you. Just leave me alone or you will regret it."

"Will we?" replied the first. "I think this kathec needs to be taught a lesson on manners." Before he had finished speaking, John's katana was out and at the throat of the first young man.

"Get lost, or I'll kill you...over a four or five day period." The young man gulped and looked down at the razor sharp edge of the Japanese blade. The others had their weapons half drawn.

"My father is very powerful," he muttered as the tip of John's sword drew a hairline of blood.

"So? He isn't here to help you, is he?"

"Jesus Christ," came Mike's voice as he walked down the steps of the bordello. "I leave you for twenty minutes and you're already picking on teenagers." He sauntered up, standing a good foot over any of them. "I told you to stop luring these kids in. The vivisectionist doesn't need any more bodies this week."

"He said he'd give me ten gold for a fair haired one," John replied, playing along.

"Oh, I don't know, we'd have to cross town..." he trailed off after seeing the look of pure terror in the eyes of the young men. Then the three of them were off and running through the crowds. "Kids these days."

"What took you so long?" John almost shouted as sweat broke out on his forehead.

"I was busy, besides, you seemed to be having fun."

"Fun, right, at least they had manners." He paused, then. "You could have caught something."

"I had protection, the Trojans backed me up." John chuckled. "I bet she was thrilled."

"She was. She kept it when we were through. She's gonna wash it out and have all her customers use it. She won't have to worry about getting pregnant or diseased." John looked at Mike out of the corner of his eye. His big friend adjusted his shirt and looked around suspiciously. "But seriously, I got the skinny on who's who around here. It seems that there is a new badass in town, who killed a councilman. A gray-eyed demon..."

John tilted his head to the side.

"Yeah," Mike replied to the knowing look. "Sounds like a certain 'artiste' we know, no?"

Regardless of Mike's digression, maybe it was turning out to be a good day.

"So you say he appeared drugged until you attacked, then he used a magical sword on you?"

"Yes sir," replied the wispy haired man before Alaric. "But you escaped?"

"You know my reputation; I am not a coward."

"I know. He must have been good."

"He killed Gral and Birel in a matter of seconds. I escaped with this." He held up his hand to show two missing fingers. "It still aches and the healer said that it will ache 'til the day I die. It is a curse."

"It seems that I have underestimated this Shadowlord. He has killed two assassins and beaten off a third. I must reassess his position in the politics of Paravel." Alaric looked up to the man. "Here, take the money and go down the coast. I want you out of the city."

The man nodded and left, relieved, after all Alaric was from Chez, where they raised dueling to a high art and he was rumored to be highly skilled with a sword himself.

As the man left, Alaric looked at the aide who sat in a deep leather chair in the corner of the room, her face thoughtful. "What do you think?"

"Myella brought him here from Helm? Teshwa? Who knows? A Lord, Duran of Qwen, has also shown up at a function of the Seat and seems to play an important role in Myella's scheming. He was with the Black Guard at Helm and also fought in some rather prominent forays. He also comes with the news that the Regent Gelion has died in mysterious circumstances last month. Gelion was apparently Duran's cousin. What the connection with Myella and Surik is we still aren't sure.

"Duran is also responsible for the circulation of four new wanted proclamations. The City and Oran Guard have been placed on alert for these men, though I doubt they will be found; the pictures are very crude."

"What is your interpretation of these events, Bale?" Alaric's amber eyes tried to pierce those of his aide, but she just looked at her notes.

"The four may have had something to do with the death of Gelion. That's just a guess, but I do not believe in coincidence and Surik's arrival in the city is enough to arouse suspicion. Is he here from the Conclave to get these four?"

"Plans within plans, it is a maze," he sighed and sat back, looking at the rough sketches of Mike, John, Tom, and Bill.

"If anyone can sort through it, you will, Lord Alaric."

"I know."

"Will that be all?"

"For now. But, let us make sure that all our members are on the lookout for these four. We may be able to use them for leverage." The woman nodded and left. Alaric watched her go, then shuffled through some more papers without really seeing them. He glanced momentarily at his saber on the wall, wondering if this

Surik was a match for him. There was always the chance.

Duran scowled and looked to the array of soldiers in the courtyard of the Seat. They were the Guards of Oran, whom he now commanded by default. Myella had promised him the Regency and he had gotten the Temple Soldiers instead. She had forced him to watch as she placed Surik on the dais of Oran, and then Surik had ritually beheaded Vilidis as the Hand of Keth.

Myella had really wanted to stir up trouble with that, though he did approve of the method.

334

The repercussions would set the Council quivering with fear. That was good; it would suppress any dissent in moving the Regency to the city of Paravel. With the Governor in their pocket and the Lord Protector preventing open rebellion, they could easily take over the largest city of the south. Then they could deal with the outlanders.

But why did she make the Shadowlord her Arch-regent? What were her plans? He knew that she had designs on the total domination of the South, but for that she would need an army, not an adjudicator or Hand of Keth. If he had been made Regent, he could bring in some of the battalions he commanded under his rule. This unknown, gray-eyed outlander couldn't command an army of swine. He wanted the White Knight first, and he would use the Guard until the last man fell, if necessary. The City Guard was good, but the Guard of Oran was better. They had orders to inform him when they found the outlanders, but they would also remain out of his way.

He smiled thinly and adjusted the fit of his leather hauberk, emblazoned with the dagger encircled by fire. If he were to lead these men, then he would do so with an iron fist. To hell with the Shadowlord! He would take care of that matter when the opportunity arose.

He looked around at the sound of horse hooves clattering on the stones within the courtyard. It was Kelvin, the Lord Protector of Paravel. Duran had first met the silver-haired man at Helm, where Kelvin held the title of Preceptor of the Black Guard. It was a position that combined the roles of Governor with Lord Protector, and Kelvin had been a harsh taskmaster even then. That was why he was made the Lord Protector of Paravel upon the mysterious death of the previous office-holder, one who had been loyal to the city fathers.

Fortunately, Myella knew that Kelvin was loyal only to the Conclaveum and, as Surrogate of the South, she could command him at will, and destroy him when she chose. What consoled Duran was that when the time came for the pendulum to swing against the Old Guard, he would be the one to slice Kelvin's throat.

Such is fortune, Duran thought as he saluted the older man. Myella had asked the Lord Protector here to meet the Shadowlord, for now even Surik was placed higher in the chain of command than Kelvin; though officially there was no link between the free-city of Paravel and the Conclaveum.

The man dismounted and extended his right hand. Duran smiled secretly to himself. He knew that the man was left handed and wicked in a duel. The custom was to proffer the fighting hand, and while Duran was mostly ambidextrous he also extended his right hand.

"Welcome to Paravel, milord," came a surprisingly soft voice. Kelvin carried himself well in the livery of the City Guard; his only symbol of rank was the gold chevrons on his epaulets. Duran professionally appraised the saber at the man's side then smiled.

"Welcome to the Seat of the Surrogate, as well as the Regency."

"Ah yes," Kelvin replied as he put one finger to his temple and tilted his head to the side. It was a signal to the stable hand, who took his horse by the reins and led it away. "Myella has invited me to a dinner of State to meet one Surik Shadowlord, the Arch-regent. I hear that he has already performed aptly as Hand of Keth." He began walking across the smooth cobbles. "The Council is quite undone. Vilidis was well liked. Now they fear a dagger in the night." He frowned, lines etching his face deeply as he walked in step with Duran toward the Hall of the Seat. "In my six years as Lord Protector, Paravel has never felt the hand of the Conclaveum so strongly. If we can bring them to tithe the Conclave and to elect a Full Seat as representation then we may find that there are possibilities for the South yet."

"Tell Myella, Kelvin, not me."

"Yes, you were, shall we say, displaced by this Surik? Who is he? Where does he come from? These are some of the questions I've been asking myself." He stepped into the cool interior of the Hall and was led past statues and busts of the former Surrogates and older relics from when the Seat was in Narn-toc. "Tell me Duran, are you jealous?"

The man from Qwen turned deep red at the insult, but held his tongue in check. He gripped the hilt of his sword and opened the wide oaken doors for the Lord Protector. "Jealousy is a trait I do not espouse, Kelvin. Especially when it interferes with loyalty. You should know that."

"Loyalty, yes," Kelvin replied. "But to whom, the Conclavator or the Surrogate?"

"The Surrogate, of course."

337

Kelvin smiled at the man's open betrayal of the Conclaveum. "Duran you surprise me, to say this to the Lord Protector of–"

"The free-city of Paravel." Duran finished.

"Touché." Kelvin entered a low-ceilinged hall, paneled richly in wood and appointed with the finest artifacts from Narn-toc. Before them was a large pine table holding some of the seafood for which Paravel was noted.

Myella looked over from the leaded windows where she stood, inspecting the milling ranks of the Guard. A man in black hose and purple tunic, carrying a large bastard sword, stood at the opposite wall regarding an open tome.

"Ah, Lord Protector, Duran, well met. I would like to introduce you to Surik Shadowlord, Arch-regent and Hand of Keth."

Kelvin watched as the man turned to him, his gray eyes piercing his own. There was something there, clouded over for the moment, but a flicker maybe, of hatred or worse; he almost flinched. "Shadowlord..." he said as he held out his hand. Surik regarded it a moment then turned back to the text.

"Forgive him, Kelvin," Myella called as she stepped into the center of the room. She was wearing a humble gown of blue velvet, a clasp of gold with a slim stiletto held by a chain about her waist. "Surik is fascinated by the Ih'dia text of the Sorcerer of Narn-toc. One of the last salvaged from the ruins of the Dead City."

"Yes," Kelvin frowned slightly but turned his gaze back Duran and the Surrogate. "I am happy that you invited me to this quaint dinner, Myella, but your invitation came at a pressing time. It seems that some of my men have spotted the outlanders that you are looking for."

"What?" Duran spun around from the table, an edge to his voice. "Where are they?"

"Oh, at an Inn. We intend to raid the place this night. Would you like to join us?"

Duran suppressed an angry retort and Myella answered for him. "My Lord Duran would most appreciate your assistance."

"Good." He paused. "Rumor has it that they killed Gelion."

"Just rumors, Kelvin, you should learn to ignore them. He died from an accident; the healer that tended him can testify to that."

"Yes, he would have been wise to wear a codpiece."

"Be that as it may, good Lord Protector, Duran will accompany you so that it may be assured they are brought to us alive."

Kelvin laughed and poured himself a glass of wine. He inhaled the bouquet, appreciating the aroma. "I can assure you we will do our best; however, there are no guarantees."

"There will be, this time, Kelvin," Duran said in a harsh tenor. "I can personally assure you that if any one of them is mortally wounded I will take measures against the soldier who inflicts the wounds. And it won't be pleasant."

Kelvin sat back on the leather divan, his saber casually placed against a Narnist hutch. He sipped the wine. "Death does occur, but I think that you will find my men much more disciplined than that rabble in the courtyard."

"They will obey me to the death if need be."

"You? Not the Hand of Keth?" He glanced at Surik who now stood by the window, gazing at the sky."

"I lead the Guard of Oran."

"Yes, but you will not lead them in my city, at least not on this venture." He stared down the pale swordsman. "You don't want to risk the propriety of the arrest. As you so rightly pointed out, Paravel is a free-city."

Duran frowned at the silver haired Lord Protector. Then, he laughed. Surik looked up startled. Myella smiled, knowing her day was not far off.

***

Again they pushed through the milling crowds. John was ready to give up and go back to the inn; they had been to four smithies and not one had met with Mike's approval. Mike now stood talking to a blacksmith at the door of his small shop. The place was wedged between two larger businesses, one a tanner and the other, to Mike's luck, an apothecary.

The smith himself was in his late forties, short and stout, and reminded the big man in many ways of Chill. He uncrossed his arms as he listened to Mike; they were large arms, obviously accustomed to the hammer and the anvil. His big hands smoothed his leather apron as he nodded. Mike noticed that the shop itself was open in the rear where the forge, his tools, and steels were located. It was a clean and well-kept place, everything as it should be.

John watched as Mike explained the diagram he held open to the man. Mike appeared to have little difficulty in explaining his thoughts and the man would often wave his hand and tell Mike to proceed. The dark eyed student turned away from his friend and looked once more over the bazaar. It was mid-afternoon now, and business was booming.

Yet he was lost in his thoughts; once again they turned to Chill. He moved his hand to his pocket, feeling the smooth curve of steel frames, the sharp fragments of broken lenses. Chill's glasses, kept for the memory and as a token for Joe when he was found. Chill had been almost as blind as a bat without them; he had always been very near-sighted. John smiled as he remembered the stout man and his slow, laconic manner. That manner often belied a quick wit. If only we had spent more time teaching him how to fight, he thought.

They had spent many nights in Galfeon Yor, more than a month, and John and Tom would practice their waza in the courtyard of Trevor's keep. Together they would go over their forms and Chill would learn. Chill had learned some forms in a day that had taken John a month to master. Obviously even this had failed the young man. Joe had pointed out one evening that if Chill were pressed too hard he might panic and fall back on his standard hack and slash. His limited skills at foil fencing would do him little good in this world of heavier swords and advanced skills. Is that what happened?

Is that what will happen to us?

341

"Lord Knight," came a soft voice and John turned to see Torec next to him. "Any news?" John asked as he adjusted his cloak and turned to the helmed man.

"Some, your pictures are circulating throughout the city. As for news of your friend, Surik, I am afraid it is not good."

"What?" John felt a sinking feeling in the pit of his stomach. The merchant looked around suspiciously and leaned closer to the outlander.

"It seems Myella is using your friend to usurp the Regency of the South. She has made him Arch-Regent and Hand of Keth, the ritual headsman of Oran. Rumor has it that he is naught more than a conjured Dhareem, how do you say? Mindless spirit-slave. Also there was an attempt upon his life and it failed. I know not of what significance that was."

John frowned. "That sort of fits with the information Mike got from the prostitute." It wasn't good, Joe being under the control of this Myella. And assassins? Why? Were they next? "What now?"

"I will try one more source, a woman I know. She owes me one last favor. Mayhap we will find the Bard and Smiling Wolf also."

Tom looked from the dark corner of the tavern. They had arrived there late the night before and, having stayed in the room all the day, decided to come out for the evening meal. They figured it would be safe as long as they were cautious and did not draw any attention to themselves.

Bill sipped at his wine and looked over the rim to gaze at Tar'elah, now dressed more conventionally in leather riding pants and silken blouse and vest. Tom leaned close to him...to whisper. "So, you like her?"

Bill nodded an affirmative and smiled. The wine was good and it only made him more aware of the feminine presence sitting next to him. As if knowing she was being spoken of, she turned and looked at the Bard.

"How are your ribs?" she asked, gesturing to the wrap beneath his shirt. "They'll be fine. Your wrap did wonders, though I'm still sore and expect to be that way for a month." He looked up and smiled as a young serving girl brought their plate of bread and cheese. It was hazy with smoke in the common room and the people were loud and boisterous.

"How do we go about finding the others?" Bill asked of Tom, as the Sioux shoved Kiera's probing head back into the fold of his tunic.

"I don't know. They're probably lying low. I wonder if they're still on their way or what. Our best bet would be to hit some of the more well-known Inns in the hope of spotting them."

Bill nodded and watched as a visible hush came over the tavern. The doors had swung wide to allow several men in the gray and red of the City Guard enter. They set their shields and halberds next to the table and sat down, gesturing to the serving girl.

"Great," Tom whispered as they received their ale and became obnoxiously loud. "We pick the tavern that's the hangout for the local cops."

"Just remain calm," Tar'elah replied as one of the guardsmen looked at their table. After a time the common room returned to normal. Most of the patrons had decided to ignore the new arrivals or had left. Of course, the three of them were prevented from leaving or retiring to their room because the guardsmen's table lay directly in their path. Tom just looked on, unconcerned until one of the guards grabbed the barkeep. He gestured wildly for a moment then pointed directly at their table.

"Uh oh," Smiling Wolf muttered, loosening the thong on his garrote.

"What?" Bill sat up, aware that something had changed, but the wine inhibited his senses slightly.

"Here is one!" shouted the guard and strode quickly to their table. He brought

Bill to his feet with the tug of one gauntleted hand. "A minstrel!"

"Yes," replied the barkeep. "They call him Bard." Tom relaxed and sat down as Bill looked around confused. He was pushed toward the center of the floor and he looked imploringly at Tom who just smiled and crossed his arms.

Tar'elah looked on, amused at the man's predicament.

"I am sorry, I don't have an Ighuire," he stalled. But, to his chagrin, the barkeep pulled out an instrument, like the one Mrick had given him and then smashed, from beneath the bar and tossed it to the blonde-haired man.

"It belonged to the last minstrel; he didna go over too well." The man shook his head and turned away. Bill felt his heart skip a beat.

"Wonderful," he sighed. He pulled a chair into the center of the floor and all eyes turned to him as a hush fell over the common room.

"Lords," he said, tilting his head to the guards. "And Ladies, and whatever is left." This brought a little laughter and he smiled nervously.

"You have drafted me from my table and I hope that I can entertain you to your high expectations." He strummed the Ighuire, tuning it as he spoke. Then he smiled and began to play an intricate set of scales that merged into a melody. It transfixed the listeners in the room, charming them, making them part of the music...or so it seemed. The notes took on a fluid form as they leapt from the instrument and went adrift on the smoky currents of air. At one moment the patrons would smile and another they would be close to tears. All were rapt with the music, even Tom and Tar'elah.

Bill felt as if he were one with the instrument, his ribs barely hindering his play. It was a catharsis that startled and excited the Bard, making him aware of his surroundings as if he were part of the sound that wrapped around all the objects within the room. The people became an instrument at his command. He could evoke this note in that person and they would cry, or this note in another and make her love. It was a strange power he discovered as he played, and he reveled in it. He turned his attention to Tar'elah and, as the song built to its climax, he sent it to her with his own feelings. He felt happiness and love in this world unlike any he had experienced in his own reality. He knew that hope existed for him and his companions.

With a flurry, he ended the melody on a happy note and those about him applauded and laughed.

The guardsmen seemed genuinely impressed and, after a pause, a handful of copper shenks rained at Bill's feet.

"Another tune, Bard," came a shout, this time from the barkeep. "If ye keep it up, ye have a place here."

Bill smiled and wondered at fate. The City Guard had gotten him a job. "This song's lyrics were written by my friend Michael, who isn't with us at the moment. It says much so listen well." His prelude was somber, low tones hinting with tremolo all on the threshold of discord.

Long lance with dripping blood, through axe and cloven head. Our independence we have won, begotten from the dead.

Is freedom really worth it?

All this trouble and this pain. Just to oust one tyrant, and let another reign.

All the dead are buried, and all the land repaired.

Shall we again allow the children to have, what? their freedom impaired.

Now all the land is burning, and the people are afire.

Shall we again oust the tyrant, to kneel before his sire?

Bill ended the song with a discord that sent shivers down one's spine. There was a nervous cough in the back, but otherwise all was silent. Treason was all that Tom could think of and the guards' faces revealed the same thought.

Then there were several nods of approval and more coins danced at Bill's feet. One of the guards scowled, but the others hushed him; after all didn't the Conclaveum threaten Paravel? Bill realized his close call, finished his set with a happier tune and then gathered his coins and headed for his table.

"You don't know how I feel," Bill croaked as he gulped his wine.

"Oh, I do, buddy, I do." Tom smiled and looked at the guards. One nodded in appreciation as they got up to leave.

"You are very good, Bard William," Tar'elah commented as she looked at the golden haired man.

"Thank you, Tar'elah." He smiled wanly, the adrenalin crashing in his system; his hands were trembling. "But right now I think I just need a breath of fresh air."

Joe lay on his back and Myella atop him, crooning her pleasure. Her fingers curled into his hairy chest as he lay there, breathing heavily.

"You are such a good slave. Even dispatching those assassins. You are proving your worth, Surik. My uncle was right in that you are indeed powerful, but not in the way which he imagines." She disentangled herself from him, letting the sheets fall to the marble floor. She strutted lightly across the room and to the balcony. It was night, but the city glowed with dim lamps that at times wound like snakes through the port city. She caressed her warm skin, which still tingled from the tumultuous liaison.

"You all possess special abilities, and these make you important to me. You are skilled in the art of war and, from what Duran tells me, you are skilled in sorcery as well. Soon I will enthrall all of your friends and use you to my own ends.

"You see, Surik Shadowlord, Master of the Shades, I control this city, and its people hold me in fear. When the time is right, I will spread my dominance west and eventually north." He groaned and tried sit up, but could not. She turned from the dark night; her eyes piercing obsidian stones, portals to the soul of a predator.

"Soon...soon. You will come to accept that I own you and your soul." She went back to him, to use him, to lead his mind to the very edge of hell itself.

John, Mike and Torec watched as the guardsmen left the Fulchard Inn, slightly drunk and very loud.

"You think that they know we're staying there?" Mike asked as he stood in the dark shadows of the alley.

Torec thought for a moment. "My men are staying at another, across town. They would not risk congregating at the Fulchard. No, I think these are probably just having a few drinks before they head home."

"I don't know, I think something's going on." Mike pulled the orb from his pouch. It glowed faintly, illuminating his face to the others. Then he thrust it away as the sound of laughter rolled up the street. A large group of sailors and dockworkers were having a good–natured shouting match as they neared the Inn.

"Do you wish me to follow them?" Torec queried, motioning to the guardsmen as they headed down the street.

"Yeah, I'll come with you." He looked at his friend. "Sir John can check the Inn." John nodded and waited for Torec and Mike to slink down the street, they kept to the shadows. Then, as the group of sailors neared the Fulchard Inn, he saw a familiar face.

"John!" he heard the shout as he and the Bard locked eyes.

"Bill!" John called back and started through the press of men and women that suddenly filled the street. They reached one another in the middle of the throng.

"Where have you been?" John asked above the din.

"It's a long story...let's get inside before–" He was cut short by a strangled yelp and the hard clap of horses' hooves. They both looked up to see the crowd open to reveal mounted guardsmen pressing their way in.

"Run!" John called and shoved Bill back toward the entrance of the Inn. Bill ducked through the door and John drew his katana. At the sight of the display the lead horseman, a man with silvering hair, smiled grimly and drew his saber.

John immediately reassessed his plans.

As the horse bore down on him, he rolled to the side and the saber passed where his neck had been. On his feet once more, he dodged a horse, pushed a sailor under the hooves, and headed into a dark alley.

"Shit!" he yelled as another rider cut him off. Turning, he darted through the nearest doorway.

The brothel was dark and suddenly quiet. He really didn't take time to notice the shocked expressions of the women as he darted through the parlor. Or the look on the face of the patron he hurdled. He ducked down a hallway and found a rear window, which he dove through, regardless of the glass.

He got to his feet in one of the more filthy alleyways and grinned at his resourceful escape. He brushed himself off and turned to leave, but the five men on horseback proved an interesting obstacle. They had obviously anticipated his decision and moved smoothly to cut him off. The silver haired leader dismounted, saber in hand, all the while watching the katana.

"Outlander, I arrest you."

"Right." John cracked a crooked grin and brandished his sword.

At that point, something smashed into his elbow and his sword went skittering across the cobblestones. He was about to turn but something tripped him and he fell to his knees. A glancing blow caught him in the side and he rolled. There was another kick to his shin as he tried to get his knife.

He felt white-hot pain sear through his shoulder and his knife fell with a clatter. Looking at his shoulder, he saw the thin blade of a saber, followed its length to a hand, and then a face.

Cruel. Hard. Smiling at him coldly. "Duran," John gasped in pain.

"Very good, Sir John," replied the bearded man as he twisted the blade. John let out a cry of agony. "I am surprised I could steal upon you so, but considering you are about the same caliber as your deceased companion...tsk, tsk. It is a shame that we will not have the chance to duel, but Myella wants you." He withdrew the blade and John watched his own blood fall from the steel. "I fear that the Lord Knight is about to find oblivion unsettling. Don't you, Kelvin?"

John felt himself being pulled to his feet, then unconsciousness took him beyond pain.

Bill rushed into the Inn, his breath of fresh air turning to a gasp. He spotted Tom in the corner and, without a word, grabbed him and took him upstairs to their room.

"Am I allowed to ask what's up?" Tom said, but the question was moot. His senses had already told him that there was danger and that Bill was responding appropriately. Down below, he could hear the startled shouts of patrons in the common room and the clatter of hooves in the street. Someone was in a hurry.

Bill slammed into the room where Tar'elah was gathering their things. She too had heard the commotion and was preparing her gear.

"We gotta go," Bill said breathlessly as he tucked Chill's knife into his belt and shoved his clothes into a pack. Tom had gone to the window, gear in hand, and was looking into the alley.

Tar'elah pulled her hair into a knot and nodded to Tom. "Is it safe?"

The Sioux nodded and took Tar'elah's gear. They watched as she dropped lithely to the ground, rolled, and came to her feet. Tom tossed her sword down and she brought it up in defense, but no assailant came.

It was Bill's turn and, with some hesitation, he lowered himself to the sill and dropped. Once he was on the ground, Tom tossed out the rest of their gear. Then the door burst open.

Tom spun, his short blade in hand. The first guardsman's momentum carried him well into the room, and Tom raked his sword across the unarmored throat. The man fell instantly. The guard behind him brought his own weapon up and warded off the Sioux's next blow. Tom fell back in a roll and came to his feet as Kiera sprang from his tunic and onto the man's face.

Yelping, the guard tore Kiera off, her claws laying open the skin of his forehead and cheeks. Then he lunged toward Tom, who sidestepped, avoided a nasty thrust, and cut through the man's hamstrings. As the guard collapsed, Tom laid wide his side from hip to spine. He ran to the window, hearing shouts from down the hall.

"Go on," he shouted, but Bill paused. "Don't worry, go on." His two friends nodded and headed off into the night. Tom turned and felt Kiera leap to his arm. Then he was out the window as the next guardsman came through the door.

The man ran to the window and looked into the alley, but no one could be seen or heard on the dank street. Nevertheless, he dropped out the window and searched the alleyway, fearing the wrath of Lord Duran.

Tom pulled himself up to the rooftop when the guard was out of sight. He tightened his muscles, gripping the shingles; it had begun to drizzle and they were quite slick. Hoping that his light skin and hair would not betray him, he crawled across the roof, Kiera chirping all the way.

"This is some weird shit," he whispered.

Kelvin looked hard at Duran, frowning at his treatment of the outlander. He roughly sheathed his sword and looked at the prostrate and bleeding young man.

"Was that necessary?"

Duran looked up and scowled. "Necessary? Oh, yes, and if it were not for my orders, I would enjoy lopping off a limb or two."

The silver haired Lord Protector knelt at John's side. He tentatively touched the wound that Duran had inflicted. It was bleeding freely and the student's breathing was labored; his tunic was now all but saturated with the blood. A vein might have been cut.

"He needs a healer or he might die."

"A shame." Duran looked toward several of his men and motioned them to attend to the fallen man. They waited for Kelvin to stand away from the outlander.

"Did you hear me, Duran? He will die."

"Myella will have him."

"Is he any use to her dead?" He stood, the vehemence of his words turning his face red. Duran just smiled and pulled off his gloves.

"Your services are no longer needed, Lord Protector."

Kelvin stood and squared off against the younger man, eye to eye. His left hand flexed involuntarily. Inches away from Duran's face he spoke in low tones for only the Lord of Qwen.

"This is my city before yours, boy. He will be healed first. There is a House not a block from here. If he isn't healed, you will be the one unable to make it even that far. I will then turn him over to you and that bitch to do with what you will."

Duran's eyes narrowed and the Guardsmen of Oran shuffled nervously. Then the pale man smiled and stepped back, waving nonchalantly. "Tis your gold to heal him, Kelvin. Your gold."

"Damn, damn, damn, damn, damn, damn, DAMN!" Mike cursed after they had followed Duran and the guardsmen to what Torec said was a House of Healing. After about an hour of waiting in the dark and stinking alley, the Lord Protector rode off with his men and Duran and the Guard of Oran brought John out on a narrow pallet.

Then it was a long trek through the streets of the city to the North Quarter. Carefully shadowing the contingent of soldiers, they were soon led to the Seat of the Surrogate. There, mounted soldiers in black patrolled the eight-block area of the North Quarter, and they were hard put to avoid the patrols, let alone attempt to free their companion. As night pulled Torec and Mike to its bosom, they watched the iron Gates of Osso close with a clang.

Torec frowned and pressed to the wall of the building where they were concealed. They had watched as the Lord Knight was taken into the hold.

"Come, we must bide our time," Torec muttered and took hold of Mike's arm. Mike followed frowning, but also feeling the reassuring warmth of the orb as it radiated in his pouch.

"Okay, what do you have in mind?" Mike watched the spike on Torec's helm bob as they jogged down the street.

"My friend. She will have to help. We will go to her."

"Why does she have to help?"

"Because." It was all Torec would say, and Mike wondered if things could get any worse.

Chapter 19

Thunder echoed in the distance as the Daedalo bumped heavily against the dock and ropes were tossed to the waiting hands. It was a low, two-masted trader and it usually carried a crew of seven, along with the post from Ionet. Now, the Daedalo carried over two score of the White Guard.

Marad jumped from the bow and landed lightly on the wooden dock. A storm had set in rapidly with nightfall, but luckily they had reached Teshwa before the cloudburst. The Captain of the White Guard looked about for a dockmaster to send for a horse, but there was none around, only the dockhands who were there to receive the post.

Kel stepped quickly onto the dock and watched as the first of their men began to disembark. Then he approached his captain; Kel was rather sullen after the cramped voyage upriver.

"Next time we will ride horses, sergeant," Marad said curtly. The smell of water and rotting fish was nauseating. He walked to the dockmaster's office with Kel in tow, but the small building was unlit and empty. He frowned and wondered why there was no one supervising the hands and, for that matter, why there was no one around to fetch horses for embarking passengers. "Fool's, awful time to take a break," he cursed, and Kel shook his head.

"There should be a carriage on the street, milord."

"Yes, there should be. You take care to billet the men properly, then join me at the Seat."

"Yes, sir." Kel turned and strolled back to his men, who were now standing in ragged formation in front of the boat.

Marad walked past several warehouses before he found himself on the main street of the wharf district. Here, the sounds of music and laughter broke the quiet night as he passed several bars and taverns. A few drunken sailors stood in the doorways or huddled in the alleys, relieving themselves. "It's good to be home again," he mused sarcastically.

He spotted a black carriage sitting on the cobbled street near a lamp; the driver was wiping down a bay gelding. The carriage was older, with tarnished fixtures and rails, and the black enamel was cracked, but it would do.

"Ho there, driver," he called and the small man turned. What the carriageman saw was a man in a dingy white cloak and sporting tangled blond hair.

"What do you want?" the driver asked in a rather grating tone. Marad thought it insulting, but then the man caught the side rail of the carriage and pulled himself into the seat as if to leave.

"I would like a ride," Marad replied.

"Ride, huh; you got shenks?" The man looked down with beady brown eyes. He held a whip in his left hand, ready to strike Marad across the face if he got too close.

Marad pulled his cloak far enough aside to reveal his pouch of coins and the hilt of his sword, but not so much as to reveal his emblem of office.

"All right then," the man said and before Marad could close the door, the coach sprang

357

forward and he was jolted roughly against upholstery within. He wondered if this man were insane.

"The Seat," he called out through the open front to the driver. The man turned around sharply with surprise.

"What? You kinnot be serious. To trespass is death."

"I know."

"Then where?"

"The Seat."

The man shook his head and snapped the reins. The horse moved faster down the street, its hooves sounding with a heavy canter. The driver even took a turn at that precarious speed and Marad had to clutch at the door. They were moving down the Avenue of the Keeps, where many of the members of the Conclave had estates along the river.

He sighed. At one time his family had had an estate here. But, with their rise in the political structure of the Conclaveum, they had moved to more ostentatious quarters. That had happened when he was very young, before the birth of his other siblings, almost thirty years ago. Now the family had nearly disintegrated. Mother was dead, Adon in seclusion, and his sister – well, that was another story altogether.

He let his thoughts wander as they rode down the avenue. Occasionally, thunder from the approaching storm would obscure the sound of the carriage as it rumbled roughly over the paving, but as of yet no rain had fallen. He contemplated the buildings as they passed into the inner city, the guard waving them through the gate that breached the seventy-seven foot wall. The inner city was slightly more alive than the wharf district, at least this section. Teshwa was an ancient city, and its size reflected a diversity of culture that was astonishing. Though they traveled on the main street, the city was also maze of alleys, byways, and catacombs. Fully three levels deep, down to the Old City itself, Teshwa was like a living, thriving being. Here, things were relatively calm, but at other levels and other sections the city buzzed with industry, crime, poverty, and political intrigue. He had never seen the entire city; it was said that only Oswaf, the Keeper of the Libraries knew it all, and he was easily over a century and a quarter old. Marad had no doubt that he would never see all the subtleties of Teshwa. There were certain areas not even the Guard of the Seat would tread; dark areas, like the underside of a sleeping beast, evil areas, that only fools or the dead went. Now, carriages and horses passed them, going about their business. People strode the sidewalks, patronizing the stores in this well-lit and kept district. This road led to the center of the city, as all roads did in Teshwa. Before him, he could see the gothic structure of the Seat rise into the night. No lights shown through the stained glass windows, and the central spire glowed with static electricity. As they came closer, the buildings gave way to the Circle of Niva. It was a wide avenue that encircled the Seat; about a five hundred spans in width it offered no unseen entrance to the large fortress.

The carriage crossed it at breakneck pace and skidded to a halt before the huge bronze doors centered in the wall.

"Out," the driver stated tersely. Marad stood forth from the cab and threw back his cloak. Thunder echoed and the gelding flared its nostrils. The driver stared aghast at the emblem, a hawk in a ring of flame, on the man's armor.

"My Lord, I had no idea," he stuttered. Marad looked up and smiled. The man clambered down and bowed low, not raising his head to meet the Captain's eyes.

"Your hand," Marad hissed. "Hold it out."

The man trembled in fear and held out a shaking hand. Marad plopped a gold shenk into it.

"Milord?"

"Your swiftness was appreciated."

"Thank you, milord."

He did not turn at the sound of the man's hasty retreat. He strode forward to the heavy doors and pulled one open with his thickly corded arm. He stepped into the ill-lit foyer and was met by two guards dressed in polished brass armor and wearing the gray livery of the Guard of the Seat. They barred the way to the hallway behind, their halberds glinting in the light of distant sconces. He turned to them.

"I am Marad." They immediately stepped back upon recognizing his name, giving him access to a fortress so rarely seen by the public. He walked through the portal and tossed his filthy cloak onto a bench. With long strides, he proceeded down the hall, flanked on either side by the marble busts of the Conclavators. It seemed to stretch on almost forever, but he turned away from the gallery, entering another hallway leading off to the side.

He came to another guardsman who curiously glanced at his sword, and then at the symbol of Tarn emblazoned on his burnished armor. The man saluted and opened the door to the Hall of the Clave and, in doing so, opened to him the memories of his youth. For a moment it was as if he were five again. He thought of his two uncles, his brother Adon, his sister. He remembered when he was but seven, the duel between his father and uncle Trevor, and then learning of the death of his mother at this very door. He remembered Trevor's capitulation and subsequent exile to the South. Only Marad remained privy to his father's compounded grief.

He shook his head to clear it and entered the room. At the far end, opposite himself, was the Seat of the Conclavator, over a hundred paces away. Tall granite columns supported the ceiling that rose into vaulted darkness. Five men with hands linked could not measure the girth of these pillars. Spaced between each column was a bowl-shaped pit, wherein danced the Souls of the Conclave: the flames that signified each of the Conclavators since passed. Along the sides of the hall rose the tiered seats of the current members of the Clave, now absent.

He walked down the right side of the Hall, between the massive pillars and the seats of the enclave. It was a long walk but his pace did not slacken. Soon he stood before the Seat of the Conclavator, and the man who had governed the Conclaveum for the past five decades.

Most notable were the last three digits of the Conclavator's left hand. Lost in that fateful duel years before, they were now crafted of silver and resembled bones, animated by some ancient necromancy. They clenched at the granite armrests of the Seat. The Conclavator himself was obscured behind the hood of his purple robe except for the sparkle of his piercing eyes.

"You have come," the voice resonated through the chamber. Yet, it was a pale shadow of the voice that Marad was accustomed to hear resonating across the Conclave. It was pained and labored with every breath.

"Adon sent for me."

"No, I have. Adon is...missing."

Marad's eyes widened slightly. "What?"

"It would not have been proper to summon you out of sentiment, but a note from your brother... the Sequestiary in the Temple of Tarn was razed. Adon is missing."

"Razed?" His thoughts flew. How could it be razed, the spiritual center of their religion?

The Conclavator shook his head. "The Sequestiary was...attacked, they say."

"So, you have summoned the Captain of the White Guard, my Liege?"

"No, I have summoned my other son." The Conclavator Ironeas stood and stepped from the Seat. Marad noticed that his father had aged much more than would be accounted for by the five years that they had been separated. Father and son were much the same height, but Ironeas was thinner and obviously frail.

"Rumors are all I have. Rumors of your sister, of Adon, and of Narn-toc. Rumors that the Tower

362

of Iss is active and the Keth have returned to spread the vileness."

"Keth? Not since Mother's death..." He noticed his father gasp and almost stumble. "Are you ill?"

"Yes, poison, so my physician says. He has done what he could to stay the venom, but he does not know how much longer he can hold it off. Do not let any in the Clave hear that emotion in your voice, boy, they will dissect you." Then he smiled. His face was somewhat sallow, but the smile encouraged Marad. Ironeas pulled back his hood, short white hair bristling. "So, my son, tell me of the North." Marad wished to learn more of his brother and of the poison, but held his questions. "We sued for peace with Bej-et and the Krim, for now. Kel seems to think that she cannot be trusted, and I would have to agree. But that is the best we can do for now. I left Barish to keep an eye on her and her fleet."

"Kel has a good head on his shoulders," Ironeas replied.

"Yes, and he reminded me of that when the Clave conceded the Archipelago of Bequa to Bej-et, so that hostilities would cease."

"The Clave does not understand the strategic importance of Bequa, they think of it as just a hunk of rock that Bej-et wanted. Now she has it and the Gangli Straits." Marad nodded. "And, she can levy us to death for safe passage. At least this may maintain the peace for a few years."

"I would it were so that the Clave shared your opinion. I am afraid that the example that your sister sets in the South causes skepticism toward

363

your activities in the North. Your sister is abusing her authority. She has seized the Regency, and made her Seat in Paravel."

"She can be no worse than Gelion, father."

"No, but I thought she would be happy as Surrogate. Obviously, diplomacy was not to her liking. She has also annexed Clef, to the displeasure of many of the merchants there. Unfortunately, many of the Clave here liked the notion and support her.

"My son, I fear that Myella had something to do with your brother's disappearance."

"Why?" Marad looked at his father, trying to fathom what crossed the older man's thoughts.

"I know not, something to do with Oran, I think. She was made high priestess of the sect last fall, and to strike at Tarn and her own brother would have been a crowning victory for that evil god. That is one of the reasons I want you to go to the South. Especially if there is the Keth."

"It might be improper for the Captain of the White Guard to infringe upon

Blacks jurisdiction, father."

"I know, my son. But, Guyle has informed me that she is the one responsible for Trevor's capture and imprisonment at Helm."

"Trevor?" Marad was stunned, shocked at the audacity of his sibling. "Yes, and I think she has aspirations for the Seat."

"She is not even of the Clave!" he shouted, appalled.

"If I were dead, by the poison, then she could claim Regency of the Seat. She has many supporters among the Clave."

"But, I would be Conclavator."

"Not if you were dead also." Marad nodded slowly, realizing the truth of his father's words. At last understanding the meaning of the dagger of fine Qwen steel. "There was an attempt on my life in Ionet, though I had thought nothing of it at the time."

"Yes? Well, soon my soul may join the others in yonder pit." He gestured to the flames that eternally burned in the depressions of the floor. Marad nodded, now was not the time for self-pity. Ironeas had always steered clear of the more decadent practices of the Clave, and he would do so with his last breath. Myella, on the other hand had followed too closely the example of the Conclaveum Nobles.

"Would that I were younger, my son, but in the past my vision was clouded with hate, and I am now forced to carry out the Edicts that your uncle Guyle set forth on that day when your mother died." He shook his head and coughed, his animated silver digits clacking together. "Now your sister has cost us peace in the South, at a time when we are in no position militarily or economically to stop her. Apparently, she earned the wrath of a group of outlanders; no more than half a dozen in number, but they killed Gelion and burned his keep in the Great Forest, near Narn-toc. Now the people of the South set themselves against her in favor of these strangers.

"These outlanders evidently possess no small magic," he continued. "Guyle said he would look into it and, as Counselor, he tells me that he feels it

365

is his duty to solve these little mysteries. I do not doubt he has ulterior motives, however.

"So, my son, you will leave with your escort for Helm on the morrow. I want you to speak with Trevor if they will permit you, mayhap he can tell you about the unrest in the South. Go with Tarn."

"And may Tarn guard you also, father," Marad replied. "My heart tells me I will see His face soon enough."

"I will miss you father." He kissed the older man on the forehead.

"And I you." He looked away for a moment. "The Clave does not meet for three more months. Then we must deal with Trevor politically. The law is the law. Trevor was exiled, and if he returns he must be tried, regardless of my, or your, sentiments. Guyle wants to put him in the Tower of Pain." He shook his head sadly, but then looked back to his son. "Would it were so that each of us could have our youthful indiscretions forgiven." He left the Hall, and Marad stared down the length of the Clave, numb.

Chapter 20

Bill kept to the wall, his breathing ragged from the long run. Tar'elah stood in front of him, cautiously peering around the corner. He collected his thoughts. They must have run across a quarter of the city, finding the streets and alleys crawling with the City Guard. It was a wonder that they hadn't been caught.

"I see no one," the bandit whispered. "But, that does not mean there is no one concealed there."

Bill nodded. They were trying to get out of the city – if they could get to the courier beast, they would fly west until they spotted Garis, his men, and the rest of her people. Every gate and postern had about a dozen of the red and gray liveried guards and, whether or not it was intended for them, it had so far proved an effective deterrent to their leaving. Now, they stood near a culvert that ran beneath the south wall of the city. Bill could only imagine what kind of filth found its way into the tunnel, and soon they too would be added to the detritus.

The Bard looked over Tar'elah's shoulder and clutched at her waist. She pressed back, gathering in his comfort and warmth. He turned her around and pressed his lips to hers; warm, moist, sensuality gripped him as she fought to suppress her desire. He laughed inwardly, realizing how absurd this was. He had, in threat of their life, embraced a moment of passion. He did not know why, maybe it was the danger, or the need for security, or just their mutual passion, but it definitely saved their lives.

"You there!" called the red cloaked guardsman as he stood up from the alcove near the culvert. He set his heavy crossbow down and shook his head. "Kinna you find another place to sate yirselves?"

Bill looked up from the kiss, startled, as the man stepped over the curb and walked toward them. He turned up the wick on his lantern as he approached. Tar'elah looked into Bill's eyes and smiled. She loosened the short sword on her hip; she was turned away from the man and her back concealed the gesture.

The guard stepped closer, holding the light high with his right hand, and peered more closely at Bill. The shock of recognition crossed his features, and he fumbled for his crossbow, clumsily trying to maintain his grip on the lantern at the same time.

Bill knocked the lamp from the man's hand and dodged behind him, locking his arms in a half nelson. Tar'elah casually and effectively cut the man's throat with one swift slash, and began going through his clothing. Bill let him sag to the ground.

"Why in the hell did you kill him? He was just doing his job."

"Indeed," the bandit replied, handing Bill copies of the sketches she pulled from the guardsman's pouch. "It seems that you and your friends were his job tonight." She wiped the soiled blade on the dead man's cloak.

Sheathing her sword she stooped and pulled the man toward the culvert. "If he had lived, he would tell his captain, and they would pursue us.

Now, we must dump the body in here and be done with it. Then we can leave the city."

Bill watched as she tumbled the corpse into the culvert. The figure rolled onto its back, white-eyed and staring, finally sliding along with the other detritus and effluvia. Tar'elah tossed the man's crossbow to Bill, who shook his head sadly as he caught it. The iron tipped arrow was meant for him, he knew, but that still did didn't make it any easier for him to accept their actions.

"Come, Bard William, we must go." She did not look back as she ducked into the tunnel.

***

The salt air was thick in the pier district of Paravel. As Torec walked, his gait took on a peculiar spring and a smile played over his hatchet features. This was where he was at home, amidst the forest of masts and the slap of waves upon the bows of ships. It was a good feeling to hear the toll of a ship's bell in the distance, marking a change in the watch and reminding him of his family's maritime tradition.

He and Mike walked through the thickening mist, searching for a certain warehouse. Mike stepped carefully on the boardwalk; the wood creaked beneath his weight and he could see the dark water below. As they neared the end of the pier, he could make out a large ship, massive ropes holding her steady. He watched as Torec gazed at her lines like one would stare at a lover. Then the man shook his head as if to clear it and walked briskly to the warehouse that now rose like a dark monolith in the thick night. He stopped at a door.

"Well," Mike quipped impatiently. "What are you going to do?"

"Knock," replied the merchant of Clef as he rapped on the wooden portal. It cracked open and a wizened old man looked out.

"Wot di yi want?" he asked with toothless speech.

"I want to speak to Bale," Torec replied. The man nodded and let them in. He uncovered the lamp and gestured for them to follow. Mike crinkled his nose and looked about at the dust-covered and musty crates that filled the warehouse. He ignored the large rats and pressed on into the narrow passage. They were led around a maze of chests and boxes, tarps and netting, until they were finally taken up a flight of stairs and down a long hall. The old salt knocked out a rhythm on the door and left them as a young girl peered out from within.

"Who?" She asked. Mike was sardonically amused at the vocabulary level of the people here.

"Torec, of the family el'Kirien, formerly of Clef. She knows me." The door closed and they waited. At least fifteen minutes passed before Mike spoke to the patient merchant.

"This is worse than a doctor's office. At least there you know you're going to get help." He grunted as Torec raised an eyebrow, but then the door swung open. The girl led them into an antechamber separated from the rest of the room by tall screens.

Mike appraised the girl. She was not tall, and she was of stocky build. Her short hair and attire gave her a boyish look. She moved through a gap in the screen and motioned for them to follow. They entered a room appointed tastefully, yet with restraint.

The woman stood in the rear of the room looking out the window and, at first, Mike thought it was Gabrielle, but then she turned. She was of medium height and about the same age as Torec. Her dark hair was bound in the back by a comb, and grew in great masses of tight curls that framed her face. She smiled seductively at Torec, her lips curving up as her head tilted to him in acknowledgement. She spread her arms and welcomed the merchant in a long embrace.

"What do I have to do to get that?" Mike muttered, watching the display with envy. She looked at him sharply, but with amusement.

"Who is your friend, Torec?" she asked as she sat on a divan. She gestured to Torec to do the same, leaving Mike to stand alone.

"Lord Michael, Alchemist and Swordsman. He is an outlander and the cause of many of Myella's current troubles."

"So, he is one of the dreaded killers that Myella so desperately wants captured. Do you know that you have a hefty price on your brow?"

Mike smiled. "It's nice to know I'm wanted." He leaned against a rather nice table, hearing it creak under his weight. The woman winced.

"That is Narnist, it is priceless..."

"Jeez, sorry. Now, let's get down to business. My companions Sir John, Lord Knight of Erie, and

Surik Shadowlord, Master of the Shades, et cetera, et cetera, have been captured by Myella. This is probably due to the fact that we castrated and killed Gelion." She looked up in surprise at that, but Mike continued. "We are also looking for our other comrades, a Minstrel and a Tracker. They are somewhere in the city. We need assistance in rescuing our friends and getting the heat off of our backs."

"What's to prevent me from turning you over to the City Guard?" She leaned back, nonchalant.

Mike smiled grimly and looked at the short sword tucked into his belt. "How about two feet of steel?" The look on his face told her he was serious.

"So much arrogance for one so young and in such desperate need of assistance," Bale smiled thinly. "I will take you to meet someone who will also find you amusing, Lord Michael. But, do not insult him in this manner, for he will not take it as lightly as I." She left the room; Torec looked at Mike and laughed.

"My friend, you handled that amazingly well."

"It's my charming personality, I'm sure. How do you know Miss Frigid anyway?"

"My family often traded with hers. We were lovers, but her appetites were unorthodox at times and we fell apart."

"Oh, really?" Suddenly Mike was finding her much more interesting.

John didn't want to turn the alarm off; he just wanted to doze a little longer. That was all he really wanted. He knew that it was cold outside, and the prospect of walking to class was a chilling

372

one indeed. Just a little more sleep would be nice. The alarm faded.

Well, he thought. It was an interesting dream, and the girl was beautiful. He let laziness take over, though he worried about classes and research. Would it be Saturday tomorrow? Did he have statistics today? He couldn't remember. He didn't care; he just let his thoughts of his thesis cascade upward and fill his mind.

Chill, was Chill going to the Event? He felt a loss that he couldn't describe. And, God, did he have to piss. Waffles for breakfast, that would be nice. He rolled to the side and felt that familiar feeling of falling. It hurt when he hit.

"Sonofabitch," he groaned. I fell out of bed.

He moaned and rose, his head spun crazily and he almost blacked out. He leaned back and breathed deeply, there was a dull ache in his left shoulder. He opened his eyes, expecting to see his bedroom; instead, the cold, damp stone of a cell wall filled his vision.

"Damn!" he muttered, too frustrated to yell. He looked at his surroundings. There was a window to his right, above the wooden bench he had fallen from. He could see the few stars that pierced the velvet vault and gave the cell the least bit of light. Otherwise, there were only four rough walls and one iron bound door.

Great. The dream was a dream.

He tried to sit up, this time a bit more slowly. As he braced himself against the wall, a sharp pain lanced down his left arm. It seemed, though, that no permanent damage had been done; he looked at the three-inch scar that now marked the spot where

Duran's saber had plunged. There was still blood on his tunic, but he seemed to be whole. He hoped.

His weapons were gone, of course, as was his armor. He still had his St. Christopher medal, and he felt much more secure for that, at least. He looked around: bunk, slop-pot, no food or water. He sat back and relaxed, he had been captured and no doubt Duran had masterminded the whole thing. "I'll kill the bastard yet," he promised himself.

The door swung open as his voice faded and he looked up to see Joe. A smile spread over John's face and he lurched up to grab his friend by the shoulders. "Joe, ol' buddy, am I glad to see you!" he stopped when he saw Duran, a woman, and several guards.

"So, this is Sir John, Lord Knight of Erie," the woman said, and John looked at her. No doubt this must be the woman responsible for Joe's capture.

"I don't believe that I've had the pleasure," John replied sardonically.

"The Lady Myella, Surrogate and Regent of the South," Duran declared, a chilling smile on his face. "I rather enjoyed the hunt, Sir John. Knowing that you carry my mark gives me great satisfaction. It might have been worse for you, had not Kelvin paid for the healer. No doubt you would have lost use of that arm. Pity." John made a move to the pale, bearded man, but Joe shoved him aside, causing him to wince at his sore shoulder. He looked into the blank eyes of his friend. What did they do to you?

"He's not much in a fight, nor to look at, my Liege," Duran said. He pulled the leather gauntlets from his hands and stepped into the cell. John stepped back, on guard.

"Tell that to Gelion, Duran." She looked at Surik. "Take him to my chambers, Shadowlord." Joe took John by the arm and dragged him from the cell. Apparently they were in some sort of tower, because he led the Knight of Erie down a winding stairwell, as Duran and Myella followed closely behind.

"What of Gabrielle?" John heard Duran ask. "Should I speak with her?"

"Yes," Myella replied. "He may be more easy to control with the proper persuasion; we may need her." She trailed off as they rounded a corner. John looked to Joe.

Nothing.

The road from Teshwa to Helm was well paved and heavily traveled. Villages and towns dotted the route and the inns were frequent and inexpensive. Marad and Kel had shaved their force of about fifty to an escort of ten. In doing so, they would save time, and not risk offending the Preceptor of Helm...or the Black Guard.

Marad's party would not reach any town until after nightfall, but the pace at which they set their horses was brisk and stimulating. On either side of the road rose heavy spruce and pine, as well as thick undergrowth. The forest was so dense that one could not see twenty feet deep. Occasionally, the earth would show her spine, and water would course freely beside the road. The day was crisp and clear and hawks circled overhead, hoping for prey.

Marad had shed his breastplate in favor of a lighter chain-mail hauberk, as had his men. The white of their livery, however, told all who they were; this was a boon in the villages, as it sped their progress.

Kel spurred his steed forward to match the pace that Marad had set. His captain nodded at his approach and gestured down the road. There was an intersection up ahead.

"The city of Acturon, not twenty leagues to the northeast. We are almost halfway to Helm."

"Aye. But, will not the Black Guard be displeased at our presence?"

"Probably, and their Commander will raise a stink with the Clave, but not too bad. It's Gythel Boern I believe. We have the papers and seals of the Conclavator himself, I don't think Boern will do anything more than breathe heavily down our necks."

Kel nodded, they had passed the intersection. There was not much traffic on the road to Helm. Beyond the merchant wains and such, very few common folk found their way to the Great Wall. Kel realized that soon the highway would fork, and the southern route would continue to Helm and the other to Baed and beyond.

Marad, though, reflected on different matters. He could not figure out why his brother would leave the Sequestiary of Tarn or whether he had simply been destroyed with all the rest; what had been the nature of the Temple's fall? What force could drive him to leave that Holy Post? Was his sister behind this? He shook his head. He knew that Myella had reached a level of corruption that

376

even some members of the Noble Houses would shun. If she were up to something that threatened their father, Adon would risk anything. Adon had always held himself away from court politics and away from the aristocracy. He was a scholar and a mage and had dedicated his life to Tarn. Marad remembered the day his younger brother had announced he was going to the seclusion of the Temple. Even uncle Guyle had scoffed, just as Myella had done, and had called him weak. Secretly, Ironeas had praised his son, and wished him peace in his new calling.

Then there was Myella's depravity. The Temple held no proscription against marriage or other intimate relations. Yet Myella had tried to seduce her own brother, and that was beyond all bounds. Adon had told him, that on the night prior to his leaving, Myella came to his room disguised as a Lady of his acquaintance. In the flickering candlelight of his bedchambers, Adon had reached out and brushed the hair away from, not the Lady's face, but his sister's. His fury had been so great that he had bloodied and bruised her, and since that day both brothers shunned their sibling. Only old Guyle seemed to continue his contact. In an effort to remove her scandalous behavior from the Clave and Teshwa, their father, Ironeas, had made her Surrogate of the South and sent her away.

At that time, the position of Surrogate was mostly honorary, being nothing more than the Diplomatic liaison to the free-states of the South. To the very Southern tip of the continent, including the Teeth of Narn, and Narn-toc, no one would lay claim. Many said that the sorcery used there had poisoned the rocks, and had spewed forth demons and wraiths. By default, the Conclaveum retained the territory; therefore it was necessary to have the Regent, who would exercise protection of the land, and the Surrogate, who would guide the diplomatic mission in the south. The Regency gave some military control to the south, and the lands that the Conclaveum held there, but it was a thankless and remote post. No one else had vied for the position, so it was given to Gelion and the family of Orr, of which Duran was also a member. Gelion had seen it as a steppingstone to power, and had gladly left Qwen with his retainers to build a fort within the Great Forest.

Unfortunately, Myella had managed to turn the South's stability into a pot of boiling oil. On the sleepless night before he had left Teshwa, Marad and Kel had poured over dispatches and letters that had reached sympathetic members of the Clave, and then to Ironeas' eyes. All the trouble began when Gelion had mysteriously suffered a wound to the groin and required the aid of a healer from Paravel. After that, things had continued to deteriorate. Gelion, with the aid of soldiers from Myella's Guard of Oran and a contingent from the Black Guard, had supposedly put down a small army in Galfeon Yor. That had led to Trevor being sent to Helm. Then Gelion had died at the hands of some outlanders who had mysteriously showed up in the south. In the absence of the Regent, Myella had removed the Regency to Paravel and named herself, and some obscure Necromancer called Surik, to the position of Arch-Regent. Just months before, she had annexed the island state of Clef to the Conclaveum, stating it was what the Council of Merchants wanted. No doubt they were in her pocket just as the Governor of Paravel was, or they were dead.

She had also risen in the ranks of the Temple of Oran, an ancient and evil cult by any standard. She would serve well as the High Priestess of that particular god. Oran was the Overseer of the Underworld and the Bringer of Merciless Justice; the cult also ran deep with undercurrents of the sorcery that had warped Narn-toc. The Tower of Iss was another manifestation of that evil; shunned even by the most brazen citizens of Teshwa.

When Myella had trampled almost every established boundary, Ironeas all but cut off contact with his daughter, only relaying information through Guyle who, as Counselor, must oversee the Surrogate.

Now the path to Paravel lay through Helm, a place where Marad had been only three times in his life. It was a large city by any standard, though not as large or ancient as Teshwa. It was built on an island that straddled the river at the base of the Great Wall. Right down the center of the city was the Breach, the great crack that split the black rampart, creating a chasm by which the Kipris River made its way from the North and joined the river South of the Wall. Deep in the recesses of this chasm shone the lights huge braziers on ancient scaffolding and lifts. If not for these, blackness would engulf a man and drive him mad. It was here that an inlet gave access to the Ocean as well as Qwen and other cities down the Coast.

The Great Wall had been erected during an age of war, when sorcerers and mages battled for control over the Conclaveum, attempting to wrest it from the mad Conclavator Untheran who, in his greed, had doomed his rule by making a pact with Oran. It was an alien construct: black, embedded with the skeletal fossils of strange creatures. Unsettling to all who gazed on it, it was always wet, as if it were weeping. Now it was the barrier between Marad and his sister.

Marad's deep thoughts made him unaware of the horsemen approaching him in the woods. Nor did Kel seem to notice, for his horse fell back a few steps and he looked askance to his men behind. No sooner had Marad rounded a bend in the road, than eight horsemen blocked their way. Marad reined in sharply, causing his horse to rear.

Marad regarded the horsemen curiously. They were all dressed in fringed black overtunics, which covered a combination of blackened chain mail and plate armor. Some carried heavy bastard swords and others spiked maces but, most notably, they all wore large helms that obscured their faces and were broken only by a visor slit. Marad tried to penetrate to their eyes and only saw a gash into hell. The black stallions stamped and snorted, foam on their flanks.

"Who dares to block the highway of the Clave?" By this time, Marad felt Kel close behind. Still the riders that blocked the road did not move. Marad turned to his second and, as he did, the dark riders charged, weapons brandished. It was all Marad could do to pull his sword free of its scabbard and fend off a heavy blow by a mace; it

380

struck so hard that it numbed his arm. But, no other attack was directed at him. Two of the horsemen flanked him, preventing him from riding off. The other six rode past and to the White Guard. Marad could not look behind, but heard the shouts and clashing of steel. One man cried out in pain, then another. It wasn't long before the fighting ceased altogether. His own sword, entangled in a spiked mace, was pulled from his grip. He lurched to the side and grabbed his opponent by the helm, trying to wrench it to the right or left to break the man's neck. A steel grip caught his arm and he was pushed from his saddle. Marad jumped to his feet, pulled a dagger from his boot and thrust it into the flank of the nearest black horse. A scream of agony tore through the beast and it reared, a flailing hoof caught Marad in the chest to send him clear of the falling horse. Then, as the rider was pinned, Marad plunged the dagger into the visor. The man stopped moving.

He looked up; the other horsemen had surrounded him. And Kel. Kel was on his steed, but his sword was not drawn. His men lay dead in the road.

Kel. Kel was with them.

Betrayed.

Chapter 21

It took them a while, but Tar'elah guided the courier beast and Bill looked carefully to spot them. They were almost ten leagues from the city, amid the rolling hills south of the Plains of Straw. At dusk, they spotted the small cooking fire and, circling low, they saw the pot-bellied form of Garis and about fifty of the bandits and mercenaries.

They brought the courier beast to the ground in a rush of air. After verifying their identity, Garis went back to eating his haunch of rabbit. He motioned for them to sit, but only Bill joined the mercenary; Tar'elah went to talk to her people.

"Bard, well met. It is good to see you again." Bill nodded and accepted an offered wineskin, letting the tepid liquid quench his thirst. "Did you find Torec and the others? And where is Smiling Wolf?"

"Things didn't go well. Tom and I were split up. I found Sir John, but the reunion was cut short by the City Guard. I think we are in worse shape than when we began."

Garis frowned and a worried look came over his face. He did not like what he was hearing. "Paravel is a big city, Bard, perchance your friends were not taken."

"Maybe, but in the time we were there, we came no closer to finding out what happened to Surik." Bill looked exhausted as he settled to the ground. Dark rings were evident beneath his eyes and he looked like he hadn't slept in a week. He stretched back and wrapped a heavy blanket about him.

"There is word of strange happenings in the city; of Myella taking over the Regency, and with her Surik, possessed like some demon, at her side." Bill perked up.

"How did you hear about this?" asked the minstrel.

"I sent two of my men into the city, one has returned, the other is looking for Torec.

"Great, just great. I wish we'd stayed here and let you do the dirty work; you certainly found out more than I did. And Surik possessed? You just raised a whole slew of questions that we don't have the answers to. Great." Bill closed his eyes; he just wanted to sleep.

"Also, we are in a poor position. Once in the city, we will have but four score men, including those already inside. That is not much compared to the City Guard and the Guard of Oran."

"What else is new," Bill muttered as he tumbled off into an exhausted and fitful slumber.

Tom moved to the edge of the crowd in the marketplace, near one of the red and gray caped guards of the city. The best camouflage was to be in the midst of your enemy, where they would least expect you. He adjusted the loose linen shirt and brown riding leathers he had creatively acquired, and sat on the edge of the fountain. As he watched the people move by, he bit into a tangy fruit and listened to the talk of the guardsmen not five feet away.

"I ave eard that these outlanders ave er werked up," one of the pikemen said. His sergeant scowled and looked over the crowds. People milled about but he seemed not to notice anyone.

"Word has it that they killed the Regent Gelion, and the lands to the west are wanting war. That is all we need, another war. It's enough that she sends her boats to the east, to Clef. That has affected the trade and business is down. Now the Westerners want a fight."

"Aye, an she sits behine the Wall of the Southern Seat. Did you see the look inna Lord Kelvin's eyes when she summoned him to the Seat?"

"Aye, an what about him going there?"

"To meet the new Arch-regent no doubt. Surik. Nhirel said that seven assassins tried to kill him and he foiled their attack. He said that when one was killed he called up the shade and had it attack the others. Now he has seven wraiths at his command."

Tom smiled at that; no doubt rumors have a way of getting greatly exaggerated as they progress. All the better though, keep them frightened and you have the advantage.

"An did you see the way that Duran rode down the outlander, and Kelvin too? He must be important, otherwise they coulda lanced im."

"Aye, an Myella has him secure behind the Gate of Osso. I'll not go within one hundred spans 'o that Keep. I dinna know how Kelvin does it. But, I wilna."

"Aye, the Guard of Oran is an evil bunch. I wish they were all behine the

Great Wall, instead o' meddlin with the Gov'nor." He shook his head. "We pull the night shift again, phaa!"

"Somethin' is afoot, all the guard are alerted. Its em outlanders I tell ya."

"Yes, Huther. But, at least we're garnerin' twice our share of silver for the duty, and you'll be whorin' some wench without complaint come payday."

"An no doubt you gamblin' it away."

"No doubt, Huther, no doubt," he smiled amiably and they walked off into the crowd.

"Hear that Kiera? They have both John and Joe in the Seat, whatever that is.

I think we're going to have to find out." He gave her a piece of meat and she chewed it complacently. Tom smiled, and waited. He guessed Tar'elah and Bill would be trying to find Garis. He hoped that things would lead them to Myella and the Seat, or else a whole can of whup-ass might open up, and lead them all right to the headsman's block.

Mike walked into the bazaar, trying to be as inconspicuous as he could manage. Tonight they would meet this Guildmaster fellow, and he didn't want to go unprepared. That was why he had ventured to the smithy and that's why he had borrowed the stone from Torec. Here a few months and already up to my ass in debt. Just like home. He grinned, yet he was tired and a furrow split his brow.

He wondered if a city this size ever slept. He supposed not, but he would like to see firsthand what the nightlife was like as long as it didn't come equipped with a squad of guards. He came to the shop, which was closed. It was later than he thought, but he rapped on the door anyway. It would not deter him from his goal.

Soon the smith opened the door, letting the big man in and quietly pouring him a cup of hot Karo. Mike sat down at a small table and looked at the balding smith, who silently cleared the table of his dinner remains, went to his cot and pulled a lock box from beneath.

"Had a feelin' you'd be back soon. Just finished it tonight, worked straight through, like you said." He unlocked the box and pulled back the cloth on top. Black metal and wood gleamed in the flickering light that fell from the oil lamp on the wall. "I finally understood it alfway through the forgin'. Do you have the gold?"

"Is it to my specifications?" the big man asked as he twisted his mustache and looked at the item.

"Aye, down to the silver hammer."

Mike picked it up, heavy, yet right. It was a very good piece of work, considering the primitiveness of the conditions under which it was made and the time constraints. He examined it closely, every last detail was right.

"How much do you think it is worth?" he asked the smith, Pellis was his name.

"Twenty gold shenks at the least," he replied warily.

"No," Mike said and reached into his cloak. "It's not worth that." The man stepped back, expecting treachery.

Mike tossed a gleaming blue gem onto the table. It scintillated wildly in the light.

"My friend tells me that this is worth about fifty of your gold. Spend it wisely, since it buys your silence as well."

The man smiled and nodded. As Mike left his shop the smith picked the gem off the table and stared at its rich color. Aye, twas worth it!

Gabrielle had spent the last weeks sitting with Trianna, assuring her that everything would be fine; that someone, anyone, would come for them. Trianna had been considerably shaken by Sir Chill's death, and they had been whisked away before they could witness the fate of Baxel and the militia. She did not know what had become of her father, nor did she know the fate of the people of Galfeon Yor.

She thought she had briefly spied Surik Shadowlord, and hope flared within her like a flame bereft of air then placed suddenly in the open. But, it could not have been him, for this man was with Myella's entourage, and Surik could most definitely not be in league with that woman.

Her thoughts wove their way down a winding path; above all else, she wondered the fate of Sir John. Had he perished at the hands of Gelion? Or was he now also a prisoner, like herself? Gabrielle could not bear to think that he also might be imprisoned, or worse. She imagined him here, in this chamber of four walls, high up in one of the towers above the Seat. She sighed and stood out on the balcony, gazing upon the courtyard where Myella's Guard drilled and practiced their swordplay. There was a brief knock on the door and she heard Trianna answer.

It was Duran; it always was.

He had come to her many times since her imprisonment, his dark eyes coldly gazing over her, his insinuations and overtures obvious. She had rebuffed him, and if it hadn't been for Trianna's presence, she did not know what might happen.

"Good afternoon, milady Gabrielle. I have come to tell you that you will be leaving soon." She turned and looked at him. She was wearing a simple blue dress, her dark hair cascaded to the side, and her beauty stirred Duran.

"Leaving? For where?"

"Helm, milady. First, however, there is something you will do for us."

"I will do nothing for you Duran."

"Oh, you will...Guard!" A man in black armor stepped through the door. "Take the wench away. I wish to speak with the Lady in private."

The guard grinned and pulled the protesting Trianna from the room. The door shut with a clang. Gabrielle gazed with contempt upon Duran.

"Now, we will talk." He casually unclasped his cloak and laid it on a chair. He walked to her and placed his hands upon her shoulders, staring into her eyes."

"I can take you away from here, Gabrielle. Far from Myella, and so far that Helm would be unheard of." He smiled. "All you have to say is yes and we will be gone. To say no, is to risk death, or worse...they say your father is destined for the Tower of Pain in Teshwa. If that is so, then your fate will follow his. I do not want that."

She shrugged and slipped to the side away from his grasp. She walked to the balcony and looked out over the fields north of the city. "If that is to be my fate, so be it. I would much rather spend it there than with you."

"You are a fool!" he snapped. "I offer you freedom."

"No, you offer me only another form of servitude. I would sooner throw myself from this tower."

At that, he moved for her and pulled her away from the edge of the rail. There was strength in his arm as he took her from the balcony and into the chamber. She looked and saw pain in his eyes, for a moment.

"She promised me the Regency. I could have given you much, and all this could have been avoided. Had you accepted my offer of marriage, and had I taken Gelion's place as Regent, I could have brought peace between the families of the West...but no." His eyes turned cold again. "Myella wants war. The outlanders have sparked it by killing Gelion, and she is just feeding the flame." His jaw muscles rippled.

"You waste your breath. I was never yours, and Sir John will come for me." She looked at him for any sign, but he just gazed at her, his face turning a deep red. "So, Sir John. I thought as much. Well, he will either succumb to Myella or die." She struggled in his grasp and he forced her to look at him, his hand gripping her jaw. Her green eyes flared. He sneered and kissed her roughly, ignoring her clouting the side of his head. She tried to scream, then the kiss was abruptly ended and he pushed her to the floor.

"I should take you right here." He toyed with the thought for a moment, then tore his cloak from the chair and flew out the door. She gazed after him and the guard shut the door.

For the first time since her imprisonment, Gabrielle wept.

***

Surik Shadowlord looked, for what seemed the thousandth time upon the Paravelian sunset. Each time he watched, it seemed to speak to him, evoking something within its coral clarity that might move him. Each time it failed in whole, but not in part. Now he watched the swollen sun, and then the ghostly image of the ringed moon a few hands to the left. Moved ever so slightly, it was now a sliver and a spear.

John watched his friend from inside the chamber, wondering what was, or wasn't, going through the artist's mind. He sat in a stone chair, hands tied.

The chamber itself was quite opulent; it was a large room, the walls and floors of gold veined black marble, polished to a mirrored surface. Behind him was a bed, and before him the balcony where the Shadowlord stood, looking over the rooftops and spires of the city. He believed they must be in the upper story of Myella's Keep. "Well, Surik Shadowlord, looks like you've hit it off with this Myella pretty well." There was more than a bit of sarcasm in his words. It almost seemed as if Joe would retort, but the blankness was there as always. He returned to look once more at the splash of red and gray that marked the sun's passage below the horizon. John sighed as the shadows deepened. Everything had such a rich and crisp luster in this world, if only he could truly enjoy it.

Myella came into the room then, wearing a white robe and silver circlet on her brow, as graceful as a dancer. By its cut, John could tell there was nothing beneath the robe, but he tried not to let that intrude on his consciousness.

"So, now that we have been formally introduced, Sir John, what do you think of my world?" John did a double take.

"You brought us here?"

"Not quite, but you serve a purpose for me nonetheless."

"Wonderful," he grumbled. Already he did not like her.

"Now, I will ask you some questions and you will answer. If not, I will cause you to experience the most exquisite pain you could imagine." She smiled and went behind him. Unlacing his tunic, she began to massage his shoulders. Her hand lingered for a moment on the side of his neck, then energy flowed from her fingers, and he doubled over as pain lanced across his shoulders. He heard her laugh as he moved his head to the side to determine if his neck was injured.

"I get the drift," he said and sat back. She walked to the front of him now and stood at an open brazier, stoking the red-hot coals.

Oh no, he thought. Here come the burns.

"What do you want to know?" he said, feeling no fear, but not wanting to give her anything she didn't already have.

"Where are the others?"

"What others?"

"The Tracker, the Bard, and the Alchemist."

"Last I saw they were at the Fulchard Inn."

"You know they are not there now. Where did you plan to regroup?"

"We didn't."

"Only fools would not plan for such a thing."

"Exactly," he said as he smiled crookedly.

"Do not play games with me." She suddenly reached forward, grabbed his testicles and squeezed. He sagged back into the chair, pain flowing from below. Now he could really sympathize with what Joe had felt. She stood there for a moment, watching his face, the grimace of pain and the flush of color. This perverted woman was actually enjoying his torment! He took a deep breath and fought to regain his composure.

"You will not lie again, Lord Knight."

"I wasn't lying. We're really not as smart as you think we are," he gasped. "Understand, Sir John, just as there are punishments, there can also be rewards," she opened her robe to reveal her lithe form. John tried not to gape; this was definitely how Joe had gotten captured.

"I'm really in no condition to appreciate it at the moment," he said as his eyes indicated his damaged groin. "Besides, from what I hear every common man and gutter slime has had that. It has no real value."

She slapped him across the face and he laughed. "Is that the best you can do? I thought you capable of a more devastating retort."

All pretense of seduction dropped, Myella re-tied her robe. "I saw Gabrielle yesterday, Lord

Knight." He stiffened and she smiled cruelly. "She is quite beautiful. It is a shame she will end up with the likes of Duran.

"It will give me pleasure to make you and your friends mine, one by one. I have need for another Hand of Keth: you and Surik, side by side. My Uncle tells me that once men finally succumb completely, they are very efficient servants." She went to the table near the bed and John craned his neck to see her pour blood red liquid into a goblet. She brought it to him and held it to his lips.

"Drink," she said and against his will he felt compelled to. The harsh liquid burned down his throat. He gagged.

"Now, Sir John, Lord Knight of Erie, you are mine. Balq..."

John heard her faintly and realized that a spell was being cast over him. Well, shit, he thought. Then there was that familiar burning on his chest and the liquid no longer warmed his stomach. He felt slightly ill, but any mind-altering effect was gone. He tilted his head back and sent a silent thanks to the heavens. Saved once again by his St. Christopher medal.

"Is that the best you can do? A naming spell?"

She stepped back in shock, realizing that her spell had failed; her face flushed red with rage. "What power do you have that wards against the spell!" she shouted, only to hear John's laughter. "Tell me or die!"

"Then you definitely won't know," he replied and the tone of his voice held a finality that reflected dangerously in her eyes.

"I can offer you riches, power, myself. Tell me!"

"Not on your life, sweetheart!"

A sneer distorted her face and she stepped back. "No, Lord Knight, it will be your life! You will have the pleasure of seeing your Gabrielle die and then you will be sent to Oran where your soul will wither in torment!" She set her shoulders and stormed from the room.

Surik Shadowlord looked out over the city as a cold wind blew his hair back. He had felt the burning in his chest also, but it was a distant touch. It smoldered. Unlike his sword, it was not instantaneous, but slow in its permanency and undoing. It would run the course.

Bale had led them to a low building not far from the warehouse in which she resided. As they walked, Mike noticed a change in the air, the cool dampness that spoke of an impending storm. Torec had said that at this time of the year a storm could come off the sea without warning, and then it was best to be indoors. Mike, however, thought differently. He loved the electricity of the storm and the unleashing of the natural forces. Having grown up on Lake Erie and watched the breakers crash over the rocks and onto the street not a stone's throw from his porch, he appreciated the energy and vitality of nature. He did not fear it.

They crossed the deserted street and were admitted to a low building that stood out over the water. After a march through a dark hallway, they were ushered into a well-lit room of distinctive taste. Heavy wood paneling was accented with brass finishings and there was a definite nautical theme to the decor. As they waited for the owner of the posh quarters, they appraised the effects.

Before them thick curtains hid the leaded glass doors that must have cost more than a few gold. These opened onto a deck that looked out over the harbor, and gave immediate access to a sloop. In front of the doors was a brass telescope and next to that a chart table and sextant, maps, and compass. The floor was covered with fine rugs, and oil lamps lit the room warmly. Before them sat a long cherry desk and a large chair awaiting its occupant. As Mike was assessing the value of the various pieces in the room, the door opened and a man passed between him and Torec to sit at the well-appointed desk.

He wore a black tunic that billowed at the sleeves and fastened with tight cuffs at the wrists. He also wore black breeches and these had gold piping. He was slender, yet his movement denoted power and speed. His black hair was curled painfully tightly and his features were sharp and chiseled; he had high cheekbones, a narrow nose, and a square jaw. His eyes were an intense shade of hazel, more amber than not.

After a few moments he cleared his throat. "You are Lord Michael?" he asked pointedly of the former physicist.

"Who else? And who the hell are you?"

The man smiled at that, and crossed his arms. "I am called Alaric. That is all you need to know for now. It seems you have a situation."

"That's an understatement."

"Tell me your story."

"Fine," and Mike proceeded to explain his travails, excluding, of course, their true origin. This kept Bale and Alaric rapt for some time, and they did not interrupt. Torec embellished the story somewhat, and soon Mike was finished. Alaric nodded his head.

"This Surik Shadowlord, he is your companion?"

"Yes," the big man replied. "He was captured by Myella. That was what precipitated my killing Gelion."

"You killed the Regent?"

"Yep, stuck him like the pig he was." At this Alaric looked to Bale, who shrugged.

"Is Surik now in league with Myella?"

"Hell no, he's under some spell, sorcery."

"I saw him kill a man."

"I've heard he killed several."

"That he did." Alaric frowned for a moment. Then, "The city's Council is frightened of Myella. They now know that her designs are to annex the city, just as she annexed Clef. Some of the Council are in her pocket, as is the Governor, but the majority are interested, like myself, in getting rid of her and the Guard of Oran. Of course, she also controls the City Guard through Kelvin. This leaves the power structure decidedly in her advantage. But what do we have? Seven out of ten of the Council and their men-at-arms will aid us if they are convinced Myella can be beaten.

"As I am sure you can understand, Lord Michael, few would risk such exposure without a guaranteed benefit. So, I must ask you, what's in it for me?"

Mike smiled and spread his arms, his eyes widening theatrically. "Why, the whole city of Paravel my friend, the whole damn city!"

Duran stood at the rail of a finely wrought oak bridge spanning a small pond in the garden of the governor's estate. He watched as a larger fish nipped at the tail of a smaller, and finally, with one gulp, swallow the fish whole. It then swam merrily along, fat and complacent. Overhead, the trees rustled in the breeze and clouds thickened. He knew that before the night was over there would be storm, just as there was the night before.

Often, a smile played on his lips, giving many to believe that he had some knowledge that they lacked; more often than not it was their undoing. It was this same smile that greeted the Governor of Paravel.

"Good afternoon, Lord Duran, what brings you to my humble home?"

Humble? Duran wondered if the fat man knew the meaning of the word. He doubted it. "Good Claybrook, naught but business as usual. Today I give Myella's regards to the Council. I was wondering if you would be attending?"

Claybrook adjusted his robe and placed a pudgy hand atop the rail. He stared at his fish below, then frowned. "I think not, good Duran. I have dinner guests tonight and I shouldn't want to spoil it with the bad taste of politics upon my palate."

He could not be more arrogant and negligent if he tried. But, Duran did not voice his thoughts, rather he gestured to the yard. There, under an elm was a guard and a small chest. Claybrook smiled.

"It is unfortunate you won't be attending, however I will give them your regards. I believe that Myella has a gift to show you just how much she appreciates your friendship."

"Yes?" he feigned surprise and waddled to the yard. Duran followed. The man knelt and Duran watched as the man's hands shook with greed. He fumbled with the latch and finally he threw the lid back to reveal one copper shenk. Claybrook looked up, a frown on his brow.

"What is the meaning of this?"

"Myella feels that you are now paid in full, and your services will no longer be necessary."

"What?" he blubbered and struggled to get to his feet, yet the guard's powerful hand held him down.

"You have been lax in the performance of your duties. And per the wishes of

Myella, we sever all ties to you."

"I will not stand for this, I will bend the Council against you. You owe–" His protestations turned to a gurgle mid-sentence as a blade flashed, then something fell into the chest with a hollow thump. Closing the lid with his toe, Duran wiped stray droplets of blood from his cheek and gestured to the guard to take up the chest.

"Well, good Claybrook, it would seem that you shall be attending the meeting after all."

Mike looked out from under the cowl to Alaric, Guildmaster Merchant, as they both sat in an antechamber. White marble was everywhere, only made dull by the lack of light penetrating the skylight; it was gray and overcast outside and a cool, moist pall had settled over the city. They were awaiting introduction to the Council that guided the city, under the auspices of the governor. Alaric had said that the governor was unlikely to attend; he rarely did so now that Myella filled his coffers. Besides, they would be addressing the Council in private, and it would be harder to sway the three youngest. Myella had gotten to them before they were appointed, but there was always that hope that they might retain a shred of independence.

They now waited inside the opulent administrative building of the city of Paravel. Pages and secretaries ran back and forth through the bleached maple doors of the council chamber, not paying any attention to the Guildmaster and those whom they took to be his man-at-arms. Mike shuffled nervously and tilted his head back. Through the window, he could see the first spattering of rain on the glass. Drip, drop, it was almost mesmerizing. He touched the orb in his pocket briefly and felt himself lifting out of his body. What the? He thought. Then, with some effort, he found himself passing through the doors and into the council chamber, yet still conscious of Alaric sitting beside him reading a manifest.

Astral projection—cool! Mike thought, pleased with himself.

But now he was also within the chamber, watching the proceedings from above the floor. This was strange indeed. He could hear and see them, but they obviously could not see him. Then, of a sudden, he was yanked back into the antechamber. Alaric was shaking his arm. It was time.

"No time to fall asleep, Lord Michael."

"What? Oh." They stood and were motioned into the chamber. Spartan in appearance, the ten councilmen sat behind a birch table, none appeared younger than fifty or so.

"Welcome, Alaric," stated the elder who chaired the Council. He held out his hand for the two to approach. The others looked on, no real emotion evident except upon the faces of the three to the far right.

Alaric bowed and Mike followed suit.

"What brings the Guildmaster and this criminal to the chambers of the Council?" asked one of men on the right. Mike glanced quickly over to see two others nodding. So, he had been recognized, and the statement was proof that they were in Myella's pocket.

Alaric looked at the other seven, pointedly ignoring the three. It was a brash insult, but he was confident that they did not have the intestinal fortitude to challenge him. "Milords. I bring to you Lord Michael, Alchemist and Swordsman. He comes to you with news of the West and happenings that are of great import."

"I object!" shouted the furthest to the right. "There is no reason we should trust the words of this outlander and criminal. I say call the City Guard and be done with him, we can only be at risk for his presence here."

The chair cleared his throat. "Ythrain, he is a criminal to the Conclaveum, not the Free City of Paravel. I will remind you that he has come only to speak, if we do not like what he says, then we will turn him over to the guard."

Ythrain scowled and looked away. The Chair motioned Mike to speak. "Come young man, tell us your story." And Mike did, for what seemed the thousandth time. He told of the fall of Galfeon Yor, the poisoning at Ord, of the death of Chill, of Gelion's demise. He told them of the disappearance of Surik, and that of Bill and Tom, and of the capture of Sir John. He told how Myella had wished conflict in the West, and how annexation would be the likely result in Paravel if something were not done to stop her. When he was finished, he stepped back and Alaric looked at him. It was a steady gaze that really said nothing. The chair frowned and looked up and down the long table. Many of the others were still absorbing what the big man had said. The three, headed by Ythrain, were chattering amongst themselves.

"You have something to share with the Council, Ythrain?"

"This is ludicrous, to think that this person and his companions have usurped Gelion and caused so much trouble to the Conclaveum that they are now wanted? More likely they are bandits from the West who had ambushed Gelion and wish to do more harm to Paravel than good."

"Hmmm." The Chair thought for a moment and looked to Alaric. "I am getting too old for this intrigue, Alaric Dirkajian. Speak with us alone. Lord Michael, will you await him in the antechamber?"

"Yes." Mike turned on his heel and left the room. Once outside he sat and waited. It was some time before Alaric reappeared, and the rain outside

401

was falling heavily, causing rivulets to stream down the glass and pool at the sill.

He looked up as Alaric walked through. The man pulled his cloak over his shoulder and walked quickly past the big man and through a side door, Mike in tow.

"Well?" Mike asked after the amber-eyed man.

"Duran is in the building, with Kelvin. We must leave by a different way. I take it we just missed a nasty confrontation in the antechamber there." Mike looked over his shoulder, wondering how close a shave it had been.

"Do not worry, the page warned us in time. Duran will not know we were here. Even Ythrain and his two lackeys will not divulge what happened in chambers."

"What was the Council's decision?" Mike asked as they passed into a rain soaked alley and pulled their cloaks about their shoulders.

"Officially they cannot help us; however," and Alaric looked askance at the big man. "You intrigued the seven of them sufficiently that they will meet with us tonight at my residence."

"The warehouse?"

"No."

"I see," Mike said, but he didn't.

Kelvin looked up as Duran exited the council chamber, sans the small chest. A smile played upon the Lord of Qwen's face, and the Lord Protector wondered what he had up his sleeve. The man almost ignored Kelvin as he passed, but saluted him nonchalantly and then Duran was gone down the hall. Kelvin looked after him a moment, shook his head, and opened the two doors into the chambers. There, on the floor was Duran's chest. Opened.

Claybrook's dead eyes stared over the edge of the box. The Council was sitting there, some in shock, some looking away. Some with hate and fury etched upon their faces.

"So, Kelvin," shouted the Chair. "You follow on the footfalls of that jackal?" Kelvin's eyes narrowed as he stepped into the chamber; something was seriously amiss.

"I take it Duran has brought more than bad tidings," he frowned at the chest and kicked the lid shut.

"It seems that Myella has found fit to dispose of her lap dog. I assume we are to take it as a warning?"

"I knew nothing of this."

"Of course not, nor of the slaying of Vilidis? No? You are a fool if you think that the Conclaveum guides her as surely as it does you. She wants Paravel, Kelvin, and she wants the whole of the South and the West."

"I am guided by the Council as Lord Protector–"

"We are not blind, but you have been a fine Captain to police the city. Do you think you will escape the same fate? If so, you are the fool, not this Council. Look, Kelvin, and remember Claybrook's end. Myella has warned us, and take care; you may be next."

Kelvin left the chamber slightly shaken by the encounter, wondering if he had misjudged Myella and Duran all along.

403

Chapter 22

The figure in black moved across the rooftops like a fleeting shadow, occasionally leaping over the narrow chasms that divided the adjoining buildings. The void filled his mind as he stretched out and landed on the opposite roof. He rolled and came to his feet. All his senses were attuned. His vision no longer bothered him, the sight of his left eye piercing the gloom with crystal acuity.

He was again wearing the clothes he had brought into this world. No more the guise of the tracker, now he was the Wind Warrior of myth. He stopped and listened, poised on the edge of the tile, near a gutter. His black cargo-pants tucked into wrestling shoes, his head wrapped in black cloth, he merged with the night. As always his chokuto style blade was at his side, as was his knife, with Kiera tucked safely into his tunic. She did not mind; she was beginning to enjoy these adventures.

He looked to the opposite wall, some thirty feet away. He had thought these buildings might come closer to the Gate Wall of Osso but no. He used the gutter to lower himself along the cornice and then climbed down the rough stone, taking every precaution not to be seen.

Once on the ground, he cleared the distance to the opposite wall and stood in the deep shadows. He felt the surface with his hand, and decided it was too smooth to free-climb. He pulled rope from his pouch and set his bow against the wall. Pulling his sword from its scabbard, he tied the rope securely to its hand guard. When he was sure no one was about he tossed the makeshift grapnel aloft.

It struck and snagged. He hoped. He tugged on it and it fell free. Swearing quietly, he caught the projectile by the hilt, luckily and tried once more. This time it held. He slung the bow and quiver and pulled himself up the length of the cord, finally reaching the top. He had only about a foot to work with up there, so he straddled it like a horse and leaned low. He quickly retrieved his rope and put his short sword away. Then he surveyed his position.

He had a clear view of the courtyard of the Seat of the Surrogate. The building across from him looked good. There were several open balconies on the third floor. He readied his bow, this time tying the cord to an arrow he had specially rigged. He aimed at what looked like a wooden beam...

...no, his vision cleared, adjusted, fused from one to two. What he thought was a wooden beam was actually a painted stone facade. But, there was a beam above it, about three inches exposed to his angle. He let fly. The rope unwound with a hiss and the specially barbed arrow struck the wood, sinking deep into the grain. He smiled and tied the other end to a piton, then pounded it into the mortar with two quick bursts from his pommel. He'd used a sheepshank to secure the rope, cutting the center cord to make it retrievable. As long as he maintained even pressure, it would hold fast, but three quick snaps would loosen it and bring the rope back to him when he arrived at his destination.

"Hold on, Kiera," he whispered. He pulled a leather strip from his pocket and wrapped it about the cord. Then he slid from the top of the wall.

His weight added to the tension on the rope, tightening the knot securely and sending him sliding toward the balcony. The leather rasped, and he felt the rush of wind as his momentum carried him through the air. Halfway to his destination, the arrow slipped to the next barb, causing the rope to sag more, dangerously slowing his pace. Just as he thought he would end his slide suspended just inches from safety, he was at the balcony, noiselessly absorbing the impact by bending his knees against the floor. Turning, he completely released the tension on the rope and then tugged it. As the far end fell free, he quickly wound it with one arm and slung it into the eaves above the arrow.

He crossed the balcony and peered into the hallway. There, at the end of the hall, a guard lounged against a pillar. The light of a small lamp illuminated the man's form as he casually sharpened a dagger on a whetstone. It would be enough sound to hide Smiling Wolf's stealthy footfalls.

Tom slipped behind the pillars and squeezed along the wall. Finally he stood behind the man. He fingered the leather garrote that twined about his hand. No, that won't work; if I kill him they'll know something's up. I have to put him to sleep. He thought for a moment, then his hand flew, his thumb striking the man behind the ear, at the base of the skull. Before the dagger hit the marble floor, Tom scooped it up and set it gingerly in the guard's lap. He then slipped past the man and into the torch-lit hallway. He smiled. Now all he had to do was find a comfortable hiding place to make brief forays from while looking for John and Joe.

Kiera chirped. He was in.

The murmur of the sea reached Bill's ears. He looked along the slate and black-pebbled beach to the distant shipping lane and the Port of Paravel. Outside the city walls, and just north of Paravel, the rocky cliff walls would hide them. Most of the group had already made their way into the city, and they would meet at a predetermined spot the next day. Torec and Garis had planned well.

He looked over the breakers to the whitecaps on the rough waters; the sky was gray and the air chill, the only warmth coming from a small fire and Tar'elah standing next to him. It was far from Daytona and Spring Break, but it wasn't so bad.

"What is your land like, Bard?"

"Please call me Bill, okay?" He smiled when she nodded. "My land is far from here. And things would seem quite different to you. But, the people, they are always the same."

She snuggled closer now, not the bandit leader, a woman. "I love the sea," he sighed.

He looked into her lucid eyes and leaned toward her. She responded eagerly and they kissed. The roar of the waves hinted at song and passion.

It was cool outside and John could make out the morning mist as it crawled past the steel bars of his cell window. A temperature inversion now meant fog later on in the day. Unholy red light illuminated the cell as the sun rose like a titan over the ocean.

Black and melancholy thoughts washed over John as he stared down into the bowl of tepid water. He set it on the stone sill and sighed.

At least she is alive, he thought. Gabrielle was alive, he knew that now and it drove him. He would not resign himself to the fate that had befallen Joe. And, as for Duran, he would not let Gabrielle fall into that monster's hands at any cost. He sat down on the berth and looked out the window. Red sky at night, sailor's delight. Red sky at morning, sailor takes warning.

He got up and paced the cell. What was to happen to him? And what was happening to his companions? He remembered his own world, the friends and family he had left behind. He wondered if he would ever return to the university and his studies; ever return to an ordinary everyday existence. He shrugged and deliberately turned his mind away from the bleak thoughts, feeling the knot of tension ease from his shoulders. He could not let the worry immobilize him.

Wow, he thought, somewhat sarcastically, we've really come a long way in this world. He smiled grimly to himself. Him captured, Joe a zombie, Mike was probably zoning in a spell, and God knew what Tom and Bill were doing. Obviously not trying hard to rescue him. That made him chuckle aloud. At least we're consistent. Once, during an Event, the Summer King's men had captured him. That had really been humiliating. But, in the end, the 'Legion of the Black Skull' had come through. That night they had gotten two of the girlfriends of the King's men drunk, kidnapped them, and traded them for his release the next day. Somehow, I don't think that'll work this time He sat down once more, trying to get into a Zen frame of mind. It didn't work. His thoughts led him to the silver medallion that hung around his neck. Had it turned into some sort of magic talisman this world? What were its properties? It had saved his life and others. But, how? And more to the point, why? Did his faith impinge on or resonate with the magic of this world?

He shook his head, trying to fathom the mysteries that this world posed. He thought coping would be hard, but they all seemed to fit, as if they were linked to this world. All of them possessed some training in the martial arts. Joe was a superb fencer and had competed with skill and daring. And Tom could make a Navy SEAL green with envy.

But where had it gotten him?

Probably killed, he mused. He sat there, hands in his lap, absorbing and slowly accepting this concept and, when the guard entered his cell, he smiled.

John released the Kiai, the spirit yell of the Samurai. It was clearly not perfect, but it sufficed. The man staggered back at the shout and John surged upwards, striking the guard in the nose with an open palm. He knocked the guard's sword aside and it clattered to the floor. He took the man by the neck and kicked him in the groin. As he doubled over, John smashed his face into the roughly hewn wall. There was a sickening crack as his neck broke.

Spinning around, the body of the guard still in his grip, he confronted the man's companion. The second soldier thrust his sword, but it was intercepted by his dead cohort. Then the body was in his face and the sword was wrenched out of his hand. The bars on the window rang as the helmed man struck them at full force.

Grabbing the sword, John rushed into the hall. He had expected more guards, but there had been only the two in the hallway. He looked around. The hallway was circular, running around the core of the tower. He soon found the stairs and was heading down. Finally at the bottom, he wrenched open the bronze door and stepped into the courtyard.

Forty of Myella's guards milled about the yard.

"Oh shit," he muttered under his breath and quickly closed the door to nothing more than a crack. He peered into the courtyard, watching the black and gold liveried guards tend their horses. They were an impressive lot, and were armed with sword and clothed in chain mail. As John scanned the walled yard and the open gate beyond, he spied a horse and rider moving toward a darkly clad, bearded figure. Duran.

The man on the horse was the one who had confronted him in the alley behind the whorehouse, silver-haired, wearing the red and gray of the City Guard and sporting a brass breastplate. He seemed incensed as he spoke to Duran in harsh, low tones. He made a cutting gesture across his neck and Duran just smiled. Then the silver-haired man leaned low in the saddle and got right in Duran's face. At this point, most of the soldiers in the yard were entranced by the argument.

John casually stepped out of the doorway and walked to the nearest guard whose back was fully exposed to him. He quietly moved toward the guard, careful to listen to any inflection in the argument that would give him away. Barely one foot from the man, he reached out and snapped the man's head at an odd angle to the side. He was feeling particularly vicious at this point.

The man fell to the ground and John swung himself up onto the horse. Now that most of the guards were watching Duran and Kelvin, John steered the horse in a wide arc around the contingent of soldiers. However, he failed to notice the figure standing on the balcony several stories above, in the very same tower that he had been in. Nor did he see the black-caped man in the doorway of the Seat opposite the tower, and the crossbow he held.

John had almost reached the Gates of Osso. There was now a narrow alley between Kelvin and the open gate and the street beyond. He was about to spur the horse into a gallop when a shrill whistling sound ended with a fletched bolt near the saddle horn. The horse reared from sudden fright. John, almost falling, spied Duran and Kelvin as they looked up sharply.

"Shit!" He slammed his heels into the beast's flanks, but now the horse angled into the throng of soldiers and sent them scrambling for arms and reins.

"No! John! Go to the gate! The gate is open!" he heard a shout and looked on high. There, in the

411

very same tower from which he had escaped, Gabrielle stood at a balcony, startled at his dilemma.

He swung his sword to the side and a close guardsman caught it in the stomach, blood splashing into the Lord Knight's face. The second got it in the neck, the blade catching on vertebrae. John wrenched it free, hoping the poor balance of the sword wouldn't impair his fighting ability. He spun the horse around and headed for the open gate. Duran was gesticulating wildly, but was pushed from the fray by his own men. Kelvin frowned and back-reined his horse to a safer vantage point. He looked on, not wishing to interfere with Duran's plight.

John spurred toward the open gate...

Surik Shadowlord, Hand of Keth, raised the crossbow and fired another bolt. It sank into the horse's neck. The beast screamed and fell to the side, pinning John's leg beneath it.

He struggled to push himself out from under the dead weight of the steed. It was no use; he was wedged firmly under the girth, his foot tangled in the stirrup.

Duran walked up and kicked the sword from his hand. "Not bad, Lord Knight. I underestimated you."

"Thanks, that makes me feel so much better."

Duran smiled as the horse was pulled off of John. The outlander was brought to his feet, surrounded by the remaining guard.

"Take him to his cell. If he hasn't killed the two who were guarding him, do it. Then replace them with four who are not idiots. This will not happen again."

Duran watched them drag John away. Gabrielle momentarily cried out and John looked up, meeting her distant gaze evenly. Then he was taken within and Duran was the one who now gazed at Trevor's daughter.

Kelvin frowned and eased his horse outside the Gate of Osso. It was clear that even the tiniest events were shaping the politics of the South.

The spell spun out, trying to reach its goal, trying to reach one point among thousands. Within his protective pentacle, Mike sat cross-legged and concentrating. It was night, the best time to access the energies of the aether. A faint silver moon could be seen through the slatted windows of the warehouse. He sat alone, amid the stacked crates, and looked into his orb.

This time it was not a summoning spell; rather it was one of location and identification. He had determined the proper formula while at one of the libraries of Paravel earlier that day. Now he drew it in his mind.

It was far less complex than the spell he had tried at Trevor's ruined Keep, and also less dangerous. He didn't have to wait long for the orb to glow a healthy amber. He felt himself drawn in, not physically, but spiritually, and hoped that nothing would separate him from his inner self.

He did not know what to expect, he thought perhaps the place and names would come to his mind as a result of the formula. It came as a mild shock to him as he felt himself rising from the warehouse floor. Yet, looking down, he saw

413

himself there, watching the orb, definitely a strange feeling of duality. So, he thought, it doesn't come to me, I go to it. Fascinating. He moved out through the window, over the top of the building and toward the north quarter of the city. It was there that he first became aware of the silver light that was akin to his aura. Faint, yet definite. Now there were two, but he recognized the strongest immediately by the talisman enhancing it. The medallion was like a beacon to Mike's tuned senses. He passed through the wall of the Seat – distances seemed to contract – dreamlike, and eased up the spiral staircase of the guard tower, seeming to float above each step. Then he came to the door and the four guards, impressed by the number. He passed one of the guards close by and noticed him shiver.

I could really frighten the bastard, he thought, but then decided against it, not wanting to arouse any suspicion. He passed through the door and saw John sleeping on the bench. He seemed in good health.

Turning, Mike flowed through the floor and down. He knew that he could not affect anything physically in this state; he just wanted to do a reconnaissance of sorts. He zeroed in on the other faint aura and passed through a series of walls, and chambers, in the last of which he stopped abruptly.

She lay on top of the bed, naked, and Joe next to her. The artist was staring at the ceiling, occasionally blinking. His breathing was regular. The woman was asleep.

What surprised the physicist was that Joe was not the owner of the silver aura that he sought;

rather Joe was not there at all, at least not in the spiritual sense. It was as if he was a shell. But where was Joe? Mike swept the room. There, a pale kernel of silver, hidden. His black bastard sword, forged by a smith from Wisconsin, sat across the armrests of a chair and within it was a faint sliver of silver energy.

Mike frowned as the woman stirred. There was a power there; Mike had felt it in her subconscious thought. Fearing she might wake, he left, passing through the wall, trying to ponder out the meaning of the sword and Joe's being.

Down another stair, floating up to the high vaulted ceiling of the Temple of Oran, Mike spotted the other strong glow of silver. It was Tom; he had camped out in an alcove at the top of one of the pillars. Apparently it was hollow and gave access to the ceiling so that painters could work on the vault. It didn't look too comfortable, but it worked.

Kiera watched him as he floated near. Tom was motionless, but not asleep. Meditating, probably. Good, he would need the rest.

As for Bill, he didn't know where the musician was. Nor would he find him this night. He turned, about to leave...wait...he looked to the dais of the temple.

Evil indeed, Mike thought, especially in the vicinity of the headsman's block, black stains darkening the granite. The Seat of the High Priestess was there and some type of sacristy behind it. He watched Myella in gossamer gown walk to this sacristy. She must have awakened and left Joe after he had come to the temple proper. He

415

didn't want to get too close for fear that she would feel him, yet he floated forward just enough to see her in the darkness of the alcove at the rear of the dais.

She spoke an utterance before the small door to the closet and it opened. Mike reeled back as if a physical wave of evil had slammed into him. Blackness oozed out of the unholy station, thin tendrils sucking away at any warmth of life. It was like a wave of madness and Myella bathed in it. Then she closed the door and Mike floated down from his vantage point next to Tom.

She isn't a bad looker, Mike thought, remembering her naked form on the bed. Too bad that Joey isn't all upstairs to enjoy it.

She went from the tabernacle to the chair and lit a purple candle with the taper, then sat and regarded the headsman's sword standing near the block. Dark iron and straight hilt, the blood groove was clean of any past impurity. She leaned her head upon her fist and thought.

He smiled to himself. He really was amazed at the clarity with which he beheld things in this state. For a moment, he wondered if he could get back to his former reality in this state of astral projection. It seemed to him that the spell wasn't difficult, the mathematical probability not bad. Just weave the formula...

Transition...

Blinding sunlight off of snow and ice. He watched an eighteen-wheel semi proceed slowly around the embankment. Pines glistened with icicles and the sky was a crisp cobalt blue. He looked down a steep embankment at the side of the road, past the modest tree line, to the rocks. There, almost obscured by the snowdrifts was a blue hood and the silver of chrome.

Curiously, his existence here was even more tenuous than in the previous reality. It was difficult to move among the aether and it was a mental drain. He tried to float down to look at the truck.

Slowly he approached from the side. He could almost see into the... Transition...

"DAMN! Shit sucking bitch!" a dark bolt coalesced near the vaulted ceiling and he felt his spirit cringe. The cord that bound him to his physical self had almost snapped with that one. If it hadn't been for the ward that he always incorporated into his workings he would surely be nothing more than a hapless ghost wandering the material plane. Myella had risen at the un-nameable disturbance; she was standing at the lip of the dais, gazing upward at his immaterial form. He could feel Tom stirring behind him. Mike had to direct her attention elsewhere or he would give away the Sioux's hiding place.

His form sank to the right, ending up on the floor behind a waist-high rail that marked the division between the nave and the dais. He stood there, gathering energy about him.

"Who are you?" she hissed, straining her eyes to see the translucent form. She warded herself with a gesture. Mike was beginning to realize that in his present state she was slightly out of his league.

YOUR GOD! His mind forced its way into hers and she took a step back. He smiled at her confusion and tried to figure out what to do next.

"HERETIC!" she screamed and a seething mass of chaos streamed towards him from her outstretched hands.

Whoops, Mike echoed and, with the swiftness of thought, was instantly back at the warehouse.

He sighed in relief as he stared at the familiar surroundings of boxes and crates. He breathed the musty air and looked about. The lantern that had supplied his light had gone out and the only illumination was the orb, which now also faded.

He squinted, peering into the dark. It's good to know where they are. As long as Alaric comes through, we have a chance. He stood and stretched. Picking up the orb, he stepped outside the pentacle to go look for Torec.

His orb glowed brightly and Mike looked at it curiously.

The chaos that had followed him through the aether struck him from behind.

Damn, he thought as he was flung full force into the crates, forgot to shut the door!

Tom watched from his lofty vantage point with curiosity. He was sure it wasn't him she was talking to. Then who? He watched as she turned away from the dark of the soaring vault to the side of the dais, screaming 'heretic.'

With bow in hand he watched as she gestured. A warping of images in front of her made his head spin. He had to clutch at the edge of his alcove to prevent himself from falling. When he looked again the woman was gone and the air was calm.

Kiera scrambled up his arm, jittery. She licked his ear and then ran into the front of his tunic, curling up on his flat stomach.

"I don't know, gal, this is certainly some weird shit." He scratched at her ear and put his bow into the back of the alcove. "Get some sleep, girl. We might as well rest while we have the opportunity." He closed his eyes, trying to find the peace of meditation once more.

A cool brisk wind whipped off the sea, a harbinger of rough weather ahead for the Port City of Paravel. Bill looked across the street, to the dark building that lay there, and to what else? He did not know. Garis had brought Tar'elah and him to this alley after meeting them at the Southern Postern.

It had been no problem getting into the city; the guards had concentrated on keeping any outlanders within the high walls and had neglected to check carefully those that wished passage within. Under cover of night and sporadic rain, they had passed through the gates in the guise of weary travelers. Garis had been waiting for them at a previously appointed place and he had guided them through the narrow city streets to a cobbled and lamp-lit avenue. Here, stately houses and buildings lined the wide street, and light glowed through the crystal panes of glass.

Garis had gone ahead. The house had looked dark, though the wrought iron gate and small yard were in good repair. The foyer held no light for the returning merchant or noble who owned the house. Garis had slunk his way to the low stone structure, keeping his bulk to the shadows and avoiding any carriage or rider that might find his way down this infrequently traveled avenue.

After a moment, a light flared in the foyer, then Garis shuttered the window, and again there was darkness.

"I like this not, Bard," Tar'elah whispered from behind, her hand pressing with urgency into the small of his back. She pointed to several plain horses that had been stabled in the alley to the right of the house. Then he noticed what was odd. The livery on the steeds was incomplete. There was saddle and bridle, but no blanket or coat. There were however the empty scabbards for sword and lance.

"Military?"

"City Guard. I know not, but these people that Garis has brought us to may not be all that trustworthy. Or...he walks into a trap."

"Garis said that his men had met with Torec and that the rendezvous was here. I do not think that Torec would betray us."

"No," she replied, and then eased back into the shadows. A light now glowed from the upstairs window of the house. "But, mayhap Garis and Torec are unaware of the trap."

"I think you worry too much." Bill tried to make out her face in the dark, but was rewarded with only seeing her outline in the dim light from the street. She hissed and he turned quickly to look down the road.

A lone City Guardsman was trotting his horse down the center of the cobbled avenue. He paused momentarily at the whinny of the horses in the alley and then continued on his way.

"Well, he didn't think anything odd of those horses. Maybe they're just the owners."

420

Tar'elah did not reply she just brushed past him as Garis flickered the oil lamp in the foyer window. That was the signal, Bill knew, and so he followed her cautiously. Soon they were at the front porch and to the door. He scratched lightly at the door. Wind swirled leaves up from the ground in a brown and green tempest that threatened their eyes. Soon the door swung open into the darkened foyer and they stepped inside.

Silence as the door shut behind them.

Harsh light and an uncovered oil lamp brought into sharp relief the four heavily armed City Guards who stood in the foyer.

"Not a trap?" Tar'elah raised an eyebrow. "I could be wrong."

Kelvin sat in his office behind a plain oak desk, looking at the parchment before him. He rolled it up carefully and set candle wax to the seam. He pressed his ring into the soft wax and then handed it to the courier who had been waiting patiently near the door. It would take several weeks for that to reach the Conclave, his last message to his allies, perhaps his last message ever. After the messenger was gone, Kelvin sat back and swirled a dark liquid within a wide-lipped glass. It had been his oldest and most prized bottle, a fine vintage, from about forty years before the fall of Bequa. How long was that? He mused. Nine decades aging? Well, if now was not the time to open it, there would never be a better. He sipped it appreciatively.

He ran a veined hand through his thinning gray hair. He was no longer the young Preceptor who governed Helm. Now he was the fading remnant of an agent plying his trade in Paravel. No doubt, he would soon be cast aside as scraps to Myella's hounds, or worse.

When she had first come to Paravel, he had thought Myella simply a spoiled and pretentious bitch, unaccustomed to the finer points of diplomacy and politics. He had been wrong. Within two years, her lust for power had upset the fine balance that he had created between the Council and the Conclaveum. There had always been an unsaid understanding between the Chair Nathal and himself.

Then she had lined the pockets of that weak Claybrook, set up three of her own on the Council, and managed to bring the Regency to the City. Like Clef, the balance was shifting from a free state to that of Regency of the Conclave; or as Kelvin was now seeing, as Regency of Myella and her lust for power.

He snuffed out the candle with his fingers and sat savoring his drink in the darkness for a few moments. The intricate clock standing on the mantle (Narnist, they had a way with such things), chimed several times and he stood, setting the glass firmly on the desk. He pulled on his cloak, adjusted the weight of his sword, and turned to leave. He knew full well that this night he would perform his duty out of loyalty to the Conclavator, nothing more.

They found him under a pile of crates and boxes that had fallen on him when he was struck by the chaos. Torec and Bale had spent a good fifteen minutes clearing the detritus to get to the big man's prone form.

"It's about time," he grumbled as they lifted a crate that had pinned his left arm. He stood slowly, checking for damage, and brushing the dust from his clothes. "What happened?" Torec asked. The merchant had found the pentacle and the signs of magic and eventually conjectured that the magician must be beneath the fallen crates. He had assumed that Mike would be dead beneath the pile and was amazed that no harm had befallen the outlander.

"Nothing really. I guess that Myella is just a tad more resourceful than I first thought. Oh well." He retrieved his paraphernalia from the floor and scrubbed out the pentagram with his boots. He then looked at Bale and the two men curiously.

"Yes?"

"We have something for you."

"Hopefully not a dagger in the back." Mike checked the orb. It was intact; he wished that he felt the same. The aether had weakened whatever had struck him from behind, yet it still had packed a wallop.

"A plan."

"Excellent."

Bale looked into his eyes for a moment and then sighed. "I wish you would not use sorcery in my warehouse. Are you certain nothing followed your trail?" As Mike shook his head, she resumed. "Now, we must be quick, we have to get to Alaric's residence; Nathal is not a patient man. We must be at the estate before the moon reaches the Fifth Place. Come."

Bale was swift in her departure. Torec and Mike followed behind. Soon they were in a closed carriage and crossing from the wharf district into the city proper. Torec leaned over to Mike and grinned.

"Garis is in the City and, by now, the Bard as well."

"Good, we'll need all the help we can get."

"That is true," Bale interrupted. "Myella has thought fit to dispense with the only thing that has separated the City from the Conclaveum. Today, the Governor made an appearance at the open Council, sans his body.

"Myella has all but openly declared that the city is hers. She has three members of the Council and the others fear retribution the likes of that which took Vilidis. Reports have it that even Kelvin was unaware of the death of the Governor. He likes not the turn of events in the South. He is a staunch supporter of the Conclaveum, not Myella's petty ambitions. Rumor has it he is not happy with what is transpiring in this city and Clef."

"And we are just pawns in a larger game?"

"Aren't we all?" she replied to Mike.

"You may be, but from now on we are not. You see, those of the Legion of the Black Skull don't take kindly to being used."

"The Legion of the Black Skull?"

"You bet, babe. And we mean business." He closed his eyes as the carriage turned onto a cobbled street.

Chapter 23

Black merged with gold and wisps of white,
slowly gliding with the incessant hiss of leather
and the steady rhythm of boots falling on marble.
Two black armored warriors dragged Marad, head
down, into the Preceptor's offices at Helm.
Stripped of his armor and weapons, he had been
beaten almost senseless and brought by the Hands
of Keth to this room, in the High Tower of the
Wall City.

The gauntleted fists opened and he fell to the
cold, unyielding floor, wondering if the red in the
texture was his blood or just the crystal veins.
Initially he had tried to resist, but as Kel just
looked on, Marad was stripped of his uniform and
dragged behind the lead horse of the Hands. Later,
he was bound and carried incognito into the city of
Helm. He vaguely remembered the Breach where,
even when it was early afternoon, no light filtered
down through the awesome canyon; only twilight
and the many lamps and flames lit the way down
the avenue. Then, up the endless steps of the High
Tower that guarded the entrance to the North. It
was square and tall, and the road ran around the
Tower and into the breach, flanked on each side by
the immense bastions of the wall. Here were the
Preceptor's chambers.

Marad tried to shift his weight onto his left
arm and fell fully on his face. His arm had fallen
asleep and he was too numb to care. He looked up,
noticed the wash of sienna and yellow across the
floor, and looked beyond to the open balcony,

seeing the last rays of sun amid the tendrils of steel clouds and salmon sky.

His gaze wandered to the secretary and the robed figure that sat there. His eyes widened in astonishment.

"Uncle..." he croaked out between cracked lips, and faltered. Suddenly the sitting figure was up and at Marad's side. Trevor lifted the prone man upright and began to rub life back into his limp arms. Then, after a moment, Marad felt cold liquid at his lips and sipped eagerly at the offered water.

He thanked the older man with his eyes as the oaken door behind them swung open once more, and this time Marad noticed the robe of purple and the shimmering images of runes upon it. Then the face...

"Isn't this a touching sight, betrayer helping the betrayed?" Veined hands clutched at the wrought staff and Guyle, Counselor to the Conclavator, half-uncle of Marad, strode into the room, his Hands standing close behind. Trevor looked up from where he knelt by Marad's side and scowled at the Mage.

"I thought a little reunion might be appropriate as you two pass one another on your separate journeys." Guyle watched as Trevor helped Marad to his feet and then to the seat at the secretary. When he had set the young man there, Trevor clenched his fists and folded his arms, his face turning dark with an anger that was hard to contain.

"Guyle, for your machinations I will have your head upon a pike."

"I doubt that, dear brother. Long ago I vowed that you would suffer in the Tower of Pain. Your crimes will only be exceeded by your punishment. Oran has deemed it so and, as I bring forth the Hands of Keth, I guarantee you will pay for that night at the Clave a score and five years ago."

"Would that I had killed you instead of maiming our brother," replied Trevor rather harshly. "No, that quarrel again leads to you and your own warped desire for Seperina and for the Seat of the Conclaveum."

Guyle's rheumy eyes looked hard and cold at Trevor, measuring the solid muscled warrior that the Mage could not even challenge now, let alone in his youth. "Desire? What do you know of true desire? I have honed my sorcerous skills down through the years in an effort to bring you and Ironeas to justice. I was the first-born, I was the one destined for the Seat of the Conclavator. But, father thought me weak and disowned me, me, to marry another.

"In begetting you and Ironeas, he shaped both your destinies. When he placed Ironeas on my throne, a plan of retribution formed before me as if a vision from Oran himself. Soon all will be in place. The power of a distant realm will be at my beck, a silver energy unlike any on Carn," Guyle used the ancient term for this world.

"You are clearly mad," Trevor stated matter-of-factly. Guyle only smiled. "No, dear half-brother, I am not mad, nor was I mad that day I pitted you against your brother, Ironeas. I manipulated your lusts and his jealousy and almost succeeded in having you both dead. But, even then you foiled me. How could I know that my own servant would kill Seperina, and that the fight would end there? Banishment!" He spat vehemently and went to the balcony, gazing out now over the darkened crags and defiles of the Rift and the last red wash of the setting sun.

"Soon, soon," he whispered. "You will be sent to the Tower of Pain. As for Marad, I will let you watch him die, dear brother-half. You will watch him spill his blood on these floors as part of my revenge against you and Ironeas. You will take this message to your brother to share with him before my poison consumes him, and will share it as you share the Tower of Pain."

He slammed his staff onto the flagstones and a shower of sparks spat from the top. The guards that had brought Marad into the office drew their swords reflexively. Marad looked up from the chair and sighed. One guard came over and took him by the arm; the other hefted his sword in both hands.

"It is a shame that your death will be so swift. But your head will be a fit message for your father."

The guard hefted his sword and the other pushed Marad roughly to his knees. The sword was raised–

"Wait!" shouted Trevor as he pushed the Hand aside. The faceless guard turned to him and leveled the blade at his chest. "You cannot."

"Don't be so dramatic. I can. Ish halam kar tuk." With that the sword was raised again and fell. But, at the last moment Marad twisted away and the sword struck with a loud clang onto the marble.

Marad grabbed the guard who held him, and swung him into the other. In the confusion of that and Guyle's yelling, he sprang toward the balcony and off, into the night.

"Fools!" Guyle hissed as the two guards looked on. "Quickly, to the Breach, before his body is discovered. We may salvage this yet." Then in passing as he turned to leave: "Dear half-brother, do not get any ideas by that noble gesture. I would gladly spend a fortnight and all the power I possess, squeezing the life back into your body just so you could spend one day in the Tower of Pain."

Trevor watched him leave and then smiled to himself. Marad was truly with Tarn.

Chapter 24

Without a second thought, Bill had placed himself in front of Tar'elah, crossbow raised and pointed at the four City Guardsmen who now stood in the foyer of the house that Garis had entered not long before. He squinted away the after- image of the harsh light and slowly focused on the figure to the rear of the four men. Garis was smiling as if the Bard were making a sad attempt at a joke. There was another man, older, thinning hair, and professional bearing, that stood before them. The man wore a richly colored robe and carried a carved rod.

"My guards will not harm you Bard, they are at my command, not Myella's, nor Kelvin's. They were hand-picked to be part of my retinue."

Bill slowly lowered his weapon and the guards mirrored his action. He noticed that Tar'elah relaxed a bit; she had been ready to spring into action.

"Bard William D'Asturien," Garis said. "This is Nathal, present Chair of the City Council."

"A pleasure Bard, I have heard much about you and your friends." Bill nodded, not quite sure what to say. He slung his weapon and the guards departed, slipping into a room adjacent to the foyer. The man turned and proceeded down the corridor; Garis motioned them to follow.

"Torec and Michael are on their way. Alaric Dirkajian waits in his study. Some of the other Council members are already there. There will be five total, as three are Myella's pawns. The two others...well—" Bill nodded, barely noticing the paintings and swords that hung on the walls, the rich furnishing. It appeared this Alaric fellow was rather wealthy.

The den was dark, but cheery. Warmed by a crackling fire and lit by sconces, the walls were adorned with shelves holding a few sparsely placed books and bejeweled ornaments. At the center of the room was a table over which several men stood. At the center was a dark haired man, younger than the rest, with piercing hazel eyes. Garis informed Bill and Tar'elah that this was Alaric, the Guildmaster Merchant of Paravel. The others were Council members, and Bill forgot their names as soon as he heard them. One scowled upon seeing Tar'elah; his mutterings were soon hushed when his gaze lit upon her short sword.

"They are discussing some matter of the City Guard, here, I will introduce you both." Garis cleared his throat and the one known as Alaric looked up from the parchment that lay before him. Amenities were exchanged and Alaric looked keenly at the Bard.

"It seems, my good fellow, that you and your friends have caused quite a stir. Lord Michael's killing of Gelion seems not so much to have earned the wrath of the Conclaveum, but rather that of Myella. I fear she is a tad more dangerous than the former at the present.

"What else?" He watched as the Bard looked on, somewhat dazed by what was transpiring. He weakly accepted some port and swiftly gulped it. "Sir John has been captured by Myella, and the Lady Gabrielle is with him. Surik, well, Surik is under some spell and meting out justice as the

431

Hand of Keth. Your friend the Tracker is nowhere to be found, but Lord Michael and Torec should be here shortly."

"And what of you, where do you stand?" Tar'elah asked of the darkly clad merchant.

"I stand with the Free-City of Paravel; a city not under the rule of the Conclaveum, or worse, the Seat of Myella.

"These gentlemen, too, come to serve the interests of the city against all who would enslave it. The Council, save Ythrain and his lackeys, is dedicated to maintaining the freedom of Paravel. And what of you? Why should we place all we hold dear in the hands of those who are obviously no more than pawns in Myella's game? She stands as centerpiece between the Conclaveum and the West, and we will not have Paravel be the playing board."

Bill turned abruptly at the sound of someone clapping his hands slowly, sarcastically. "Well said, Al," drawled Lord Michael, Alchemist and Swordsman, as he entered the study. He quickly looked around, saw the decanter of port, and took a swift swig right from the bottle. "That was a mighty impressive speech." He looked to Bill and raised his eyebrow at the sight of Tar'elah.

"Billy boy, how ya doing?" He clapped the blonde haired man on the back. "Good. I guess."

"Know how ya feel." He nodded to the bandit. "Looks like you have a story there. Can't wait to hear it."

"Where's Torec?"

"He's with Garis, checking on the men."

"Right, well, you're here and that's that. These guys are supposedly gonna help us. Isn't that right, Nathal?"

Nathal looked up from a deep conversation with one of the other Councilmen. "Young man, we intend to help the City of Paravel. Our interests lie solely in that. When Duran brought the severed head of Claybrook to our chambers, we knew that things were finally coming to a peak. With Ythrain making ever-stronger attempts to intimidate the other two members of the Council, we could not hold a majority to rule on what to do about Myella's killing Claybrook and Vilidis. Nor could we rule to have the Seat removed from the city."

"However, we can decide to have Ythrain, Quinz, and Gyergo removed from the Council, if not by altogether legal means," another Councilmen said. "If Myella can do it, so can we. And if they are removed, at least those on the Council who are afraid to make any overture will not bother us in this venture."

"Where do we come in?" Bill asked as he watched the man tap his rod of authority on the table.

"As Alaric said, you are just pawns in a larger game. Leave it to the Generals, lads."

"Generals rarely know the test of battle, Chair Nathal," Mike piped in. "More often than not it is the squire or the pikeman who decides what side will win." Nathal frowned and looked to Alaric who shrugged. "They do have a stake in it Nathal."

"They are outlanders."

"These outlanders managed to kill Gelion and destroy his keep. They managed to upset Myella so much that she has the City Guard and the Guard of Oran crawling all over Paravel looking for them. No, they have the right to be involved in this."

"That they do," came another voice from the door. They all turned to see a silver-haired man cloaked in gray. Bill did not need to see the regalia of the office to know that this man was the same man that had run John down outside the Fulchard Inn. It was Kelvin, Lord Protector of Paravel. Both Mike and Bill raised their brows at this new conspirator.

"Welcome, Lord Protector," Nathal said in a more subdued tone than he had used previously.

"Nathal...gentlemen. I see we have reached the point of no return. I am at your disposal as Lord Protector of Paravel."

Mike looked suspiciously at the man who was at one time under the command of the Conclaveum and Myella. Was it a trap? He didn't know. Bill just sat down hard in his seat and looked at Tar'elah. She seemed to be aloof from the conversation as she admired a few choice weapons hanging on the wall. Then: "You're the one that ran Sir John down."

"Yes...Bard? I did. It was my duty at the time. But now Myella's design unravels like the thread of some unwholesome tapestry. I fear that soon I would be the one falling under the sword of Oran. Vilidis was a warning to the merchants. Claybrook, to the Council. Would I be that to the Conclave?

"Yesterday I confronted Duran in the Seat. I asked him why? And the man smiled. He said: 'Kelvin, you of all people should know why. Once the Conclave ruled the provinces with an iron fist.

434

When Narn-toc fell, the spirit of the Conclaveum fell with it.' He said that when the Conclaveum pulled back behind the Wall it forsook everything that lay beyond. Now, Myella has claimed it. Phaah, if she only knew that her father has dispatched Marad to the South to rectify things."

He looked pointedly at Mike and Bill. "Your friend, Sir John, is rather resourceful. I saw him attempt escape while I was at the Seat. And by Tarn he would have made it if it weren't for the one called Surik. Still, he killed a few of the Guard of Oran, almost ran down Duran. Heh. I'm surprised we caught him so easily the first time.

"I slipped out of the Seat before they closed the Gates of Osso up tight. Now you see me before you, a servant of the City of Paravel."

Alaric smiled and shook his head. Nathal nodded and the others of the Council looked on. "I am hesitant in believing that you of all people, Kelvin, would plot against the Conclaveum," Alaric said as he sat down.

"Listen well, Guildmaster. My loyalties are still to the Conclave. It is Myella and Duran who conspire against it to build themselves and independent empire in the South and West. The Conclaveum has its hands full with the Krim of the North. The only care that Ironeas has with the South is that peace is maintained and that the revenue from trade continues to flow. The last thing they want is war on two borders, however meager that war be.

"I offer the aid of the whole of the City Guardsmen that are loyal to me. Five score and ten, and that includes the Council's personal guard.

435

That is just over a third of the Guard of Oran. I fear that since Duran returned with additional men we had little time to muster a militia. However, there are others about?"

"Yes," replied Alaric. "I have a few men. Enough to stir up trouble. They will take care of the Guard of Oran that are stationed at the posterns, as well as those of the City Guard that aren't loyal. Lord Michael there, apparently he has about thirty or so men headed by Torec el'Kirien and Garis."

"Torec?" Kelvin perked up. "Myella ran him out of Clef last I remember."

"Yes, well, that was some time ago and is another story. I remember Myella coming to Paravel after that, as Surrogate." Nathal sighed. "Would I had known then that this was coming."

Alaric continued. "The Bard here has brought us over a score of bandits from north of the Ghisik Pass; rough country, frequented by Watchtower and the Black Guard. I believe that Duran has raided there in his younger years."

"He was weaned among the best of the Black Guard. His family in Qwen suckled him and that bastard Gelion on swords and daggers. They are both alike."

"He shouldn't be too hard to take, then," muttered Mike as he looked at his nails.

"Be that as it may," replied Kelvin. "He now has the Guard of Oran at his beck, and they are to be feared more than the Black Guard. Trained in the belly of Oran and vomited from the Tower of Pain, they are fearsome in combat."

436

"So what's the plan? We rescue John and Gabrielle?" Bill asked; he was looking somewhat sick.

"Yes, and that will set the stage for the expulsion of Myella from Paravel. Here." Alaric tossed Mike and Bill two black tunics and robes. Both were emblazoned with the dagger and fire of Oran.

"What's this?"

"It is your pass to the Seat."

"Pass?" asked Bill.

"I think Duran and Myella have something further planned for the White Knight. Two days hence, we will be in the Seat; there is a hidden way, beneath the city."

"I know of it, Alaric, but my men sealed it off."

"We put in a false door."

"Oh."

"What else?"

"Well, here is the rest of the plan." They all huddled together, conspirators in the freeing of Paravel.

Chapter 25

"It was a valiant effort, Lord Knight. I have gained new respect for your resourcefulness. And, I dare say, so has Myella."

John turned back from the grate that gave him a wonderful view of the ocean. Wishing he was in St. Croix and not imprisoned in the Seat's tower, he had failed to notice that Duran had entered the chamber. Now he turned to his nemesis and skewered him with an angry glare.

"I thought rats didn't like high places." The man smiled and fingered the embroidered tunic he wore. John had noticed the regalia of the Guard of Oran earlier.

"Do you like it? You should. Because of you, I have lost the arch-regency and your companion Surik sits as a Hand of Keth."

"So I noticed. It's not like I wanted it this way, Duran. You should have left us alone in the first place."

"Were that possible, I would have made it so," Duran mused. "But, Myella and Guyle have other plans. What am I but their humble servant?" He smiled cynically as John sat on the bench, keeping a wary eye on the pale-skinned man. "Ere this is over, Lord Knight, your hatred of me will seem small in comparison to your fear of Myella. She will wrack the power from your being, before she gives what's left of you to Oran."

"Ere this is over, Duran, I will kill you. For Sir Chill."

A cold smile grew on his lips and he rubbed the fringe of his black beard. "We two are much

438

alike. Both idealistic in our own way and, in that, honorable. You and I were cast from the same mold. Early on our paths took a turn. If things were different, we might have been brothers."

"On the surface alike, Duran; however, we were never cast from the same mold. The difference between us is inside. You have no conscience, no remorse. You take your orders and reap pleasure from the game. I, on the other hand, gain no pleasure from the fight."

"You may think that is the case, Sir John. I know better. Tomorrow, either you will willingly accept the role of Hand of Keth, or Myella will break you before the Seat, and send you to her uncle, Mage Guyle. The Turning will not be easy, for his is the Tower of Pain.

"I just wanted to see you once more, before you are no longer aware or perhaps destroyed. They say a man is not the same after he has become the Hand." Duran turned and left. The solid ironbound door shut with a dull thud.

"Great," John muttered and slumped back.

Chapter 26

Yhtrain slept, but his dreams were not pleasant. Visions of Claybrook's head in that chest on the Council room floor kept interrupting his repose. "You are next," those eyes said accusingly. He jerked awake and stared blearily at the dark ceiling; the soft samite sheets had slipped down about his waist. His breathing eased and he caressed the shoulder of the prostitute that his aide had brought to him. Undoubtedly she was the loveliest he had ever been with: dark hair, curly, with a smile that would disarm a man quicker than could the Guard of Oran. He noted the smoothness of her back and the tight muscle of her arm. She had performed well for him that night, bringing him to the heights of ecstasy before he had collapsed from utter exhaustion.

Now, as he watched her, she smiled and her eyes fluttered open. Turning onto her side, she exposed the curve of her breast and again he felt a stirring in his loins. She reached beneath the covers and stroked him.

"Are you not a great Councilman?" she asked. She had questioned him earlier in the evening and he had eventually told her how he had become more powerful than even Nathal. He had gained that power through an alliance with the Seat and Myella, and that was what had brought him wealth. Now, as she asked again, he replied: "I am the greatest of the ten."

She smiled and her hand gripped harder. He arched his back in pleasure, but she did not abate. He looked at her with worried eyes and she let go.

He smiled then and urged her to continue. She leaned her head close to his, to whisper, as she reached down once more.

"You are nothing, Ythrain."

Pain sliced up into him. Cold, unyielding fingers of steel grasped his innards and his eyes rolled back. He convulsed once, twice. Then went totally limp.

Bale leaned back. She shivered for a moment then a smile spread across her lips and her heavily lidded eyes glazed somewhat. She wiped the blade of the stiletto on the sheet. Her friends would also have Quinz and Gyergo's ears on silk cords this night.

My ass is killing me. Tom mused as he watched the light streaming in through the crystal panes across from his precarious perch. Another day had passed and, by the angle of the light that streamed through the windows it was early morning. During the night, he had sneaked down to the nave and warily stretched his stiff muscles. Then he had explored what was the Temple of Oran, giving a wide berth to the tabernacle. It was large by any standard, and reminded him of the pictures he had seen of the Hagia Sophia. At sunset, acolytes had locked the obvious entrances into the Temple, but in the course of his inspection he had found several well-hidden doors that led to dark and dusty passages, only one of which had seen footsteps in a while. So it was that he stretched and poked about, until the dim light of dawn began to illuminate the vault near the stained glass windows. He soon found himself crawling up the narrow passage within the hollow pillar and taking his position near the vault.

He nibbled on a granola bar and Kiera graciously accepted a quarter of it. Below, in the center of the temple, acolytes had opened the door and, as was their routine, scrubbed the marble dais and polished the headsman's sword that sat near the humble seat. Occasionally, a priest (for that was what Tom took the purple- robed men to be) would order an acolyte away from the tabernacle on another errand. The temple was now clean and sparkling, unlike the dark and evil chamber of the past two nights.

"Looks like they're getting ready for something, girl," he whispered to the ferret. It was uncanny how she looked into his eyes, then returned to her preening. His attention was caught as a woman (the one who had caused all the ruckus the other night) stalked into the nave. Behind her was a black cloaked and armored man. He thought he recognized the sword...

He almost fell from the alcove as he realized that Myella had Joe in tow. Then he remembered what the guards had said, about Surik, the new Arch-Regent that had killed several assassins. But how?

Smiling Wolf cleared his mind; vaguely he heard her talking, but the distance was too great. Then as he relaxed and cleared all other ambient noise from his surroundings, he began to pick up the conversation...

"...and tonight he will be mine, or he shall see his beloved face the Hand of Keth. He will succumb. I do not know what power he has to hold the Naming at bay, but when he agrees willingly he shall become Oran's eternally, just as you have." She went to the cabinet from which that awesome presence had emanated two nights before. She opened the grate and stepped back.

Above, the sky darkened and a cloud passed before the sun. Kiera chittered nervously.

"Come, Surik Shadowlord, Hand of Keth and Arch-Regent. Bathe in that which is Oran."

Tom watched Joe step forward, next to Myella. Black tendrils, like coal dust spun about her feet. Outside the sky had darkened causing any light within to fade and be replaced by shadow and darkness. Then Joe reeled back as a tendril struck his chest. He fell.

Tom had to restrain himself from rappelling down the pillar and going to Joe's aid. He watched as a somewhat shocked Myella knelt to Joe's side and pressed her hand to his chest. He convulsed once then gasped.

"Truly, you are chosen by Oran, Surik. He has touched you from his realm." She looked up. "Guards! Take the Hand to his chambers."

As Tom watched Joe being carried from the hall, Myella closed the cabinet grate and exited the nave. Smiling Wolf closed his eyes and prayed to his ancestors. He prayed to them and whatever good and decent spirits were about.

He prayed for Joe's soul.

Kelvin, Lord Protector of the Port City of Paravel, stared with sleep-laden eyes at the body lying on the bed before him. Ythrain, blood draining from his gut, lay dead in his own bedchambers. The Lord Protector held no remorse for the death of this petty man. Power had corrupted him, and power was his undoing. This man had been as much the cause of Paravel's problems as Claybrook or Myella.

Now, the Lord Protector heaved a sigh and turned his attention to one very angry captain of the Guard of Oran. Supposedly, the man had called on Ythrain's house and found the body. No doubt he was the man's lackey or a messenger from the Seat. On finding Ythrain dead of violence, he reported it to the City Guard, and Kelvin's lieutenant had informed him that morning when he was just arriving back from Dirkajian's.

Yet, there was no time for wandering thoughts. The Council had taken care of their problem in the ranks, and it would eventually be seen through for what it was: a reprisal for the act against Vilidis. It was also a clear statement to the Seat of who should be in control of Paravel.

Now, one of Myella's own guard was in his face. What was it that he had said? Threatened the Lord Protector if the culprit was not found. Kelvin laughed then. He was getting on in years but he was not that old. He grabbed the man by the scruff of the collar and shoved him aside.

"It was a prostitute, Guardsman; no doubt Ythrain here could not satisfy her."

"A whore? We are not blind Kelvin. Your attitude will be reported to the Seat.

We all know to whom you answer, and she will not be happy. I should take you to her myself." The man's sword was half drawn when Kelvin's lieutenant had his own steel at the man's throat. His eyes bulged as Kelvin waved his own lieutenant's hand away.

"When I was your age, I saw a young guard like you insult a member of the

Conclave. At that time, it was the duty of the Guard – of which I was also a member

– to quell any dissent and protect any honor. I took no pleasure in the act, but I struck him down with my dagger and I was honored with the post of Second Commander of the Black Guard. From there I became Preceptor of Helm.

"Now, killing is not pleasurable to me, but I have had my share of it in the past. You tell Myella that this was the work of a prostitute. Or, I may consider it an insult to my honor." With that the lieutenant's sword was sheathed and the Guardsman left.

"Any other deaths, lieutenant?"

"Quinz and Gyergo were found. The former was hung. The latter drowned in his bath. A shame."

"Yes," replied the silver haired man. "Are the men ready?"

"Yes, and loyal to you."

"Now comes the test."

The shackles were snapped into place by a surly old guard as two more looked on from the door. They weren't taking any chances this time, per Duran's orders. John was hauled roughly into the hall and down the winding stairs. Late afternoon had brought heavy clouds and the hint of an impending storm. John wondered what else lay ahead, but drove that thought and any other despair from his head.

He passed several other doors, one of which he knew must be Gabrielle's, but he was in no position to find out for certain. They marched him through the courtyard, where two days ago he had killed several men and stolen a horse in an attempt to escape, and was in turn thwarted by one of his best friends, Joe. He looked at the Gate of Osso. Is that what they had called it? Now a spattering of rain crossed from the gate to his entourage. He realized that it would soon be pouring. From the courtyard, he was led to the Seat. Here another escort joined them, flanking four on the left and four on the right.

Maybe it was the tingling in his chest; maybe it was intuition, or the hint of many voices on the edge of his senses. Whatever it was, he knew he was headed for the Temple of Oran.

His guards took him through side corridors that must have paralleled the length of the temple. Occasionally, he would glimpse a doorway and in doing so see a milling group of guards and soldiers in the livery of Oran. There were others, civilians loyal to the Conclave or to Myella or, no doubt, to that evil god. He was led into a room. Ironically, it reminded him of the antechamber of a church, but all resemblance ended with the woodwork. The tools and instruments were not the chalice and the miter, but rather were the flail and the dagger. Nice combination, he thought.

There were several masked priests checking over the items of the temple, and his gaze was directed to Joe, good old mindless Joe. Myella sat next to him.

The Surrogate of the South looked up from the chair and appraised the White Knight. "I see that you made it to the Temple, Sir John. No reprieve like the other day?" She smiled when he did not reply. "It is unfortunate for you that you did not die in your endeavor. The Wracking is a thousand times more painful than any death you could imagine."

"You tried the Naming–"

"And I failed, yes?" She looked down at the floor a moment, as if choosing her thoughts carefully. "The Wracking is unlike the Naming. You see, after the victim has succumbed, by his own agreement, he is first physically beaten, and then what is left of his soul is peeled away.

"You know, in the past it was said some sorcerers could do this to the recently deceased. You, Lord Knight will be painfully aware of the entire process. Ere this night is over, there will be a second...make that third, Hand of Keth in Paravel. After that, the rest of your companions will be easier."

"Gee, thanks Myella, but you don't have to go to all the trouble."

"It is no trouble, that I assure you." She smiled and caught the look on John's face when he saw his katana hanging from a peg on the wall behind her. "It is a nice weapon, Lord Knight, but you won't be needing that for a while. I trust you have made your peace. It is the only peace you shall know for a long time. Oran's hands are not very gentle for his enemies."

"As if you care."

"No, I don't. Yet, you will pay tenfold for the men whose blood you shed on the Temple Grounds."

"Your threats are beyond frightening me, Myella."

"Mayhap that is true, but what of Gabrielle?"

John's eyes were cold as he looked at the High Priestess of Oran. If the shackles weren't binding him, he knew he would strangle her with his own hands.

"Where is she?"

"Not yet, outlander." She moved from the chair, the grace of a cat. She stood before him. "One last chance. Tell me of your power. Acquiesce to me and all will be yours. You shall have all you wish."

"What I want, I doubt if you could give me."

"Anything."

"My sword."

She jerked him forward by the collar; her tawny muscles were much stronger than he had thought. "Do you hear that?" she hissed.

He vaguely heard the growing murmur from within the temple. He strained to be away from her; sensuous lips strained into a rictus of hate.

"They rush to the Temple of Oran like the tide. They come as witness to the power of Oran. If you will not yield to me, then I will cast the design my uncle has set forth and you will be bound by the Wracking."

She pushed him away and strode from the chamber, Joe gazed at him for a moment then he too followed. Through the opening door, he caught a glimpse of Duran and someone else.

"Gabrielle!" he shouted and tried to dodge to the doorway. One of the priests snaked a staff out and he fell against Myella's chair. Blackness enshrouded him and the last thing he saw was Duran striking the daughter of Trevor to her knees.

Mike nodded and murmured something he was sure sounded profound as he passed into the Temple of Oran. His pants were too tight and the collar strained his neck, but he made do. It wasn't often one had the opportunity to be one of the Guard of Oran. The uniforms made the group just one of many. Bill, Torec and Garis all tried to push to the head of the nave, but the going was tough. It seemed that rank dictated how close one sat near Oran, and they were nothing more than common soldiers. He made sure that all the gear was in place as he nodded to Torec, and they finally positioned themselves near the dais, just to the front of a heavy pillar.

Torec tried not to be too conspicuous, he had feared that his chain hauberk might be too noisy, but the babble that greeted them was enough to drown out an occasional clink of metal.

Bill looked nervous, Mike noted with a frown. Tar'elah and the others were being led to a secret passage by Bale; she had looked rather worn that morning, as if she had been working all night, but she was glowing fiercely, evidently in anticipation of the fight to come. The mercenaries and bandits would bring up the rear if any trouble arose and with the looks of the crowd within the Temple of Oran that was highly likely.

Mike touched the orb tentatively and was pleased to note that John was in the rear of the

449

temple and Tom...Tom was directly above him at the summit of the pillar. He wondered what surprise the Sioux had in store for the party.

Above, Tom had watched the group of guards push their way to the front of the temple. He had noticed something about them that was curious; they had seemed familiar. Then, it hit him. The largest of the group was wearing soft leather moccasins, not the polished black boots of the Guard. It was Michael.

Why, that little sneak. Looks like we're all here, Kiera, he said quietly to the ferret as she peered at the growing throng. He had already seen Joe among the Temple Guard, but the face was as blank as ever. He readied his rope and placed his bow near at hand. Ready to rock n' roll.

***

Alaric ducked into the tunnel that led almost directly from the foundry to the Seat. It was a long-forgotten way, used formerly for transporting building materials and supplies. Faintly, he heard the reverberating sound of several ships in the adjacent docks exploding, as the naphtha and tallow were set afire. That would occupy the guards at this end of town for the rest of the evening. The fire would no doubt take three of four ships and foreign traders. Now, he had to sprint quickly to meet with the others, who must be awaiting him at the appointed place beneath the Seat.

A frown spread over Duran's countenance as he watched a fireball erupt from the vicinity of the docks and recede to a bright glow in the eastern portion of the city. He had dispatched several men to investigate the fire, but from this chamber in the temple he could not see far beyond the rear Wall of Osso. He sighed and turned; it was probably nothing but a warehouse going up, just trouble for the militia. At this time he would not even bother Myella with it. She stood before Gabrielle, fire in her eyes as she anticipated the fall of Sir John this night.

"Today I will teach any who would defy me a grievous lesson. Your outlander friend will be the object lesson, and you will be the catalyst. Tonight the City of Paravel is mine. The Council knows it; the Lord Protector knows it and now all the lands to the West will know it.

"Paravel will go down in history as the place where the New Conclaveum was birthed. The old has withered and will soon fall, and the new will be born here, in the Temple of Oran. From here Oran will spread his dominance to the West. Narn-toc will be a reminder of the power of Oran, rising from the ashes to regain its lost glory. Tonight I will proclaim myself Conclavatrix of all that is. Tonight even Helm shudders." The Surrogate looked at the woman before her, dressed in the leather jerkin and breeches she had worn when Galfeon Yor fell. Dark rings beneath the eyes told the priestess of Gabrielle's exhaustion, yet there was fire in her eyes as she stared defiantly at her captor.

"You won't be needing those," Myella said, gesturing to her clothes. Gabrielle stepped back and into Duran's arms. She craned her neck, trying to peer beyond the closed door to where Sir John had been. She felt Duran's hands on her shoulders and shivered in revulsion.

"Remove them, Duran." Myella smiled coldly at the expression on the Lady's face.

Duran spun the dark haired Gabrielle around and looked into her eyes, almost as if to say, Last chance. Then he abruptly clutched at the bodice of her jerkin and with a sneer ripped it down the center. His hand grazed her breast.

Gabrielle kicked him in the groin. The man doubled over in pain and staggered back against the wall. Myella chuckled from behind.

"Very good, cousin." She gestured to the two masked priests that were in the room. They grabbed Gabrielle by each arm as Myella took a plain white shift from the bench.

"You will wear this," she said in a low voice.

Kelvin mounted his stallion; a contingent of City Guard milled around his horse then finally formed up in a column behind him. Eighty guards on horseback rode through the streets of Paravel.

Few people were out this early evening, the impending rain and swirling rumors had led to most people shuttering their windows and bolting their doors. Only a few merchants were about, and they were forced to move their wains hastily out of the way as the City Guard passed.

Regardless of the few spits of rain falling from the cloud-heavy sky, Kelvin let stream his whitest cloak. He looked over his shoulder, hearing the rumble that was not thunder, but the signal that Alaric had set their plan in motion. The Council's guardsmen were in similar position throughout the city; to prevent any backlash that might occur from the Guard of Oran who were stationed outside the Seat.

As Kelvin rounded the north square and spied the Gate of Osso, he pulled forth his saber and considered the writ tucked into his belt. At least it would all be nice and legal.

His men flanked him as he stopped before the gate. He knew that no engines of war lay behind the wall, but there were almost two hundred men, most seasoned warriors. Strangely enough, the gate was closed, which was unusual for even this hour of the evening. Yet, this did not deter him. His lieutenant rode ahead and pounded sharply on the bound iron gates with the butt of his halberd. After a few moments a lone guard in black livery peered over the postern. Upon seeing the eighty horsemen he frowned, then his gaze lit upon Kelvin. Without hesitation, the man disappeared and was soon cracking open the gates. Once they were wide, he strode smartly up to the Lord Protector and stood square in front of him. Kelvin turned his horse slightly to the side and leaned down to address the man.

"Milord Kelvin, what brings you and these men to the Seat?" the guardsman said with some authority, resting his hand on the hilt of his sword. It was as if eighty men at the Gate of Osso were not out of the ordinary.

"Read," the Lord Protector said as thrust the writ into the face of the guard. The man eyed it suspiciously but did not raise his hand to take it.

"What is it?"

"A writ, declaring that Myella and the Seat are to remove themselves from the Free City of Paravel by sundown this evening or they shall be removed by force of arms. It also charges Duran and Myella in the deaths of Vilidis the merchant and Claybrook the Governor. They have been implicated in the deaths of Councilmen Ythrain, Gyergo and Quinz as well." Kelvin let that soak in for a moment and the guard just looked from the paper to the silver haired Lord Protector, wide-eyed.

"That is ridiculous!" the guard finally spat out.

"I thought you'd say that." Kelvin leaned back and his sword flashed out; the flat of the blade struck the man in the temple. He fell to the ground, unconscious before his back struck the cobbles.

"At least he was good enough to open the Gate," muttered the lieutenant. Kelvin smiled and waved the horses in.

"Let us hope that the others are in place," he called as the Gates of Osso shut with a clang behind them. They were in the Seat.

John was bound and led out onto the dais where he was tied most effectively to the humble seat near the headsman's sword. One of the guards slapped him in an effort to revive him from the blow to the head, and it worked to some extent. His head throbbed and he knew from the tickle on his cheek that he was bleeding. When his eyes focused, he looked out over the several hundred people in the temple proper. Black and gold uniforms mixed with a few civilians; a crowd of faces, some mocking, some hateful, some blank. And as he looked about, a hush fell over the crowd,

454

no more the murmur of spectators, rather a low susurration, the anticipation of impending doom.

He shook his head, in part to clear it, yet also to shake off some of the blood that had managed to find its way into his eyes. The guards had bound him to the arms of the stone chair with leather straps. When he strained at them, the effort almost cost him his consciousness, a moment of dizziness. He breathed deeply and looked about the dais.

The headsman's blade, the bench, the tabernacle, if you could call it that. He sighed inwardly, not knowing if he was going to get out of this one.

He looked up to see Joe, clad in black armor, staring straight through him. Then the artist went to stand directly behind the heading block. He grasped the hilt of the flat-tipped blade, letting his own bastard sword lie sheathed in its scabbard at his side.

Several masked priests stood behind the Hand of Keth. Their faces were blank as they folded their arms and closed their eyes. Lightning illuminated the crowd through the crystalline windows. Rain had begun to strike them creating white noise for the masses.

He spotted Duran, in the livery of the commander of the Guard of Oran. He looked good, John thought. He caught the others eye and smiled wickedly. Maybe I can kill him with kindness.

Myella walked from the antechamber. She gestured and flames soared from the braziers to the vaulted ceiling. A hush befell the crowd.

"Subjects of Oran!" All within the temple heard, though to John her voice was barely above a whisper. "Tonight marks the beginning of a new era. Not long ago I brought you the Arch-regent of the South, designee of Narn-toc and Hand of Keth. Tonight I bring you this man, to become a new Hand of Keth.

"He will resist, but together we will speak the ancient words. We shall Wrack him. He will become the servant of Oran, and, in doing so, shall lead you and others against the West.

"The Conclaveum has grown weak and fettered in its old age. No more does the Conclavator care for the South, nor does he care that the West breeds war. Armies are massing to the West and pose a danger to Paravel, and to its sister city Narn-toc that, with time, we will bring back to its former glory. These armies would wipe the Conclaveum and those of it from this land and into the sea. But, like Clef, we will not allow dissention to spread.

"Tonight I proclaim that I am Conclavatrix of all that was and all that is. No more shall the doddering fool of a man in Teshwa guide our destinies. No more will a body of decrepit and sodden men rule the provinces without care for what happens south of the Great Wall. You shall carry the message to the North. You who comprise the eyes and ears of the Clave shall whisper dissent to those that gather at the Enclave. Already the Conclavator is dying, and soon those loyal to me shall sweep through the cities North, and all that is Carn will be under our sway.

"Tonight, under my orders the Guard of Oran has taken Helm as its main garrison. Now control of the Black Guard belongs to them. Tonight, all that is the Great Wall and South belongs to Oran. Narn-toc fell because we were weak. It shall rise once more, it shall withstand all, even if we have to set fire to every city-state and sacrifice every man, woman, and child who oppose Oran!"

The throng shouted its approval, their voices reverberating in the cavernous temple. John felt a tingling in his chest and immediately a warmth suffused his being, clearing his head and, to some degree, diminishing his exhaustion. He thanked God for that little comfort.

"Bring out the girl," Myella called and two of her masked and armored priests brought forth a struggling young girl. John watched as Trianna was forced to kneel at the headsman's block, her neck lay exposed on its stained surface. He swore under his breath as the girl tried to rise but was forced down again. She looked about, wild-eyed, until she saw Surik and the sword.

"Oran! I call upon thee. Bring justice to those who would bring ruin to you." John waited and tensed as shadow overlapped shadow near the rear of the dais. Dark tendrils seem to form and phase near the pseudo-tabernacle. Thunder boomed outside the temple and there was another crack as lightning struck near the Seat. The storm seemed to rage outside as well as within.

"Balhq, Ak'hu nictu, Balhq es tuien, Oran," Myella shouted and Joe hefted the blunt tipped sword in both hands.

Trianna screamed.

Tom readied his bow. Was this the moment? He asked himself as his friend and comrade lifted the awkward blade. Fortunately, it was not one of the priests, who wore a heavy type of armor that his arrow would not pierce. Was there anything left to Joe, anything at all? If he could catch the artist's left shoulder. He pulled the string taut, rolling it over his middle and forefinger. Kiera nipped at his ear. He paused.

"No!" shouted John as the blade began its descent toward the girl's neck. "Take me instead."

Surik Shadowlord stopped and looked to Myella. She turned to the Lord Knight of Erie. "Very well. We will take you instead. You have made the first self- sacrifice, a necessary step on the path to the Wracking." She gestured for the two priests to take Trianna back into the antechamber.

"Your title of Knight is well earned, yet you will not trade your life for that wretched girl's. You have another role, and will not find solace in simple death. Tonight you will dance in the power of Oran, Wracked to His will, and it is mine to break you so that it may be done. Only wait, and you will see that which you most desire destroyed."

John strained at the straps that held him in the humble seat.

Tom sighed in relief at what had transpired. John had called Myella's bluff, and was no worse for the wear. The Sioux readied his rope and sword, waiting for some signal from the others.

Chapter 27

There were many passages beneath the city of Paravel. Some even stretched outside the wall proper, and most were constructed long before the Seat was built within the walls. Yet, the ones that concerned Alaric were the ones directly beneath the Seat.

The Guildmaster Merchant slogged through knee-deep sewage, knowing every twist and turn of the tunnel by heart. This was the escape route one would take if he were to commit a crime on Delph Street; the other led to the Lord Protector's keep. If he continued to his right, that would take him to the Maze, to the left was the Temple.

He had caught up with Torec's men, Tar'elah, and her bandits. Now they all followed him, three score at the most when he counted Bale and a few others. With the fires at the docks and the warehouses burning, it was hoped that the Guard of Oran outside the Seat would be occupied. It was also hoped that Kelvin and his men had gotten past the Gate of Osso; if they did not, all would be lost.

He stopped and looked up, the sound of the storm muting the echo in the flooded passage. His lantern flickered in the draft that flowed from above. He called to several of his men. Above, the cistern cover would be heavy and they would have to create a living ladder. That was no problem; the hard part would come when they removed the cistern cover.

They would be in the Seat Guardhouse.

***

"I have a special gift for you," she whispered for only John to hear. "You participate in my theater well, Sir Knight. But, now the real spectacle begins. Bring her in," Myella ordered. She smiled venomously at John. He'd gotten that sinking feeling in the pit of his stomach when he saw the look on Myella's face. He watched helplessly as two priests escorted another woman from the antechamber. He saw her dark, curly hair, and forest green eyes. Blood lubricated his bonds as the leather bit into his straining wrists.

"Gabrielle!" he called, his voice cracking. She tried to go to him, but the two priests held her tightly, pulling her toward the block where Joe stood. He felt utterly helpless.

"Myella, anything. I'll give you what you want, just free her." He knew his words were the beginning of the end but, although she smiled, Myella paid him no heed. The priestess walked to the Lady Gabrielle and caressed her arm. Then she spoke in an almost sisterly tone.

"You shall be his undoing. He will succumb. Then I will peel all that is him away and he will be an empty shell for me to fill."

She looked to Joe as she backed away, the priests held Gabrielle to the block. Surik looked down, his gray eyes squinted and his brow furrowed. He looked at the blade, the curved quillions, the blood groove and flat tip. He looked at her neck, exposed but for her straining and her hair. His own sword swung to the side, and he paused.

Then he raised the sword high above his head, sweat beading his brow. He gasped.

The tendrils of blackness reached from the tabernacle.

John shook with rage. He closed his eyes and concentrated on his St. Christopher medallion. Envisioning white searing light, he hoped all would be burnt away. He opened his eyes. Yet, all was the same, stopped in time for him to witness.

No, not all was the same. The blackness that was at the rear of the dais had abated. Gone from the place, as if the evil presence had fled.

"Myella!" Joe paused at John's shout. The Surrogate looked to the bound knight. "The Power you seek. I can give it to you. It is in my medallion, the talisman around my neck. You can have it, just free Gabrielle!"

"The Power? Around your neck? What trick is this?" She hesitated, but then ordered Surik to lower the sword. "If this is a trick Lord Knight...I warn you. Surik, attend to it." Joe handed the flat blade to one of the priests. The bearded man went to Sir John and leaned forward. Sweat splattered from his brow and he was breathing heavily as if in a fever. He leaned close to his friend and felt around his collar.

"Joe, you bastard! Remember who you are!" John whispered it fiercely, trying to get it across to his friend as he fumbled at his collar. "You have your own fencing school. Because of your fuck-up, a rare Dutch painting burned!"

Joe stepped back, without the medallion, anger and confusion crossing his face.

"Fool!" hissed Duran as he came from behind. Duran pushed John's head back roughly and grabbed at his neck. He had the medal...for a moment...then white-hot fire burnt his hand and tore it from his grip. He jumped back, almost falling off the dais. Myella watched with growing impatience.

"Only he can give it to you, is that not obvious? Un-bind him."

"But–" began Duran.

"Do it, Surik, but take care." Joe looked to Myella and nodded. He swiftly cut the leather with his dagger and John rubbed his abraded wrists.

"The medallion, Sir John," Myella called as he stood. "Go to hell!" he shouted as he shoved Joe to the side. "Kill him Surik!" she shouted.

Joe drew his own black bastard sword.

He paused as blue fire coursed up its length; silver light flowed within it and into him. The ember was no longer dormant and he suddenly remembered a story. It was the story of the catatonic who would stand all day with his hand out, palm upward. He would never move from that position. When asked in a moment of lucidity why he stood that way, he answered: "Why, the forces for good and evil are battling for dominion on my hand. I fear that if I tip it one way or the other, good might lose."

Joe smiled, never one for polemics, he tipped his hand to the side. "Kill him Surik!"

Joe shook his head. His sword glowed an ethereal glow; the Power of their realm manifested in this reality. "I don't think so, Myella. Your magic doesn't work too well on us outlanders."

She looked at the Shadowlord, seething with rage. Everything seemed to be falling apart around her. She spun, her eyes falling on Gabrielle and the black- armored priest who now held the sword.

"Kill her!" she shouted. The sword flashed back in an arc. Joe and John froze, hypnotized by its glittering surface. It began to descend.

A loud report shattered the silence that had fallen on the Temple. The priest sagged and dropped the sword over his back, clutching at a hole that had appeared in his forehead. The smooth surface of the tabernacle was splattered with a pink and white collage as the man fell onto it. Myella looked wildly into the crowd.

Mike smiled nonchalantly down the smoking length of the black barrel; the modified flintlock had worked flawlessly. At the sound of the gunshot, Torec, Bill, and Garis had thrown back their cloaks and revealed their weapons and armor. In seconds they were ready to fight. Above, Tom smiled, knowing that from his angle it would have been difficult at best to kill the priest. He watched as Mike and others sprang toward the dais.

Joe turned to John. "Figures that asshole would bring gunpowder to this world." He smiled at his friend and tossed him the dagger. "Sorry about me being away."

"So am I," John replied. He looked about. The temple was in utter chaos. The Guards in front were turning to intercept Mike and his group. John heard a whirring noise and looked up to see Tom rappel down from the rafters. He landed amid a group of the Guard of Oran.

John and Joe looked at each other and grinned. Then they turned and made a rush for where Gabrielle was being held. Joe ran in front, blocking the first priest into John, who struck him under the sternum with the dagger. He soon was over the dead priest, grabbing the headsman's sword from the ground.

Two guards near the rear of the dais drew their swords and rushed into the melee. Joe intercepted them with a quick riposte, then a parry and the guard fell, clutching his side. The Shadowlord turned, his glowing sword sheared through the blade of his second assailant and cut deep, through the chain mail, and into the stomach.

Rain slashed the courtyard of the Seat as Kelvin's men secured the Gate of Osso and rode their horses dispassionately at the few guards that were stationed at the gate. His men drove their lance and halberd into the black-clad men, and Kelvin slashed one of the remainder that had gotten through.

Some had poured from the Tower, half-clothed and unprepared for an assault from the City Guard. Kelvin ordered his men onward, and saw that the Guards were also being assailed from the rear, as Alaric bit into them from the basement of the tower. Soon, the dreaded Guard of Oran spilled their lives onto the rain-soaked flagstones.

Alaric quickly dispatched a guard and turned from the fray, leaving Kelvin and his men to take up the contest. With Bale and Tar'elah at his heels, he crossed the courtyard to the steps of the Seat. Alaric Dirkajian lunged and feinted, slicing through the guard that tried to block the door. The guard shouted and his companion turned, only to be cut down by Tar'elah's short, but lethal blade. Blood sprayed across the heavy doors as they were flung open and Alaric entered.

Duran drew his basket-hilted saber and leapt to defend Myella from the fray. There was a harsh shout as more guards appeared at the rear of the Temple. He smiled at the thought of killing Sir John himself. He watched the man go to Gabrielle. For now he would wait, then when the chance presented itself, he would strike. He smiled as he killed one of Torec's mercenaries.

Tom Smiling Wolf rolled and threw out some shuriken, needle thin spikes. They sprayed into the six guardsmen he had landed amidst, confusing and stunning them. He rolled to the side, his sword blade snapping up and out, into the first man's jaw. The second offered a bit of a fight, but after the stomp-kick and a lunging slice, he offered his head. Tom dodged another blade and headed to where Mike and the others stood.

"Myella!" Joe called as he leveled the bastard sword, its black edge glinting with fire. "Payback time."

He attacked the guards around her ruthlessly. Hate filled his eyes and his blade leapt effortlessly, spinning a web of death. He struck down another guard and parried two blows from yet another.

Mike and Bill could not get a foothold on the dais; the Guard of Oran had seen to that. Torec had tried to position them as a wedge in front of the advancing mercenaries, but a contingent of the Guard of Oran had flanked them and quickly drawn their weapons. The guards seemed to be coming from everywhere, and the companions were hard put just to defend themselves against the flashing blades. They were slowly being beaten back against the wall of the Temple when Tom sidled up from behind and nodded to Mike as he held his sword in the ichimongi. He fended off a long sword, but had no room for attack.

"Seems to be a little tight," the Sioux remarked as he slid past a hack and nicked the guard on the arm. The bearded guard flinched and struck back, missing the tracker and striking the pillar.

"I knew a girl like that," Mike huffed as he spun his short sword in one hand while trying to tuck the flintlock into his belt. He was almost impaled by a guardsman.

Alaric and Tar'elah spread their people through the rear of the temple. They wanted to flank the throng, half of which was trying to push its way to the front and half of which just wanted to escape by the nearest exit. Avoiding the majority of the milling crowd they soon forced their way in and began to hack and cut guards who stood amid the congregation, causing mass confusion. One of the bandits fell, his viscera spilling onto the floor, and then he too in a heap. Alaric's saber flashed and it stabbed into the guard's visor, through the eye.

Torec sliced at a black-clad guard and heard a clunk as his curved sword struck the helm of the armored man. The guard stumbled back into a priest, and Torec's scimitar slashed across his chest, opening a wide gash. The man attacked once more, only to find Mike's short-sword in his way.

It bit deep. As the man fell to the blood-slick floor, another replaced him. They were soon surrounded.

Joe was forced back to the block, where John quickly cut Gabrielle's bonds and gave her the dagger. He slipped and almost fell, then recovered and looked about him. Mike, Torec, Bill, and a few of their men formed a knot, surrounded, near the dais. Other knots of men fought individual battles throughout the congregation. John watched as the Guard of Oran made their way to the tabernacle area. He lifted the awkward headsman's sword in his hand and parried a heavy hack. His arm shuddered from the blow. Then he lifted the blade high and it fell with a crunch into the man's shoulder, shearing clear to the hip. The man screamed in agony and fell.

Things certainly seemed to be taking a turn for the worse as Myella and

Duran issued succinct commands to their guards.

"If we could make it to the doors!" John shouted as he nodded to the twin doors that flanked the nave. But the artist just frowned and parried as their route was cut off by six more in Temple guards.

***

Kelvin's men were flanking the main building of the Seat. No resistance met the City Guard beyond the few guardsmen who patrolled the grounds. The main body of the Guard of Oran was inside the Temple or out in the City entirely. What concerned Kelvin for the moment were those inside the Temple, the ones that vastly outnumbered the mercenaries and bandits who were in the rear of the large structure.

Kelvin heard the gates slamming open before he could see them. Peering back through his men in gray and red, he saw a group of guardsmen in black. Apparently the ruse at the docks had not been enough. There was a contingent of about thirty. He motioned for half of his men to take them. The lieutenant nodded and broke off with his men; their horses charged the guards on foot. It wouldn't be pretty.

Kelvin kicked his steed in the flanks and his horse leapt forward, toward the doors of the Temple of Oran.

"There are too many!" Tar'elah shouted. She was having difficulty defending herself from the long blades of the Guard of Oran. Bill, at the other end of the temple, may as well have been a league away for the men in black that stood between her and the dais.

Alaric just shook his head and ducked as the blade of a halberd sliced near. He struck back, missing the man and getting cut on the shoulder for his error. He frowned, his amber eyes squinting through some splattered blood. Striking again, he cut up from the man's thigh, effectively crippling him.

"Get ready to retreat!" he barked. The oak bound doors of the temple were against their backs. He saw Tar'elah shake her head, her sandy hair streaming out; she pressed forward into the fray. Not caring that her back was exposed she made her way toward the front of the temple. Alaric swore heavily and leapt to guard her back. "This is foolish, even for a bandit!"

"Even to us, honor is more valued than life, merchant!" she shouted back. Her short sword plunged into the gut of a guardsman. Alaric barely blocked a blow that was meant for the woman's back.

"There are a lot more of these guards than I thought," Tom yelled to Mike who was too busy to answer.

"Oran has many worshippers, most are the Guard, others are those civilians who are trying to get out of the Temple," grunted Torec. He avoided a thrust and sent the man back without a hand.

"No shit?" Tom dove to the side, between two guards and came up behind them. He cut them down and dodged a few others, trying to make his way to the dais.

Suddenly the awkward sword that John used was knocked from his grip. He looked up to see a guard grinning triumphantly. The man was about to strike again when Joe's black blade neatly sliced through his neck.

"Thanks," John called as the man fell back.

"That's two you owe me," Surik responded, rather winded by the exertion. Then he staggered to the side as the halberd bit him in the thigh. It had gotten through his armor, but it was not serious. The guards were pressing in more closely now, and the floor was thick with blood and effluvia.

"What the hell?" Joe heard John mutter. He watched as John grabbed up the headsman's sword and swung it awkwardly. It effectively cleared the guards from his view. Joe glanced to where John was looking.

As lightning washed through the windows high up in the temple, the sound of the twin doors bursting inward was augmented by the thunder. Oak and steel splintered as several large horses slammed against it. Kelvin and his City Guard trampled in on horseback.

"We're done for," John called. "That's the guy that captured me!" But he was astonished to see the Lord Protector not helping the Guard of Oran, rather cutting them down from atop his mount. Several of the City Guard on horse were now in the temple, trampling as well as cutting at the guards. John heard Mike whoop and howl as the City Guard attacked the minions of Oran.

Mike and Torec stood near the pillar as Kelvin plowed through on his stallion, clearing a wide swath in the congregation. Bill sighed and relaxed against the smooth stone surface. Torec smiled at Garis and the Bard.

"It looks like the tide is turning," Garis bellowed, but his expression abruptly changed. Twisting to the side, a halberd full in his back, Garis fell to the floor.

Bill howled in rage and leapt at the guard who had struck down his friend. Up to this moment Bill had refused to acknowledge the imminence of the death and pain. He refused to allow himself to become part of this reality, but now his acquired long sword arced down and he collided with the other man. The blade crashed between the man's neck and shoulder, and he struck again, and again. It struck the same place and the man shouted in agony, finally to lie still at Torec's feet. Bill stood over the body, letting the hate and the pain flow out with the man's blood.

"He has always been at my side." Torec's voice broke with sadness. He noticed his own bloody arm and how the blood dripped with that of Garis'. "He was my brother, Bard. I shall avenge him against these Ish-deme!"

***

With the advent of Kelvin charging his horses into the temple, the fray had begun to thin. Joe could clearly see the gap between him and John, Mike and the others. From the rear of the temple Alaric and Tar'elah were pushing the guardsmen to the middle, where the Lord Protector and the City Guard could strike them with greater ease. There was a sizable group at the dais, surrounding Myella and Duran. Joe stepped to the side and spun a sword out of the way, slicing deep to the man's side. The melee was getting wearing on him, and he hoped it would end soon.

"The cavalry?" Tom shouted to Bill. Bill only looked to the rear of the temple to catch a glimpse of Tar'elah. Her short sword flashed, and she soon neared Bill and Tom, forcing her way through the battling crowd with Alaric at her back. The throng had finally begun to dissolve with the onslaught of Kelvin and his mounted men. Then the rear doors burst inward and more of the City Guard poured through the breach.

Tom watched as Bill coldly and carelessly began to strike to and fro, smashing the sword into any of the black-clothed guard that came near. Something had changed in the man; but, there was no time to think of it now as several of the Guard of Oran ran toward him with fire in their eyes and swords in their hands.

***

Joe struck with savage enthusiasm at the last guard standing between him and Myella. The man fell in two at the Surrogate's feet and Joe looked into her cold, black eyes.

"Now, your holiness," growled the gray-eyed man. "It's time for you to meet Oran!" His blade sang as it cleaved a horizontal path through the air, fire flickering at its razor edge. Myella smiled, and at the last instant coruscated into nothingness. There was a thunderclap as the Shadowlord's sword passed through empty air.

"Now I'm pissed!" he said calmly and turned to the rear of the temple. Anyone who stepped in his path died painfully.

John pushed Gabrielle before him and into the antechamber. He discarded the heavy and awkward headsman's sword and grabbed his own Samurai sword from the peg on the wall. The polished steel shone like velvet in the dim illumination, the hamon on the blade glinting a ghostly white.

Gabrielle clutched him and pressed her lips to his; he smiled then looked about. "I knew you would come for me, Sir John!" she spoke and joy filled her voice. Momentarily her green eyes transfixed him.

Footsteps behind him.

"You!" came the angry shout.

Sir John, Lord Knight of Erie, spun and confronted his foe. Lord Duran of Qwen, Commander of the Guard of Oran, brandished his saber and appraised the outlander. He was wide-eyed as he approached the couple, then they narrowed. He wiped a splash of blood from his pale cheek and flourished his blade. John pushed Gabrielle behind him.

"This is the last mistake you will ever make in this land, Sir Knight!" Duran rasped. "Twice I let you live when I had the opportunity to kill you. I will not let the chance pass a third time. I knew when I was in Galfeon Yor that you and your companions were trouble, but Myella wouldn't listen. The Power, hah! Well she is gone and it is just you and me. No power will be between us, aye." He smiled and looked to Gabrielle. "Like Sir Chill then?"

With that the man leapt agilely forward, his saber slicing down. John slapped the blade to the side, being careful not to damage his own by parrying full on the edge. Duran's blade struck Myella's chair and a flash of sparks rained to the floor. John thrust back and Duran slid along the length of the blade to strike at the White Knight. The saber was blocked by the katana's hilt, and John jumped back. Duran paused, feinted, thrust. John responded with several quick steps forward, pushing Duran back into the dais area. Duran moved to the side, John overcompensated and almost ended up impaled on the saber. Duran's sword swung down; striking the edge of the headsman's block, stone chips shot into the air. John slashed at the man's hand but Duran pulled away too fast. He then lunged into Duran, who stepped aside once more and cut a streak into the outlander's forearm. John winced in pain. "You will not easily beat me, Lord Knight," Duran hissed between ragged breaths. Duran spun to strike at John's back, but the former student rolled to the side, coming back up to face the man.

"As long as I kill you, I'll be satisfied," John replied. Then he focused and tried to center himself. This fight was not in dojo on a practice floor. This was real, and he could not risk losing. As the two squared off again, the surrounding melee seemed out of place, disjointed, unimportant.

Duran's blade came up, faster than John cared for, yet he parried the blow and struck back viciously, slicing through Duran's ear and nicking the neck. Duran grunted and pain etched its way into his face. He stepped back, but not quick enough as John struck again, this time slicing through the left deltoid and immobilizing that arm.

Duran lost his balance and John struck the saber from his hands. As the man fell off the dais, his feet struck out, tripping John and causing him to stumble to his knees.

Duran staggered back and caught himself on the saddle strap of a horse, jarring the rider. He looked up to see Kelvin staring back at him, but before the Lord Protector could strike, the Lord of Qwen shoved him from the saddle and took the reins in hand. With one good arm, he swung himself up and slammed his heels into the steed's flanks. The horse reared and charged down the center aisle, Duran hunched low over the saddle.

"DURAN!" John shouted and all heads turned. Tom Smiling Wolf also saw the pale man fleeing down the middle of the nave on horseback. He quickly swung his bow off his shoulder and snatched a broad-headed arrow from his quiver. With one quick motion, he drew a bead on the man and let fly. It caught the pale man in the shoulder, but did not unhorse him. He galloped harder and was soon passing through the doors. A few men on horse began to follow but were blocked for the moment by other Guardsmen of Oran.

"Sonofabitch!" John swung his blade to the side as he got to his feet.

Chapter 28

Lightning flared about Helm, more from Guyle's anger at not finding Marad's body than from the storm clouds that ran low against the summit of the Great Wall. Guyle presumed that either the body had caught up in some crevasse to be a feast for scavengers, or it had fallen into the river at the base of the Tower, washing out to sea. So, as Helm slept, Guyle raged.

"Come!" he called to the five Hands of Keth who attended him. "I must speak with Oran's servant." Down the endless steps he flew, his Hands in his wake. Helm was built in ages past, during a time of change in the Conclaveum. Cathedral-like spaces gave way to wide, winding stairs, and broad avenues. At this time, it was all but deserted of common folk. Now, only the Black Guard and a few others inhabited the city, and they stayed near the docks and the warehouses, outside of the crushing, empty weight of the Wall City. Only the administrative level remained active, and then only during the day. Courier Beasts patrolled the summit and their riders lit the watch fires. Once, tens of thousands had filled the city; now only a legion and a half.

But it was not to the heights that Guyle headed, rather to the foundation and roots of the Wall, where sorcery was still the strongest, as strong as it had been when the earth disgorged the wall, centuries ago. He passed the Black Guard of the Wall; the pattern of the Wall and sunburst on their tunic. They halted abruptly. Their faces were hidden by heavy helm, but their eyes showed fear

476

as he passed by. The mage's wizened head did not even turn to acknowledge the Guard. They had grumbled and complained about the five hundred Guard of Oran billeted in Helm and since returning from their foray to Galfeon Yor, the city had taken on a more ominous character.

One of the guards muttered under his breath as Guyle's party passed into the darkness of an unlit passageway and Guyle's staff flared with an unholy white light. His sergeant summarily hushed him and the Guards continued on their way.

Guyle was heading for the Inlet, the bowels of the Wall. This was where the sewage system met with the river and was washed away to the north by an underground waterway. This was where the spine of the wall bared itself to the world, and where the sorcery of the Heaving was the strongest. Abruptly the hallway ended. Here, there was no sconce or torch; only the light from Guyle's coldly flaming staff threw dark and dancing shadows over a heavy iron door, its hinges rusted by the ages.

Guyle barked a command to the Hands and all five moved to the door. They strained for a moment to budge the heavy portal and then suddenly the door moved with a screaming grind of metal. Air rushed into the hall, putrid and rank, but Guyle did not flinch or gag. He just stepped within to the chamber that lay beyond.

The thunder here would have deafened any man, and the darkness could drive one mad. Guyle slammed his staff onto the rock and light flared everywhere. He stood in a vast chamber, several stories high. Above in the darkness the wings of bats rustled. Around him was a pool of turbulent water. The effluvia and waste of the city churned in the water and was swiftly swept away to Guyle's right, into a tunnel of stygian darkness. To the mage's left came the falls. Above there was a semi-circular opening, about seven stories up, and this was where the river drifted into the Breach, and into this dark gap that ran beneath the Wall and into a cavernous abyss. Through this rent he could occasionally make out the flash of lightning, but the water that cascaded into this natural spillway drowned out any thunder from the storm far above.

He knew that he and his guard were several hundred yards upstream from the Breach and the docks of Helm, and few actually knew of this place beyond the city engineers and the former Lord Protector. This was the only flaw in the Great Wall's defense, but the fury of the falls made invasion all but impossible.

This was where the Summoning would occur.

The ledge he stood on was covered with the filth and detritus of human waste, and the water lashed not ten feet from his robes. The Hands stood near the door, awaiting any command he might give; they were without fear, their souls already in Oran's care.

Mage Guyle held his staff out in both hands and turned a full three hundred and sixty degrees. Fire encircled him at the span of his staff, erupting green and ugly from the rock. Flickering, it seemed to fade, but then caught strength and formed an unbroken circle about the rheumy-eyed man.

He touched his signet ring to his forehead and leaned on his staff, the carvings etched in the wood glowed an eerie green. Then he waited. He was beyond the point of verbally summoning the servant of Oran. He knew it would come; all he had to do was wait.

And wait he did, until beyond the incessant white noise of the falls he heard a rustle of wings. Not the bats, this sound was outside his senses and outside thought. Then the sound of scales on stone and rumbling of the earth. From the river of waste that flowed away to his right he heard the shriek of slaughter, the sounds of death and hideous torture.

Guyle smiled. The Daemon was coming.

He had passed the point where he was in any danger from the creature. Long before, in his youth, he had forged a pact with Oran and His servant. Guyle had known at an early age that his strength lay not in skill at arms, but rather the skill of the Dark Arts. And knowing that his father intended another for the Seat of the Conclave, he channeled his energy into learning secrets that were kept from before the raising of this Great Wall. That first time with the Daemon he had nearly lost his life and his soul. Only through quick thought had he promised his survival and his powers to Oran and the eventual downfall of his own father and half-brothers.

The Daemon had told him that Oran knew of a power lying beyond the aether, one that could be tapped and used. He had taught Guyle the use of the Naming. Thus the Hands, centuries old creatures, were reborn in the current age. Guyle knew that this was the way that the Power could be harnessed, and he had spent more than several decades formulating the path he might take to bring the power into his realm.

Now he was on the brink.

Before him rose the specter of the Daemon, blacker than the eldritch darkness of the underground river. The creature, corrupt in thought and spirit, heaved itself up before him. Its taloned wings brushed the rough rock wall and its plated belly dragged like nails on slate across the floor. Even though darkness enveloped the entire being, its eyes shone like black coals in the night. Guyle knew that this was not the only guise it wore, just one of the more malevolent.

You have summoned me, and Tarn retreats. Its voice was like silk being torn. "The six are broken," Guyle called. "Their power is asunder. One wracked, another Named. When will the Power course?"

Power? Indeed the six are now not. The stout has fallen. In symbol power resides, not in body corrupt. The Shadowlord is Named but un-Named. As is the White Knight. Four still hold Power, until the White is broken, and the Saint's soul die.

"You have lied!" Guyle shouted as he barely controlled himself from stepping from the circle of flames that licked about his feet. "You promised that the Power would be mine once they were drawn to this realm. Once they were sundered and Named. Do you recant? Is the pact broken?"

No! hissed the Daemon. And Guyle could almost feel the creature reel back from the energy that threatened at the tip of his staff. The pact remains as Oran bade, or shall I go and become shade? No. The White must break, or the

Ensorceled. If it be the White, the Key is the Saint. If the Other, the Mind.

"Do not riddle me!"

And test me not! Or Oran I shall call!

"Then what?"

Give unto Oran the White, if you can.

The Daemon was gone; the thunder of the falls engulfed them but the air was lightened its absence. The stench of the sewage did not bother Guyle quite as much, now that he knew the way to the power.

The lone horseman sat on the ridge north of Paravel. The horse, all but exhausted at the ride, wobbled on its legs and was ready to collapse. Lather whitened its flanks and its sides heaved with greater effort than thought possible. The horse was scared; wolves roamed the hills north of the City. The rider did not care. He slid off of the saddle and almost fell. Pain shot through his arm and shoulder. He was certainly no better off with that dull throb in the side of his head either.

It had taken all his effort to evade the City Guard and get past the walls of Paravel. Even now he watched a score of Guards ride onto the four roads that spread from the city, their torches winding along the road, chasing what Guard of Oran that were left. Gratefully, he knew that they would not find him this night. He had left the road early on and had ridden from copse to copse, staying to the trees and fields north of the city.

Now he just grunted in pain as he broke the arrow shaft in his shoulder. The broad head had gone clean through the muscle, clearing anything vital. He almost passed out from the pain of it. He sat heavily on a large stone as he tossed the bloody arrowhead into the bushes.

He laughed, almost hysterically, but then stopped. He wrapped a torn piece of cloth around his head. He had lost his ear to that bastard's sharp sword. He would also need stitches in his shoulder, where the man had made his left arm useless. He had underestimated Sir John. Not again, though. Not ever again.

He had discarded the tabard of the Guard of Oran half a league from the city's west wall, but kept the black coat for the chill air of the night. He would have to find a healer or physician in one of the villages along the coast, but tomorrow was good enough for that. He would go to Qwen, and from there he would catch a felucca to Helm. Or he could go inland, along the Crevasse.

He had a few choice words for Myella, especially after she deserted him. She should have known better than to trust Surik and expect the same from Sir John.

He shrugged and leaned back. No sword, no blanket. Luckily the night was not too cool, he couldn't risk a fire. So, he wrapped himself in his cloak and eased himself to the grass. From here he could spy the lights of the city, and if he could see them, they could see him. He leaned back against the cool rock. There was plenty of time. Time to plan. Time to heal. Lord Duran of Qwen was not one easily beaten.

He smiled, and once more his laughter rang out. Even the distant wolves shied away from the wounded man.

Chapter 29

Gabrielle surveyed the length of the temple. Smoke lay like a haze over the vast chamber, smoke and the smell of death; but the evil pall that had hinted at Oran's presence was all but gone. More than one City Guard stood, resting against the wall, or sitting on one of the few blood-free spaces on the floor. She watched as John paced back and forth, his bright sword now in its scabbard, a drawn and angry look on his face. She knew that he desperately wanted to kill Duran. He had even wanted to follow on horseback, but his friends had persuaded him against that course of action. There were more than a few Guards of Oran left in the city proper. No doubt there were also some of the City Guard loyal to Myella, though few would admit it now.

Kelvin had gone, with most of his men. Many of them were posting the Edict around the city of Paravel. It stated simply that the Seat was no longer welcome to the City of Paravel. That Myella and Duran were wanted for the murders of Claybrook, Vilidis and three other Council members, and that any remaining Guardsman of Oran found in the city past noon on the morrow would be summarily executed. The hidden message being that anyone who vowed allegiance to the Surrogate of the South would be sought out and killed. Yet, Kelvin and the other Council members had worded the Edict neutrally enough that it would not offend the Conclave or those merchants and citizens that were loyal to trade, not the sorceress.

As the men from the charnel house began to dispose of the dead, and as those left alive but injured were tended to, Gabrielle's gaze shifted to the large knot of people in the center, where John was standing.

"It stinks of death in here, or worse. We should leave," Tar'elah said to Bill, who massaged his shoulder. He looked at her, his eyes weary and his face ashen. He nodded, but did not make a move for the shattered doors and the courtyard beyond.

"The stink of Oran still fills this place," Torec muttered, but his eyes were downcast and his thoughts drawn inward. He now would have another scar, this one on his right cheek, to match the one that ran beneath his eyes and across the bridge of his nose.

"Well John, we managed to pull your ass out of the frying pan," Mike chimed. He sat on the step of the dais, and lit his pipe; at least the smell of the tobacco would inure them to the charnel. He puffed twice and thought better of leaning back; the floor was covered with a coagulating film of red.

"Where is Surik? Is he alive?" Alaric asked. He was as noble in bearing as ever and the fight did not seem to ruffle him in the least.

"Over here," Joe said as he waved a hand and limped over to the knot of people. The temple was all cleared out now except for them and about twenty City Guardsmen who were getting their wounds tended to by a physician. The place seemed empty, but not oppressive.

Joe sighed. He was tired. His armor was chipped and dented, and covered with gore. His hair was matted with blood, but when he saw his friends he smiled. "I was watching the City Guard escort those sons-a-bitches that served Myella outa here. Said they were gonna strip em' naked and trot them through the city. I guess most of the common folk never liked having the Seat here. What a shame," he drawled sarcastically. He was about to sheath his bastard sword when Mike stayed his hand.

"Hold on there, buddy. That little trick where you snapped out of lala land? That happened when you drew mister magic sword there. How do you know you won't snap back when the sword slides home?"

"You gotta be kidding me. You're not, are you." The thought of perpetually holding his sword in hand brought a sudden chill over him.

"Well, let me do a little once-over." Mike held out the amber orb and passed it over Joe from head to foot. "Okay, all clear. It should be fine now."

"Should be, Blotto?" Joe slowly sheathed the sword. Suddenly his eyes rolled back.

"Joe!" Mike snapped, scrambling for his orb.

"Gotcha," Joe laughed at the big man's discomfiture. Tom Smiling Wolf chuckled at the exchange.

"We thought you were a goner, Joe," Smiling Wolf observed as he scratched Kiera. He had retrieved her from her perch high above the fray soon after the last of the fighting had stopped; now, stoic as ever, he sat with the animal. Her very presence would help him heal.

"Me? Come on, Tom. The Shadowlord, a goner? Riiiiight. If you had some spell cast over you, you'd find a way around it. I did." He smiled tiredly and sat next to Mike, favoring his injured leg. "I knew you'd corrupt this land with something like that," the artist said as he gestured to the flintlock tucked into Mike's belt. "There goes the neighborhood."

Mike smiled and patted the weapon. "Anything for an edge." Joe looked around, there seemed to be somebody missing.

"Hey, where's Chill?" he asked, expecting the stout man to pop up anywhere. Silence fell over the group.

"He's dead," Bill said without emotion. "Duran killed him, when they sacked and destroyed Galfeon Yor."

Joe, stunned, dropped his sword, a hollow sound in the open temple. Even the voices of those Guards near him seemed to be muted. Chill gone? Dead? They weren't supposed to die. This was just a dream, wasn't it? He tried to comprehend that. It didn't seem possible that Chill could be gone. No. He shook his head. NO. Something inside was not right. He suddenly got nauseous and thought he would vomit. He bit back the bile, swallowing hard. This whole world was a nightmare.

Chill gone.

He was aware that the others were watching him and John finally pressed something into his hand. It was Chill's glasses, now broken and twisted, but still Chill's. He wasn't sure how he should feel. He should have expected this to happen. We should have known. But, they hadn't expected it. It was too much.

He felt sick. Chill gone. Dead.

"We aren't finished," Tom said, breaking the silence. "We still have to find Trevor. We still have to find the one that brought us here. We still have to find a way home."

"Guyle, his name is Guyle. He is Myella's uncle," Gabrielle said it. She knew more than she put to words, they saw that in her eyes, but they did not press.

Mike nodded, feeling the bulge of the orb in its sack. He was glad that the Sioux had changed the subject. It wasn't good for Joe to dwell on Chill's death at this moment. Not here, not in the Temple of Oran. "I know a way to find him, I think," he said between puffs on his pipe.

"Then I guess we'll find out what's really going on, when we find him. There are a lot of pieces here. The power we have. Myella...her uncle...the Conclaveum..." Joe trailed off. There was an edge to his voice.

"I never thought you would be the one to carry that flame," Tom interjected. "I have a few debts to collect on," Joe replied quietly.

"Well, with the help of Tar'elah and Alaric, I'm sure we can accommodate you," Bill echoed. He noticed that the smell was growing even more fetid in the temple. He watched as the remaining Guards made their way to the door. The fires were guttering and it was growing dark. Alaric and the others were slowly moving to the side of the nave and toward the courtyard. Mike got up with a grunt and helped Joe to his feet. They walked slowly, all of them, their muscles tired and stiff. Bill felt numb, too numb to feel the pain. What has changed? He tried to look at himself, to examine his feelings. He tried to see past Garis' death.

Garis had been a good man, and he did not deserve to die in manner he did. Garis had not questioned their motives nor did he pull back from their venture. Bill supposed that was what had changed him. He 'd lost something when Garis died. Tar'elah had noticed it, especially in the way he had pulled from her at the end of the melee. What pained him the most was that he didn't know he could kill, especially like he had; it soured in his stomach.

Gabrielle paused at the shattered remnants of the oaken doors. Cold, fresh air greeted her. The storm had passed and stars broke through the thinning clouds. Sir John however was not with them. He had gone ahead, into the night.

"He needs someone to be with him. He's by the tower." It was Surik. He stood near her side, leaning in the doorframe. "I'd go, but my leg hurts too much." She smiled her thanks.

He stood, his back against the tower, watching the clouds give way to the ringed moon of this reality. The black cobbles of the courtyard were silky with the wetness of the passing storm; pools of water now reflected the yellow of torches that flared in the night. The strained laughter of the City Guard at the Gate of Osso broke through the night. Beyond the wall, he could hear the muted voices of people as they took to the streets after learning that the Guard of Oran and Myella had been expelled from the city. He cradled something in his hand: his medallion. It had saved him and the others.

It seemed as though a thousand years had passed since they first ventured up the embankment and beheld the Great Forest. A thousand years since they had come to Galfeon Yor and its people. But it was only months. In those months they had caused more trouble than anyone had thought possible. They had killed, stolen, and loved. It was a rich life, but a fee had to be paid. They had all paid, especially Chill, the one who deserved it least.

He sighed. What was it he had to work out? What required him to be away from his friends, his brothers? They were there for him, yet he was out here, why? It was something else he was sure. Was it Duran?

That touched a nerve. After tonight – he remembered how he had casually snapped that guard's neck when he had tried to escape. Maybe he wasn't so removed from the Lord of Qwen after all. Maybe they were alike. It was almost as if he and the other were linked somehow, and it rankled him that the man had gotten away from him, and from the City Guard, possibly from Paravel itself.

His thoughts wandered down the long road of the past months, to the journeys and the wonders they had beheld. But always his mind turned back to Gabrielle.

"Sir John," she whispered. He smiled, but did not turn.

"There's blood on it," he said, gesturing toward the medal in his hand. "It will wash away."

"Will it?" There was a touch of irony in his voice.

"What is wrong?" she asked. "You have won."

"Have we? For now, maybe. It's not over, though. I just hope it was worth the cost. In coming to this land we have wrought such change. Such death."

"You cannot change the past," she said. She hugged him close, ignoring the dried blood, the sweat. "What have you lost, Sir John?"

He reflected on what he had done and squeezed her tight. "My innocence. My dreams were naive fantasies."

They both turned, a hawk alighted atop the wall. It eyed them for a moment then with a few thrusts of its pinions was off into the night again.

"It is a good sign, that hawk. My father would say Tarn has blessed us." She looked to him and smiled. Even in the aftermath of battle her smile heartened him. Uplifted his spirits. He half expected to hear a chorus of angels in the background as he gazed into her eyes. He found himself laughing. She brought the medallion up and tucked it beneath his tunic, kissing him as she did.

"Will you be my Champion, Sir John, Lord Knight of Erie?"

"With the greatest pleasure, My Lady," he replied, and kissed her again.

He heard his friends clapping as they stood in the courtyard, but it didn't matter. Even the stars glowed a million times brighter.

Epilogue

Guyle had waited long moments in the freezing cavern beneath the Wall. Eyes closed, long had he concentrated on what the Daemon had riddled. He had pondered the words and the meaning and, like the flaring of the ward still encircling him, it appeared dimly at first, and then with crystalline revelation.

"Nin aqu' et twia," he spoke to the Hand with the horned helm. The guard moved back and motioned the others to leave. Only the most senior Hand, the oldest and most powerful, would remain to witness Guyle's task. The remaining Hand pulled the heavy door to the charnel chamber closed and waited.

Guyle concentrated, and the sigils on his staff warped and flared. It was not so much the conjuring, but the unmaking that was the difficult task. The Hand smiled knowingly as he watched the surface of the frigid pool suddenly calm before the feet of the Mage. As Guyle muttered the last of the arcane incantation, a single ripple appeared in the surface of the water. Slowly, a figure rose from the rank and icy depths, until it stood, enshrouded, upon the glassy surface. The wet caul slid away and, as Guyle's spell encircled it, a gaping wound in the figure's chest sucked itself closed.

"You shall be the undoing," Guyle said sonorously.

The stout face stared forward, a wicked scar at the temple. Tousled black hair over dead white skin gave the face an empty look — blank, frozen.

Guyle allowed himself to hope. Was this not the one who would break them?

"Aptly named, Sir Chill," Guyle chuckled. Sir Chill the Cold.